D0862827

NEANDERTHAL SEEKS HUMAN

KNITTING IN THE CITY BOOK #1

PENNY REID

WWW.PENNYREID.NINJA/NEWSLETTER/

This book is a work of fiction. Names, characters, places, rants, facts, contrivances, and incidents are either the product of the author's questionable imagination or are used factitiously. Any resemblance to actual persons, living or dead or undead, events, locales is entirely coincidental if not somewhat disturbing/concerning.

Caped Publishing

Made in the United States of America

Third Edition: March 2013, May 2014; June 2016

ISBN: 978-1-942874-48-5

DEDICATION

To my computer: I couldn't have written this without you.
To the software developers responsible for spellcheck: You are my everyday heroes.
To Karen: I hope this makes you laugh and makes you proud.
To my readers (all 3 of you): Thank you.

CHAPTER ONE

I LOST IT in the bathroom.

Sitting on the toilet, I started to panic when I noticed the graveyard of empty toilet paper rolls. The brown cylinders had ostensibly been placed vertically to form a half oval on top of the flat shiny surface of the stainless steel toilet paper holder. It was like some sort of miniature-recycled Stonehenge in the women's bathroom, a monument to the bowel movements of days past.

Actually, it was sometime around 2:30 p.m. when my day exited the realm of *country song bad* and entered the neighboring territory of *Aunt Ethel's annual Christmas letter bad*. Last year Aunt Ethel wrote with steady, stalwart sincerity of Uncle Joe's gout and her one—no, make that two—car accidents, the new sinkhole in their backyard, their impending eviction from the trailer park, and Cousin Serena's divorce. To be fair, Cousin Serena got divorced every year, so that didn't really count toward the calamitous computation of yearly catastrophes.

I sucked in a breath and reached inside the holder; my hand grasped for tissue and found only another empty roll. Leaning down at a remarkably awkward angle, I tried to peer into the depths of the vessel, hoping for another yet unseen roll higher up and within. Much to my despair the holder was empty.

"Shit," I half whispered, half groaned, and then suddenly laughed at my unanticipated joke. How appropriate given my current predicament. A bitter smile lingered on my lips as I gritted my teeth and the same three words that had been floating through my head all day resurfaced:

Worst. Day. Ever.

It was, no pun intended, an extremely shitty day.

Like all good country songs, it started with a cheatin' fool. The "cheatee" in the song was obviously none other than me, and the cheater was my longtime boyfriend Jon. Realization of his philandering arrived via an empty condom wrapper tucked in the back pocket of his jeans as I, the dutifully dumb girlfriend, decided to do him a favor by throwing some of his laundry in with mine.

I reflected on the resulting debate after the found condom wrapper was smacked to his forehead by my palm. I couldn't help but think Jon had a good point: Was I upset with him for having cheated on me, or was I disappointed that he was such a dummy as to put the wrapper in his pocket after taking out the condom? I tried to force myself to think about what I'd said earlier that morning.

"I mean, really, who does that, Jon? Who thinks, *I'm going to cheat on my girlfriend, but I've got too much of a social conscience to leave my condom wrapper on the floor—heaven forbid I litter*."

I stared at the blue and white Formica door of my stall, tearing my bottom lip through my teeth, contemplating my options, and trying to decide if staying in the stall for the rest of the day was actually feasible. Hell, at this point, staying in the stall for the rest of my life seemed like a pretty good option, particularly since I didn't really have anywhere to go.

The apartment that Jon and I shared belonged to his parents. I insisted on paying rent, but my paltry $500 contribution plus half of the utilities likely didn't cover one-sixteenth the cost of the midtown two-bedroom two-bath walk-up.

I think part of me always knew he was a cheater; otherwise, he was too good to be true. He appeared to be all the things I always thought I wanted in a man (and still believed I wanted). Smart, funny, sweet, nice to his family, good looking in an adorkable kind of way. We shared nearly identical political views, ideological views, and values; we were even the same religion.

He put up with my eccentricities and he even said I was cute, whereas weird was the word I was most used to hearing about myself.

He made romantic gestures. He was a wooer in a time when wooing was dead. In college, he wrote me poetry even before we dated. It was good poetry, topical, related to my interests and the current political climate. It gently warmed my heart, but it didn't make my sensibilities explode; then again, I wasn't an exploding sensibilities type of girl.

One major difference between us, however, was that he came from money—lots and lots of money. This was a thorn in our relationship from the beginning. I carefully measured each expense and dutifully tallied my monthly budget. He bought whatever he wanted whenever he wanted it.

As much as I loathed admitting it, I suspected that I owed him a lot. I always wondered if he or his dad, who always wanted me to call him Jeff, but whom I always felt more comfortable calling Mr. Holesome, pulled the strings that landed me an interview for my job.

Even after our fight, for it was the closest we'd ever come to a fight, this morning he told me I could stay, that I should stay, that he wanted to work things out. He told me that he wanted to take care of me, that I needed him. I ground my teeth, set my jaw, firmed my resolve.

There was no way I was going to stay with him.

I didn't care how smart, funny, or accepting he was. It didn't matter how certain my head had been that his welcoming surrender to my oddities meant that he was the one; or even how nice it was to be out from under the crushing burden of Chicago rent, thus freeing money to spend on my precious Cubs tickets, comic books, and designer shoes. There was absolutely no way I was staying with him.

No way, José.

An uncomfortable heat I'd suppressed all day started to rise into my chest, and my throat tightened. The empty toilet paper roll that broke the camel's back stared at me from the receptacle. I fought the sudden urge to rip it from the holder and exact my revenge by tearing it to shreds. After that, I would turn my attention to the Stonehenge of empties.

I could see it now: the building security team called in to extract me from the fifty-second floor ladies' room, decimated toilet paper cardboard flesh all around me, my panties still around my ankles as I point accusingly at my coworkers and scream, "Next time replace the roll! Replace the roll!"

I closed my eyes. *Scratch that—my ex-coworkers.*

The stall door blurred as my eyes filled with tears; at the same time, a shrill laugh tumbled from my lips. I knew I was venturing into unknown, crazy-town territory.

As country songs do, the tragedy of the day unfolded in a careful, steady rhythm as I methodically worked my way through a mental checklist of all that had happened:

No conditioner leading to crazy, puffy, nest-like hair: *Check.*

Broke heel of new shoes on sewer grate: *Check.*

Train station closed for unscheduled construction: *Check.*

Lost contact after being knocked in the shoulder as crowd hustled out of elevator: *Check.*

Spilled coffee on best, and most favorite, white button-down shirt: *Guess I can cross that off my bucket list.*

And, finally, called into boss's office and informed that job had been downsized: *Double check.*

This was precisely why I hated dwelling on personal problems; this was precisely why avoidance and circumvention of raw thoughts and feelings was so much safer than the alternative. I hadn't wallowed—really wholeheartedly wallowed—since my mother's death, and no boy, job, or series of craptacular events could make me do it now. After all, in the course of life, I could deal with this.

Or so I must tell myself.

At first, I tried to blink away the moisture in my eyes; but then I closed them and, for at least the third time that day, I used the coping strategies I learned during my mandatory year of adolescent psychoanalysis.

I visualized myself wrapping up the anger and the hurt and the raw, frayed edges of my sanity in a large, colorful beach towel. I then placed the bundle into a box. I locked the box. I placed the box on the top shelf of my imaginary closet. I turned off the light of my closet. I shut the closet door.

I was going to remove the emotion from the situation without avoiding reality.

After multiple attempts at choking back tears and doing so with a great deal of effort, I finally succeeded in suppressing the threatening despondency, and I opened my eyes. I looked down at myself and pointedly took a survey of my appearance: borrowed pink flip-flops to replace my broken pair of Jimmy Choos; knee-length gray skirt, peppered with stains of coffee; borrowed, too tight, plunging red V-neck to replace my favorite cotton button-down; my raucous, crazy curls.

I pushed my old pair of black-rimmed glasses, replacement for the missing contacts, farther up my nose. I felt calmer and more in control despite my questionable fashion non-choices.

Now, sitting in the stall, the numbness settling over me like a welcome cool abyss, I knew my toilet paper problem was surmountable. I squared my shoulders with firm resolve.

All my other problems, however, would just have to wait. It's not as if they were going anywhere.

As I approached my desk—*scratch that, my ex-desk*—I couldn't help but wonder at the circle of curious faces that lurked around my cubicle, wide eyes stealing glances in my direction. They hovered at an appropriate blast radius: close enough to watch my shame unfold but far enough to pass for a socially acceptable distance. I wondered what this kind of behavior said about my species. What was the closest equivalent I could draw as a comparison between this action and the lesser species in the animal kingdom?

Was it sharks circling around a hint of blood? I imagined, in this analogy, the sharks would instead be hoping to feast on my drama, my dismay, and my discomfort. I indulged my ethnographic curiosities and studied the hovering group, not really feeling the embarrassment that should have precipitated my exit, but instead observing the observers. I tried to read clues on their faces, wanting to see what they hoped to accomplish or gain.

I was wrapped in my detachment, and I drew it close around me.

I didn't register the drumming of approaching footsteps behind me, nor did I realize that a hush had fallen over cubicle land until two large fingers gave my shoulder a gentle, but firm, tap. I turned, feeling steady but somewhat dazed, and looked from the hand, now on my elbow, up the strong arm, around the curve of the bulky shoulder, and over the angular jaw and chin, until my eyes met the breath-hijacking sight of Sir Handsome McHotpants's piercing blue eyes.

I cringed.

Actually, it was more of a wince followed by a cringe. And his name wasn't Handsome McHotpants. I didn't know his name, but I recognized him as one of the afternoon security guards for the building—the one that I'd been harmlessly admiring-slash-stalking for the past five weeks.

I had never learned his name because I had a boyfriend, not to mention that McHotpants was about twenty thousand leagues out of my league (at least in the looks department), and, according to my friend Elizabeth, likely gay. Elizabeth had once told me that men who look like McHotpants usually wanted to be with other men who look like McHotpants.

Who could blame them?

More often than I was comfortable admitting, I reflected that he was one of those people who were just decidedly too good looking; his perfection shouldn't have been possible in nature. It wasn't that he was a pretty guy; I was certain he would not look better dressed in drag than ninety-nine percent of the women I knew.

Rather, it was that everything about him from his consistently, perfectly tousled light brown hair to his stunningly strong square jaw to his faultless full mouth was overwhelmingly flawless. Looking at him made my chest hurt. Even his movements were gracefully effortless, like someone who was dexterously comfortable with the world and completely secure with his place in it.

He reminded me of a falcon.

I, on the other hand, always hovered in the space between self-consciousness and sterile detachment; my gracefulness was akin to that of an ostrich. When my head wasn't in the sand, people were looking at me and probably thinking *what a strange bird!*

I'd never been comfortable with the truly gorgeous members of my species. Therefore, over the course of the last five weeks, I'd been incapable of meeting his gaze, always turning or lowering my head long before I was in any danger of doing so. The thought of it was like looking directly at something painfully bright.

Therefore, I admired him from afar, as though he was a really amazing piece of art such as the kind you only see in photographs or displayed behind glass in museums. My friend Elizabeth and I affectionately referred to him as Handsome McHotpants; more accurately, we knighted him Sir Handsome McHotpants one night after drinking too many mojitos.

Now, looking up into the endless depths of his blue eyes through my black-framed glasses, my own large eyes blinked and the protective cloak of numbness started to slip. A tugging sensation that originated just under my left rib quickly turned into a smoldering heat that radiated to my fingertips then traveled up my throat, into my cheeks, and behind my ears.

Why did it have to be Sir McHotpants? Why couldn't they have sent Colonel Mustard le Mustache or Lady Jelly O'Belly?

He dropped his hand to his side and then he cleared his throat, removed his gaze from mine, and glanced around the room. I felt my face suddenly flush red, an unusual experience for me, and I dipped my chin to my chest as I mocked myself silently.

I finally felt embarrassment.

I took stock of the day and my reaction to each event.

I knew I needed to work on being engaged in the present without becoming overwhelmed. It occurred to me that I was demonstrating more despair over a stall of empty toilet paper and the presence of a gorgeous male security guard than discovering that my boyfriend had cheated on me, thus leading to my present state of homelessness, not to mention my recent state of unemployment.

Meanwhile, Sir McHotpants appeared to be as uncomfortable with my surroundings and the situation as I should have been. I could sense his eyes narrowing as they swept over the suspended crowd. He cleared his throat again, this time louder, and suddenly, the room was alive with self-conscious movement and pointedly averted attention.

After one more hawk-like examination of the room, as though satisfied with the effect, he turned his attention back to me. The stunning blue eyes met mine, and his expression seemed to soften; I guessed most likely with pity. This was, to my knowledge, the first time he had ever looked directly at me.

I had watched him every weekday for the last five weeks. He was why I started taking a late lunch, as his shift started at one thirty. He was why I now frequently ate my lunch in the lobby. He was why, at five thirty on days when Elizabeth met me after work, I began loitering in the lobby by the arboretum and fountain; I would peek at him through the squat tree trunks and tropical palms, knowing my friend would not be able to meet me in the lobby any earlier than six o'clock.

McHotpants and I stood for a moment, uneasily, watching each other. My cheeks were still pink from my earlier blush, but I marveled that I was able to hold his gaze without looking away. Maybe it was because I'd already put most of my feelings in an invisible box in an invisible closet in my head. Maybe it was because I realized this was likely the twilight of our time together, the last of my stalkerish moments due to the recent severing of gainful employment. Whatever the reason, I didn't want to look away.

Finally, he placed his hands on his narrow hips and lifted his chin toward my desk. In his gravelly deep voice, which was just above whisper, he asked, "Need help?"

I shook my head, feeling like a natural disaster on mute. I knew he wasn't there to help me. He was there to help me out of the building. I huffed, spurning his offer. I was determined to get my walk of shame over. I turned, pushed my black-rimmed glasses up my lightly freckled nose, and closed the short distance to my desk. The borrowed flip-flops made a smacking sound against the bottom of my feet with each hurried step: *smack, smack, smack.*

All my belongings had been packed into a brown and white file box by some employees from the human resources department while I waited, as told, in a conference room. I glanced at the empty desk. I noted where my pencil cup had once been; there was a clean patch of circle surrounded by a ring of dust. I wondered if they removed the pencils before packing the cup into the box.

Shaking my head to clear it of my ridiculous, pointless pondering, I picked up the box, which, unbelievably, held the last two years of my professional aspirations, and walked calmly past McHotpants and straight to the reception desk and the elevators beyond. I didn't meet his gaze, but I knew that he was following me even before he stopped next to me, close enough that his elbow grazed mine as I tucked the box against my hip and jabbed a finger at the call button.

I thought I could feel his attention on my profile, but I did not attempt to meet it. Instead, I watched the digital red numbers announcing the floor status of each elevator.

"Do you want me to carry that?" His gravelly voice, almost a whisper, sounded from my right.

I shook my head and slid my eyes to the side without turning; there were about four other people waiting for the elevator besides us.

"No, thank you. It's not heavy; they must've taken the pencils." I was relieved by the flat, toneless sound of my voice.

Several silent moments ticked by giving my brain a dangerous amount of unleashed time to wander. My ability to focus was waning. This was a frequent problem for me. Time with my thoughts, especially when I'm anxious, doesn't work to my advantage.

Most people in stressful situations, I've been told, have the tendency to obsess about their current circumstances. They wonder how they arrived at their present fate, and they wrestle with what they can do to avoid it or situations like it in the future.

However, the more stressful my situation is, the less I think about it, or anything related to it.

At present, I thought about how the elevators were like mechanical horses, and I wondered if anyone loved them or named them. I wondered what steps I could take to remove the word 'moisture' or even 'moist' from the English language; I really hated the way it sounded and always went out of my way to avoid saying it. I also really didn't like the word slacks, but I felt vindicated recently when Mensa came out against that horrible word in an official statement proposing that it be removed from the vernacular.

Sir McHotpants cleared his throat again interrupting my preoccupation with odious-sounding words. One of the herd of elevators was open, its red arrow pointing downward, and I continued to stand still, lost in my thoughts, completely unaware. No one else had yet entered the elevator, and I could feel everyone watching me.

I shook myself a little, attempting to re-entrench in the present. I felt McHotpants place his hand on my back to guide me forward with gentle pressure. The warmth of his palm was soothing, yet it sent a disconcerting electric shock down my spine. He lifted his other hand to where the door slid into the wall, effectively holding the elevator for me.

I quickly broke contact and settled into one of the lift's corners. Sir Handsome followed me in, but loitered near the front of the elevator, blocking the entrance; He pressed the Close Door button before anyone else could enter. The partitions slid together and we were alone. He pulled a key on a retractable cord at his belt and fit it into a slot at the top of the button pad. I watched as he pressed a circle labeled BB.

I lifted an eyebrow, asked, "Are we going to the basement?"

He made no sign of affirmation as he turned to me and regarded me openly; we were standing in opposite corners. I imagined for a moment that we were two prizefighters; the spacious elevator was our ring, and the brass rails around the perimeter were the ropes. My eyes moved over him in equally plain assessment. He would definitely win if it came to blows between us.

I was tall for a girl, but he was easily six feet and three or four inches in height. I also hadn't worked out with any seriousness or intensity since my college soccer days. He, judging by the large expanse of his shoulders, looked like he never missed a day at the gym and could bench press me as well as the box I was holding, even if it contained the pencils.

His eyes weren't finished with their appraisal, but instead lingered around my neck. The tugging sensation beneath my left rib returned. I felt myself starting to blush again.

I tried for conversation. "I didn't mean to be imprecise; I imagine this building has more than one basement, although I've never seen the blueprints. Are we going to one of the basements and, if so, why are we going to one of the basements?"

He met my gaze abruptly, his own unreadable.

"Standard procedure," he murmured.

"Oh." I sighed and started tearing at my lip again. Of course, there was a standard procedure. This was likely a common experience for him. I wondered if I were the only ex-employee he would be escorting out today.

"How many times have you done this?" I asked.

"This?"

"You know, escort people out of the building after they've been downsized; does this happen every day of the week? Layoffs typically happen on Friday afternoons in order to keep the crazies from coming back later in the same week. Today is Tuesday so you can imagine how surprised I was. Based on the international standard adopted in most western countries, Tuesday is the second day of the week. In countries that use the Sunday-first convention, Tuesday is defined as the third day of the week."

Shut up, shut up, shut up!

I drew in a deep breath, clamped my mouth shut, and clenched my jaw to keep from talking. I watched him watching me, his eyes narrowing slightly, and my heart pounded with loud sincerity against my chest in what I recognized—for the second time that day—as embarrassment.

I knew what I sounded like. My true friends softened the label by insisting I was merely well read; everyone else said I was cuckoo for Cocoa Puffs. Although I'd been repeatedly urged to audition for *Jeopardy* and was an ideal and proven partner in games of Trivial Pursuit, my pursuit of trivial knowledge and the avalanche of verbal nonsense that spewed forth unchecked did little to endear me to men.

A quiet moment ticked by, and for the first time in recent memory, I didn't try to focus my attention on the present. His blue eyes were piercing mine with an unnerving intensity, arresting the usual wanderlust of my brain. I thought I perceived one corner of his mouth lift, although the movement was barely perceptible.

Finally, he broke the silence. "International standard?"

"ISO 8601, data elements and interchange formats. It allows seamless intercourse between different bodies, governments, agencies, and corporations." I couldn't help myself as the words tumbled out. It was a sickness.

Then, he smiled. It was a small, closed-lipped, quickly suppressed smile. If I had blinked, I might have missed it, but an expression of interest remained. He leaned his long form against the wall of the elevator behind him and crossed his arms over his chest. The sleeves of his guard uniform pulled in taut lines across his shoulders.

"Tell me about this seamless intercourse." His eyes traveled slowly downward, then, in the same leisurely pace, moved up to mine again.

I opened my mouth to respond but then quickly snapped it shut. I was suddenly and quite unexpectedly hot.

His secretive yet open and amused surveillance of my features was beginning to make me think he was just as strange as I was. He was making me extremely uncomfortable; his attention was a blinding spotlight from which I couldn't escape.

I shifted the box to my other hip and looked away from his searching gaze. I knew now that I'd been wise in avoiding direct eye contact. The customs and acceptability of eye contact vary greatly depending on the culture; *as an example, in Japan, school-aged children...*

The elevator stopped and the doors opened, rousing me from my recollection of

Japanese cultural norms. I straightened immediately and bolted for the exit before I realized I didn't know where I was going. I turned dumbly and peered at Sir Handsome from beneath my lashes.

Once again, he placed his hand on the small of my back and steered me. I felt the same charged shock as before. We walked along a hallway painted nondescript beige gray with low-hanging fluorescent lights.

The *smack smack smack* of the flip-flops echoed along the vacant hall. When I quickened my step to escape the electricity of his touch, he hastened his stride and the firm pressure remained. I wondered if he thought I was a flight risk or one of the aforementioned crazies.

We approached a series of windowed rooms, and I stiffened as his hand moved to my bare arm just above the elbow. I swallowed thickly, feeling that my reaction to the simple contact was truly ridiculous. It was, after all, just his hand on my arm.

He pulled me into one of the rooms and guided me to a brown wooden chair. He took the box from my hands with an air of authoritative decisiveness and placed it on the seat to my left. There were people in cubicles and offices around the perimeter; a long reception desk with a woman dressed in the same blue guard uniform that McHotpants wore was in the middle of the space. I met her eyes; she blinked once then frowned at me.

"Don't move. Wait for me," he ordered.

I watched him leave and their subsequent exchange with interest: he approached the woman, she stiffened and stood. He leaned over the desk and pointed to something on her computer screen. She nodded and looked at me again, her brow rising in what I read as confusion, and then she sat down and started typing.

He turned, and I made the mistake of looking directly at him. For a moment he paused, the same disquieting steadiness in his gaze causing the same heat to rise to my cheeks. I felt like pressing my hands to my face to cover the blush. He crossed the room toward me but was intercepted by an older man in a well-tailored suit holding a clipboard. I watched their exchange with interest as well.

After pulling a series of papers off the printer, the woman approached me. She gave me a closed-mouth smile that reached her eyes as she crossed the room.

I stood and she extended her hand. "I'm Joy. You must be Ms. Morris."

I nodded once, tucking a restive curl behind my ear. "Yes, but please call me Janie; nice to meet you."

"I guess you've had a hard day." Joy took the empty seat next to mine; she didn't wait for me to answer. "Don't worry about it, hun. It happens to the best of us. I just have these papers for you to sign. I'll need your badge and your key, and then we'll pull the car around for you."

"Uh…the car?"

"Yes, it will take you wherever you need to go."

"Oh, ok." I was surprised by the arrangement of a car, but I didn't want to make a big deal out of it.

I took the pen she offered and skimmed over the papers. They looked benign enough. I hazarded a glance toward Sir Handsome and found him peering at me while he seemed to be listening to the man in the suit. Without really reading the text, I signed and initialed in the places she indicated, pulled my badge from around my neck along with my key, and handed it to her. She took the documents from me and initialed next to my name in several places.

She paused when she got to the address section of the form. "Is this your current address and home phone number?"

I saw where I had filled in Jon's address when I was first hired; I grimaced. "No; no it isn't. Why?"

"They need a place to send your last paycheck. Also, we also need a current address in case they need to send you anything that might have been left behind. I'll need you to write out your current address next to it."

I hesitated. I didn't know what to write. "I'm sorry, I—" I swallowed with effort and studied the page. "I just, uh, I am actually between apartments. Is there any way I could call back with the information?"

"What about a cell phone number?"

I gritted my teeth. "I don't have a cell phone; I don't believe in them."

Joy raised her eyebrows. "You don't *believe* in them?"

I wanted to tell her how I truly loathed cell phones. I hated the way they made me feel reachable twenty-four hours a day; it was akin to having a chip implanted in your brain that tracked your location and told you what to think and do until, finally, you became completely obsessed with the tiny touch screen as the sole interface between your existence and the real world.

Did the real world actually exist if everyone only interacted via cell phones? Would Angry Birds one day become my reality? Was I the unsuspecting pig or the exploding bird? These Descartes-based musings rarely made me popular at parties. Maybe I read too much science fiction and too many comic books, but cell phones reminded me of the brain implants in the novel *Neuromancer*. As further evidence, I wanted to tell her about the recent article published in *Accident Analysis & Prevention* about risky driving behaviors.

Instead, I just said, "I don't believe in them."

"O-o-o-o-k-a-y," she said. "No problem." Joy reached into her breast pocket and withdrew a white paper rectangle. "Here is my card; just give me a call when you're settled, and I'll enter you into the system."

I stood with her and took the card, letting the crisp points dig into the pads of my thumbs and forefingers. "Thank you. I'll do that."

Joy reached around me and picked up my box, motioning with her shoulder that I should follow. "Come on; I'll take you to the car."

I followed her, but like a self-indulgent child, allowed a lingering glance over my shoulder at Sir Handsome McHotpants. He was turned in profile, no longer peering at me with that discombobulating gaze; his attention was wholly fixed on the man in the suit.

I was dually relieved and disappointed. Likely, this was the last time I would see him. I was pleased to be able to admire him one last time without the blinding intensity of his blue eyes. But part of me missed the heated twisting in my chest and the saturating tangible awareness I'd felt when his eyes met mine.

CHAPTER TWO

THE CAR WAS a limo.

I'd never been in a limo before, so of course I spent the first several minutes in shock, the next several minutes playing with buttons, then the subsequent several minutes after that trying to clean up the mess made with an exploding water bottle. It tumbled out of my hands when the driver hit the brakes behind a yellow cab.

The driver asked me where I wanted to go; I wanted to say Las Vegas, but I didn't think that would go over very well. In the end, he'd graciously consented to drive me around while I made some calls using the car's phone. One of the nice things—or not so nice things, depending on your perspective—about not having a cell phone is that you have to know people's phone numbers.

Additionally, it keeps you from making meaningless acquaintances.

It is nearly impossible for most individuals to remember a phone number unless they use it frequently. Cell phones, like the other social media constructs of our time, encourage the collecting of so-called friends and contacts similar to how my grandmother used to collect teacups and put them on display in her china cabinet.

Only now, the teacups are people, and the china cabinet is Facebook.

My first call was to my dad; I left a message asking him not to call or send mail to Jon's apartment, explaining very briefly that we'd broken up. Calling my dad, in retrospect, was more cursory than critical. He never called, and he didn't write except to send me email forwards. Nevertheless, it was important to me that he knew where I was and that I was safe.

The next call was to Elizabeth. Thankfully, she was on break when I called. This was a stroke of luck, as she was an emergency department resident at Chicago General. I was able to communicate the salient facts: Jon cheated on me, I was now homeless, I needed to buy some conditioner for my hair, I lost my job.

She was outraged about Jon, generously offered her apartment and hair conditioner for my use, and expressed stunned sympathy about my job. She had a nice apartment in North Chicago; too small for long term but large enough that I wouldn't smell like fish after three days.

I was relieved when she quickly asserted that I could stay at her place, as I didn't actually have a Plan B. Elizabeth also noted that she frequently was forced by necessity to sleep at the hospital, so I would likely be at the apartment more than she would.

We decided on a course of action: I would stop by Jon's, quickly box up the essentials, then head to her place. I would go back over to Jon's the next week to pack up everything else. I had plenty of time, since the construct of work hours held so little meaning at present.

I hesitated asking the driver to wait for me while I packed a bag, but in the end, I didn't have to. He'd been eavesdropping on my conversation and offered to circle back in two hours.

As I packed, I was stunned by my lack of material possessions. Three boxes and three suitcases were all it took to assemble the entirety of my worldly goods. One suitcase, the largest one, was full of shoes. One box, the largest one, was full of comic books. This plus my brown and white box from work was the sum total of my life.

When I finally arrived at Elizabeth's place several hours later, the limo driver—his name was Vincent, he had fourteen grandchildren, and he was originally from Queens—helped me carry all my belongings up the two flights of stairs to the apartment.

Elizabeth greeted us at the door and helped Vincent with the suitcases. She was all smiles and profanity.

When we unloaded the last box, Vincent surprised me by taking my hand and placing a kiss on my knuckles. His deep chocolate eyes gazed into mine, and he spoke with an air of knowing wisdom. "If I ever cheated on my wife, she'd have my balls cut off. If you don't want to castrate this guy after what he's done, then he's not the one for you." He nodded as though affirming the truth of his words and turned precipitously to the driver's side door.

Then, like the end of a B-movie, he left us standing on the street watching the limo depart into the sunset.

Elizabeth told the story several times that night to our knitting group; it was her turn to host, so I helped her procure snacks and red wine. With each retelling, Vincent became younger, taller, more muscular, and had thicker hair; his Queens accent was replaced by a sultry Sicilian brogue; his black coat was removed leaving only a gauzy white shirt open to mid-chest.

The very last time she told it, he gazed longingly into my eyes and asked me to run away with him. I, of course, replied that he would be of no use to me castrated.

I didn't mind that Elizabeth was so open with the ladies about my day. I thought of them as our knitting group even though I knew not one stitch about knitting. I felt a great deal closer to each of them than I did to my own sisters for two simple reasons: none of the ladies was a felon (to my knowledge), and I thoroughly enjoyed their company.

I loved how open and supportive and nonjudgmental they were. There is just something about women who spend hours and hours knitting a sweater with mind-blowingly expensive yarn, when they could just buy a sweater for a fraction of the price—not to mention the time saved doing so—that lends itself to acceptance and patience for the human condition.

"Who puts the condom wrapper back in their pocket? I mean, hola, Señor Dumb Ass!" Sandra, a feisty redhead with a mostly concealed Texan drawl, pursed her lips, her brows rising expectantly as she glanced around the room. She was a psychiatry resident at Chicago General and liked to refer to herself as Dr. Shrink.

"Exactly." I felt slightly vindicated so I nodded, as did everyone else in the room.

"I think you're better off without him." Ashley didn't lift her blue eyes from her scarf as she offered her thoughts; her long, straight brown hair was pulled into a clever twist. She was a nurse practitioner originally from Tennessee, and I loved listening to her accent. "I never trust a Jon without an *h* in his name. John should be spelled J-o-h-n, not J-o-n."

Sandra pointed at Ashley and added, "And his last name: Holesome. It should be Assholesome or Un-holesome. He's a turd."

"I think we should ask Janie how she feels about the breakup." Fiona's pragmatic assessment was met with agreement. A mechanical engineer by training, a stay-at-home mom by choice, Fiona was really the leader of the group; she made everyone feel valued and protected. She owned a commanding presence even at a mere five feet tall. She looked like a fairy with her large, heavily lashed eyes set perfectly in her small, impish face topped by the practical pixie haircut she always wore. Both Elizabeth and I knew her from college; she was the Resident Advisor in our freshman year dorm, ever the mother hen.

I shrugged as all eyes turned to me. "I don't know. I don't really feel all that mad about it, just…annoyed."

Marie peered at me over her half-knit sweater. "You seemed pretty shaken when I arrived." I met her large blue eyes before she continued, "Between Jon and losing your job, I think you're more upset than you want to admit." Marie was a freelance writer and artist; I envied how her blonde curls always seemed to behave. Every time I saw her, she looked as if she'd just finished shooting a shampoo commercial.

I sighed. "It's not that. I mean, yeah—I wish I hadn't lost my job because now I have to find another one. But it's not like I was really able to do what I wanted there. I went to school to become an architect, not to become a staff accountant at an architecture firm."

"At least it was at a firm; jobs are scarce." Kat, the most soft-spoken of the group, shook her head full of brown waves. I introduced Kat to Elizabeth when I discovered her passion for knitting. Kat also worked at my company—*scratch that, ex-company*—as an executive administrative assistant to two of the partners. "But they are going to miss you, Janie. You were, by far, the most competent of the business group."

"Do they always give their terminated employees limos for the afternoon?" Ashley asked Kat with plain interest.

"Not that I've ever heard of. But then layoffs have always happened in groups of five or more." Kat wrinkled her nose. "It does seem extremely strange. I'll look into it."

I wondered at the limo as well. The whole day bordered on ridiculous, so, in comparison, the limo and Vincent seemed like a minor bump on my roller coaster of anomalies.

"Do you have any idea why they did it—why they let her go?" Sandra reached for her red wine, directing her question to both Kat and me.

"No, but I'll try to find out what I can." Kat lifted her brows as she slid a gaze laced with suspicion in my direction. "Although, I heard that you were escorted out by one of the security guards from downstairs. Is that true?"

I nodded, feeling uncomfortable and studied my wineglass with pointed interest.

"Wait, what? Security?" Elizabeth sat forward and placed a hand on my arm. "Who was it?"

I took a swallow of the wine and lifted my shoulders in a noncommittal shrug. "Uh, just one of the guards."

The room was quiet as I tried to sink farther into the couch. Elizabeth tossed her knitting to the side and started bouncing up and down with excitement. "Oh…my…God; it was him, wasn't it? It was HIM!" Her blonde ponytail wagged back and forth.

"Who is him?" Sandra stopped knitting and crossed her arms over her chest as she looked from Elizabeth to me to Kat, her large green eyes darting around the room like a Ping-Pong ball.

Elizabeth stood up abruptly and ran to her kitchen. "Wait! I have a picture!"

My eyes widened as I watched her go. I called after her, "What do you mean you have a picture?"

All knitting ceased abruptly. The last time they all stopped knitting mid-row was when a good-looking pizza guy arrived, and they all wanted to give him the tip. This time, everyone started talking at once, but their chatter trailed off when Elizabeth reentered the room with her phone and flopped down on the sofa next to me.

"I Kinneared him a couple times," Elizabeth said as she thumbed through photos on her phone. She looked up at our silent, blank faces and lifted a single brow. "You know, to Kinnear: to stealthily take a clandestine picture of someone without them knowing. Hello? Don't any of you read the Yarn Harlot's blog?"

"Oh yeah, I heard about that. Didn't the Yarn Harlot do that to Greg Kinnear at the airport or something?" Ashley placed her knitting on her lap, pointing at Elizabeth.

"Yes, yes. She wrote about it on her blog then it was put in Urban Dictionary and the *New York Times* yearly review thing or something or other." Elizabeth turned to me and looked from my open mouth to my eyes. "Oh, don't look so shocked about it."

"I still want to know who *him* is." Sandra stood up and leaned over Elizabeth's shoulder as she paused on the first in a series of pictures of Sir Handsome McHotpants. I drank another swallow of my wine. All the ladies clustered around the couch as Elizabeth drew her thumb over the touch screen of the phone; only Fiona stayed seated, waiting for the drama to pass.

The group let out an audible gasp.

"Holy hotness, Batman. Who is that?" Ashley's blue eyes were as round as saucers.

"That's Sir Handsome McHotpants." Elizabeth sounded almost proud. "He's a security guard at Kat and Janie's building. Janie's been lusting after him since he started a few weeks ago. I don't know his real name, but Janie might."

Kat nodded, a small smile curving over her lips. "I recognize him. Janie isn't the only one who has noticed."

Marie laughed as she straightened and moved back to her discarded yarn. "No wonder you're like: Jon who?"

"Damn, Janie, did he cuff you?" Sandra punched me on my shoulder. "Did you have hot elevator eye sex? Is that why you're the shade of my red sweater right now?"

I didn't realize that I was blushing until that moment. I put my wineglass aside and pressed my hands to my cheeks. It wasn't that I was embarrassed by their comments; quite the opposite. I enjoyed their good-natured teasing.

I knew I was blushing due to the memory of his gaze and the intensity of his blue eyes as they moved over my body and the warm, charged strength of his hand on my back and arm. I felt more affected by him than all the other events that preceded his presence, even all these hours later, after my day from hell. I moved my hands to cover my face and shook my head.

"Janie, did something happen?" I felt Elizabeth shift her weight on the couch as she addressed me, her voice contrarily laced with excitement and concern.

"No, nothing happened. I just talked to him, and you all know how well that always goes." I left my hands on my face and sighed.

"What did you talk about?" Fiona's soft voice made me feel a little calmer.

"I…I talked about the days of the week and the international standard for assigning numbers to days of the week." My hands dropped from my face and I met their stares.

"Oh, geez, Janie! What brought that up?" Ashley snorted as she laughed, moving her attention back to the soft mass of stitched yarn on her lap.

"No, wait, tell me everything," Elizabeth said as she passed the phone to Fiona so she could see the pictures. Elizabeth grabbed my hands in hers and forced me to meet her pale blue eyes. "Leave nothing out. Start at the beginning and repeat what happened word for word—especially everything he said."

So I did. I tried to stay focused as I repeated the story without allowing my mind to wander and expand on some meaningless tangent. When I repeated the part about ISO 8601 and how he'd asked me to expand on the seamless intercourse between government bodies, they all gasped.

"Ah! What did you say?" Sandra was leaning forward in her seat. "I can't believe he flirted with you! Did you flirt with him back?"

"What? No, no, he wasn't flirting with me!" I shook my head emphatically.

"Oh, Janie, *au contraire mon frère*, he was most certainly flirting with you." Ashley wagged her eyebrows at me, her teeth sliding to the side in an impish grin. Everyone giggled at her thick Tennessee accent applied to the French colloquialism. "He sounds like the strong and silent type. You must have made an impression. Kinda weird, though —flirting with you right after you've been fired."

Kat nodded. "I agree his timing could have been better, but you must have made an impression."

"Of course you did; look at you—you're stunning." Fiona's tone and expression was matter-of-fact as she gestured to me with one hand.

I stared at her wide-eyed. "You call this big bottom of mine stunning?"

Marie giggled. "One man's big bottom is another man's idea of stunning; don't hold it against this guy if he likes curves on his girl. On second thought, do hold it against him."

The room roared with laughter, and I couldn't help the small, breathless chuckle that abdicated my lungs. I couldn't fathom that he was attracted to me, let alone flirted with me; it all seemed too strange. I interrupted their merriment to finish the story, and everyone frowned when I explained that I left with the female guard and hadn't talked to him or said goodbye.

"But he told you to wait," Kat said. "Why didn't you wait for him?"

"I'm sure he didn't mean it that way; he meant 'wait here' or 'wait for the papers,'" I explained.

Ashley shook her head. "No, didn't he say," she lowered her voice to a manly tone which actually sounded a lot like Batman, "'*Don't move. Wait for me.*'?"

"I think you're reading too much into that." I stood and began collecting empty wine-glasses, stretching as I did so. The weight of the day made my shoulders feel heavy; I was tired.

"I wonder." Fiona gave me a sideways glance. "You've always been clueless with guys."

"Oh really?" I countered.

"Yes, really," Elizabeth said, chiming in. "You are beautiful, even if you don't believe it. A lot of guys, and, I mean, *a lot* of guys, like the big boobs, small waist, big butt, long legs, amazon woman thing you have going on. Pair that package with your curly auburn hair and big hazel-green eyes, and some people, me included, would call you gorgeous."

I tried, with varying levels of success, to change the subject as the evening came to an end. These were all women who loved me just as I was; of course, they believed I was beautiful. The truth was I just didn't especially like dwelling on my looks. So, I didn't.

As I lay on Elizabeth's couch that night, I was surprised by the nature of my thoughts. I couldn't stop thinking about him. I played the mostly one-sided elevator conversation over and over in my head trying to discern if he had actually been flirting. Not that it mattered, as I would likely never see him again.

I felt almost normal as I obsessed about something as mundane as whether a guy I liked, albeit based on physical attractiveness alone, thought I was attractive enough to flirt with me. However, before I let myself believe I was behaving completely rationally, I reminded myself that I just ended a long-term relationship with someone I thought I was going to marry, and lost my job in the same day.

A normal person would have been obsessing about one or both of those life-altering events.

My last thought before I succumbed to sleep was to check the definition of *to Kinnear* on Wikipedia.

CHAPTER THREE

It was announced to me Friday morning, one-and-a-half weeks after the worst day ever, that Friday night was going to be outrageous. And by outrageous, Elizabeth meant that she'd secured VIP passes to a much sought after "club experience" as she put it, which I think was the trendy way of saying "we're going to a new bar."

I was very motivated to find a new job and new apartment, although Elizabeth hadn't made any complaints against my presence. In fact, she'd gone so far as to mention that her lease was almost up, and she suggested we find something larger and continue to room together.

The idea appealed to me. Living with Elizabeth would be excellent prophylaxis against my natural reclusive, agoraphobic tendencies.

Even in my relationship with Jon we'd both recognized that I required a generous amount of space and alone time in order to behave with appropriate affection when we were together.

Maybe that was why he felt the need to cheat.

The idea struck me as one with merit. I tucked it away as a data point.

Over the last several days, I'd done a fair amount of practiced focusing on my present state of "lessness"—homelessness, joblessness, and relationshiplessness. Less was not more. Less was an unstable, uncomfortable place to be.

Jon was my first boyfriend. I went on dates with guys in high school and college, but they were all first dates. Jon was the first guy who didn't seem put off by my rampant randomness; he seemed to bask in it. I wondered if he would be the only one.

ught didn't trouble me as much as it should have. In fact, it bothered me far the thought of never experiencing something like the smoldering warmth of ess I experienced during my seven to twelve minutes with the blue-eyed security d.

I'd spoken only briefly to Jon since the breakup, and I still needed to evaluate what I actually felt during our conversation. He was mad at me; in fact, he was outraged, and he'd yelled at me for the first few minutes of our conversation. He said he'd found out about my job loss from his dad, and he wanted to know why I hadn't asked him for help.

I couldn't believe my ears; it took me a few seconds to respond. "Jon, is that an actual question? And how did Mr. Holesome—I mean, how did your dad know?"

"*Yes. It is an actual question. You need me, you are my girlfriend—*"

"No—" I shook my head as if convincing myself.

"*Nothing is decided. I want to take care of you. I still love you. We belong together.*" He sounded resolute and a little sullen.

"You cheated on me. We are not together." I was starting to become aggravated, which was the closest I came to anger.

I heard him sigh on the other end, and then his tone softened. "*Janie, don't you know that changed nothing for me? It was one time. It meant nothing. I was drunk.*"

"You were sober enough to put the condom wrapper in your pocket."

He half growled, half laughed. "*I still want to take care of you—let me take care of you.*"

"That's not your role—"

"*Can we be friends*?" He cut me off, his voice somewhat gentler.

"Yes." I meant it. I didn't want to lose him as a friend. "Yes. We should be friends."

"*Will you let me take care of you?*" His voice was pleading. "*Will you let me help you?*"

I thought about what he was asking; I knew he meant financial support. "You can help me by being a good friend."

"*What if I can't be just friends?*" I could sense his renewed annoyance with me as he spoke. "*I can't think about anything but you.*"

It was my turn to sigh; I couldn't think of anything to say. Well, more accurately, I couldn't think of anything to say related to our topic of conversation, but I could think of plenty of things to say about the climate of New Guinea or the prehistoric ancestors of the African secretary bird.

After a moment of silence, he cleared his throat. When he spoke again, his voice sounded firm. "*Nothing is decided,*" he said again. "*When can I see you?*"

We arranged a time to meet on Saturday morning at a neutral spot, then we said our goodbyes, during which he told me again that he loved me. I didn't respond.

I reflected on all that had happened. I didn't feel an acute need to grieve the loss of him or the five years of our life together. In order to be confident of my feelings, I made sure the invisible closet door in my head was open, the light was on, and the box was unlocked, but detachment remained.

I knew that my preoccupation with the trivial was a direct result of my mother's death, as well as what my therapist called an already natural propensity to observe life rather than live it. He called it self-preservation.

My paternal grandmother, ever a fangirl of pharmaceutical products and medical intervention, insisted that I needed therapy when my mother died. So, I started therapy at the ripe age of thirteen.

I thought therapy meant sitting on a couch being shown inkblots shaped suspiciously like blobs of ink and being told I was angry with my mother for her affairs; angry with her for running off with her latest lover; angry that she had gotten herself killed in a motorcycle accident; angry that she had left me with my somewhat dimwitted—albeit well-meaning—father and my two siblings, both of whom were prone to criminal activity; and angry at her for cooking veggie tacos on the Tuesdays of my childhood instead of the hot dogs and potato chips I craved.

The therapist did all those things even though I hadn't felt particularly angry; I just felt sad, enormously sad.

It was why, the therapist said, my brain always took a hard U-turn when I was faced with difficult or uncomfortable emotional situations. Nevertheless, during that year, I also reluctantly learned strategies that worked. I learned that when I was overwrought with emotional distress, small things could be a trigger, like finding a bathroom stall bereft of toilet paper. The mundane became as insurmountable as moving Mt. Fuji.

However, I felt certain that I was doing my utmost to spend some time marinating in the end of my relationship. The most emotion I could conjure over its end was a wistful melancholy over the possibility of losing Jon as a friend. Admittedly, I also felt a twinge of regret when I realized I'd already bought him a birthday present.

Maybe that made me shallow.

Elizabeth thought I was in shock.

Whatever the truth was, I reasoned, once enough time passed, the truth would out. I liked to think of myself as Launcelot Gobbo from Shakespeare's *The Merchant of Venice*; even a foolish man will produce some wisdom, given enough time to drone on and on in unchecked soliloquy. Since most of my time was spent in unchecked soliloquy, I held out hope for some wisdom.

The job search was in its infancy. Nevertheless, I sent out at least a hundred resumes, applied for every job on craigslist for which I might be the least bit qualified, and contacted all the temp agencies I could find in the Chicago area.

I was determined to be employed.

I had a meager savings account, but it wasn't just the money at issue. I could not take a prolonged sabbatical from the working class because my temperament required that I be, at all times, gainfully employed.

The recognition that my temperament was less than ideal for appropriate integration into society was the reason I started tutoring elementary school kids in math and science every Thursday afternoon and evening. Admittedly, it wasn't why I continued. I continued for selfish reasons: the kids liked comic books, they were funny, and I liked doing it.

If left to my own devices, I would eventually become a hermit, sans my weekly tutoring on the South Side. I knew the longer I was out of work, the more despondent I would become. I even considered learning to knit. I think this last revelation is what led Elizabeth to insist that we spend some time being outrageous.

And, therefore, we were destined for an outrageous night at an outrageous club.

The only items she approved of in my wardrobe were my shoes. In fact, she borrowed a pair of orange faux-crocodile leather wedge heels with a turquoise bow at the toe. I wore a zebra printed spiked heel; the rest of my outfit came from her closet. She said I owned the clothes of a radiologist and the shoes of an OB/GYN, which is like the medical doctor equivalent of saying that I dressed like a librarian with a propensity for fuck-me boots.

We wore the same shoe size, but she was at least a size smaller everywhere except her waist. She owned a mere two dresses that actually fit over my expansive derriere: an olive-green, button-down, *Mad Men* throwback, 1950s-style housedress and a cinch-waisted, almost backless, simple black dress that gathered and flowed nicely over her shoulders and hips but that merely stretched and puckered on mine.

The black dress ended mid-thigh. I looked at myself in the mirror, then gazed longingly at the olive green dress still hanging in the closet; it was knee-length.

Elizabeth met my eyes in the mirror and gave me a dirty look over my shoulder. She'd seen my attention stray to the closet.

She won. I wore the black dress. Even with the addition of thigh-high stockings to cover my bare legs I felt exposed and, if I must admit, a tad sordid.

We were able to enter the club with little difficulty, even though a long line of party-goers snaked around the length of the building. Elizabeth walked to the front and handed two large tickets to a man wearing sunglasses flanked on either side by two beefsteaks of man-meat.

As far as I could tell, the man in the sunglasses didn't look at the tickets, but I got the distinct impression he was studying us behind his dark lenses. He nodded his head just once, and then moved to the side so we could pass.

Elizabeth tossed me a bright, carefree smile as the clicking of our heels was swallowed by the jungle sounds of the club. I gaped at our surroundings in uneasy wonder; it was definitely going to be an experience. She didn't communicate to me that the name of the club was actually *Outrageous*. To be honest, *Overwhelming* would have been a better name.

The inside of the club was quite literally a jungle. Twenty-foot replicas of trees native to the rainforest towered above us, and I followed the line of one of the taller trunks as it reached to the ceiling, which had been painted or canvassed to look like the canopy of a rainforest.

Strategically placed lights filtered through the pseudo-branches creating the effect of twilight in the heart of the Amazon. The ground slanted downward from the entrance, and it was impossible to tell how big the room was; I guessed rather than saw that the majority of the walls were covered in mirrors, which multiplied the jungle atmosphere in every direction.

A total of 428 amphibians and 378 reptiles have been classified in the Brazilian rainforest; I wondered how many were represented in Club Outrageous that night disguised as human beings.

Unlike most clubs I'd had the misfortune of attending, the music in Club Outrageous wasn't oppressive or omnipresent. I recognized the music playing unobtrusively over the sound system as *The Mix-Up* by The Beastie Boys, specifically the song *B For My Name*; intermixed with the 2007 Grammy award-winning album for instrumental pop were wildlife calls of the Brazilian rainforest.

Just as the bass strummed a low rhythm, a call wrenched forth from what I guessed was the giant leaf frog indigenous to the western and northern regions of Brazil.

It could have been a different frog species; admittedly, I was not at all familiar with all Amazonian frog calls. But, since I recently read an article about the giant leaf frog and the medicinal potential of its waxy secretion leading to biopiracy of the species, it was the first frog that came to mind.

At the center of the expansive room was a massive arch that was obviously meant to resemble an eroded sandstone canyon or cave, and underneath it was an impressively large bar that also appeared to be carved out of eroded sandstone. A waterfall cascaded over the top of the arch into a pool at the base of the bar.

The floor around the bar was illuminated with blue lights, and even from our place at the entrance, we could see the water flowing beneath clear glass tiles. A furry movement caught my eye, and I turned my attention to a previously unseen cage between our location and the center of the room.

"Look," I leaned close to Elizabeth and pointed to the cage. "Wait, that's a person. There is a woman in there with the monkey, and she is...she is naked!" I covered my mouth as I realized the woman was not alone. "Oh, my God, that looks like...oh, my God."

Elizabeth laughed, presumably at my expression and lack of speaking ability.

On closer inspection, I noticed the club did an admirable job of making it appear that the woman was in the cage when, in fact, she was encased in a separate Plexiglas shell within the cage. There were multiple cages in the club; some were at floor level and others were suspended in the trees. Each of the cages held one or more exotic primates or monkeys and a Plexiglas cylinder in the center of the enclosure.

However, the woman was not alone within the cylinder.

I did a half-spin and gaped around the room, my wide eyes as they moved from cage to cage, my mouth hanging open. Behind, or next to, or in front of, or wrapped around each naked woman was a man dressed in a furry suit that obviously was meant to match the primate or monkey in the cage; the woman and man were engaging in what I only allowed myself to term as open displays of affection. It was hard to tell for certain what they were doing without venturing close to one of the cages and studying them for a prolonged period. I felt a little sick to my stomach.

"That's distressing." I swallowed hard, trying to look anywhere but at the strange theater surrounding us. Elizabeth just chuckled lightly as she pulled me into the room, and I shot her a hard glare. "You knew about this, didn't you?"

She shook her head; tears of hilarity were pooling at the corners of her eyes as we navigated around trees. "No, no—I swear I didn't! I think they're just making out. I don't think they're…you know, doing it."

We stopped at the bar and stood in front of two stools that looked like they were covered in fur. I couldn't bring myself to sit down. I glanced at Elizabeth from beneath my lashes and couldn't help the small smile that pulled at my mouth. She made no move to sit either.

I couldn't speak any further due to my extreme discomfort with the situation, and Elizabeth couldn't speak as she was caught in a new tsunami of giggles. Her amusement finally became too contagious to ignore when the soundtrack of jungle noises included a brief call from a macaw. I couldn't restrain the laugh when it bellowed from my chest.

Elizabeth leaned her elbow on the bar and turned her smiling eyes to mine. "I had no idea what to expect, honestly. One of my patients gave me the tickets. All he said was, 'Be prepared for something outrageous.'" Elizabeth turned to the bar and signaled to the bartender, briefly inclining her head toward me. "I think they switch it out every few months and try to outdo themselves each time."

"Is it always a jungle theme?" I twisted my lips to the side in an effort to keep from laughing as I offered a sympathetic tilt of my head toward one of the cages. "I feel so sorry for the poor monkeys. I don't want to see that, and I can't even begin to imagine how they feel about being stuck inside with those gyrating bodies." Suddenly, the fine hairs on the back on my neck stood at attention and I shivered inexplicably.

I had the overwhelming impression that I was being watched.

My attention skimmed the floor of the club as I tried to quell that omnipresent pressure associated with uncertainty and nervous expectation, but I couldn't find any eyes pointed in my direction. I tried to shake off the sensation. I hoped it was just the combination of being an unwilling voyeur as well as the lingering distress I felt about my state of undress.

Elizabeth's smile faded when she saw my expression, and she frowned. "Hey," she placed one of her hands over mine. "We don't have to stay. Why don't we have one drink then get out of here?"

I pressed my lips together and shook my head. "No, no. It's ok. I'm good. It's just…" I sighed and let my eyes move over the room, allowing myself to look beyond the cages to the crowd of clothed club-goers that I somehow missed when I entered.

No one was dancing, which was understandable because the music was low and inconspicuous; instead, they sat on large circle shaped cushions that looked like giant lily pads. Other groups, mostly in pairs, were snuggled together in booths that had been carved into the bases of the trees.

Everyone was gorgeous, every single person, in that glossy, shiny, plastic way. It was like being in a room of animated mannequins. Their mouths moved, but rarely did their expressions change. I'm sure there were famous people present, but I didn't immediately recognize any faces. I began to feel a familiar comfort envelope me, as I became an observer. No one would notice me in this room of plastic women and perfect, sinewy limbs.

"I'm good." I finally met Elizabeth's worried gaze and smiled as the bartender approached.

She eyed me with plain contemplation then nodded once. "Ok. But if you want to go, just say the word."

Before we could order, a bleach-blond bartender with big brown eyes placed two glistening glasses of what I surmised was champagne on the bar. He gave us a crooked grin that was somehow perfectly paired with his Australian accent.

"Ladies, these are for you. I've also been instructed to put anything else you order on the same tab as well. I'm David. Let me know if you need anything."

Elizabeth recovered faster than I did. "Uh, I don't know if we can accept these without first knowing who our benefactor is."

His smile widened and his gaze moved in conspicuous appreciation over her silky turquoise dress. "I can't divulge that."

"Then we don't want them." Elizabeth pushed the glasses back to the bartender, but he stopped her by leaning over the bar and leveling his lips with her ear. He whispered something that I couldn't hear, and I frowned; my attention was diametrically split between their exchange and the rest of the room.

When he leaned back, her gaze followed his movements with obvious suspicion. He merely smiled the same crooked smile and winked at her, and then he added before leaving, "Like I said, let me know if you need anything."

I met her pensive expression with one of my own. "What did he say?"

"He asked me to drink the champagne. He said if I didn't drink it, he might get in trouble." She lifted the golden liquid to her lips, her inky lashes hiding the movements of her eyes as they surreptitiously swept over the inhabitants of the bar with renewed interest.

"This is unexpected," I said, dutifully picking up my glass.

A short laugh escaped her throat followed by an extremely unbecoming snort. "Not really; we look hot." She tipped her glass against mine and lifted it in a toast. "To looking hot and getting free stuff."

I tapped my glass against hers and we took a sip of the champagne. Elizabeth continued her survey of the room over my shoulder when, suddenly, I saw her eyes widen as she almost choked on the bubbly liquid. She set her flute down clumsily and coughed. Her hand went to her chest, but her gaze was still transfixed over my shoulder.

"Janie." She coughed, cleared her throat, and tried to speak again. "Don't turn…"

"Let me get you some water." I started to walk around her, but her arm reached out and held me in place.

"Don't!" She coughed, swallowed, lowered her voice to a hoarse whisper, and added, "Don't move—don't. He's here!"

"Hey." A male voice spoke from behind me, and it sounded strangely familiar. I turned my head toward the greeting and was met by the towering form of Sir Handsome McHotpants clothed in a black suit and open neck black shirt, his startling blue eyes directed squarely at me.

CHAPTER FOUR

MY HEART SKIPPED two beats. I turned fully around.

Oh my God, it's you.

"Oh my God, it's you." I realized too late that I said and thought the same thing in unison.

He gave me a whisper of a smile, his blue eyes moving over me: lips, neck, shoulders, chest, stomach, hips, thighs, legs, shoes. The slow deliberateness of his perusal made me shiver even as I felt a dismaying hot flush rise to my cheeks.

His gaze lingered on my shoes before it traveled upward again.

After a long pause, his blue stare met mine again, "Yep. It's me."

I was speechless; my usually cluttered brain was blank. I could only gape at him. Thankfully, Elizabeth spoke from behind me. "Hi, I'm Elizabeth."

His eyes moved beyond me to where she stood. I took the opportunity to make some semblance of an attempt to gather my wits from where they lay scattered: on the floor, on the bar, on the ceiling, like blood from a gunshot victim.

"Hi, I'm Quinn." He gave her a closed-lipped, socially acceptable for the situation, friendly enough smile, and I tried to think of something to say as Quinn and Elizabeth shook hands over the bar.

Quinn. His name is Quinn. I must remember to call him Quinn, not Sir Handsome McHotpants.

The best I could come up with was, "What are you doing here?" Then I tried not to cringe when I realized it sounded somewhat accusatory.

His attention moved back to me. "I'm working."

"Are you a bouncer?" My brain, like a skipping record, seemed to be stuck on stream-of-consciousness questions.

"My company…" He paused for a moment as though considering something, and then he continued. "My company does the security for this place."

"Oh—the same company that does the security for the Fairbanks Building." I stated this rather than asked. The Fairbanks Building was where I used to work.

I started to feel marginally more relaxed in his company as his presence at the club made more sense. However, his presence at the bar, with us, was still a mystery. Before I could stop myself, I asked, "Are we in trouble?"

His eyebrows lifted. "Are you in trouble?"

I nodded. "What I mean is, did we do something wrong? Is that why you were sent over here?"

He shook his head, not answering right away; confusion and something akin to uncertainty flickered over his features. "No, no one sent me over here."

"Oh," I said, and my mind went blank again.

He was watching me in that measured way he'd employed in the elevator after my episode of verbal nonsense. A moment passed as we looked at each other. Then, he tipped his head toward our champagne glasses on the bar. "Are you two celebrating something?"

I looked to Elizabeth for help, but she was pretending to read the drink menu.

"No." When I met his gaze again, I found him watching me with unveiled interest.

His attention was maddeningly distracting; my unresponsive brain felt covered in molasses. My body, however, felt rigid and aware. I felt every stitch of clothing I was wearing touching me: my backless, strapless bra felt too tight; the caressing silky softness of the dress caused goose bumps to rise over my neck and arms; the friction of my lace undergarments and stockings burned my inner thighs.

I swallowed with a great deal of effort and forced myself to speak, not really paying attention to my words. "One of Elizabeth's patients gave her the tickets, and she wanted to take me out because she thinks I need cheering up."

"Because of your job?" He prompted, shifting closer to me, resting his hand on the bar between us.

His new proximity caused my heart to gallop, effectively kicking my brain into overdrive. Words tumbled forth unchecked. "Yeah, that and I just broke up with my boyfriend. Although, I don't know if broke up is the right term for it. It's hard to find words and phrases which really accurately reflect actions. I find verbs in the English language to be lacking. What I really like are collective nouns. The nice thing about them is that you can use any word in the English language as a collective noun, which allows you to ascribe both features, as well as character traits to the collection or group. Although, some collective nouns are well established. As an example, do you know what a group of rhinoceroses is called?"

He shook his head as he tilted it to the side, watching me.

"It's called a crash. I like to make up my own collective nouns for things; like, take that group of women over there." I indicated across his shoulder, and he turned to see where I pointed. "See the plastic-looking ones on the purple lily pad? I would call a group like that a latex of ladies, with the word latex being the collective noun. And those cages, with the monkeys and the couples—I would call them collectively a vulgar of cages, with the word vulgar being the collective noun."

He lifted his hand to get the bartender's attention as he spoke. "I would switch them. I would call the cages a latex of cages and the women a vulgar of women."

I considered his comment before responding. "Why is that?"

He leveled his gaze on me and gifted me with a small smile. "Because that group of women over there are more vulgar than what is happening in the cages, and the couples in the cages are wearing latex."

I watched him for a moment, my brow wrinkling, and then I moved my eyes to one of the cages to watch the couple. I chewed on my lip as I studied them. "The women look completely naked, and the men are in monkey suits. Where is the... the—" I sucked in a breath, my wide eyes moving back to his. "Are you saying... they're, are they...?"

He laughed and shook his head; a bright, full smile lit his eyes with amusement. "No, no. I guarantee they're not engaging in any monkey business." He laughed again as he watched me. "I know for a fact it's all choreographed. It's a show."

I narrowed my eyes at him. "It's a show?"

His laugh was deep and open, and it was doing strange things to my insides, especially since I suspected he was laughing at me. My stomach fluttered with a mixture of embarrassment and apprehension. I narrowed my eyes at him, trying to ignore my body's continuing hysterics. "It's still disconcerting. I mean, would you want one of those cages in your house?"

He continued to grin at my incredulousness and answered, "Not with the monkey in it."

"The man or the primate?" I countered.

"Neither." His gaze narrowed, mimicking mine, and he leaned still closer.

I swallowed unevenly and managed to croak, "But you would want the woman?"

"Not that woman." His voice was so low I almost didn't hear his response. His eyes moved from mine and traveled over my hair, forehead, nose, cheeks, then remained on my lips for longer than I felt was necessary... or appropriate... I wasn't sure which, but there had to be a word that adequately conveyed my discomfort at that moment.

"What do you need?" The bartender's polite query sounded from my left, which, to my dual relief and disappointment, caused Quinn to move his attention from my lips.

"Hey, David, please put whatever these two are having tonight on my account," Quinn said.

David shook his head slowly, his eyes flickering upward then back to Quinn. "I can't do that, Mr. Sullivan."

Quinn frowned. "Why not?"

"Someone else already volunteered to cover their tab." The bartender grimaced, his shoulders stiffening.

"Who?" Quinn asked.

David's voice was tinged with uncertainty when he responded. "I can't tell you that."

The bartender's response surprised Quinn; I could tell by the narrowing of his eyes. I saw the muscle tick at his jaw before he murmured in a low voice, "Yes, you can."

I turned to Elizabeth, but she was distracted by her pager. I didn't notice until that moment, but it must have been going off. I gave her a questioning glance as I listened to Quinn and David's discussion.

I heard David sigh. "Alright, listen, I'll tell you, but don't look at them, ok? They've been really great with the tips."

"Who is it?" Quinn didn't raise his voice, but his tone clearly betrayed impatience.

"It's the guys on the second floor—don't look up there—the ones in the Canopy Room." David sighed again.

I sensed rather than saw Quinn step closer to me as I suppressed my urge to look up to the previously unnoticed second floor. I wondered where the Canopy Room was. Before I could give this much thought, I felt a shock as Quinn placed his hand on my arm above the elbow and turned me to face him.

His gaze was no longer warm and friendly; in fact, it almost looked hostile as he addressed me. "You need to leave."

His touch, his closeness, the intensity of his stare all made my insides feel like lava. I couldn't understand my erratic and completely unintentional reactions to him; it was as if I was someone else, some daft dimwit.

I resolved to pull myself together, and opened my mouth to respond but, before I could, Elizabeth chimed in from behind me.

"Yeah, actually, we do need to go." She waved her pager, stepped to my side, and gave me an apologetic frown. "I just got paged. They need me to go in. I'm sorry, Janie."

I looked between Elizabeth and Quinn, a confused frown securely in place. "Wait—why do I need to go?"

Quinn's hand moved down my bare arm, causing me to immediately shiver, and engulfed my hand; his fingers linked through mine. He tugged impatiently and began leading me toward the entrance as he spoke.

"Because your friend is leaving, and it's not safe to be in a club like this by yourself, looking the way you look."

"But…" I sputtered, trying to understand what was happening and the meaning of his words, but my body was still achingly sentient, focusing on where his hand held mine, and my mind was decidedly distracted. Again, I looked to Elizabeth for help, but she was already some distance behind us, and I wasn't certain she could hear our conversation. He wasn't moving particularly fast, so we walked side-by-side holding hands.

Finally, I said, "What's wrong with how I look? And aren't I safe with you?" My skipping record of stream-of-consciousness questions seemed to be spinning again.

He glanced at me from the corner of his eyes and hesitated a moment before speaking, as though he were about to give away a secret reluctantly. "Not necessarily."

"Can't I just stay here?"

He withdrew his hand from mine and placed it on my back, pressed me forward as he answered, "No. You can't." His firm strength at the base of my spine reminded me of how he'd escorted me to the basement on my worst day ever, and I felt aggravated. My annoyance spiked when he added, "Someone like you shouldn't be in here anyway."

I stepped abruptly away from him and stopped walking; we were approximately ten feet from the entrance.

His words felt like a snowball to the face. "Someone like me?" I asked, squaring my shoulders, even as I felt an irritating blush spread up my neck and over my cheeks. I glanced around at the perfectly formed animated mannequins in the club and knew exactly what he meant.

I was used to remarks about my strangeness, and I'd long ago resolved to rejoice in the awkwardness of my appearance, but the offhand comment, coming from him, the benighted source of my weeks-long stalkerish fantasies, chaffed against a wound I thought had healed into a concealed scar long ago.

His attention followed my movements as I pulled away, a mixture of surprise, annoyance, and confusion apparent in his features. He took a step to close the distance between us and reached for my hand, but I crossed my arms over my chest to avoid further contact.

I wondered at my seesaw of emotions; hot then cold. I didn't enjoy how unbalanced I felt, especially when he touched me. I didn't like that I'd given him some strange power over my inner mechanics and chemistry just because he was beautiful. I didn't like how my body seemed to be intent on sabotaging my brain, especially since my brain was so good at sabotaging itself. The burning in the pit of my stomach was replaced with a cold ache. I felt seasick and truly absurd.

"I think I can navigate the last few feet just fine without an escort. I do know how to walk."

I tried not to notice how very nice he looked in his black suit, and I gave him what I hoped was a withering glare, but I suspected it was merely a stiff stare, and I walked around him and headed straight to the door. I didn't look back as I exited the club, and welcomed the windy, Chicago city air.

Elizabeth must have been a significant distance behind me, because she didn't join me for what seemed like several minutes. This gave me ample time to work myself into a tornado of heated annoyance and embarrassment.

When she finally arrived, she was on her cell phone, obviously talking to the hospital. She gave me a huge smile, nudged my elbow with hers, and mouthed *oh my God.* I frowned at her elated expression and shook my head. Elizabeth covered the receiver of her phone to block our conversation from whoever was on the other end; a questioning crease was between her eyebrows, her smile replaced with meditative concern.

"I thought you'd be over the moon," she said in a loud whisper, indicating the club with a quick nod of her head. "He was flirting with you!"

I sighed and turned away from her. "No, he wasn't."

"What, are you crazy? He's completely into you. Did he…yes…" I listened as Elizabeth turned her attention back to the voice emanating from her cell. "Yes, I'm still here."

I ignored the rest of her phone conversation. My thoughts were a black cloud of grumpiness focused on my maladroit personality disorder and gargantuan features. There were very few times in my life I truly wished I looked different, and simply *was* different from the person I am: the middle child in a family of three girls, and the one who is universally acknowledged as the smart plain Jane of the bunch.

We were the Morris girls. My older sister, June Morris, was the pretty one; I was the smart one; my youngest sister, Jem Morris, was the crazy one. Jem's first arrest came when she was nine, shortly after our mother's death. She stabbed one of her teachers in the hand with a cafeteria knife, then told the police she had a bomb hidden in the school.

Even from an early age, I was at peace with my family and my place in it. In recent years both June and Jem had become known, collectively, as the criminal ones. June had just been found not guilty in California for her part in running an organized escort service as my dad called it. He was too polite to call it what it was—her prostitution business.

The last time I heard from Jem, she was calling the shots at a chop shop in Massachusetts just outside of Boston. To their credit, June and Jem were both leaders in their respective fields, masterminds at their craft. I, meanwhile, went to college to become an architect, and the closest I'd come to realizing my dream was securing a job, bought by my at-the-time-boyfriend's dad, as a staff accountant at a mediocre firm.

I wasn't even sure it was my dream anymore.

Elizabeth pulled me back into the present with a tug on my arm as she led me toward a waiting taxi. "Here." She shoved cash into my hand. "Just go to the apartment. I'll take a different cab to the hospital; it's in the opposite direction." She gave me a quick hug as I looked from her to the money in my hand. "We'll talk tomorrow. I won't be home 'til the afternoon."

I nodded dumbly as she shoved me into the open door, closed it, waved through the window, then turned to hail another taxi.

The car was moving. I frowned at the pile of bills in my fist. I wondered why my sisters were so fearless. I wondered if I had missed out on that gene along with June's beauty gene and Jem's crazy gene. I wondered why everyone—Jon, Elizabeth, and even to a certain extent Sir Quinn McHotpants—felt like I needed oversight: someone to escort me, to take care of me, to tell me what to do and point me in the "right" direction.

"Where to?" The cabbie's baritone cut through my dazed preoccupation, and I realized we'd already gone two blocks. "Where are we going?" his voice sounded again from the front.

I quickly considered my options. I could go back to the apartment, read my new book on the history of viral infections, and embrace my hermit tendencies, or I could ask the driver to turn the cab around, take me back to the club, and—just for one night—live my life unescorted while I tried to unlock my Morris Girl fearless gene.

"Take me back to Outrageous."

CHAPTER FIVE

THERE ARE TIMES, after drinking too much alcohol, I wonder if the prohibitionists were on to something when they coined the term "demon liquor." It felt like I had a demon inside of me who was stabbing my eyes with a corkscrew, scooping out pieces of my brain with a spork, twisting cotton in my throat, and wearing soccer cleats as it jumped up and down on my bladder.

This was only my third time with a hangover and, like all the other times, I promised myself it would be my last. The first time was not my fault; my younger sister, Jem, diluted my breakfast of orange juice with vodka on the morning of the SATs. She said it was a protein drink, and it would keep my brain alert. I ended up throwing up all over my examination, and the proctor screamed that I'd ruined his perfect test administration record.

The second time I was with Jon at a tiki bar near his parents' house in the Hamptons. He ordered me a drink called "The Hurricane," which didn't taste like anything but fruit juice. I ordered several, liking the little umbrellas and other accoutrements that donned the rim of the glass, and ended up getting sick on the beach. I passed out on the sand, and Jon, being just my height and of a lean build, wasn't strong enough to lift me. He had to call two of his friends over to help him pick me up and carry me back to the guesthouse. When I woke up, I wanted to die.

Now, lying face down on a strange bed with my mouth tasting like whatever the Grim Reaper served at Thanksgiving, I knew three things for certain: I was not in Elizabeth's apartment; I was wearing only my bra, thigh-high stockings, and underwear; and I wanted to die.

I squeezed my eyes shut tighter, wanting to postpone my collision with reality for as long as possible, and willed myself back to sleep. I wasn't certain how much time passed as I lay there hoping that my fairy godmother would appear along with little talking birds and mice, clothe me in jeans and a T-shirt, put me in a pumpkin carriage, and send me to Starbucks for a soy latte. When I finally opened my eyes, all my earlier unpleasant assertions proved true.

I wasn't in Elizabeth's apartment. In fact, I had no idea where I was. Swallowing with a great deal of exertion, my mouth free of saliva, I slowly moved my gaze around the room. My eyeballs felt like sandpaper, and I had to blink several times, both in response to the unforgiving brightness of the world and the dryness resulting from sleeping in my contacts.

When my eyes were appropriately lubricated, I scanned my surroundings from where I lay. It was huge, with walls of exposed red brick, and it was sparsely decorated. The ceiling was tiled tin, rusted in a few places, beige everywhere else. There were no overhead light fixtures; rays of sunlight poured in through tall windows along two adjacent sides of the room. Near the bed was a floor lamp, which was currently off. The floor was sealed cement.

From my vantage point, I saw only five other pieces of furniture besides the mattress and the floor lamp: a drafting desk, a tall wooden chair for the desk, a bookshelf, a brown leather couch, and a side table. The drafting table was covered in papers, and the bookshelf was littered with what looked like machine parts.

I was wearing only my bra, stockings, and underwear. I confirmed this belief by peeking under the white sheet pooled at my mid-back. I glanced again around the room and found my dress folded in half over the back of the wooden chair and my shoes neatly settled under the desk.

I struggled to sit upright and find equilibrium in the vertical world. My hands automatically went to my chest to adjust the strapless bra and ensure it covered my breasts, minimal modesty intact.

My hair fell to my lower spine in a puffy, untenable tangle of curls; it must have come completely loose sometime during the night. Elizabeth called it my mane of hair; I called it my bane of hair. I kept it long, though, because—paired with my freckles—I looked like Orphan Annie when it was short, sticking straight up or out at awkward angles. At least when it was long it almost obeyed gravity.

I wanted to die. Almost as soon as I was in a sitting position on the mattress, but before I was fully able to bring the world and my current misadventure into focus, I perceived the sound of running water, emanating from a door to the right of the bed. A sudden thunderbolt of panic struck my heart and I stiffened, immediately regretting the ungraceful movement and the resulting stab of pain in my temples.

I closed my eyes and took a deep breath. I took several deep breaths. I went to the invisible closet space in my head and went through the motions of wrapping up the panic in the beach towel, somehow fumbled with the lid of the box, finally found the damn key for the box, and inserted it into the lock. I tried to ignore the shaking of my hands as the pretend me in my head put the box on the top shelf of the closet, quickly turned the light off, and ran screaming from the make-believe closet.

I needed to focus. I *really* needed to.

I had to get out of here before the mystery person emerged from the bathroom. *Avoid confrontation at all costs!!* My memory was drawing a complete blank. I had no idea if the mystery person was a man or a woman. At this moment, I wasn't sure if I really had a preference in their gender, but I drew some hope from the fact that I saw no discarded monkey suits by the bed or littering the floor.

I raced to the chair, grabbed my dress, and quickly pulled it over my head. It felt just as inadequate in daylight as it had the night before. I shimmied into my shoes just as I heard the water cut off in the bathroom.

"Oh, God." I couldn't find my handbag.

My gaze swept over the desk and the chair, but they proved to be purse-free zones. My eyes darted to the brown leather couch and side table—again, no handbag. I tiptoed to the queen mattress and lifted the sheets. The box spring was lying directly on the floor; otherwise, I would have crawled around looking under the bed.

I gave up my search for the bag and instead started hunting around the room for a phone. Before I could initiate my first sweep, I heard the handle on the bathroom door turn, and I sucked in a sharp breath.

This was it.

This was going to be my second walk of shame in two weeks. I just hoped that whoever was on the other side of the door didn't insist on a no-eye-contact breakfast. The worst part wasn't just the fact that my stupidity had resulted in a one-night stand (and maybe a plethora of incurable venereal diseases) or my immediate embarrassment at the situation. It was that Jon and Elizabeth had been right: I needed an escort. I had reclusive tendencies for a reason; I couldn't be trusted to live in the world and make decisions on my own.

I swallowed again, my hand on my stomach, as I turned to face the door.

When he emerged, I thought I was hallucinating or, at the very least, still passed out from my night of drunken disorderliness. I had to blink several times to understand, and several more times to accept that McHotpants was standing in the doorway, clothed only in a white towel wrapped low around his waist as if it didn't matter to him whether it stayed in place or pooled on the floor.

I vote for the floor!

Even through the lingering, pounding pain of my hangover, I couldn't help but gape at the perfection of him, of his bare chest, arms, and stomach. Every part of him looked Photoshopped.

Finally, after what felt like an hour, but what actually might have been four seconds, I realized I'd been staring at not his face and moved my gaze to his eyes. He wasn't smiling. In fact, his expression wasn't cool or warm or disgusted or pleased; it was completely unreadable. We stood, watching each other; me with a burning unfamiliar mixture of lust, mortification, and complete astonishment, him with a marble mask of calm. This stalemate lasted for an indeterminable amount of time.

He was the first to break the stare, his eyes moving over my now-clothed form. I shivered involuntarily.

Finally, he removed his attention from me and walked farther into the room, crossing to the bookshelf. "I believe you are looking for this."

I watched him, how the muscles in his back moved, still struck dumb by his sudden appearance. He easily reached to the top of the bookshelf and retrieved my bag. His bare feet made hardly any noise as he moved to where I stood and handed it to me. I took the offered purse and tucked it under my arm.

"Thank you." My voice was surprisingly calm given the fact that my brain and heart and lungs and stomach and lady bits were all rioting. I was determined to stay off the seesaw of crazy; I was going to be unaffected by him.

"You're welcome." He replied, his eyes skimming over my face. Without warning, he brazenly reached out, pulled a thick puffy tendril from my mass of bedraggled hair, and looped it around his forefinger. "You have a lot of hair."

Suppressing a swarm of butterflies in my stomach, I nodded and cleared my throat. "Yes. I do." Before I could stop myself, I continued. "Hair is one of the defining characteristics of mammals." I quickly bit my lip to keep from telling him that there were only four species of mammals still alive that laid eggs; among them were the platypus and the under-publicized spiny anteater; everyone always forgets about the spiny anteater.

He released the lock of hair and crossed his arms over his chest. "What are the other characteristics of mammals?"

I watched him intently for a minute, about to tell him about sweat glands and ear bones, but then a flash of memory from the previous night penetrated my consciousness. I suddenly felt sure that he was making fun of me. I remembered the absurdity of my innate response to him; I remembered the way my brain and body were in complete discord. I remembered his words to me just before the first time I left the club—that someone like me didn't belong there. I was determined to remain in control, detached, invulnerable to his glittering physical perfection and soul-baring blue eyes.

I focused on his teasing. I didn't especially enjoy being teased when I couldn't be certain of the person's intentions, so I shrugged.

His eyes narrowed for the briefest of moments as he studied me, his mouth curving into a frown; he looked displeased. Then he said, "What do you remember about last night?"

I lifted my chin, gritting my teeth. "I remember you making me leave the club."

"Can you remember anything after that?" His tone was guarded.

My attention drifted to the left, and I blinked, trying to figure out precisely what I *did* remember from the previous night. I had been so preoccupied with my hangover and my escape that I hadn't stopped to think about how I'd ended up in his apartment, in his bed, in my underwear. I was talking as I was thinking, and before I realized it, I said, "Not much. You were there, and I remember leaving the club."

"Which time?" he interjected.

"With Elizabeth—I left with Elizabeth, and she put me in a taxi. I asked the driver to take me back. When I got back, sunglasses man waved me in; then I…" My eyes lost focus as I tried to pull the memories forward. "When I walked in, I bumped into a man; he said he was looking for me. He…" I cleared my throat and squinted. I felt sure that I had bumped into someone I knew, a man I recognized, but I couldn't remember his face. "I think someone took me up some stairs; it actually looked like a tree at first, with a tree house in it, but it was a room."

"The Canopy Room." Quinn's voice was matter-of-fact, but a veiled sharpness in his tone brought my attention back to him. He moved his hands to his hips, his blue eyes dark with some unreadable thought. "What else do you remember?"

I studied him for a moment, and my own thoughts, before I continued. "Not much." I licked my lips. It was the truth; I didn't remember much. I remembered being offered and then drinking a shot of something that burned, but I couldn't really make out the size or shape of the room or any of its tangible, physical characteristics. I knew that several people had been present because I remembered hearing them laughing, but I couldn't remember what they looked like. It was like I walked into the tree-house room and was swallowed up by a black fog.

A sudden thought occurred to me, and I quickly wrapped my arms around my center. "Does that happen a lot? After drinking?"

"What? Losing your memory?" he asked.

"Yes." I nodded.

"No, not after drinking. When I found you upstairs in the Canopy Room, not long after I *thought* you'd already left, you were still awake, but you weren't making any sense, so I carried you out."

"Wait, you carried me?" My body responded strangely to that information.

He nodded. "Yeah, one of our…" He seemed to struggle for the right words. "One of the club patrons was dancing with you, but you weren't exactly cooperating so much as critiquing his dance moves. I think someone must have slipped you something." He surveyed me as though he were carefully studying my reaction, or bracing for a freak-out.

"You mean someone gave me bendothi… bethnzodiath… benzodiazepid…" I huffed, gritted my teeth, took a deep breath, and sounded out the word slowly. "Ben-zo-dia-zepines?"

"Yes, I think someone slipped benzodiazepines into whatever you drank up in the Canopy."

"Oh." I twisted my mouth to the side and thought about someone giving me a date-rape drug. It seemed far-fetched but not out of the realm of possibility, especially considering my lack of memory. I felt it would be best to be certain. "Do you have any pharmacies nearby?"

Quinn nodded his head. "I imagine you could use some aspirin. There is some in the bathroom."

"Oh, thanks, but I was thinking I'd pick up a test. Did you know that pharmacies will sell you over-the-counter tests to detect whether you have benzodiazepines in your system?" He lifted his eyebrows in what I interpreted as confusion, so I felt the need to clarify. "It's a urine test, not a venipuncture."

He frowned deeply, his tone incredulous. "How do you know this? Has this happened to you before?"

"No, no, I've never lost my memory before, and I'm not much of a party/club/bar person. One time my sister spiked my orange juice before the SATs, but that was just vodka; the other time I got drunk was also an accident."

"The *other* time? You've been drunk two times?" His frown eased, and he blinked at me. I noted again that his eyes were very blue, and his chest was very naked.

I didn't respond immediately, as I was not really sure what to say, especially because I was feeling mounting discomfort under his bared-chested scrutiny. At last, I shrugged, using a tactic introduced to me by Sandra, the psychiatry intern in my knitting group, and I answered his question with a question. "How many times have you been drunk?"

He smiled faintly. "More than two." His gaze was inscrutable. I wondered how he could be so comfortable in nothing but a towel in front of a complete stranger. "Do you remember how you got here?" Quinn tilted his head to the side; the movement reminded me of our bar conversation and the way he'd tilted his head last night.

I searched my memory, my head starting to hurt with the effort, before I slowly shook my head. "No, I don't remember coming here or," I said, and then swallowed before adding, "or anything else."

He shifted closer to me, his voice low. "Nothing happened." My eyes widened, not immediately understanding his meaning. "Nothing happened last night."

I blinked at him again, opened my mouth to speak, and then closed it again.

Nothing happened.

My eyes moved to his chin then lowered to his chest.

Nothing happened.

Of course, nothing happened.

I licked my lips involuntarily and nodded. "I know." My voice sounded like a croak.

"Really?" he asked.

I nodded again; my heart twisted in my chest, and I shifted on my feet. I couldn't meet his eyes. I couldn't understand my reaction to his statement. *Nothing happened.* Why did I feel suddenly disappointed when I should have felt nothing but relief? I didn't understand myself. I should have known that nothing had happened between us as soon as I saw him coming out of the bathroom door.

Of course, nothing happened. Of course, he wouldn't be interested in me. Of course, he is ten thousand leagues out of my league.

Just as swiftly as these horribly unhealthy thoughts swelled within my mind, a more rational notion clamored over them: *Or—and consider this, you weirdo—thank God he's not a creep who takes advantage of drugged women. If he'd touched you, he'd be an A-hole of the first order.*

"How do you know nothing happened?" he countered, sounding defensive.

I took a step back and tried to run a hand through my hair, but my fingers encountered stubborn tangles again, "I get it, ok? I, uh, I need to get out of here. What time is it?" I turned from him and started walking toward the couch, looking for the front door.

"You don't look like you believe me. This is my sister's apartment. I promise; nothing happened between us." I heard his voice close behind me, and knew he was following me.

Nothing happened because you're out of my le— GAH! *Stop it, Janie. For the love of Thor, stop it.*

In order to silence my inner crazy, I decided both were true. Nothing happened because he was a decent guy who didn't touch drugged women *and* nothing happened because he was out of my league.

I turned to face him, not quite meeting his gaze. "No, I really believe you. I know with certainty that nothing happened." I added under my breath. "Of course nothing happened."

He didn't seem to hear the last part. Quinn came to a stop in front of me again, standing at least several feet away this time. "Good." He nodded, his hands gripping the towel at his waist.

"Let's go get some breakfast."

"You want to go get breakfast?" I couldn't keep the surprise from my tone as I finally met his eyes. He nodded again, and I stammered. "Like—like this?"

He gave me a small sardonic smile. "No, obviously I'll get some clothes on."

"But—" I blinked again in confusion. I needed to stop blinking so much. "But, why?"

He shrugged, and before he walked back to the bathroom, he said, "I'm hungry. You need eggs and bacon for that hangover. And, I'm hoping you'll tell me more about the defining characteristics of mammals. I'm pretty sure you know more than you've let on."

CHAPTER SIX

Giavanni's Pancake House was an extremely small, open-air eatery with no tables. An L-shaped, waist-high, speckled gray countertop ran the entire length of the establishment, and short, circular stools upholstered with red vinyl were bolted in place on the wooden floor along the counter's edge.

The place was packed.

A line extended down the block, around the corner, and out of sight. People stood patiently, sipping Dunkin' Donuts coffee and reading papers as they waited for a spot to eat breakfast. Rather than find the back of the line, Quinn walked up to two conspicuously empty stools at the farthest end of the counter, pulled a RESERVED sign from the top of each seat, and motioned for me to sit on the stool adjacent to the wall.

Before I complied, I asked, "Did you call and make reservations?"

He shook his head no. "Come. Sit," he said, and he placed his hand on my arm above the elbow and pulled me to the red vinyl seat. "I want to know more about mammals." His mouth hooked to one side in a poorly hidden smile.

I complied, frowning at him and his teasing.

Before we left the apartment, but after Quinn finished dressing, he suggested I look through his sister's clothes if I wanted to wear something to breakfast besides my little black club dress. All her personal things were located in a room adjacent to the bathroom, but it was really more like an oversized walk-in closet. I had to walk through the bathroom to get to the closet. I didn't feel especially comfortable digging through someone else's things, so I grabbed the first casual outfit I saw: a blue cotton knee-length skirt and a V-neck black T-shirt.

Her feet were a full size smaller, so I wore my zebra print stilettos out to breakfast. Thankfully, the skirt fit perfectly. The shirt, however, was snug over my chest. The strapless bra I wore was surprisingly supportive, but it was also a push-up.

Therefore, paired with the snug fit of the V-neck, my usually well-concealed cleavage was brazenly, visibly ample. I thought about removing the strapless push-up bra, but I was never one of those girls who could go comfortably braless; there was too much jiggle in my wiggle.

I washed my face and used my finger to brush my teeth then paused to look in the mirror. My mishmash of Northern European coloring was especially pastel under the bright, fluorescent bathroom light: pale skin that burned instead of tanned, a light smattering of freckles, and red-brown hair, eyebrows, and lashes.

I felt marginally better after the brief ministrations; my hair, however, was a complete disaster. I thought about asking Quinn if his sister owned any hair ties or barrettes or rope or anything I might be able to use to tame the wild beast. In the end, I just wore the fuzzy mess of knots loose down my back, over my shoulders, and at times in my face. I figured that, worst-case scenario, I could use it to cover my ample bosom.

As we walked to the breakfast cafe, however, Quinn brushed it back from my cheeks when it became too unruly, which invariably caused my skin to burn from pale pastel to scarlet, and I would lose all semblance of thought or focus. Directly following these interactions, I prattled on about the concept of leap seconds, nanotechnology, and the inevitable space elevator that would allow the moon to rival Disney World as a tourist destination.

Quinn didn't talk much but seemed to listen with interest as I expounded on these various and sundry topics. He asked questions periodically; the moon space elevator in particular drew an avalanche of questions. When I didn't have all the answers, I promised I would email him a link to the NASA update page for the project.

And now here we were, seated quietly at the counter. I was trapped between him and the wall, and stared at the menu without seeing it. Maybe it was the fact that I was silent for the first time since leaving the apartment, but I found myself attempting to ignore the sudden, uncomfortable, yet omnipresent self-awareness that was alternatively giving me goose bumps and making my neck hot.

His thigh brushed against mine; his elbow grazed mine lightly. I leaned against the wall to gain as much distance as possible, but I couldn't avoid the small touches in the tight space. I glanced at him from the corner of my eyes; he appeared completely at ease, studying his menu, oblivious to the gentle torture his careless closeness was causing. I was so absorbed in my discomfort that when the waitress spoke to me, I was visibly startled.

"Hey-ya, Quinn. Where's Shelly? Who's yer friend?" A short, dark-haired woman in her late fifties or early sixties gave me a brief, friendly smile as she placed two mugs of coffee in front of us. She had the unmistakable rasp of a smoker, and, paired with her thick Midwest accent, she sounded like Mike Ditka.

"Shelly left early this morning and couldn't come. This is Janie. Janie, this is Viki."

I dumbly reached my hand over the counter and tried to look and sound more composed than I felt. "It's nice to meet you, Viki."

She held her hands up. "Oh, baby, my hands are covered in grease. You don't wanna shake deeze unless you wanna wash yer hands with turpentine." A deep, gravelly laugh escaped her lips as she pulled out an order pad and pen. "But it sure is nice to meetcha. Are you a friend of Shelly's?"

Before I could answer that I didn't know Shelly, Quinn interrupted me. "She's here with me."

Viki lifted her brow, for it truly was a single brow, in what I guessed was surprise, and her mouth formed a small O. I felt her eyes move over me with renewed interest, which made me blush… again. I gripped the menu a little harder and tried to swallow but found the simple action difficult.

"That's…" Viki blinked. Her big brown eyes continued their open assessment, and her mouth moved, but she seemed to struggle for words. Finally, she murmured, "Well, that's a surprise."

My cheeks burned; I could hear my heart drum and the blood rush between my ears. I knew that this Viki person didn't mean to be rude. She looked honestly perplexed, and, if I was reading her awkward soundlessness correctly, she was obviously stunned at the possibility that Quinn and I could be there as a couple. I felt the need to distance myself from the notion and make certain she believed that the very idea was beyond ludicrous to me as well.

I need to make certain that she knows that I know that he knows that he isn't interested. I was starting to confuse myself.

Before I realized that I was speaking, the verbal diarrhea spilled forth. "Oh, we're not together. I mean, we're sitting together and we came here together, but obviously, we're not *together*. How could *we* be together? I'm probably never going to see him again after today. We're not even friends. I don't even know him. I mean, you know, not *really*." I inclined my head toward her and a small laugh burst from my lips. "Can you even imagine? It'd be like *Planet of the Apes*. He's Charlton Heston with all the muscles and such, and I'm that girl ape. They could never be together because it'd be like a Neanderthal with a human, cross-species breeding…and that's just not right. Although Neanderthals are closely related to humans and are in fact part of the same species. If you want to be precise, they are a subspecies or alternate species of human."

I glanced at him and gave him a closed-mouth smile. I categorically hoped it dually conveyed confidence and cheerful ambivalence to the obvious disparity in our compatibility. His eyes, however, narrowed as they watched me. I wondered if he found my analogy to be imperfect. Maybe he didn't like Charlton Heston because of his NRA involvement.

Conversely, Quinn did seem like the sort to like guns.

I cleared my throat and continued. "And why would Charlton Heston want to be with the ape? No one would, even though she has this huge…huge…brain."

Viki blinked at me and looked at Quinn. "Where didja meet this one?"

Before Quinn could speak, I felt compelled to answer, hoping to make up for my gaffe. "I met him last week, and before that I saw him a few times at my building where he works as a security guard. I used to work as an accountant there before I was downsized."

Viki's unibrow crinkled over her nose until it came to a point. "A security guard?"

I gulped and gave her a tight smile as I reached for my coffee, wanting to change the subject. "I love coffee. Brazil is now the world leader in the production of green coffee, but in East Africa and Yemen, coffee was used in native religious ceremonies that competed with the Christian Church. Because of this, the Ethiopian Church banned secular consumption of coffee for many years." I brought the mug to my lips and sipped the bitter black brew, mostly to keep myself from talking. The coffee burned my tongue. I ignored it. "Mmm, coffee."

Viki's eyes moved between Quinn and me, her unibrow still suspended on her face. "R-i-g-h-t," she finally said, drawing out the word.

I heard Quinn clear his throat, and then he placed our order. "She'll have eggs over easy, bacon, sausage, hash browns, and toast with extra butter. I'll have the usual." As he ordered, he pulled my menu away and handed it to Viki along with his, and I noticed his voice sounded different, distant. Viki gave us both a small, quizzical smile, and then she left.

I sipped more of my black coffee and glanced again at Quinn. He wasn't looking at me. His mouth was a precise straight line, and his temple ticked as he flexed his jaw. I couldn't read his sculpted features. I had a hunch that I embarrassed him or said something inappropriate. This was not a new feeling for me—regretting my words—but this time, I felt remorse on his behalf.

I set the cup down and sighed. "I'm sorry." I tried pulling my fingers through my hair but again abandoned the effort when I encountered unruly knots. "I have a bad habit of saying what I'm thinking and—"

He held his hand up and shook his head. "No—no need to apologize." He gave me a tight smile that didn't reach anywhere near his eyes. "You were just being…honest. It's not the first time I've been called a Neanderthal."

"You're not a Neanderthal." I frowned at him. "For one thing, you're far too tall. And, I was comparing myself to a Neanderthal due to my physical features—you know, the size of my head, for one."

"So, you're saying your head is larger than mine?"

"Yes—no—what I mean is, they have big awkward heads, or are believed to have had big awkward heads that were too large for their body. Then, there is also the hair."

"Hair?"

"Yes, hair. It is hypothesized that red hair…" I gestured to my crazy-town curls, "… comes from the Neanderthals interbreeding with the earliest humans."

"So, Neanderthals and humans did breed?"

"Yes. Female humans and male Neanderthals may have bred successfully, which, if you think about it, isn't as far-fetched because bigheaded men and small—er, normal-headed—women still breed quite often today. But, currently, scientists believe that the male humans who mated with female Neanderthals created sterile offspring. They believe this because there is a lack of Neanderthal mitochondrial DNA present in modern humans. So, as you can see, and if you reflect on it, awkward headed-females mating with beautifully normal headed-males is a bad idea."

He blinked at me once, frowned, then turned his attention to his coffee. Unbearable silence lay like a thick blanket of fog around us. I figured he was regretting his decision to invite me to breakfast. I thought about comparing myself to a donkey and him to a horse, but instead bit my lip to keep from speaking.

I noted his cheeks, neck, and the bridge of his nose were tinged with a faint shade of pink, likely due to annoyance with my fumbled conversation. I searched my brain for anything that would distract him. An abrupt thought came to me and, for lack of a better strategy, I decided to resort to a parlor trick that usually either amazed people or endeared me to them. It would also be an excellent demonstration of my freakishness, but I didn't really have anything to lose.

I licked my lips before speaking. "So, uh, want to see a trick?"

He shrugged his shoulders, his tone unenthusiastic. "Sure."

I turned in my seat to face him, resting my elbow and arm along the counter. "Give me any two numbers and I can give you their value in addition, subtraction, multiplication, and division."

He turned toward me and met my gaze with a disbelieving one of his own. "What—in your giant brain?"

I noted that he sounded interested more than sardonic, which I felt was an improvement, but I chose to ignore his giant brain comment. "Yes, in my brain. No paper."

His mouth hooked to the side just barely. "Any two numbers?"

I nodded once. "Try me."

He turned his body to me completely, and I tried to ignore how his legs bumped into me, one of his knees settling between mine as we faced each other. "Hmmm..." his gaze narrowed speculatively. "Ok, four hundred and seven hundred."

I wrinkled my nose. "Here you go: addition—1100; subtraction—negative 300; multiplication—280,000; division—.57 yada yada yada. Ok, give me a hard one now."

He blinked at me, his mouth slightly open, then he smiled a small albeit real smile and rubbed his hands on his thighs. "Fine, a hard one then: twenty-one and five-thousand-one-hundred-twenty-four."

I let out a breath of relief; our earlier unpleasantness seemingly forgotten. "Ok, in the same order as before, the answers are 5145, 5103, 107,604, and .004 yada yada yada. That wasn't a hard one, either."

He half-laughed half-sighed. "How do you do that?"

I shrugged. "I don't know. I've just always been able to. It comes in handy on Thursdays."

"What happens on Thursdays?"

"I tutor math and science at the Kids' Club on Thursday afternoons. Sometimes, if I can't get them to focus, I distract them with my 'freakishness.'" I used air quotes for the word freakishness then frowned at myself for doing so. I hated it when people used air quotes. It was like when someone says '*we*' instead of '*I*.' As in, '*We would be so delighted... we just did the laundry... we have a yeast infection.*'

"Why did they downsize you? It seems like you would make an incredible accountant."

"I don't know that either. My friend Kat—she still works there—she was going to try to find out but hasn't been able to for some reason."

He took a sip of his coffee and said, "Has anyone else been let go?"

"No. I'm the only one. But you have to admit, I'm pretty strange. Maybe they were just looking for an excuse to get rid of me. I have a tendency to make people uncomfortable with—you know— the plethora of trivial facts." I was about to air quote '*freakishness*' again but successfully suppressed the urge to do so.

"Hmm." His clear blue eyes narrowed as they studied me. "Are you…?" He set his cup down and leaned a little closer. "Do you have a photographic memory?"

I laughed despite myself, mostly from nervousness due to his proximity. "No—God, no. I'd forget my name if it weren't on my driver's license." Then I frowned at the inaccuracy of my statement. "Actually, I don't have a driver's license since I moved to the city, but my name is on my credit card and my state ID, so that helps."

He continued to survey me for a long minute, and then he asked, "Have you found a job yet?"

I shook my head and rolled my lips between my teeth. Even though it had only been a week and a half, and I was eligible for unemployment, I felt anxiety about being out of work.

He reached for his coffee and watched me over the rim of the cup as though he were considering something, or more specifically, considering me for something. When he put his cup down, he reached into his back pocket and pulled out a business card and a pen. "I think I might be able to help you." He wrote a name and number on the back of the business card.

"What? Do you think I should get into the security business? I am pretty tall for a girl. And I can be fierce when I need to be."

He tilted his head to the side in a gesture that I was becoming used to, and then he handed me the card. "I don't doubt it, but my company always needs someone good in the business office." He closed his pen and set it on the counter. "I've written down the name and number of our director of business operations. You should call him; send him your resume. I can get you the interview if you want, but you'll have to get the job on your own."

Viki returned with our food as I studied the card. I turned it between my fingers and read the front:

Quinn Sullivan

Cypher Systems, Inc.

UNDER HIS NAME was his phone number and business email address. I flipped the card to the back and stared at his handwriting rather than the name and number he'd written. His letters were all capitals, severe and precise; he put little dashes through his sevens but not through his zeros; his words were in a straight line rather than drifting up or down in the absence of lined paper.

I liked his handwriting. I imagined reading a handwritten letter from him. I thought about him writing it—about taking the time to think of me enough to want to sit and write something to me. It made a volcano of warmth erupt in my stomach.

When I looked up, he was frowning at me, his gaze guarded. "Of course you don't have to apply if you don't want to."

I placed my hand on his arm without thinking. "Oh, no, I'm going to apply. Really, thank you. Thank you for thinking of me." His eyes moved to my fingers, and I withdrew my hand quickly and tried to tuck my hair behind my ears as I turned to the plate of greasy food left by Viki. I stared at the plate for a moment before I spoke. "I'm very grateful for everything you've done for me, last night and this morning, and now this." I gestured to the card on the counter. I met and held his gaze as I added with a thankful smile, "You're a really nice guy."

His frown deepened as though I'd just insulted him. His attention moved over my face, hair, and neck, and then he sighed and looked upward in an almost stealthy eye-roll.

He mostly mumbled, "I'm not that nice."

DESPITE ONE MORE EXTREMELY AWKWARD moment when Quinn wanted to give me a ride home on his motorcycle and I somewhat freaked out, stubbornly refused, and insisted on taking a cab, the rest of our morning together was actually really nice. Rather, more precisely, it was as nice as it could be considering I spent most of the time distracted, attempting to think of a way to get him shirtless again. During one weak moment, I contemplated throwing my coffee at him.

Later that night, as I lay on the couch in Elizabeth's apartment trying to concentrate on reading my book and failing miserably, I thought about my debate with Quinn about the motorcycle. If he'd offered to drive me home in a car I likely would have said yes.

As it was, he owned a motorcycle.

I've never been on a motorcycle, and since my mother died on one, I have absolutely no desire to ride on a motorcycle, ever. Obviously, I didn't tell him that. I don't like to think about, much less talk about, my mother's death. I doubted that Quinn, who probably already thought I was a complete nutcase, wanted to hear about it anyway.

"Janie? Janie, are you here?" I heard Elizabeth burst through the door just as I was getting up to brush my teeth, for the tenth time that day, and go to bed. There was an unexpected urgency in her voice, so I met her at the hall.

"Yeah, I'm here; are you ok?"

When she saw me, she stepped back and closed her eyes, her hand over her chest. "Oh, God. I'm going to kill Jon."

I lifted my eyebrows in confusion. "Jon? My Jon? What happened?"

Elizabeth sighed and let the bag on her shoulder fall to the ground. "He called me, like, eleventy-thousand times today; he kept paging me, too. He said the two of you were supposed to meet today, and you didn't show up."

It took me approximately five seconds to remember the planned meeting with Jon that I had obviously forgotten about earlier in the day. The sight of Quinn's bare chest must have wiped my memory.

"Oh, geez, I totally forgot!"

Elizabeth rolled her eyes. "You need to get a cell phone. I'm blocking his number from mine."

"I am so sorry, Elizabeth. I'm sorry he bothered you at work."

"Don't worry about it; I was more worried about you." She laughed lightly as she pulled off her work clogs. "But you might want to send him an email or call him on Skype. He said something about calling in a missing persons report." She stopped to give me a brief hug before walking to her room. "I'm glad you're ok."

I nodded and turned to my laptop. It was already ten o'clock at night. I knew he would be up, but I didn't particularly want to speak with him, so I opted to send him an email instead. When I opened my account, I saw that he'd already emailed me five times, with each message progressing in level of anxiety. The last was sent less than a half hour ago and read:

Would you please call me and let me know you are ok? I am going crazy with worry. I love you, Janie, and just want to know you are ok. I get that I hurt you and that you are mad, but please don't punish me like this. This isn't like you. If you're trying to make me upset, then you've succeeded. If you don't want to see me, just say so. I'm scared to death that you are somewhere hurt. If you get this and you are ok, then we really need to talk about getting you a cell phone. Please call me. Jon

I sighed and gritted my teeth. I was annoyed by his presumption that we "needed" to talk about "getting me" a cell phone (as if I couldn't do that myself if I wanted to) as well as at the pinch of guilt I felt as I typed my response:

Jon, I'm ok. Honestly, I forgot about meeting you today. I'm sorry I didn't call, but there is no reason to worry. Elizabeth just came home and said that you were calling her at work. Please don't do that again. You know that I usually check my email at least once a day, and you also know how I feel about cell phones. I have no problem meeting you, I don't want to upset you, and I'm not punishing you. I really do want us to be friends. Let me know if you want to try to meet up next week sometime. Talk to you soon, Janie

I stared at my cursor and re-read my email. I decided to delete *Talk to you soon* then I sent it. I didn't want him to think I was promising to speak with him soon. I took a moment to skim down the list of emails in my inbox, and I noted with a great degree of frustration that none of them contained responses to the hundreds of employment queries I'd sent.

My thoughts drifted back to Quinn, and I remembered the card he gave me at breakfast. I reached to the coffee table in front of me and pulled out the card, letting my thumb caress his name before flipping it over to read the contact information he'd written on the back. My mouth curved into a wistful smile when my eyes met with the image of Quinn's handwriting. I really was ridiculous.

I clicked the Compose button and typed a quick letter of introduction, making sure to attach my resume to the message. As an afterthought, I decided to copy Quinn on the email. I wanted him to see that I was actually very interested in the position and thankful for his recommendation.

Just as I hit Send on the email, my account chimed with a new message from Jon. I stared at the subject line:

I'm sorry. I love you.

I sighed and crossed my arms over my chest. Shaking my head, I closed my laptop without opening his message. I was tired. I huffed again. I wanted to brush my teeth and go to bed. I didn't like how uncomfortable and guilty Jon made me feel when I was certain—well, mostly certain—that he was the reason we were no longer together.

"You keep sighing; I can hear you in my room." Elizabeth came around the couch and flopped down next to me, stretching her arms over her head as she did so. "What happened with Jon?"

I shrugged and unthinkingly expelled another loud breath. "I emailed him. I don't really want to talk to him right now."

"You need a cell phone."

"No. If I had a cell phone then I'd have to talk to him. Since I don't have one, I get to put that conversation off until I'm ready to have it."

"Fair enough." Elizabeth lifted her hands in surrender. "I don't want to talk about old soggy pants anyway."

I laughed and rolled my eyes; Elizabeth started calling Jon soggy pants when he accidentally sat in a wet seat at a movie theater once, and spent the whole movie with wet pants after confirming the liquid was soda.

"So…" Elizabeth wagged her eyebrows at me. "I have something for you." She pulled a card out of seemingly thin air and squealed as she forced it into my hand. "Look! It's Quinn's card! He gave it to me last night before we left the club."

I stared at it for a minute before I responded. "Oh. Are you going to call him?"

Elizabeth frowned at me then hit me on the arm. "What? No! You left the club so fast that he stopped me and asked me to give it to you." She nudged me with her shoulder. "He wants you to call him. Ah! Janie and McHotpants, sitting in a tree, k-i-s-s-i-n-g and f-u-c-…"

"Wait!" I exclaimed, cutting her off. "No, no—he gave you the card because he wants to help me find a job. He thinks there might be an opening with the security firm he works for."

Elizabeth smirked. "Oh, really? That's preposterous! What would give you that idea?"

I pulled an identical card from next to my laptop and handed it to Elizabeth; "Because he gave me one too; he wrote the name of a business manager on the back and told me to apply for a job."

Elizabeth looked from one card to the other, speechless, then demanded, "Wait—when did he give you this?"

"This morning."

"When did you…? Ok, start from the beginning. What happened? When and where did you see Quinn this morning?"

I told her about going back to the club last night and everything that transpired thereafter: the blackout, waking up in Quinn's sister's apartment with no clothes on, the fact that he'd wanted to be sure I knew he hadn't made a move on me, breakfast, and the business card. Elizabeth listened, frowning in disapproval and surprise, but confusion mostly, and didn't interrupt even when I knew she was anxious to get to the origin of my matching business card.

She contemplated me for a moment after I finished. "So did you pick up the test to see if you'd been drugged?"

I shook my head. "No, I meant to, but I…" I sighed and let my head fall back to the couch. "I was so tired when I got home."

"Oh! Thank God Quinn found you!" She squeezed my hand with hers. "Wait—did anything happen? How did he find you? When did he bring you home? Did anyone…are you ok? Did you go to a doctor?"

"Yes—I mean no." I sighed again. "Yes, I am ok. No, nothing happened. No, I didn't go to a doctor. I think Quinn found me before anything happened."

"Oh." She squeezed my hand harder then let go and rubbed her eyes. "This is a lot to process. I'm exhausted. I can't believe you went back to the club. He obviously likes you. He was flirting with you. Why would he take you to his sister's place? Who does that? And what was with the reserved seating at breakfast? Did this waitress woman really have a unibrow? I'm really glad you're ok."

I could tell she was tired because her usually well-ordered thoughts were bouncing all over the place. I smiled at her. "You need sleep; we can talk about it in the morning." I pulled her up and she gave me another hug.

"I am glad you're ok. Jon really scared me." She released me from the hug and held my shoulders as she pinned me with her pale blue eyes. "If something happened to you, who would help me finish the pitcher on Mojito Mondays? Who would be my partner in Trivial Pursuit? Who would clean my bathroom?"

We both chuckled as I pushed her toward her room. "You did just fine cleaning your bathroom before I moved in."

"No, I didn't. I hadn't cleaned it in several months before you moved in. I told everyone it was my bacteria wet lab." Elizabeth yawned. "Goodnight, Janie. I love you."

"Goodnight, Elizabeth. I love you too."

CHAPTER SEVEN

BING, BANG, BOOM—I got a job.

To my surprise and, quite frankly, utter disbelief, I received a return email from Carlos Davies, Director of Business Operations at Cypher Systems, on Sunday morning, followed by a rapid-fire series of events: Carlos responded to my message and requested that his secretary, Olivia Merchant, also included on the email, arrange an appointment for Monday morning. She responded Sunday afternoon requesting that I be at the office by 10:00 a.m.

Olivia included directions to the office in her email, an informational document on benefits, and instructions for my arrival. I immediately noted that Cypher Systems was located in the Fairbanks Building, the same building as my previous job. I responded Sunday evening confirming my appointment for Monday at 10:00 a.m.

The benefits package contained a salary offer for the position of Senior Fiscal Project Coordinator, which I read three times before I actually comprehended that the number was real and that I wasn't misreading the placement of the decimal point in relation to the zeros. I tried to Google Cypher Systems but, other than finding a very slick, graphics-heavy web page facade and an inquiry form for potential clients, the search results were unhelpful.

The lack of information available left me feeling pensive and unprepared for the interview. If they asked me why I was interested in the position, I wasn't sure how I would answer the question honestly. I didn't know anything about the company other than that they provided security for the Fairbanks Building and Club Outrageous, and the position apparently paid twice my previous annual salary.

Oh, and they hired supermodel security guards *a la* Quinn Sullivan.

Cypher Systems was located on the top floor of the Fairbanks Building. Olivia's instructions indicated that I should check in with security on the lobby level, after which a security guard would escort me to the Cypher Systems offices.

It seemed one needed quite a lot of escorting experience in order to be a security guard for Cypher Systems.

My escort's nametag labeled him as Dan, and he was shorter than me, especially as I was wearing sky-blue silk stilettos. He appeared to be my age or a few years older, stocky, and was thick-necked with swirling tattoos just visible beneath the blue collar of his uniform. Dan gave me a plain once over as he walked me to an elevator. When we got to it, he didn't push a button as one would normally do, but instead placed his palm against a glass screen. The screen retracted to reveal a keypad. Dan then punched in a series of numbers and waited.

"You're very big," he said.

I gave him a cursory smile. "Yes. I ate all my vegetables as a child." This was my standard response when someone remarked on my size. For some reason, it always irked me when people felt it necessary to draw attention to my height as though I wasn't aware of my larger than average stature. I once responded, "Yes, and you're very small." That didn't go over very well, even though it was true.

Dan chuckled at my canned response and waved me into the elevator. I realized I'd never noticed this lift before. When we walked in, I further noticed there was only one destination button. Dan was quiet the rest of the ride even though his eyes continued to move over me in unhidden appraisal, and the corner of his mouth curved in a friendly, lopsided smile. I was silent and had to half-yawn in order to pop my ears as we traveled upward.

The elevator doors opened to an impressive view of the city behind an all-glass reception desk. The light was almost blinding. I swallowed nervously and smoothed my free hand down the hips of my beige tailored jacket and skirt as I stepped onto the landing. My other hand gripped the letter-sized portfolio at my side, which contained copies of my resume and letters of recommendation from college professors.

Dan didn't leave the elevator but rather spoke from behind me. "Keira at the reception desk will take care of you."

I turned to thank him, but the doors had already closed. Straightening, I walked to the glass desk and paused before it. The woman, who I presumed to be Keira, was on a phone call.

She lifted her brown eyes to mine, raised a single finger, and said into her headset, "Just one moment; let me track him down for you." She then pressed a series of buttons on a phone that looked very high-tech. The first thing I noticed about Keira was that her black hair was in such a tight bun that it looked painful. It seemed to pull at the corners of her eyes and mouth, giving her the appearance of a perpetually smiling cat.

She turned a Cheshire grin on me and said, "May I assist you?"

"Uh, yes. I have an appointment with Carlos Davies."

"Oh? An appointment? And what is your name?"

I swallowed again; my mouth was very dry. "I'm Janie Morris. I'm here for an interview."

Keira moved her attention to an impressively large monitor on her desk and nodded. "Yes, here you are. Today is your first day, right?"

I opened my mouth and a small squeak came out before I said, "No, no—I'm just here for an interview."

She moved her attention back to me, confusion clouding her angular features. "But, didn't Mr. Sullivan recruit you?"

"I wasn't recruited. Qui—I mean, Mr. Sullivan arranged for the interview."

I was interrupted by a new voice. "Ah, you must be Janie Morris."

I turned to my left and tried to smile warmly at the approaching man but was struck momentarily speechless. With my heels on, he was exactly my height, and he was the definition of what my friend Ashley liked to call a brown sugar hottie. His dark chocolate eyes were framed with long, black lashes, his skin was warm olive, and he had a slow, easy smile bracketed by dimples. He wore a gray suit, a white shirt, and a silver tie.

"Yes, I'm Janie," I half croaked as I extended my hand. He enclosed my hand in both of his and gave it a firm, professional shake.

"I'm Carlos. I'm so glad you could start on such short notice. Come with me; I'll get you settled in."

"I—start?" My voice was strained and hoarse, so I cleared my throat. "Um, wait. I—that is, I was under the impression that this was an interview."

Carlos blinked his pretty lashes at me, his smile waning but not disappearing. "Oh, I see." His eyes moved between mine, his gaze still warm. "Certainly, we can start with an interview if you wish." He turned and motioned for me to follow him down the hall.

If I wish?

I matched his stride and tried to suppress a new flutter of uncertainty as I walked next to him. "I have extra copies of my resume if you need them."

He chuckled softly. "No, no need. We've done a background check; you're very qualified, and you have excellent references."

My face warmed at the compliment, but I wasn't sure I deserved it. He led me past a series of offices, and I noted the lack of cubicles. He paused at one office and asked me to wait a moment. I heard him ask the inhabitant to join us, and then we continued.

Carlos's office was moderately sized, not huge, but not small either, and seemed to be only slightly larger than the rest of the rooms we'd passed. He motioned for me to sit in one of two brown leather club chairs as he walked around his desk.

"So, Ms. Morris, why don't you start by telling me about yourself." His voice was very soothing, and his brown eyes sparkled as he leaned back in his chair.

I was doing my best to give a good impression, choosing my words carefully and trying to stay on topic, when another man entered. He was tall and lean, and his blond hair was disheveled as though he'd been running his hands through it. His gray eyes peered at me from behind fashionable black horned-rimmed glasses perched on a nose that was a little too pronounced for his thin face.

He immediately crossed to me and held out his hand. "Oh, thank God you're here! I'm Steven; we're going to be great friends." He gave me a single shake then half sank, half collapsed into the empty brown club chair next to mine. "These people! There is so much to do. I spent this morning summarizing the projects for you."

Carlos cleared his throat and gave Steven a friendly smile. "Ms. Morris is here for an interview. I don't believe she has accepted the position yet."

Steven looked between Carlos and me, his face betraying his inner horror. "What?"

Carlos dipped his head. "Steven." His voice was thick with warning.

Steven affixed his attention squarely on me. "Janie—can I call you Janie?" I nodded, but he didn't wait for me to give verbal assent before he continued. "Janie, I need help. As Carlos explained it, you are a numbers person. You have experience managing client accounts. Your references say you are a hell of an accountant. You have no criminal record. You tutor children once a week, so that means you're good with big babies. You look like a Scandinavian version of Diana Prince." I coughed at the allusion that I was Wonder Woman's alter ego, but Steven continued. "And, assuming you can string three words together, you'll be a smashing success with our business partners. I'll be honest, Janie; they don't like me. I'm not pretty enough to go out in public. I'm a hard worker and I'm a tax wizard, but I make the clients uncomfortable. You'll do nicely."

"Steven, Ms. Morris was just telling me about her work experience."

Ignoring Carlos, Steven scooted his seat closer to mine and drew my attention to an iPad on his lap. "Now, these are all the current accounts," he said, as he trailed his finger down a column of number codes that denoted account names, and I noted that the columns had no title headings. "And these are the payment terms…the filing terms…and here are the estimated expenditures for this quarter and the actual expenditures for last quarter. This is the project balance for the year. Got it?"

I nodded, looking over the spreadsheet. "Why don't you use column headings?"

"They slow me down."

"Hmm." His response made no sense. I tried not to focus on the gargantuan size of the dollar figures but instead scrutinized the veracity of the calculated amounts. "Your formula is wrong here…" I pointed to two separate boxes on the spreadsheet. "…and here. Also, when did this account open? The balance should be negative if the projected expenditure column is correct."

When I looked up at Steven, I saw that his thin lips were pressed together in a quivering smile. "Good girl. Test passed. I think I love you, Janie. Let's get married and not have children."

My eyes widened for a brief moment. I felt sure he was teasing me, but when I looked into his dancing gray eyes, I knew he meant it as a compliment. I returned his smile. I liked Steven.

Carlos broke the silence. "Ms. Morris, the job is yours if you'd like it."

"Oh, please say yes." Steven's smile widened.

"To the proposal or the job?" I asked.

"If you have to pick one, let it be the job." Steven handed the iPad to me then reached out his hand to shake mine again. "I snore and you're too tall; we'd divorce within a year."

I laughed, stood, and shook his hand, not minding that he'd remarked on my height. "Fine, then; I accept the job." I turned to Carlos, who was also standing by now. "Although, I'd like to see a job description. I'd like to make sure I can actually do the job you've apparently hired me for."

Carlos gave me another disarming, dimpled smile, which could only be described as adorable. "Of course. You get settled in with Steven, and I'll have Olivia email it to you." He came around the desk and, like before, shook my hand with both of his. "And if you have any questions, please don't hesitate to find me."

♥♥♥

It was decided that, instead of meeting at Kat's apartment for knitting night, as it was her turn to host, we were all to meet for drinks, then dinner at South Water Kitchen for a Janie-is-once-again-able-to-pay-income-taxes celebration. It was a Tuesday, it was the second day at my new job, and it was exactly two weeks since my worst day ever.

Almost immediately after settling into our seats, Elizabeth introduced the subject of Quinn along with Friday night, monkeys, naked cage dances, Saturday morning McHotpants breakfast, and the business card that led to my new job.

"You all remember McHotpants, the security guard? Well, Janie and I saw him at that new club where the naked ladies dance with the monkeys—yes, that club called Outrageous! Anyway, his name is Quinn, and she went home with him after being drugged. They had breakfast together Saturday morning, and he got her the interview for her new job."

It was like throwing *Hustler* magazines at sex addicts. After a two-second lull of stunned silence, everyone started talking excitedly at once. Elizabeth sent me a sweet smile over her ice water.

The entire first half-hour of the evening was consumed by me regaling the ladies with the events of my weekend, plus the Monday non-interview job interview. A few questions interrupted my story, largely relating to trivial clarifications, but mostly they sat and listened with a grave, almost reverential silence. Every time the waiter came by to take our order, Sandra and Ashley shooed him away by demanding wine with quiet, urgent whispers.

As I neared the end of my story, I could feel the tension building in the group. I sensed that they were restless with questions, but Elizabeth seemed to have an agenda and, when I finally reached my conclusion, she interjected.

"This is what I don't understand: How did Quinn know you were up in the Canopy Room? Or did he? Did he go up there to get you, or did he just happen to go up there and see that you needed rescuing? And is that why he was suddenly like 'you need to leave' when he found out the Canopy Room people bought us drinks? He must have known the people up there were shady. Furthermore, since we suspect that you were slipped something, what is to be done about it?"

She glowed with an almost Sherlock Holmes-esque satisfaction and sat back in her seat while the group speculated on her questions. Undeniably, Elizabeth seemed to have given the entire encounter a great deal more thought than I had.

Although I tended to obsess about topics like the English vernacular, the height of the average Brazil nut tree, and international date standards, I had a habit of ignoring important details, such as who drugged me and how I felt about blacking out only to wake up mostly naked in a strange apartment with seven pieces of furniture.

I shivered a little, finally feeling the weight of my recklessness and truly understanding what a dangerous situation I'd been in. Likewise, my stomach flipped at the thought of Quinn finding me, carrying me out the second-story room, and taking me to his sister's place, all while I was blacked out.

Maybe I wouldn't need to be rescued, escorted, or coddled so much if I focused on actually important details rather than dreaming up an appropriate collective noun for every plural eventuality.

In the end, I promised the ladies I would attempt to corner Quinn when I saw him at work, at which point I would question him about the Canopy Room, as well as actions taken to ensure the safety of unsuspecting female guests in the future. The waiter reappeared and, thankfully, everyone placed her order, thus giving me a reprieve from the hour-long investigation into my weekend.

"Have you seen him yet? In the office I mean?" Marie asked, leaning toward me and fixing me with her bright blue eyes.

"Quinn? No, today was only my second day. Mostly, I just filled out paperwork, met with lawyers, and settled into my office."

"You met with lawyers?" Fiona's steady voice sounded from my right.

"I had to sign a non-disclosure agreement and a non-compete agreement."

Fiona frowned. Her eyes met Marie's for an instant then moved back to me. "Why did you need to sign that?"

"Well, basically, I'm not to disclose the nature of my work or who I work with."

Fiona's frown deepened. "You mean their names? You're not allowed to talk about your coworkers?"

I shook my head and finished a thirsty sip of my wine. "No, I mean I'm not allowed to discuss any of the clients I work with: their names, how much they pay us, what we do for them, or what services we offer—that kind of thing."

I recalled my conversation with two lawyers from earlier in the day. They were both egg-shaped men in their early thirties and reminded me of Tweedledee and Tweedledum in appearance. But when they spoke, their French accents clouded my earlier impression.

Le Dee and Le Dum both made it extremely clear that I was not to disclose any details about the clients with which I was soon to interact: no names, no characteristics, no impressions, no nothing. I was also not allowed to discuss what I did at work, including my job description or duties, or what services Cypher Systems offered. I could, however, communicate my job title if asked.

It was Marie's turn to order; I took the opportunity to glance at the menu, but Fiona pressed me on the subject. "I guess it makes sense…" Her voice trailed off as though she expected me to fill in a blank.

I turned my attention to her and found her elfin eyes softened with concern. I gave her a comforting smile. "Oh, it does; it does make sense. It's not really a top secret I'd-tell-you-but-I'd-have-to-kill-you kind of thing; it's more of a proprietary thing—trade secrets and such."

That answer seemed to pacify her, because she returned my smile and let me go back to studying the menu.

CHAPTER EIGHT

To my dueling chagrin and girlish glee, I didn't have to wait very long to talk to Quinn. It happened during my second week on the job.

Cypher Systems was an extremely efficient, well-oiled machine of a company, and it was very secretive. Almost immediately, I learned the necessity of the non-disclosure agreement I signed on my second day, and at the end of the first week, I was beginning to feel confident in the general maintenance of my accounts, systems, and the structure of the business office.

I loved my new job.

I managed what Steven called all the public accounts, which were mostly moderately large businesses that used a subsidiary of Cypher Systems called Guard Security.

Guard Security provided security for various corporate properties and buildings, and personal security details for CEO types. I quickly discovered why Steven didn't use column headings on his spreadsheets. Steven told me that Cypher's firewall was under nearly constant attack; all data files and identities were coded. Thus, for the first half of the coming month, during the bulk of my training, I wouldn't know whose account I was working on; I would only know the code. Steven said that after the first two weeks, he would provide me with a code key on a flash drive and give me only one day to memorize which code belonged to which customer for each account.

Steven managed the private accounts, which, from what I could infer based on his vague description, were contracts with individuals, private citizens, and high-level families. In addition to security, the contracts also often included investigative work. This subsection of Cypher Systems was also a subsidiary, and was referred to as Infinite Systems.

In addition to Guard Security and Infinite Systems, Cypher Systems had other holdings and was the parent company to a number of other businesses, but Steven and I were the only two accountants in the security division. In fact, Cypher Systems was actually quite small, if you didn't count all the sub-companies, with only nineteen staff members in the office.

Even so, my company exclusively occupied the entire top floor, and every office was a window office along the north perimeter of the building. According to Steven, the offices and location were new; the company had moved into them just a few months prior.

There was no view of the lake from my window, but the northeastern corner office likely had a respectable panorama. Regardless, part of me wanted to move into my office and live there; I found myself distracted by my amazing view of downtown, and frequently pinched my arm to remind myself it was real. The rest of the space was mostly blocked off with only one heavy door as an entrance. In order to gain entry you needed to pass a five-finger and retina identity scan.

When I asked Steven what was inside the room, he shrugged noncommittally and said, "Data storage."

I had met almost everyone by my second day. I counted Quinn among my eighteen coworkers even though I didn't know his role yet, and I hadn't seen or spoken to him since the Saturday before I was hired. Eight of the eighteen were accountants; some of them shared my title of Senior Fiscal Project Coordinator, and some were titled just plain Fiscal Project Coordinator.

In addition to Carlos, there was only one other director in the office, Director of Human Resources, and she didn't seem to have any staff other than her administrative assistant. The rest of the group included Keira, the receptionist and something of a telephone operator, one desktop support guy named Joe, two computer programmers, and another administrative assistant named Betty, who I never spoke to but did see every so often when she walked by my office.

Betty worked for the company CEO, who also happened to be the CIO, CFO, and COO, but everyone just called him the boss.

It became clear to me that Betty and the boss, or as Steven called them, B & B, didn't interact much with the rest of the staff. The boss, it seemed, didn't come into the office much. No one seemed surprised by his absence the entire first week or the second week of my employment, so I never actually met him.

Betty was very stylish, and looked to be in her mid-sixties. She had steel-gray hair and black eyes, and she wore pearls every day with a tailored skirt suit. She didn't come across as unfriendly; she just seemed very busy all the time.

My Quinn happenstance occurred on the Wednesday of my second week at Cypher Systems.

I noticed that I'd never seen Betty leave the office. She was there when I arrived, no matter how early, and she was still there when I left, no matter how late. Betty's perpetual busyness prompted me to offer to pick her up some lunch that day. I think I confused her at first because she repeated the word lunch several times, as though it were a mythical thing she'd heard of in a bedtime story long ago.

Finally, with a plainly grateful smile, she accepted the offer and requested a bowl of vegetable soup, a side salad, and a giant oatmeal cookie from a deli called Smith's Take-away and Grocery. It was a well-known deli and sandwich shop, with a few grocery items for sale, just one street over from our building.

I left early so that I could eat out and still return before noon. The deli had a few tables, all along a far wall. I was sitting at the corner table rereading one of my favorite comics, an anthology of a series in a bound paperback.

When most people think of comic books, they recall the small pamphlet style with only a few pages and, at the beginning of each pamphlet, the story picks up where the previous one left off in another comic book that always ended with *to be continued.* The larger, paperback bound anthologies are like watching an entire season of a TV show on Netflix or on Amazon Instant Videos. You can gorge yourself on the entire series and immerse yourself in graphic novel goodness in one epic sitting.

I had lent the anthology to one of the kids I tutored, and he'd just returned it to me last week. Over the past two years of tutoring, I'd become something of a comic book lending library for the kids. I didn't mind; they took excellent care of them and loved to discuss the stories after they were done.

My thumb moved back and forth over the place where I'd torn the cover several years ago as I sank deeper into the story. My legs were curled under me, and I was just getting to the part where the really bad guy is about to kidnap the good guy's best girl when I heard a voice immediately to my left.

"What are you reading?"

I stiffened, my heart leaping, and I automatically turned toward the voice. I found Quinn looking down at me, his expression guarded and neutral except his eyes. His eyes always seemed to be a shade of up-to-no-good blue. I struggled to make sense of his presence and blinked at him several times.

Acutely, I became aware that my mouth was hanging open. I snapped it shut and looked away, habitually running a hand over my hair. It was pulled into a severe bun and seemed to be on its best behavior, which was more than I could say for any other part of my body.

I cleared my throat and showed him the cover of my book then glanced at him again. I noted that he wasn't wearing a security guard uniform. Rather, he was dressed in a very nice wool gray suit, white shirt, and gray tie with threads of blue silk running through it. If we had been in Victorian England, I would have called him dashing; but, since we lived in the twenty-first century, I had to settle for the wordier *GQ*-model hot.

"Hmm…" He craned his neck and leaned closer to read the cover then he straightened, his expression impassive. His eyes skimmed over my face. "You read comics?"

I nodded, absentmindedly stroking the cover. As usual around his aura of handsome manliness, my mouth felt dry when I finally spoke. "Yes, I do."

"Hmm," he said again. We watched each other for a moment and, like clockwork, I could feel the warm awareness that always accompanied his presence start spreading from my lower belly to my neck, toes, and fingertips.

Suddenly, he said, "Scoot over." Then he abruptly picked up my bag, which had been resting on the bench next to me, and placed it on the bench opposite. Setting down his food next to my empty sandwich wrapper, he took off his suit jacket, folded it with care, and draped it over my bag.

"I—uh—" Flustered, I could only push myself farther into the corner of the booth as he slid in next to me, but my efforts did little good. The booth wasn't really meant for two people. It was maybe meant for one and three quarters, which meant that even with my back pressed to the wall behind me, a big guy like Quinn and a big-bottomed girl like me barely fit. When he finally settled, his leg pressed against mine from upper thigh to ankle.

I chewed on my bottom lip and set the book on my lap. It must have been the effect of the graphic novel paired with Quinn's sudden closeness and being quite trapped by his large form, but whatever the cause, I felt like swooning.

"Kind of a tight fit," he remarked with a small smile, turning toward me, his face inches from mine as he unwrapped a sandwich.

"Yeah, well, I can go if—"

"No, no. Stay. How do you like the job?" He bit into his sandwich and turned the whole of his attention to me.

"I like it." I had to focus on breathing normally; being so close to him was maddening. I couldn't seem to look anywhere without seeing some part of him, so I settled for looking at his hands. One held the roast beef sandwich and the other gripped a napkin. "I like it a lot. I just started, and…uh..." I frowned, then huffed out a breath. I wasn't sure if I was allowed to talk to Quinn about work. I hadn't seen him at work, and to my knowledge, he didn't have an office on my floor.

I must have debated the issue a little too long because, after a few moments, Quinn asked, "What's wrong?"

"It's nothing. It's just…" I met his searching gaze. "I'm not sure what I'm allowed to tell you."

His eyes narrowed at me. "What do you mean?"

"I'm not supposed to talk about what I do with anyone."

He blinked at me. "What?"

"I signed the non-disclosure agreement last week." I gave him an apologetic grimace.

He set his sandwich down and looked at me with something resembling disbelief. He opened his mouth to speak but then closed it and gave a short laugh. "Janie, trust me. You can talk to me. It's my company."

My shoulders sagged a little. "I know you work there too. I'm sorry; I've never had to sign a non-disclosure agreement before, and I don't want to make a mistake."

His smile widened subtly as his gaze moved over me. His eyes brightened with what looked like laughter, and then he pulled his phone from his pocket. "I'll call Carlos. If he tells you it's ok to speak to me freely, will you?"

Unthinkingly, I put my hand over his to still his movements. "No, don't do that. You're right; I'm being silly. I really don't want to mess up, and everyone seems so nice —like too good to be true nice—and the office is too good to be true, and how I got the job is too good to be true, and when you add all that together, I'm just waiting for the other shoe to drop." I sighed. "No, the first shoe hasn't dropped, so that's not the right idiom to use, even though it originated in cities like Chicago." I slid my hand away from his and to my book, nervously picking at the cover.

Quinn shook his head, and I noticed that his usually detached, hawk-like gaze seemed softer and unguarded. "Janie, what are we talking about?"

"About the origin of the idiom I just used: waiting for the other shoe to drop. Did you know it originated in cities like Chicago and New York?"

"No, I did not." He tilted his head, his mouth hooking upward to one side as though he were trying not to laugh. "Tell me about it."

He was teasing me again. "Well, it did. So…"

He lifted his eyebrows. "That's all? You're not going to tell me the specific details of how it originated?"

I shook my head. "I don't know the details."

He mimicked me and shook his head in response. "You're lying. You do know."

"Nope, I don't."

"This is just like the mammals." He sighed and placed his phone on the table. Before he took a bite from his sandwich, he said, "You're stingy with information."

My frowned deepened. "No, I'm not."

His words were somewhat garbled as he spoke between chewing. "You're an information tease."

"What?"

"Or maybe you don't really know the origin, and you're just making things up to impress me." He took another bite.

"I am not! It originates from the late industrial revolution in the late nineteenth and early twentieth centuries. Apartments were all built with the same floor plan and with a similar design so that one tenant's bedroom was under another's. Therefore, it was normal to hear one shoe hit the floor, then the other, when an upstairs neighbor undressed at night."

"I wonder what else they heard." His gaze held mine and seemed to burn with a new intensity.

"I suppose anything that was loud enough."

He gave me a full grin followed by a deep, rolling belly laugh. I liked the sound of his laugh and smiled reluctantly in response; nonetheless, I was fighting the warring feelings of being pleased that I'd made him laugh but concerned that I was being laughed at. The latter feeling eclipsed the former, and I frowned then glanced at my lap and picked self-consciously at the cover of my book again. I could feel the heat of a blush spreading up my neck.

The intensity of my reaction to him continued to confound me.

It wasn't just his good looks, which verged on angels-singing-on-high miraculous, that unnerved me so—not anymore, at least. If he'd been a gorgeous jerk or a good-looking moron, my reaction would have cooled and normalized rather quickly. Inopportunely, he was not a jerk, and he was most definitely not a moron. He was thoughtful, clever, and confident, and the most adroitly sexy guy I'd ever met. I didn't like to think he was laughing at me.

I heard his laugh falter abruptly before he said, "Hey, Janie—look at me." I lifted my chin but couldn't quite manage to meet his eyes. A hint of a grin was still on his face when he said, "I was just teasing you."

I forced a small laugh and shrugged. "I know. I…uh…" I looked at my watch purposefully. "I have to get back to the office; my lunch break is over."

His grin faded. After a moment, he cleared his throat. "You still haven't told me how the job is going."

"It's great, but I don't want to be late getting back."

He swallowed and pushed his sandwich to the side. "Don't worry about being late. I'll give Carlos a call."

"Don't do that."

"I don't mind."

"But I do."

He watched me for several moments and, despite the thunderous beating of my heart, I silently endured his perusal. I felt too hot, too self-aware, too everything. When I finally met his gaze, I noted that his face had settled into an impassive mask, but, as ever, his blue eyes seemed to burn with intensity. At last, he stood. I released a breath that I didn't know I was holding. As I moved to stand, he reached out his hand and grabbed mine to help me from the booth.

"Listen," he said, and then he cleared his throat again. He was still holding my hand and thereby holding me in place. "Over the next week you'll be going out with me on a couple of stops. It's part of your training."

I opened my mouth in surprise. A little pang of pleasure and pain twisted in my chest as I thought of spending more time with him. Finally, pulling together enough of my wits to form words, I stuttered, "Wh—what kind of stops?"

"I'll be taking you to meet some of the corporate clients."

"Steven didn't mention anything about that in his training schedule," I said.

"He must have forgotten."

"That doesn't seem likely,"

Quinn lifted his eyebrows in challenge. "Is there some reason you don't want to go?"

"We won't be taking your motorcycle, will we?"

"No, we'll be taking a company car."

"Oh. Ok." I looked down at our hands, still linked together from him helping me out of the booth. His hand was very large; mine was small in comparison. It was a strange sensation to feel that any part of my body was small. I'd always felt so big around Jon. My hands were the same size as his.

Quinn must've noticed my gaze because he abruptly let my hand drop and reached over to the bench where his coat lay across my handbag. He moved his jacket to the side and picked up my bag. He seemed to study it for a few brief moments before he handed it to me.

"Thanks," I took the offered purse but made no move to leave; instead, I gave him a small, closed-lipped smile and shifted under the weight of his steady gaze.

"You're welcome. And thanks for letting me interrupt your lunch."

I shrugged. "Oh, no problem; feel free to interrupt anytime."

"Really? Anytime?" The corner of his mouth hooked to the side and he dipped his chin as though to force me to meet his gaze. "That's a dangerous thing to say if you don't mean it. I might interpret that to include lunch, dinner, and breakfast."

His question, then statement, and the manner with which both were posed, made my bun feel too tight and my neck hot. I glanced at him through my lashes, unsure of where this was going. Even after our various, albeit limited, encounters, everything about Quinn made me hypersensitive and self-conscious.

Undoubtedly, if he expected me to retort with something coquettish and droll, then I would fail completely. I didn't know how to engage in flirtatious banter. My mind wandered to conversations with Elizabeth in which she'd continued to insist that Quinn was interested in me, and I continued to find the assertion ridiculous. Therefore, faced with such a man speaking to me in such a way, I was wholly unprepared. All previous attempts in similar situations, mostly relegated to college, had been disastrous and painfully uncomfortable. They were either ill-timed, or the topics I had chosen were ill-conceived.

As an example: the pheromone excretions of termites.

Now, standing awkwardly, avoiding eye contact, trying to postpone my response, I didn't even know if flirtatious banter was what Quinn expected or wanted. Men in general unsettled me; this one in particular turned my insides into a brouhaha of chaos simply by glancing in my direction.

Finally, while ignoring looming feelings of trepidation, I decided to answer with candid earnestness. There was nothing wrong with honesty, and it was his choice to read as much or as little into my answer as he liked.

Not quite able to meet his eyes, I finally responded. "Yes, I mean it. Feel free to join me anytime." I was surprised by how soft my voice sounded.

A slow, hesitant grin spread over his features, and I had difficulty drawing breath. It was a sexy grin—a very sexy grin. His eyes dropped to my mouth, and he licked his lips almost imperceptibly. I felt a little woozy.

"Good. I'll do that." Still giving me his grin, Quinn reached over and grabbed his jacket from the booth. "I'll walk you back."

♥♥♥

Quinn carried Betty's lunch as we walked the short distance back to the Fairbanks Building. I was in the middle of explaining a potential improvement to the billing structure of Guard Security to Quinn as we approached the security desk. Dan, the security guard with neck tattoos who'd escorted me on my non-interview first day of work, nodded at Quinn. Then Dan winked at me.

I smiled and waved warmly in return, and then I finished explaining to Quinn the impetus for the cost analysis I was working on. "The best thing about the proposal is that the software is free." I glanced over at Quinn to gauge his reaction to this great news, but to my disappointment, he was frowning at me. We stopped in front of the elevator, and I turned to face him. "You don't think it's a good idea?"

Quinn's expression was rigid, and he looked past me to the lobby; he motioned toward the security desk with his chin. "How do you know Dan?"

"Who?" I glanced over my shoulder to follow Quinn's gaze and found Dan looking at us, at me, and I gave him a closed-mouth smile then turned back to Quinn. "Oh, Dan the security man; just from the building. On my second day at Cypher Systems, he helped me bring up my box of paraphernalia."

"You two talk much?" Quinn still wasn't looking at me and, for that, I was glad. He looked like a hawk about to devour a mouse and, standing this close, I could see that his eyes were a fiery cerulean.

I shook my head. "Not really. Just every once in a while when I arrive in the morning or go get lunch. Why? Should I be worried?" I hesitated, frowning. "Is there something I should know about him? Is he a bad guy?"

Quinn returned his attention to me and it sent warmth from my nose to my toes; his expression softened, and he seemed to debate what to say next. Finally, he sighed and said, "You read too many comics."

"What?" I thought about denying the accusation, but instead I asked, "How can you tell?"

The elevator opened and he held the door then followed me in. "Bad guy, good guy—most guys fall somewhere in between."

I lifted an eyebrow at his assertion. "I don't think that's really true. I think you can say someone is good or bad based on their actions."

This was a subject I spent a lot of time considering. Both my sisters were criminals. My mother was a serial cheater who had abandoned her family. I liked labels; I liked putting people and things into categories. It helped me calibrate my expectations of people and relationships. If I didn't label my sisters as bad, I would be an enabler of their behavior, just like my father was. I didn't plan on spending my life as a doormat, or living in the waiting room of perpetual disappointment, hoping they would change.

"So, does one bad action make a person bad?" Quinn placed his palm against the five-point fingerprint screen; he then punched in the code to call the elevator.

"No, a person is the sum of his or her choices, and therefore, is largely defined by his or her actions."

"No one makes all good choices, and everyone makes mistakes."

"Ah, ha! Yes, that's why I also consider intentions as the defining denominator in my good-people, bad-people confidence interval."

Quinn's mouth pulled to the side. "What does that mean—your good-people, bad-people confidence interval?" He leaned his shoulder against the wall of the elevator.

"Well, obviously, everyone makes mistakes, but if you only see it as a mistake because you've been caught, then that's bad. However, if you realize that you've made a mistake because you recognize the error of your ways and you make an effort to change, then that is good. There is a big difference."

"So, really, you think a person is the sum total of his intentions and not his actions."

The elevator opened and I stepped out as I continued my philosophizing. "No. Without action, even good intentions are meaningless."

I was abruptly struck by the comfortable progression of our conversation. Strangely, the ever-present pins and needles I usually felt around Quinn seemed to dissipate the further we ventured into this topic. I felt almost relaxed. We walked past Keira, who nodded at me but then suddenly stopped typing when she saw Quinn.

Before I could do a double take and ask Keira if she were ok, Quinn asked, "What would a person be if he had good intentions and no actions?" His free hand pressed against my lower back, and we continued down the hall to my office.

"Lazy."

Just inside my door, he pulled me to a stop with gentle pressure on my elbow. "And what do you call someone who has bad intentions and good actions, or good intentions and bad actions?"

"Stupid."

He considered me for a long moment; his brow was furrowed, but there was a small smile on his lips. "Let me get this straight; according to you, there are four kinds of people: good, bad, lazy, and stupid. Is that right?"

My eyes drifted over Quinn's face as I contemplated his summary of my philosophy. "More or less; that's about right. Think of it like a four-quadrant scatter plot graph."

He blinked at me. "Use a different analogy. I don't work much in four-quadrant scatter-plot graphs."

I laughed and walked to my desk. "Ok. Imagine a map of the United States. Divide it into four quadrants: north, east, south, and west. Let's say I typically always take trips due north but sometimes I go east. Sometimes I go northeast and, on rare occasions, I go south. Each trip I take is a dot on the map. The quadrant with the most dots represents my personality."

"Therefore, someone could be a good person with a tendency to be slightly stupid."

I nodded slowly. "Yes, precisely. Take me for example. I feel confident saying I'm a good person with a tendency to be slightly lazy and a precipitous tendency to be stupid, especially when it comes to non-work related decisions and actions."

"And what kind of person do you think I am?"

My gaze met Quinn's as he leisurely crossed to stand in front of me; his features were set in a detached mask of indifference, but his eyes were piercing and steady. The pins and needles immediately returned; my heart quickened and my neck was hot.

"Uh, well." I let out a slightly unsteady breath and rested my fingers on the desk, mostly for balance. He stopped less than a foot from me so that we were both standing behind the desk. I had to tilt my head backward to maintain eye contact. "I don't think you're stupid or lazy."

"Hmm." A whisper of a smile briefly passed over his face. "So that leaves either good or bad."

"I tend to think good."

"Why is that?"

"Because you helped me at the club, and you put in a good word for me here." I licked my lips; my mouth felt dry. "I still need to return your sister's clothes, and I didn't get a chance to thank you for arranging the interview."

His eyes lost focus and he frowned. Abruptly he took a step back and affixed his attention to the floor; he lifted the hand that held the take-out order. "I'm going to get this to Betty and stop by Steven's office about your training this week. I'll…" He rubbed the back of his neck with his free hand. "I'll see you tomorrow."

Suddenly I remembered my promise to Elizabeth regarding the Canopy Room incident and some unknown person's alleged inclination to drug women. Without thinking, I took two steps forward. "Wait; before you go, I need to ask you something."

He stopped, lifted his eyes once more, and waited with patient interest for me to continue. I attempted to swallow, but my throat felt tight. I didn't know how to bring this up so I just started talking. "So, about what happened at the club last week; I wanted to ask you…what I mean is…what happened to the person who, you know, who dosed me with the benzodiazepines?"

"He was arrested," he answered matter-of-factly.

I couldn't cover my surprise as I gaped at him. "He was arrested?"

Quinn nodded. His expression was neutral and unreadable.

"But, do I need to do anything? Should I file a report?"

"No. He wasn't arrested for drugging you. He was arrested for something else."

"Oh." I frowned, then sighed as I thought about that. "Who is he? What was he arrested for?"

"Just some guy. Don't worry; he won't have the opportunity to bother you again." With that, Quinn turned and left my office.

I stared at the door, confused and relieved, but mostly confused, not really sure what to make of the last part of our exchange. Before I could dwell on it with any exactness, Olivia Merchant stepped into my office. She wasn't looking at me but rather down the hall in the direction of Quinn's departing form.

"Was that Mr. Sullivan?" Olivia sounded as befuddled as I felt.

I'd interacted with Olivia, as Carlos' administrator, a number of times. She didn't strike me as good or bad or stupid. She wasn't terribly efficient with her work, but she seemed to make a good show of it whenever Carlos was around. I didn't mind her; I just needed to figure out a way to improve her responsiveness to my requests or discover a work-around for her work-lethargy.

"Yeah, that was him." I stood next to my desk and leaned against it, somewhat dazed. If I hadn't been so dazed, it might have occurred to me that this was the first time Olivia had ever gone out of her way to speak to me.

"What was he doing here?" She turned to me, placing her hands on her hips. Again, if I hadn't been so dazed, I would have noticed the accusation and suspicion lacing her tone.

"Taking lunch to Betty."

She straightened and let her hands fall to her sides. "Oh. Well, that was nice of him."

I nodded. It was nice of him. It was nice of him to sit with me at the deli, it was nice of him to walk me back to work and indulge me in my silly philosophies. He didn't exactly look safe, nice, or approachable, but Quinn Sullivan *was* a nice guy.

He was a good guy.

Olivia mumbled something about checking in with Keira, and then she left, but I didn't pay much attention to her. I was excited, nervous, and disoriented.

I would be spending some part of tomorrow with Quinn.

CHAPTER NINE

I RAN HOME to tell Elizabeth my news and engage in what I surmised to be completely typical female behavior: nitpick every detail of my conversation and time with Quinn Sullivan, a.k.a. McHotpants. Alas, when I arrived home, I found a note indicating that she'd gone to the hospital for an unexpected shift and that I should start looking for reasonably priced two-bedroom apartments.

Instead of indulging myself in girl talk, I had to settle for watching a chick-flick period drama on BBC America and sifting through craigslist for new living arrangements. Truth be told, I wasn't in any real hurry for us to vacate her current place. I liked sleeping on the couch; it made every night seem like a sleepover. I liked the non-permanence of it.

The next day I was racked with excited nervousness. I woke up way too early, and left the apartment late after trying on every piece of clothing I owned. Finally, I settled on a scoop neck white shirt, dark blue pants, and matching high heels. I felt I'd achieved my goal of business professional without trying too hard, but I worried, as I waited for the train, that I'd not tried hard enough.

I worried that I looked boring.

Almost immediately, I pushed the thought out of my head. I reminded myself: *Quinn Herr Handsomestein Sullivan is my coworker; he isn't interested in me, and he doesn't care or notice what I am wearing.*

The reminder made me feel both better and slightly worse.

When I arrived at work, I stopped by Steven's office to ask if I should prepare or bring anything to the training session.

Steven only shrugged and said, "No. Mr. Sullivan didn't tell me much about it, but then, he's not much of a talker, is he? He'll probably just show you one of the properties and have you back within the hour." Steven pushed a button on his phone to get on a conference call and then shooed me out of his office.

I waited all morning for Quinn to call. I stayed within earshot of my office phone and jumped every time I heard someone else's phone ring. Around three o'clock, I glanced at my watch and frowned for the forty-second time that day.

Still no call and it was past lunch. I hadn't eaten since breakfast at six o'clock in the morning, and that had consisted of two hardboiled eggs. Additionally, I had to be on the South Side in three hours for my Thursday night tutoring session. I decided to bury my disappointment in an Italian beef sandwich from Smith's Take-away and Grocery.

Things went awry when I ran out to pick up lunch for Betty and me, since we were the only ones in the office who hadn't yet eaten. In the seventeen minutes it took me to pick up lunch, Quinn left me two messages on my office phone.

The first was a gruff, "Call me back ASAP."

The second call was less verbose.

He must've called as soon as I left. My heart leapt at the sound of his voice when I checked my voicemail with one hand and held my to-go meal in the other. Then Keira came into my office. A Bluetooth headset was clipped to her ear. She told me that Mr. Sullivan was on the phone, and wanted me to meet him downstairs at the Starbucks on the corner.

I abdicated thoughts of eating and promptly took the elevator to the bottom floor. I was agitated. I was tense. As it turned out, both sensations were warranted. My stomach plummeted when I caught sight of him and noted his stern expression and the object he held in his hand.

As we stood across from each other next to the coffee counter, I could see my doom in his hand: a small, sleek, black rectangle with a shiny screen and only one perceivable button. Virtually everyone at Cypher Systems had a business cell phone.

I knew it made sense, but I still didn't have to like it.

My hands were on my hips, and I eyed the cell phone with contempt. "What is that?"

His smile was reluctant, as though he really wanted to maintain an impassive mask but found it impossible to do so. "What does it look like?"

"I don't believe in cell phones," I said.

I might as well have said that I didn't believe in the laws of thermodynamics.

"I don't understand." His gaze felt remarkably penetrating, and the smile fell away from his features. His usual stoic mask of detachment was tinged with confusion.

I shifted awkwardly on my feet, twisting my fingers together. "It means I don't want to carry a cell phone."

"I'm not asking." He reached out with his large hands and placed the phone in my palm.

"What about Carlos? What does he say?"

"It was his idea."

His rebuttal left me unfazed. Maybe it was because I'd woken up in his sister's apartment half-naked, or because we may or may not have engaged in flirting the day before, or maybe it was my very real resentment at the thought of having to carry a cell phone. Whatever it was, I seemed abruptly semi-impervious to the usual pandemonium his proximity administered to my insides.

I countered, "No, it's not Carlos's idea. It's your idea. You probably talked him into it."

"Fine, yes—it is my idea, and Carlos thinks it's a great one. And, since Carlos is your boss…" he lifted his eyebrows and waited for me to fill in the blanks.

My chin lifted in defiance while he cradled my hand with both of his. I tried not to be affected by his touch, but the incongruence between the gentleness with which he held my hand and the obstinate quality of his glare was unnerving. His thumb was also moving in slow circles over the back of my hand. I clutched my anger to my chest like a last pair of marked-down Jimmy Choos in my size.

Finally, I said the only thing I could think of. "It's a personal choice. I don't want it."

He sighed, visibly annoyed. "Why not?"

"Because…because…" I held my breath, not wanting to explain my unconventional repugnance for conventional technology, but I couldn't help myself. His closeness, his hands holding mine, the dastardly small circular motion of his thumb, even his slightly perturbed glare unleashed the floodgates of my nonsensical verbosity.

"Because—are we really here, alive, if we interface with the world via a small black box? I don't want my brain in a vat. I don't want to be fed with input from the equivalent of a cerebral implant until I can't tell fiction from reality. Don't you see those people?" I motioned with my free hand to a line of customers waiting for their coffee orders to be filled. "Look at them. Where are they looking? They're not looking at each other, they're not looking at the art on the wall or the sun in the sky; they're looking at their phones. They hang on to every beep and alert and message and tweet and status update. I don't want to be that. I'm distracted enough as it is by the actual, tangible, physical world. I've embraced the efficiency of a desktop PC for work and research, and I even use a laptop on my own time, but I draw the line at a cell phone. If I want social media, I'll join a book club. I will not be collared and leashed and tracked like a tagged Orca in the ocean."

I was a little breathless when I concluded and withdrew my fingers from his, leaving the phone in his hand. I tried to look everywhere but at him and his damn tenebrous blue eyes.

He placed the phone in my hand once again. "As much as the idea of collaring and leashing you sounds promising, the purpose of the phone is to ensure you're reachable."

I interrupted him. "You mean bound and restrained."

"Janie, if I wanted to restrain you, I'd use rope." When he spoke, his voice was low and softened with what could only be described as intimacy.

I met his gaze abruptly, startled by his tone, but his gaze struck me momentarily mute. He'd shifted closer, towering over me so I had to tilt my head back to meet his stare, his mouth curved into a whisper of a smile that felt more menacing than a scowl. I blinked under the scalding stare and leaned one elbow against the counter for balance.

I felt heat rise up my throat and over my cheeks as I frowned at him. "I know what you're doing." My own annoyance bolstered my confidence.

He lifted a single eyebrow and leaned against the counter, mimicking my stance. "And what's that?"

"You're teasing me again, like yesterday; you're trying to distract me." I placed the phone on the counter.

"I'm not trying to distract you." His eyes traveled slowly over my face.

I gritted my teeth to get my blush and the beating of my stupid heart under control. "Yes, you are, and it won't work."

His smile grew, but it was still just a small curve; his gaze continued its searing yet leisurely perusal of my features. "And why not?"

Recovering my voice but not entirely in control of my brain, I started talking without really paying attention to my words. "Because they don't use ropes; they use nets. They track the Orcas between Alaska and the Hawaiian islands to establish migration paths, mating patterns, and birth rates. It's actually fascinating. Did you know that most male killer whales that are raised in captivity—which is about sixty to ninety percent of them—experience dorsal fin collapse?"

"Really? How interesting. What is dorsal fin collapse?" His voice was deadpan, but he was still giving me that dangerous smile.

I took a step backward. "It's where the dorsal fin—you know, the usually stiff fin on their backs—droops to the side, and they can't get it up. Scientists think it's because when the males are in captivity, they can't swim to an adequate depth, and so their dorsal fins droop. That is why I don't want a cell phone. I don't want a droopy fin."

The purposeful languorous caress of Quinn's gaze faded during my litany, as had his smile. He met my eyes and blinked at me as if I'd said something completely crazy or horrifying. Quinn shook his head and glanced away, presumably to clear his thoughts.

"Look," he said, almost in a growl, and he picked up the phone from the counter and smacked it into my palm once more. He quickly crossed his arms over his chest, his hands balling into fists. "You're going to carry that phone." His tone left little room for argument even as he made concessions, but his characteristic up-to-no-good stare had slipped back into place. "You don't have to look at it; you just have to answer it when it rings. No one will text you; I promise. And if they do, you can ignore the messages. Use it just like a landline; in fact, you can use it for personal calls if you want." If possible, he looked even more preoccupied and detached than usual.

"But you can still use it to track my whereabouts, so I'll still be like a whale with..." I swallowed hard as my hand closed around the stupid smart phone, accepting my fate. "I'll still get a droopy fin. Do you want me to have a droopy fin? Can't you tell Carlos it's a bad idea? Tell him you made a mistake; he might listen to you."

His eyes moved down to my neck and lingered there. Then he said, "Do you know what your problem is?"

His question made me frown, insta-glower actually, and I instinctively crossed my arms over my chest. "I have a problem?"

"Yes. You have a problem." He lifted his piercing blue gaze to my glowering frown, and I was somewhat stunned to see that he didn't look agitated any longer; he looked intent and very determined. It aggravated me.

Without thinking, I said, "Oh, really? I can't wait to hear what my problem is. You've known me a total of three weeks and you've already diagnosed *the problem*. The suspense is killing me. Well, please enlighten me, oh great identifier of problems." As soon as the words were out of my mouth, I suppressed a gasp by gulping hard. The level of my annoyance-fueled sarcasm was reaching critical mass, and I couldn't seem to control it.

"You are incredibly talented, and you're one of the smartest people I've ever met."

I interrupted him. "Yes, that sounds like a real problem. I see your point."

"But you are completely blind to the obvious."

I could feel heat rising into my cheeks again. I clenched my teeth. "Well, *obviously* you're right. *Obviously* I should just carry the cell phone." I slipped the cell phone into my pocket. "Thank you so much, Quinn, for pointing out the *obvious* error of my ways." I gave him a sugary sweet smile and started past him, intent on the door.

Before I could move more than a step, he reached out and stopped me, gripping my arm above the elbow. "Damn it, I'm not talking about the cell phone."

"I need to get back to work." I stepped back and shrugged out of his grip; he took a step forward, effectively trapping me against the counter, and I refused to meet his eyes.

"You're angry with me." I heard him sigh.

"I'm not angry. I don't get angry."

"Then you do a really good impression of angry."

Am I angry? I wondered. I couldn't remember ever being really angry, not even when my mother left, not when Jem spiked my orange juice before the SATs, not when Jon cheated on me with random bimbo number two. I was flustered and agitated and more annoyed than I'd ever felt in my life.

I lifted my hand to my forehead and rubbed my temple. "Look," I huffed. He was standing too close. I couldn't think with my brain when my body wanted to climb him like a tree. "I'm not angry. I just have a completely irrational hatred of cell phones. And you are just the messenger."

"It won't be as bad as you think." He sounded remorseful.

I looked at him then, narrowed my eyes unhappily. "It's already pretty bad."

"Now I can text you daily jokes." Again, his voice was deadpan, but his eyes were alight with mischievousness; he placed his hands on either side of me, my back still against the counter, and filled every inch of my immediate vision.

I cleared my throat to gain composure. My annoyance was melting into something warmer even as I tried to stay focused. "I thought you said there would be no texting."

"Only from me, and you don't have to answer."

"I won't answer, and I won't read your jokes."

Then he smiled that slow sexy grin that always penetrated my defenses. "Yes you will. You'll read them." He nodded slowly, just once, as though to emphasize his certainty.

I tried not to smile and only half succeeded. "I'm still angry with you."

"You said you weren't angry."

"In retrospect, I think I was angry…" I tried to take a step to the side and met only the immobile granite of his arm. "…am angry."

"What can we do about that?" His eyes moved between mine.

I tried to keep my voice steady. His closeness was twisting my stomach into knots. Didn't he understand the concept of personal space?

"You can start by moving out of the way. I've been gone for too long, and my very late lunch is now cold."

I let out a breath of relief tinged with a semi-subconscious note of disappointment as he stepped back; he straightened and let his arms fall to his sides. It was suddenly clear to me that our short time together had helped me to become slightly more at ease around him. If he'd cornered me like he'd just done when he escorted me from my old job, I think I would have spontaneously combusted with lust or fainted into a coma of bliss.

It felt like we were becoming friends or, at least, friendly. I didn't see him as just a delicious piece of man meat anymore. I saw him as Quinn: pushy, intelligent, frustrating, sexy Quinn who liked to tease me and thought I was smart and talented.

The corner of his mouth pulled upward just a fraction. "Yesterday you said I could interrupt your meals anytime."

I grunted a non-answer and wrapped my arms around myself. Without his closeness, I felt cold, and something about his eyes made me shiver.

He sighed, suddenly becoming serious. "Listen, I was calling earlier to cancel for today, but I'll pick you up tomorrow morning at ten for training." He pulled a hand through his hair, causing the locks to arrange themselves with adorable awkwardness before settling back to their tousled perfection. "You go eat your cold lunch. I have to go to a meeting."

"Go then." I shrugged. "And if you lock yourself out of your car, don't call me. I won't be answering my cell phone."

His eyes narrowed threateningly in response. "You'll answer. Besides, I'm taking the motorcycle."

I frowned. "Be careful on that thing."

He nodded once, gave me a half smile, and left. I stood in place for several minutes after he left, motionless except for intermittent smiles and frowns alternating over my features. I replayed our conversation in my head; the phone felt heavy in my pocket. I thought about appealing to Carlos about the phone. As Quinn said, Carlos was my boss, and if he decided the phone was unnecessary, then maybe I could get out of having to carry it around.

On my way back to my office to eat my now cold lunch, I felt the phone vibrate against my thigh. At first, I didn't know what it was, and jumped in startled surprise. I fished out the contraption and glanced at the screen; true to his word, he'd sent me a joke:

There are 10 kinds of people in the world: those who understand binary numbers, and those who don't.

I shook my head and said to no one in particular, "What a nerd."

By the time I departed the elevator to my floor, I had a silly grin on my face, and any thoughts of appealing to Carlos had vanished.

WHEN I ARRIVED home that night after tutoring, Elizabeth was still gone, and it looked like she hadn't yet returned to the apartment. This was fairly typical for her, and I think it was one of the main reasons why she and I were able to cohabitate in a small one-bedroom apartment with no issues or drama. That and we were drama-free by nature. I plowed through my Chinese takeout then dutifully opened my laptop and began searching for two-bedroom apartments.

Three hours later and no real progress made, I navigated instead to my email. As usual, I had an email from my dad; it was a forward of some joke. This was how he communicated with me. I often wondered if my dad knew he could modify the content of messages, as he'd never sent me anything but forwarded emails.

There was also an email from Jon.

Jon and I were speaking every few days and meeting for coffee or lunch or dinner since his freak-out a week and a half earlier. It was almost as if we were dating again, except we lived separately and the nights didn't end with soft kisses and caresses but rather awkward goodbyes and weird staring contests.

Each time we saw each other, he indirectly, or sometimes quite directly, brought up the possibility of us getting back together. I hoped that over time he would realize our romantic past was exactly that: the past.

This particular email from Jon was in response to my suggestion that we change a lunch to a dinner.

Jon and I were scheduled to meet for lunch on Friday afternoon, and I was planning to bring Steven along. One day at work, after reviewing the corporate account structures and during a particularly funny story about one of Steven's most recent dating disasters, I mentioned to Steven that Jon and I were still friends. Steven said he wanted to see what an amicable breakup looked like. With his gray eyes narrowing in plain suspicion, he insisted the concept was as mythical as odor-free cat litter.

However, since Quinn's announcement less than forty-eight hours ago that my days would now include afternoons spent meeting corporate partners, I emailed Jon earlier in the day and canceled the lunch. Instead, it was settled that Jon, Steven, and I would all have dinner together tomorrow night at a new Ethiopian restaurant near my place.

Before I closed my inbox, another message popped up. I blinked at the screen several times before the words made sense.

It was from my sister Jem.

The body of the email was blank, but the subject line read *I'm coming to visit. I want to see you.*

CHAPTER TEN

THE NEXT MORNING I woke up, took a shower, and was dressed in ten minutes; then spent twenty minutes contemplating my shoe selection. I arrived at the office early and set to work sorting through emails, pending tasks, and preparing for my upcoming business trip to Las Vegas in less than two weeks. Minutes ticked by at a cruelly slow pace. My mind wandered to Jem's strange email.

I was so engrossed in my meanderings that the ring of my cell phone made me jump. Frantically and fumbling, I answered it, finally. It was ridiculous. My office phone never made me nervous.

"Hello?" I said when I finally brought it to my ear.

"Hey, it's me. Come downstairs." Quinn's gravelly tenor sounded from the other end. There was traffic in the background and the roar of a large truck.

I sighed as I stood, gathering my portfolio from the desk. "Why didn't you just call my office phone? I'm in my office."

"I wanted to make sure you were reachable on the cell." I could hear the smile in his voice. I felt half-heartedly annoyed.

"Next time just call the office phone." I hung up on him before he could respond and felt a little twinge of satisfaction. If he could initiate a conversation with me whenever he wanted, then I could end it whenever I wanted.

A black Mercedes was illegally parked at the corner, and Quinn stepped out of the back seat as I exited the building. He wasn't wearing his guard uniform or a suit; instead, his tall form was clothed in black boots, dark jeans, and a blue T-shirt; as normal, his hair was expertly tousled, his face was a mask of indifference, but his eyes were hidden behind a pair of aviator sunglasses. I took a moment to appreciate the sight of him. He looked really yummy. I may have sighed. I may have licked my lips.

I walked out to the car, feeling a little conspicuous in my capped sleeve red oxford shirt, gray pants, and red satin stilettos. I'd opted to wear my glasses instead of contacts; for some reason, I always felt a bit more invisible when I wore glasses, like I blended into the scenery behind the frames. My hair was once again in a tight bun. As I approached, I saw my reflection in his sunglasses, which only increased my unease. I thought he was going to lecture me for hanging up on him, but instead he smiled as I approached.

"Hey." He nodded once.

"Hi." I gave him a half wave, gripping a portfolio notebook to my chest for taking notes, just in case. Neither Steven nor Carlos proactively briefed me on the scope or purpose of the training. I thought of Steven's statement yesterday when I asked him if I should prepare or bring anything for the training; he'd said that we would tour a property, but it should take only an hour.

Steven was half-right. Quinn did show me one of the properties, but we were not back within the hour.

The car took us a short distance to the League Center. The League Center is your typical arena concert venue, and Guard Systems was acting as a security consultant for the managing security company.

There had been a number of breaches in physical security during the past six months. The most recent included an impressively enthusiastic fan that posed as a roadie and serenaded the early audience with a drunken/stoned rendition of a teen pop song called *Girl, I Love You Hard.*

When we arrived, we were given a comprehensive tour, and the visit ended up being part business meeting between Quinn, the lead Guard Security liaison, and the onsite supervisor of the security management company; part training-slash-information session for my benefit; part review and tour of newly implemented measures.

Quinn was very quiet in the car on the drive to the League Center, and very businesslike, abrupt, and authoritative with everyone we encountered at the venue. He was not the Quinn I knew from Club Outrageous and the morning after at his sister's apartment and Giavanni's Pancake Diner, or the Quinn at Smith's Take-away and Grocery, or even at Starbucks. If he didn't look bored, he looked unimpressed. People called him Mr. Sullivan or sir. At one point, I thought one of the ground staff was going to salute.

He was actually quite intimidating.

However, throughout the entire visit, businesslike though he was, Quinn took special care and time to define concepts and acronyms that he thought I might not understand. He clearly identified and described weaknesses in the venue's security, and he provided context and background to purchases, personnel, and any other topic that he felt related specifically to my management of the account.

By the time 5:30 p.m. rolled around, my brain felt full and my stomach was growling. We just finished an inspection of the site's server facility, and Jamal, the Guard Security liaison, was leading us down a narrow, low-ceilinged hallway to the elevator.

He glanced at his cell phone and said, "The gates will be opening for tonight's concert in one hour, so now is the time to eat if you're hungry. The first act is onstage at 7:10 p.m."

I looked imploringly from Jamal to Quinn; aside from being ravenously hungry and suffering from crippling stiletto-related foot pain, I had plans with Steven and Jon at seven o'clock.

"Um, are we staying for the concert?"

Quinn nodded, his expression of impassive detachment firmly intact.

This was news to me. I chewed on my top lip during the silent ride on the elevator and debated what to do next. I was with Quinn, and I didn't particularly mind that I'd be stuck with him for several more hours, even if it would be *Mr. Sullivan* Quinn instead of shirtless, smiley, teasing Quinn.

The elevator reached our floor, the top floor, and Quinn placed his hand on the base of my spine to guide me from the lift. He'd been doing this all day, and I was still getting the warm fuzzies each time. I was so preoccupied with Quinn's hand I didn't notice where we were until Jamal opened the door to a private box and motioned me inside.

"Here—we have dinner set out. I'll be back in an hour to take you through the gate procedures, and then I'll show you the new crowd control measures we've instituted." Jamal didn't enter the room and was gone before I could turn and thank him or say goodbye.

I took three steps into the impressive box and stopped, my eyes moving over the spacious suite with unbridled wonder. It was very large. There was a full kitchen with a bar, several high-top circular tables and stools as well as five rows of stadium leather seats facing a large picture window overlooking the stage.

A small buffet of fruit, green salad, hot dogs, hamburgers, condiments, barbeque potato chips, and canned soda was placed on the bar. This was not fancy food by any stretch of the imagination, but two of my favorites happened to be represented: hot dogs and barbeque potato chips.

Quinn crossed to the steps leading down to the picture window and scanned the floor of the arena beyond.

I glanced at my watch and fiddled with the strap. I was having what my sister Jem calls a champagne problem: a champagne problem is when something good happens but it interferes with something else, usually planned, which is either very important or also good. I wasn't really sure what to do.

Quinn must've noticed my disquiet because he asked, "Are you hungry?"

I nodded as I eyed the food, and in confirmation, my stomach rumbled audibly.

"Is the food ok? I can order something else."

"It's just…" I twisted my mouth to the side. "It's just that I actually have dinner plans for tonight."

"With who?"

"With Steven from work and my friend Jon."

"Jon." Quinn repeated the name and shifted on his feet. His eyes moved between mine. "Isn't that the name of your ex?"

I nodded. "Yes, it's the same person. The three of us were supposed to go out to lunch, but instead we moved it to dinner because I thought I'd miss lunch due to the training today, and so…" I sighed, assuming the aloofness in his expression meant I was boring him. "Sorry—I'm sorry. You probably don't care about any of this. Anyway, I just need to call them and cancel for tonight."

Quinn watched me for a moment; as usual, his features seemed to be carefully expressionless. Then he said, "Are you and Jon back together?"

"Oh, no. We're just friends now. But Steven wanted to see what an amicable breakup looked like, so we are all going out for sustenance."

"You still see this guy—Jon?"

"Mmm-hmm."

"All the time?"

It felt as though I was being interrogated. "No, not all the time; just two or three times a week."

Quinn's eyebrows shot up. "Are you sure you're not still dating this guy?"

"Yes. I'm sure. I think I would know if I were having sex with someone." I bit my lip as soon as the words were out of my mouth; feeling very abruptly mortified, a remarkable blush spread its warm tentacles up my neck and behind my ears. I fiddled with the zipper of the portfolio.

We stood silently for several moments, and I had to continue biting my lip to stem the tide of random sex factoids that threatened to spill forth. I was annoyed by his questioning and even more annoyed with myself for feeling the need to answer.

I didn't like that he knew every detail about my lack of a love life, but I knew absolutely nothing about him, whether he was seeing someone or had a girlfriend or a fiancé—or a wife.

Without really meaning to, I glanced at his left hand; his third finger was bare. When I spoke, I was surprised by the sound of my voice. "You're not married."

"Was that a question?"

I lifted my chin and met his gaze, hoping that if I appeared confident, then he wouldn't notice my unending mantle of awkwardness. "No…yes."

"No. I'm not married."

His response further aggravated me. I already knew he wasn't married. When he didn't continue, I pressed him. "Well?"

"Well what?"

"What about you?" Either my empty stomach or annoyance augmented my confidence.

"What about me?"

"Are you having sex with anyone?"

His mouth fell open in obvious shock and he actually stuttered. "Wh—what—why do you want to know?"

"Well, you now know who I'm not having sex with. I think it's only fair."

He narrowed his eyes in a very hawk-like manner before answering. "I'm not dating anyone."

I wrinkled my nose at him. "Well, that's not an answer. I didn't ask you if you were dating anyone. I asked you if you were having sex with anyone."

"Not at this moment."

I pursed my lips and tried my very best to give him a withering glare. He responded by mirroring me; the only difference was that his stare really was withering, and would have been quite effective if he hadn't also been suppressing a smile.

It wasn't my finest moment, but I rolled my eyes and actually huffed. "Fine, don't answer. I don't even know why I asked."

"No. I am not having sex with anyone."

"Oh." I shrugged nonchalantly, but for some reason his response filled me with glee. It was as if a unicorn had appeared beneath a double rainbow and started tap dancing. Despite my best efforts to maintain a neutral expression, I could feel my mouth curve into a mutinous grin.

Quinn tilted his head to the side as though studying me and my reaction to his statement. Then he said, "Now it's your turn."

"My turn?"

"Yes. How many people have you had sex with?"

It was my turn: my turn to be shocked.

My jaw dropped but no sound came out for several seconds; my mind stopped, and at one point, I was uncertain if I'd heard him correctly. When I finally spoke, my voice sounded like a squeak. "Could you repeat the question?"

He laughed and took a step closer to me. "You heard me the first time."

"That's not any of your business." I took a step back.

"No? You asked me—"

"You asked me first—"

He crossed his arms over his chest. "No, I didn't. You volunteered."

"You *asked* me if I was still dating Jon."

"But you're the one who brought up sex."

I opened my mouth to argue but then realized he was right. I considered the question as I glared at him. I wondered if he would reciprocate if I answered. But I didn't want to answer, because Jon was the only guy I'd been with. I didn't know how to feel about that, how normal or abnormal it made me to be a twenty-six-year-old woman who'd had only one sexual partner. And I didn't want to give Quinn more ammunition for additional ambiguous teasing.

"Fine." I started chewing on my lip, stalling, hoping that we'd be interrupted again by one of the managers, or by a bear attack, or an earthquake, or giant snakes.

When I waited too long, he prompted. "Well?"

"So, slept with…right?"

"No, the question was: how many people have you had sex with?"

"Are we using the Bill Clinton definition?" Not that it would have mattered.

"No, the Hillary Clinton definition of sex."

"Ok, stop saying the word sex!" I glanced around the room looking for something to save me from this conversation. I didn't even know how we got here.

"Well?"

"So, how does this work? If I tell you will you have to tell me?"

Quinn shook his head. "Not unless you ask, in which case I get to ask you another question." He really looked like he was enjoying himself. He was merciless.

"What would your next question be?"

"Janie, stop stalling and answer the question."

"Fine, fine, one—ok? One person, and to be honest, I don't even know what the big deal is. If you ask me, society really does make way too much out of it. It's like we want to glorify the process of procreation. You have these authors like Byron who make physical familiarity out to be some amazing, soul-consuming, meaning of life, like an end-of-the-world thing, and it's not like that. It's…" I waved my free hand in the air, trying to find the right words. "It's like having someone else pick your nose or floss your teeth. It requires a lot of coordination and planning. For instance, you can't do it unless you've had a shower within so many hours ahead of time. If you fall out of that time window, then you have to stop reading comics or whatever you're currently doing, go take a shower, dry off, get dressed, blah blah blah. What a hassle. I think bacteria have the right idea; humans should procreate via binary fission."

I was sure my shirt and my face were the same color red. I hazarded a glance at him again through my lashes to find him watching me with no trace of his earlier amusement. I couldn't read his expression, which only served to unsettle me further. I turned completely away from Quinn and started walking toward the door; the single knot in my stomach had turned into a million-man march of knots, and I couldn't quite bring myself to look at him anymore.

"I need to find a phone. I'll be back." I left my notepad on a high top table and continued toward the exit.

I heard him take a step behind me. "Where is your phone?"

I waved him off, walking faster. "I left it at the office."

I was almost out the door when I felt his hand close around mine and turn me around. "Janie, you should carry it with you."

I pulled my hand from his and gained a half step back. "Well, you said you were the only person who would call me on it, and since you and I are here, together, there is no reason for me to carry it."

He frowned at me. "And when were you planning to pick up the phone before the weekend?"

"I wasn't." I crossed my arms over my chest.

"Does that mean we're spending the weekend together too?" He took a full step toward me. I was forced to lift my chin to maintain eye contact.

At his words, my stomach felt like it was full of honey-drunk bees; I swallowed with effort and stated what I felt to be obvious. "As far as I know, we're not working this weekend. Why would you need to call me during non-business hours?"

He opened his mouth as though he was going to say something but then clamped it shut, his jaw ticking as he ground his teeth. His eyes were half-lidded and piercing. After a long moment, he pulled his cell phone out of his pocket and handed it to me. "Here, you can call your *friend* on my phone."

I glanced at him then at the phone, then back at him again. Reluctantly I took the phone from his hand. "Thank you." I muttered before I turned my back on him and dialed Jon's number. For some reason it felt wrong to call Jon using Quinn's phone. I pushed the discomfort aside, reminding myself that Jon and I were broken up and Quinn and I were coworkers. Coworkers could lend each other their phones. It was not unseemly. It was normal.

Jon's phone rang four times, and then he answered with a somewhat hesitant, "*Hello?*"

"Hi, Jon, it's me, Janie." I took a few steps away from Quinn, keeping my voice low, although I didn't precisely know why.

"*Hey, I didn't recognize the number. Sorry I took so long to pick up. Are we all set for tonight?*"

"Um, that's why I'm calling." I glanced over my shoulder; in my peripheral vision, I could see Quinn standing by the bar a few feet away, facing me. "Listen, I have to work tonight, so I can't make it. Can we reschedule for tomorrow?"

"*Oh, ok. Well, that's too bad...*" I could almost see Jon's frown. I heard him sigh. "*What time tomorrow?*"

"Do you already have plans? Don't cancel your plans; we can always—"

"*Janie, I want to see you. Of course, I'll cancel my plans. You come first.*"

I felt my throat tighten, half from frustration, half from guilt, and I walked a few more steps away from Quinn. I was careful to keep my voice low but still above a whisper. "Jon, you can't say things like that."

I was acutely aware of Quinn's presence and, as though sensing my discomfort, I heard him say quietly, "I'll be back." He walked by me and out of the private box.

"*Who was that? Are you with someone?*" Jon's tone changed slightly, his voice rising. "*Janie, is this really about work?*"

It was my turn to sigh. "Jon, I am at a site visit with one of my coworkers."

"*A male coworker?*"

"Yes, if you want to get technical about it, I'm here with literally dozens of male coworkers." I rolled my eyes.

"*And you are all working late? Where are you?*"

"I can't tell you that; you know I signed a non-disclosure agreement. I can't tell you about any of my clients." I spun around and stalked to the other side of the room.

"*This is ridiculous. No one ever works late on a Friday night. If you would just let me take care of you, I would—*"

"Jon." I hoped he heard the warning in my voice.

"*You know what? Fine. Fine. You have to work late—I get it.*" He sounded frustrated yet resigned. "*I still want to see you tomorrow. Listen, I'm sorry, Janie. I'm sorry. Can we just start over? I want to meet your friend Steven. Can't we just meet for dinner tomorrow and have a good time?*"

I stared unseeingly at a spot on the wall, my guilt winning over my frustration. "Yes," I said on an exhaled breath, and I glanced over my shoulder when I heard movement from behind me. Quinn reentered the room, gave me a brief once over, and then turned to the buffet of food. "Yes, that sounds good; we'll try to make tomorrow work. I'll call Steven next and see if he is available. Listen, I need to go."

"*Ok, but let me know if you need anything—money or anything. I'll see you tomorrow.*"

"Ok. Bye Jon."

"*I love you, Janie. Don't forget that.*"

I closed my eyes, my mouth curving into a frown. I said, "I'll see you tomorrow," and then I hung up.

I punched Steven's number into the cell and only had to wait one ring for him to pick up. "*Mr. Sullivan?*"

"No, no—it's Janie. Listen, we're still at the site, and I have to work late, so that means dinner is off for tonight." The words came out in a rush. Quinn crossed in front of me to a table with two plates in his hand, and the wafting smell of hot dogs made my mouth water.

"*Oh...*" I heard Steven audibly shuffle papers on the other end of the phone. "*Wait a minute, where are you?*"

"I'm—"

"*You know what, scratch that. I don't want to know. No problem about tonight. We'll reschedule for after the Vegas trip.*"

"Can you get together tomorrow for dinner instead?" Without really meaning to, I walked closer to where Quinn sat eating his food. I watched him take a large bite of his hamburger. His jaw flexed, and the muscles in his cheeks and neck were strangely mesmerizing. I may have been staring.

"*Sorry, no can do, babycakes. I've got a hot date.*"

Movement from the suite door pulled my attention from Quinn; I watched with perplexed interest as two girls entered, both wearing skintight T-shirts, which showed off their midriffs, and too short shorts. They each carried a tray laden with what looked like various glasses of alcoholic beverages.

"Um—" I was distracted by the presence of the girls and had to refocus on my conversation with Steven. "Um...that's ok. We'll just reschedule then."

"*Ok, sweetums. I'll see you on Monday. And don't let Mr. Bossy make you work too late. Buh-bye.*"

Before I could respond, Steven's line clicked off. I let the hand holding the phone drop to my side, and I watched as one of the girls, who I shall call Girl #1, carried three large glasses, filled with what I assumed was beer, over to Quinn as the other girl, who I shall call Girl #2, unloaded the other glasses from the trays onto the bar. Girl #1 smiled at Quinn. It was what I recognized as a take-my-panties-off smile. My sister June had used it quite frequently on members of the football team when we were in high school.

It made me glower.

Much to my surprise and relief, Quinn didn't seem to notice her smile. Instead, he offered a curt "thanks" and immediately lifted one of the beers to his mouth and took a long drink. Girl #1 loitered at his table, watching him. I loitered at one side of the room, watching them. Girl #2 loitered by the bar, watching us all.

After a short moment, Quinn looked from Girl #1 to Girl #2 then briefly to me. He shifted on his seat then dismissed them. "I'll let Jamal know if we need anything else."

I didn't miss the disappointed frown cloud over Girl #1's face as she left. I also had some difficulty explaining to myself the small smile tugging at my lips when the door closed. I stood in place, Quinn's phone still in my hand, and continued to watch him eat. He took big bites. Every time he took a bite, a quarter of the hamburger disappeared. I think he actually finished it in four bites.

I was abruptly pulled from my musings by the sound of his voice. "So, you finished your calls?"

I blinked at him then nodded. "Yes. Yes, calls all finished." My thumb moved over the smooth screen of his phone. I walked over to his table and placed his cell on the surface. "Here is your phone. Thank you again for letting me use it."

"Anytime." His eyes moved over me in that way he sometimes employed: a plain, open assessment. He did this a lot, and it always made me feel uncomfortable and warm and flustered. He lifted his chin toward the bar. "I don't know what you drink, so I ordered a few things."

I moved my attention to where he indicated and scanned the glasses sitting on the end of the bar. "Should we…?" I cleared my throat and motioned with my hand toward the three glasses of beer in front of Quinn. "Should we be drinking while we're working?"

Quinn took a bite of his hotdog and shrugged. "We're not working now."

"But we're not done; we still have the review of new crowd control measures."

Quinn interrupted me with a wave of his hand. "I spoke to Jamal. That part of the tour is off, so we're done for today." As though to emphasize this fact, Quinn took a long swallow from his glass and finished another third of the contents. He set it down firmly and looked at me.

"Oh." I blinked. I was befuddled, and when I am befuddled, I tend to speak my thoughts as they occur to me rather than engage in an internal dialogue like a normal person. "So that means I didn't need to cancel my dinner plans?"

Quinn's jaw ticked and his mouth curved into a frown. "I guess not." He placed three chips in his mouth and made a loud crunching sound as he chewed. His eyes were trained on me as his jaw worked, and I felt a now familiar anxiety under the piercing weight of his gaze.

"Well, then—" I cleared my throat, "I should call Jon back and see if we can still get together." I said the words, but I didn't particularly want to follow through on the action. I stalled by glancing at my watch.

"Or," Quinn leisurely reached over and plucked his cell phone from the table then slipped it into his pocket, "you could stay here and enjoy the concert with me."

I lifted my wide eyes to his. "You're staying for the concert?"

He nodded.

I opened my mouth to ask if we were allowed to stay but then thought better of it. I contemplated the current state of things. I contemplated Quinn; he looked relaxed yet somehow on edge. It also struck me again at that moment how startlingly and even painfully handsome he was. A fresh stab of awareness sliced through me, and I desperately wanted something to drink. Pulling my attention away from him, I eyeballed a martini glass on the bar filled with a bright yellow liquid and lemon twist garnish; the rim was coated with either salt or sugar, or a combination of both.

I crossed to the bar and lifted it toward him. "What's this?"

"That's a lemon drop."

I picked it up and sniffed it. It smelled good. "What's in it?"

"Lemon juice, sugar, and vodka."

"Vodka?"

"My sister, Shelly, says it tastes like lemonade." Quinn took a large swallow of his beer and finished it, and then he reached for the second glass next to his plate.

I thought about mixing vodka and Quinn; it would make *Quodka*, which sounded to me like some sort of Bulgarian card game involving gangsters and prostitutes. I put the lemon drop back on the counter and motioned to his glasses of beer. "Are there any more beers?"

"These aren't beers; they're boilermakers—beer and whiskey."

My eyebrows lifted of their own accord. "Oh."

Considering my options, I took a sip of the lemon drop. It didn't exactly taste like lemonade, but it was delicious. I moved to the buffet and picked up a plate with my free hand, but before I could start heaping on piles of potato chips, Quinn's voice stopped me.

"I fixed you a plate already. It's over here on the table."

I turned to face him. "Oh" was again all I could think to say.

I put the empty plate back in its place, picked up a second martini glass full of the bright yellow liquid, and crossed to where Quinn was sitting. I slid onto the stool opposite him. The plate he'd fixed contained two hot dogs with generous amounts of both ketchup and mustard, a cornucopia of berries, and a perfect portion of barbeque potato chips.

I smiled at the plate, my stomach rumbled again, and I took another sip of the lemon drop before setting both glasses down. "That is exactly how I like my hotdogs."

His mouth hitched to the side. "Fan of hotdogs, are you?"

I nodded as I bit into the sausage. It was still warm, and it was delicious. I finished chewing and said, "It was my favorite dinner as a child. I think I would have lived off hotdogs if my mom had let me."

"But she didn't?"

"No, she was very body conscious, even when we were kids." I licked mustard off my index finger.

Quinn followed the movement, and his eyes stayed on my mouth as he asked, "How many siblings do you have?"

"Two sisters; I'm in the middle." I took another bite, licking the side of my mouth then washing all the nitrate goodness down with a generous wallow of lemon drop. I could barely taste the alcohol. "How about you?"

"Um, one sister and…" Quinn took a gulp of his second beer.

I waited for him to continue; when he didn't I prompted, "And?" then took a very unladylike bite.

"And a brother, but he died a few years ago."

I stopped chewing and, not thinking about my very full mouth, said, "Erm ser serrie erbert er beerder."

Quinn half smiled. "What was that?"

I swallowed my food, took another gulp of my drink, and said again, "I'm so sorry. I'm sorry about your brother."

He watched me for a moment then glanced away; he took a large swallow of his beer, finishing the second one off and starting on the third.

My head was starting to feel light, most likely from the addition of vodka to an empty stomach, but I attempted to push the sensation away and focus on our conversation. "Were you very close?"

He nodded then cleared his throat. Still he didn't look at me; still he said nothing. Without thinking, I reached up and covered his hand where it rested on the table with mine. "That completely sucks." I finished my lemon drop, raised the elbow of my free arm to the tabletop, and rested my chin in the palm of my hand.

He met my gaze. His was serious, searching. He turned his palm so that we were holding hands and agreed very quietly. "It does."

My eyes moved over him in open surveillance; I felt warm and loose-lipped, likely also due to the alcohol, and therefore didn't think twice before I asked in rapid-fire succession, "What was he like? Was he like you? Was he older or younger?"

"He was older. He wasn't like…" His attention moved to our joined hands and he frowned, as though considering something; I noticed his unhappy expression and tried to withdraw, but he increased his grip—not painfully, just firmly—and glared at me. He tugged on my hand as though to ensure that I didn't attempt to escape again. Without a word, I slipped off my seat and took the one next to him. When I was settled on the stool, he seemed to relax. "We weren't alike," he said. "He was a police officer in Boston." He faced me so that one of his legs was between mine; his foot rested on the bottom rung of my stool.

I tried to focus on his words, but the world seemed fuzzy. "His being a police officer meant that the two of you weren't alike?" I took a drink from the second lemon drop, licking the residual sugar from my lips.

His eyes moved to my mouth, stayed there, and seemed to lose focus. "Yes and no. He was honorable. I think he wanted to be a police officer because he always wanted to do the right thing."

I lifted an eyebrow at him and tilted my head in much the same way I'd witnessed him do a number of times before. "I still don't understand; you'll need to be more precise." I mostly succeeded at not slurring when I asked, "Are you saying you're not like him because you didn't become a police officer?"

His eyes didn't move from my lips as he responded. "No. I'm not like him because usually I don't want to do the right thing."

Either his proximity or my glass and a half of sugary-sweet alcohol were responsible for the heated deliberateness of my beating heart; I guessed it was a little of both. The air seemed to change and become slower—thicker. I felt like something important had just happened, but I was too foggy to grasp it. I did know that the way he was looking at me made my lower belly feel delightfully achy and full.

However, before I could consider the issue further, he kissed me.

CHAPTER ELEVEN

HE CAPTURED MY mouth, pressing his lips to mine softly, then tilting his head and repeating as though he wanted to taste me from every angle. We were joined only by our lips and our clasped hands. This lasted just briefly before Quinn released my hand in favor of digging his fingers into the small of my back, pulling me from my seat and fully against him. I was between his legs, half-standing and half-leaning on his chest.

Without thinking, I inclined forward; my hands rose and gripped his shirt, partly for balance and partly because the opportunity presented itself. His lips were warm and yielding. He kissed me gently at first, slowly, savoring each touch; but his grip on me was forceful, crushing me to him as though I might collapse or try to push him away.

My brain and my body were disconnected, and I didn't immediately respond to the current situation with appropriate enthusiasm, which, in all honesty, might have been a stroke of luck. Had I been prepared for the kiss and known it was coming, I likely would have become flustered, overeager, and ended up with half his face in my mouth.

However, as it was, a small, involuntary moan escaped me. This turned out to be a very good thing because, almost immediately, I felt his tongue sweep gently against my mouth. I parted my lips and he responded with a low growl, his arms sliding completely around me as he claimed my mouth. His hand moved up my back and fisted in my hair; he pulled my bun out of its twist sending rascally curls in every direction. He looped a length of it around his hand and held me in place as he explored my mouth. The kiss turned hungry, and my hands, trapped between us, could only grip the front of his shirt.

My reactions were entirely medulla oblongata-based. I was so engrossed in the sensations of Quinn—his hands, arms, mouth, chest—that I didn't hear the door open behind me, and I didn't understand why Quinn stiffened suddenly then pulled his mouth from mine. My eyes were still closed, my chin was still tilted upward, and my lips were still parted when he disentangled his hand from my hair and I heard him speak.

"What is it?" He sounded angry.

My eyes flew open, not comprehending his meaning, believing initially that he'd meant the words for me. It wasn't until I realized he wasn't looking at me but rather over my shoulder that my mind was allowed to engage. This time I recognized the voice behind me.

"Sorry, it's nothing. Shit. We thought you wanted—never mind." I heard the door close as Jamal exited the box.

It was in that moment that I knew my glasses were askew. I tried looking up into Quinn's face, but the frames of the glasses blocked my vision casting black, horn-rimmed lines in every direction. Quinn's arms were still around me in a pseudo vice-grip, and I gave myself until the count of six to enjoy being pressed against the hard planes of his body. When I reached six, I kept counting until twelve.

Quinn made no movement; he was so still I thought he might be holding his breath. I gently pushed against his chest, readjusting my glasses as gracefully as possible. He loosened his grasp but kept his hands at my waist as I straightened. I let my glance flicker to his face and endeavored to read his expression through my lashes.

His eyes were dark, unreadable, and half-lidded, watching me; and his mouth was reddish and mussed from our earlier kiss. I was wobbly on my legs and tried unsuccessfully to balance as I stood; it was likely that I would've fallen backward without his hands on me. He licked his lips. I had to suppress another moan. I closed my eyes again and dipped my chin to my chest.

The dark shelter provided by my eyelids should have allowed me to make a concerted effort to sort through the house party of pandemonium and dinner party of doubt dueling for my attention; however, Quinn's continued closeness, the weight of his hands curled around my middle, and his chest beneath my fingers was, once again, driving away my higher brain function.

One thought galloped around and around in my brain: *I can't believe that just happened.*

Eventually it was accompanied by another thought: *How can I make that happen again?*

Once I was fairly certain of my balance, I opened my eyes and reluctantly lifted them, but I could only make it as far as his neck. I felt Quinn's hands briefly tighten then fall to his sides. He took a shuffling step back, then another; he pulled his fingers through his hair leaving small spikes of disheveled disorder. As though not knowing quite what to do with them, Quinn placed his hands on his hips.

He said, "That shouldn't have happened."

His sobering words had an immediate effect; the alcohol and Quinn-induced tropical weather system that had spread through my body was blanketed by an arctic blast. With surprising dexterity and speed, I was able to distance myself from my starchy feelings of disappointment before they became unmanageable: *box locked, light off, closet closed.* My eyes lifted and met his only briefly; I looked over his shoulder.

"Well, you did have three cement mixers." My voice was a little breathless, so I swallowed and crossed my arms over my chest, hoping to steady my stream of words. "Alcohol is a depressant and depressants target a chemical called GABA, the primary inhibitory neurotransmitter within the brain. It has also been found that drinking increases levels of norepinephrine, the neurotransmitter responsible for arousal, which is believed to account for heightened excitement when you begin drinking. Norepinephrine is the chemical target of many stimulants, suggesting that alcohol is more than merely a depressant. Elevated levels of norepinephrine increase impulsivity which, in turn, leads to pleasure seeking behaviors you likely wouldn't engage in without the introduction of alcohol into your system."

I chewed my lip; feeling conflicted about my very logical explanation. Explaining the kiss away via alcohol-induced madness made my head feel better, as though the world had been righted on its axis, and inalienable truths still existed. It also made my heart plus all the girly parts of me feel bad, like when you find out Santa is a myth or that Superman doesn't really exist.

Throughout my lecture on the culpability of alcohol, Quinn had watched me with preoccupied oblectation and, when I finished, he audibly sighed. "What just happened had nothing to do with alcohol."

I decided to cling to inalienable truths. You can't be disappointed if you cling to inalienable truths. "You can't be certain of that," I turned away from him, tugged on the hem of my shirt, and searched for my notepad, not especially wanting to have this conversation. "Our impulsivity control is still currently compromised by the introduction of alcohol into our systems." I searched the floor for my hair tie.

"Is that why you kissed me back? Because your impulsivity control was compromised?" I could feel his eyes on me as I abandoned my pursuit of the hair tie and walked to the table holding my discarded notepad and portfolio case. I picked them up.

"Logic dictates that both my participation and yours was due, in large part, to the consumption of alcoholic beverages." I glanced at my watch unseeingly then crossed to the door. I needed to leave and sort through the events of the day and evening. I wasn't feeling particularly stable or steady the longer we talked, despite my cool bravado.

He stepped in front of me before I made it to the exit, halting my escape and holding up his hands so I had to take a step back. "Let me be clear about something: I kissed you because I wanted to. I've been thinking about kissing you since I first saw you in the lobby of the Fairbanks Building weeks ago."

His declaration, if one could call it that, caught me completely by surprise, and therefore, a small, surprised sound escaped from my throat. My upstairs brain and my downstairs brain engaged in a game of risk, and it was downstairs's turn to roll the dice.

I shifted on my feet, not certain what to say or do, so I took a deep breath, releasing it slowly, and met his gaze. My stomach twisted at the slightly guarded expression he wore; his eyes seemed to be searching mine.

I cleared my throat. "You just said it shouldn't have happened."

He hesitated for a moment, as though considering a chess move, his eyes still wary. "It shouldn't have happened."

I tilted my head to the side, ignoring the very obvious fact that I was beginning to pick up his mannerisms, and challenged him. "And do you think it would have happened if we hadn't been drinking?"

He pulled in another audible breath; I watched as his chest expanded, and his gaze dropped to my mouth. "Eventually."

I blinked at him, twice. "I…" I couldn't get out another word. North was down and south was up. "I don't know what to say."

He pulled his hand through his hair again and mumbled so that I could barely make out his words. "I don't have much experience with this." His features were serious, cautious.

"With what?" I blurted.

"I want to take you out." He swallowed and added, "Out to dinner."

"I…" East was west and west was somewhere in the Andromeda Galaxy. "You want to take me out for dinner?" This was some kind of mistake. My eyes were wide with confusion and disbelief. I was certain the next words out of my mouth were going to result in my complete mortification; but being a glutton for punishment, I said them anyway, and my voice cracked on the last word. "Like a date?"

He didn't smile; he didn't look amused; he just nodded his head and repeated, "Like a date."

I stared at him for an indeterminable amount of time, waiting for him to take it back or clarify that he was referring to the dried and candied food *date* not the event *date* or for someone to wake me up from this bizarro perpendicular universe. Finally I said, about ten decibels too loudly, "YES!"

In actuality, I yelled it. I yelled the word yes.

Quinn let out a breath. "Good."

"YES, I'LL GO OUT ON A DATE WITH YOU, QUINN SULLIVAN, TO A PLACE WHERE WE HAVE DINNER." I couldn't stop the shouted words. I was having an out-of-body experience, which, for some reason, made me shout my sentence.

He laughed lightly. "Good! I'm happy to hear it."

I nodded, not speaking until I was sure I had control over my volume. "Ok then. That's that." Not really sure about proper protocol in cases such as these, I stuck out my hand for him to shake.

He studied my offered hand and enclosed it in his own, tugging me forward instead of shaking it. He leaned down and kissed me again, this time just a quick, brief brush of his lips against mine, and then he straightened. That small but enchanting kiss made my toes curl, my spine shiver, and my heart jump to my throat. I instinctively swayed forward as he retreated.

I blushed for the seven-hundred-and-thirty-first time. "I should go."

"You don't want to stay for the concert?"

"Oh." I'd completely forgotten about the concert.

He pulled my notebook from my grip and motioned toward the picture window. "The first act should be starting soon."

I hesitated.

"Let's finish eating; then we'll watch the concert. We can leave whenever you want."

I glanced around the room. Much had happened in an extremely short period; the events warranted analysis.

Quinn tugged on my hand where he'd entwined our fingers until I met his gaze; his eyes were warm and unguarded, even sparkly. "I promise: no monkey business and no more compromising impulsivity control..." His now trademark sexy, meandering smile shone down at me, and then he added, "Unless you want to."

I could only nod, rendered mute by the glittering intensity of his grin, and allow myself to be coxswained in the direction of his choice.

True to his word, there was no monkey business. Even though we both consumed additional alcoholic beverages, neither of us initiated any physical intimacy beyond brief touches every so often. From time to time, Quinn would brush my hair away from my shoulders or face and lay his arm along the back of my seat.

It felt strange to listen to a concert rather than to be actively engaged in it; we didn't sing or dance or clap. In fact, we spoke through most of it; it might as well have been background music on a stereo system. At one point, we ignored it altogether and spent forty-five minutes debating my good-bad-stupid-lazy philosophy.

It was Quinn's belief that, if I included both good and bad, I should add intelligent and motivated. I countered that the absence of stupidity implied intelligence, but the absence of bad did not imply good.

When he caught me yawning for the second time, he decided it was time to take me home. A black Mercedes met us when we arrived downstairs; to my astonishment, we were greeted by a familiar face.

It was Vincent—Vincent the limo driver who helped me move the contents of my belongings from Jon's apartment and had taken me to Elizabeth's apartment on my worst day ever. I couldn't believe my eyes at first, but then, as he held the door open, he winked at me. I could only stare at him dumbly.

Quinn and I spent the first half of the car ride in separated silence, sitting on opposite ends of the long leather bench seat. My brain hurt. It was tired of trying to keep up with so many changes and gauging the appropriateness of my reactions. Nevertheless, I attempted to sort through the last several hours. I glanced at the back of Vincent's head, and once or twice, he caught my eye in the rearview mirror. At some point, I would need to ask Quinn if he'd arranged the limo that had taken me home all those weeks ago, or if Vincent's presence tonight was merely a fluke.

At a stoplight, Quinn pulled me out of my musings by unbuckling my seat belt. I met his gaze, the clear blue of his eyes appearing opalescent in the dark car; he silently pulled me to the center of the bench. He wrapped his arms around me, guided my back to his chest, and fastened the middle buckle around me. I felt warm and safe, which, paradoxically, made me shiver and made my heart race with apprehension.

When we arrived outside my building, Vincent the driver opened the door and offered his hand. I smiled up, then down at him as I climbed out. "It's good to see you again."

"You too. You are looking very beautiful." His brown eyes twinkled at me under the street lamp; he brought my knuckles to his lips and gave them a kiss, just like he'd done before.

Quinn stood from the car behind me and I walked forward, turning to continue my conversation with the driver. "And how is your wife? Your grandchildren?"

"Ah, the days are long but the years are short." He shook his head and looked to the heavens.

Quinn looked from him to me, then back again. He raised an eyebrow but didn't say anything. I said my farewell to Vincent, and Quinn placed his hand on the small of my back and guided me to the steps of my building. We stopped at my door and I fished my keys from the portfolio case.

"How do you know Vincent?" One of Quinn's hands was in his pocket; the other was scratching the day-old stubble on his jaw.

"I was meaning to ask you about that." I paused as I separated the front door key from the others. "Vincent was driving the limo that took me home on the day I was downsized."

Quinn's eyes clouded over then his brow lifted in sudden understanding. He looked away from me and to the door of my building.

I eyed him suspiciously before I asked, "Did you arrange for the car that day?"

He hesitated then nodded, still not making eye contact. "Yes."

"Why did you do that?"

He met my gaze. "You seemed… upset." He sighed.

"You didn't even know me."

"But I wanted to." He countered, shifting closer, his hand lifting and tucking a curl behind my ear.

I swallowed with effort and lifted my chin to maintain eye contact as frenzied warmth twisted in my chest. "Why didn't you just talk to me then—ask me on a date?"

Quinn's eyes narrowed and considered me; he looked particularly hawkish as he said, "I don't date."

I frowned at him, but before I could process his response, he bent and kissed me for the third time that night. This one was different; not the slow, savoring sweetness of our first kiss and most definitely not a quick caress of lips like our last. This one was hungry, immediate, and demanding.

He fisted his hand in my hair and backed me into the door of my building, trapping me in place. It was the kind of kiss that drove away all coherent thoughts; like a bloodthirsty wolf chasing a bunny rabbit. My body responded in a way that I didn't know possible, my back arching, wanting to press every inch of myself against his taut form, with the painfully delightful ache in my lower stomach winding its way around my limbs.

Just as suddenly as it had begun, it was over; he ended by nipping at my bottom lip and waiting for me to open my eyes so he could stare into them. I felt him slide something into my pocket.

He smiled almost imperceptibly. "I had Jamal pick up your cell from the office. I'll call you tomorrow so we can make arrangements for dinner." I opened my mouth to respond, but he stopped me with another quick kiss. Quinn took my keys out of my hand and opened the door; he pushed on it and guided me inside, placing my keys into my palm.

I complied mechanically, pausing at the steps to glance back at him hovering just outside the door. He was still grinning in that secret, quiet way of his. Then, he turned and was gone.

♥♥♥

I WALKED INTO Elizabeth's apartment feeling like a zombie. I needed brains. The Quinn Sullivan rollercoaster had left me completely exhausted. Nevertheless, instead of sleeping, all I wanted to do was sit, stare into space, and obsess about everything that had occurred. I embraced this desire to obsess because I knew it was what normal people did.

Elizabeth was lying on the carpeted floor with her legs up against the wall in an excellent Viparita Karani yoga pose. She was listening to music on oversized headphones that were connected to her stereo system via a remarkably long cord.

Elizabeth had an impressively strange record collection and would frequently relax by listening to records while sprawling on the floor, contorting into yoga poses, knitting, or reading medical journals. She loved boy bands, and had vinyl records for most of her collection, starting with New Kids on the Block. She must have noticed the movement of my entrance because she turned just her head and gave me a quizzical smile. She brought her legs down from the wall, sat up straight, and pulled off the headphones. Her eyes moved over me in open assessment.

Elizabeth frowned. "Were you just with Jon?"

I shook my head, and then I sat dazedly on the couch. I picked up a decorative pillow and clutched it to my stomach. "No, I was with Quinn."

She shot up and claimed the seat next to me on the couch; I could hear the faint sounds of a One Direction album coming through her headphones. "Oh my God. What happened? Was this for work? Where were you guys?"

My face fell to my hands and I shook my head. "Elizabeth, you are not allowed to take concurrent shifts at the hospital ever again."

I started by telling her about bumping into him on Wednesday at Smith's, and I included the ambiguous arrest details Quinn had given me about the alleged girl-drugger from Club Outrageous.

I covered our somewhat unpleasant exchange on Thursday, and the fact that I was now forced into the bondage of carrying a cell phone.

I ended with a very short version of our day, our training session, and then the after part where everything went from calm to a cavalcade of crazy.

When I told her about the sex conversation, she hit my shoulder and said, "You didn't!"

When I told her about the kiss, she gasped, her eyes grew wide, and she covered her mouth.

When I told her that he'd asked me on a date, she started bouncing up and down on the couch. "Who called it? I called it! That's right, uh huh!"

I skipped over most of the concert, and when I told her about Vincent and what I learned regarding Quinn's part in arranging the limo, she frowned, blinked, and said, "I guess that was nice of him in an overreaching kind of way."

Then, I told her about his last comment of the evening: that he doesn't date.

Her frown grew more pronounced, and she leaned back into the couch and crossed her arms. She was silent for a moment then sighed. "You know, I kind of guessed that about him."

It was my turn to frown. "What do you mean?"

"Some guys just aren't boyfriend material."

"Well, then, what kind of material are they? Suede?"

The corner of her mouth hitched as one of her eyebrows lifted; she gave me a knowing look. The problem was I didn't know what I didn't know. I shook my head at her. "What? What's that look for? What don't I know?"

"He's a Wendell."

A Wendell.

"What is a Wendell?"

Elizabeth quickly added, "He's a hottie player—a Wendell—someone you don't date."

"What am I supposed to do with a Wendell?"

She pushed me on my shoulder. "Janie! You have mind-blowing sex with a Wendell! You have your way with him and spend hours in orgasmic paradise taking advantage of his hard body and each fantastic orifice and pleasure-causing appendage until you get tired of him."

I blushed and glanced at my hands. "I don't—I mean, I don't think—"

"Yes. That's right. Don't think. Just let yourself have a good time." She covered my hand with hers and patted it until I met her gaze. "You deserve this. Repeat after me*: I, Janie Morris, deserve splendiferous orgasm therapy with Sir McHotpants.*"

My eyes widened and I took a brave breath. "This is madness."

Elizabeth's eyes narrowed. "Say it!"

I shook my head. "I can't! I can't say it!"

"You're not just going to say it; you're going to do it—with frequency!"

I laughed in spite of myself. "You want me to have intimate relations with a man-whore."

"Alleged man-whore. And, yes, I do." Her face turned serious. "You've only ever been with Jon and…" She huffed. "And I know he wasn't so great in the bedroom department."

"I never said that."

"You never had to. The fact that you didn't say anything at all spoke volumes."

I bit my lip. The truth was that I thought Jon was fine in the bedroom department. Just fine. He was… just… fine. And what was wrong with fine?

"Janie, sex can be great. It can be *really* great and fun and amazing. This thing with McHotpants—this could be a great thing. This could help you become more comfortable around guys and experience what sex and physical intimacy can be like when it's really good. Wendell—I mean, Quinn—Quinn is being honest with you about his intentions. When you get tired of him, you don't have to worry about his feelings; how great is that? Then, when you meet a non-Wendell who you like and who likes you, you'll know how to command yourself in the bedroom."

I shook my head. "I don't think I can be that person. I don't think I can have sex with someone without knowing that he cares about me and wants to be with me for… without something more. I know it sounds Victorian, but I don't want great sex if it doesn't come with— with—"

"Love?" Elizabeth supplied, her voice tinged with sarcasm.

I twisted my lips to the side. "Mutual care, respect, compassion, and commitment, and yes, hopefully all of that adds up to love of some kind."

The truth was being that person, the person who could value the physical aspect of a relationship more than emotional commitment and consistency, scared me. The untamed and unpredictable nature of it scared me. It reminded me of my mother, of how she abandoned her family with alarming frequency in favor of temporary sex partners. It was important to me that I never have anything in common with that woman. And if it meant that I ended up without a partner at all, or if I spent the rest of my life in a staid, passionless albeit reliable and dependable relationship, then I was really ok with that.

She huffed. "You can get all of that with a dog or a cat. You say these things and think this way because you've never had great sex."

I laughed at her discontented scowl. "Then, oh well; I guess I'll never have great sex."

She huffed again then pulled me to her for a hug. "I love you, Janie, and I could give you great sex, but I'm just not into girls."

I smiled into her shirt. "Well, let me know if you ever change your mind."

She withdrew and held me at arm's length, her face and tone serious. "If you don't want hot Wendell sex then, I have to tell you, you need to be careful with this guy. He's being honest with you when he says he doesn't date. You should believe him."

I nodded and tried not to betray the sadness I felt. "I do. I do believe him."

She watched me for several moments, considering me. "What did he say after the no dating comment?"

I swallowed, my fingers drifting to my lips of their own accord. "Then he kissed the hell out of me."

CHAPTER TWELVE

I FINALLY RESPONDED to my sister's email on Saturday afternoon after a great deal of procrastinating.

I slept in 'til nine thirty, then laid on the futon for another twenty minutes thinking about Quinn Sullivan's lips of magic and mystery. I decided, on an odd whim, to go for a run along Lake Michigan. The weather was still nice, especially for late September, and the wind felt clarifying. I distracted myself with sights of Millennium Park, the Aquarium, the Natural History Museum, and I reflected on my city.

There is something really special about Chicago.

Chicago is the proverbial middle child of large U.S. cities. Some might consider this analogy only in reference to Chicago's geographic location in the middle of the country. However, the analogy is multifaceted; like most middle children and like books between elaborate bookends, Chicago can sometimes be easy to overlook. It is smart and genuine, but it is always compared, for better or for worse, to its older and younger siblings, New York and Los Angeles. It's the less notorious but smarter sister to New York; it's the less ostentatious but considerably more genuine sister to Los Angeles.

It is breathtaking and beautiful and yet somehow caught in the blind spot of popular consciousness.

I've always wondered if Chicago prefers to shy from the onerous and usually dysfunctional limelight of notoriety. I hypothesize that it is more than content to be smart, genuine, and breathtaking, without attracting the attention that plagues cities that are notorious and ostentatious.

On my way back, I picked up coffee from Starbucks and indulged in my incessant

Quinn Sullivan obsessing. Eventually, I stopped outside of Utrecht Art Supply and accomplished window-shopping. When I arrived home, I found Elizabeth cleaning the kitchen. I felt a little disappointed; I had been planning on spending time procrastinating by tackling that exact chore. Instead, I took a shower and shaved everything that could be shaved. I plucked my eyebrows then decided to give myself a pedicure.

Elizabeth eyed me with suspicion as I sat on the couch and propped my foot on the coffee table. I attempted to ignore her pointed gaze.

After a period of tense silence, she said, "So, what do you need to do that you don't want to do?"

I huffed, liking and disliking that she knew me so well, and confessed. "Jem sent me an email."

"Jem?" Elizabeth didn't suppress her surprise. "When?"

"On Thursday."

"What does she want?"

I uncapped the nail polish remover and applied a liberal amount to a cotton ball. "She wants to visit."

"Who?"

"I'm guessing me. She said she wanted to see me."

She shook her head. "This is so strange. She doesn't even like you."

I shrugged. "I know."

It was true. My own sister didn't like me. It wasn't that we didn't get along; Jem just didn't seem to *like* anyone. Sometimes she pretended to like people but only for as long as was necessary to obtain what she needed from them. I felt that there was a distinct possibility that she was a sociopath.

Abruptly I placed the cap back on the nail polish remover and pulled out my laptop. I needed to rip off the Band-Aid of fretfulness and just answer her damn email. I responded:

Jem, I'm in town all next week, but will be gone part of the week after for a business trip. When do you plan to arrive? How long are you staying? Do you want to see or do anything in particular while you are here? Let me know the details when you are able. Talk to you soon, Janie

It seemed benign enough, but I was pretty sure it would annoy the hell out of her. She didn't like confiding her plans even when they directly affected someone else.

That issue settled for now, I decided to email Jon about dinner. Even though Steven couldn't make it, I felt compelled to keep my dinner arrangements with Jon, especially after cancelling two times in a row. As I began composing an email, something in my vicinity began to chime.

I stopped typing and looked to Elizabeth in confusion. "What is that? It sounds like an ice cream truck."

Elizabeth paused loading the dishwasher, holding a dripping plate. "It actually sounds like a cell phone. Is that your new phone?"

I started, remembering the phone, and began ransacking the living room trying to find the blasted thing. At one point, it stopped ringing, but then seconds later, it began again. I was cussing and was mid-single-syllable, four-letter word when I found the cursed contraption.

I answered breathlessly. "Yes! Hello?"

"Hey."

Outwardly, my body stiffened; inwardly, my bones dissolved. "Oh, hi-hi-hello! How are you?"

"Good. How are you?" Quinn sounded like he was smiling. An image of him smiling flashed across my consciousness, causing the hairs on the back of my neck to prickle.

"I'm well. It's, uh—" I glanced over at Elizabeth. She was making suggestive gestures with her still wet hands. I gave her a dirty look then turned completely away. "It's good to hear from you."

"Even via cell phone?"

I smiled despite myself and responded, "It would be better if it weren't via cell phone."

"I agree. I'm calling about dinner. What time should I pick you up?"

"Dinner?"

"Yeah, dinner."

"Tonight?"

"Yes. Dinner. Tonight."

"Um…" I frowned and glanced at the message still open on my laptop that I'd been typing Jon.

"Janie? …Are you backing out?"

"No—no. I'm not backing out. It's just that I can't tonight. I already have plans." Movement from Elizabeth caught my eye, and I found her glaring at me and mouthing, *What the hell are you thinking?* I shooed her away.

Quinn didn't respond immediately, so I pulled the phone away from my ear and looked at the screen, attempting to decipher if I'd hung up on him. None of the symbols seemed to indicate anything of value, so I spoke into the phone again. "Quinn? Are you still there? Did I hang up on you?"

"Yeah, I'm still here." I heard him sigh. "These aren't the same plans you made yesterday with your ex, are they?"

Inwardly, I cringed. Then, outwardly, I also cringed. "Yes."

His response was silence.

"Quinn?"

"I'll come too." It didn't sound at all like a request.

"Uh, what?"

His voice was business-like and brusque. "You and I will go out tomorrow. Tonight I can meet your friend Jon."

"You want to meet Jon?" Instinctively my gaze searched for Elizabeth, and I think I must have looked as stricken as I felt. She just stared at me with wide eyes.

"I want to see you."

His words made my heart skip; I had difficulty forming a coherent thought. "Well, I guess— I mean—I suppose it's—I mean it's not like— maybe we could—I just don't think that…"

"Where are we going? What time are we meeting him?"

"I was just emailing him to work out the details."

"Ok. How about Chez Jean? I'll pick you up at seven o'clock."

"No, I'll meet you at the restaurant." I didn't want to arrive with him. It would feel too much like a wheelbarrow date: two wheels and a kickstand.

"Do you know where it is?"

"It's a block west of Al's Beef, right?"

I could hear the smile in his voice. "Your landmark is Al's Beef?"

"How can you miss Al's Beef? It's yellow and black and has a giant plastic cup in the center of the sign. I think they have franchise opportunities available."

He laughed. "I'll see you at seven o'clock."

His laugh made me smile like an idiot. "Ok. Seven it is. I'll see you then."

When the call ended, I stared at the cell phone without seeing it for several moments. I felt light, as if my feet weren't touching the ground and I could cloud-hop if the desire so struck me. I felt like running through a field and spinning around while an orchestra played in the background. I felt like clicking my heels together and sliding down an impressively large and steep banister. I felt like picking apart a daisy while reciting, "He loves me…I love him…he loves me."

Elizabeth's concerned voice brought me out of my meandering reveries and a bit closer to reality. "You've got it bad. I've never seen you like this."

Goofy grin still in place, I sighed. I knew what I looked like and sounded like. A small voice in the recesses of my overactive brain screamed at me: *You are infatuated! Infatuated I say!*

I'd never realized before how glorious infatuation could be. Perhaps I'd never been presented with the opportunity until Quinn came along.

♥♥♥

THAT NIGHT'S DINNER began with one of the most awkward silences I've ever experienced in my life. I had to bite both my cheeks to keep from filling the black hole of unsaid words. After introductions were made, Jon sat next to me on the booth along the wall and glowered at Quinn. Quinn, from his chair opposite us, smiled at Jon.

It was a smug smile tinged with a certain amount of swagger. I didn't know how to feel about it, so I just ignored it for the time being. I just hoped that my excessive nervous swallowing went unnoticed. Finally, feeling as though I was going to burst, I excused myself from the table and half-bolted to the ladies' room. I stayed there until I felt capable of reining in the overflowing list of factoids related to black holes that was running on a loop in my head.

When I left the ladies' room, I noticed for the first time how really nice the restaurant was. It smelled like garlic and roux, and the walls were a pale yellow except for the crown molding, which was a dark, natural stained wood. Windows were framed with sheer burgundy curtains. Beautiful oil landscapes, of what I assumed were the French countryside, added intimate elegance without making the place feel cluttered or like an art museum.

The tables were covered in white cloths; rows of forks, spoons, and knives spread like petals on either side of a series of plates stacked one on top of the other; largest on the bottom, smallest on the top. A delicately folded linen napkin, which looked like a swan, spilled out of a water glass to the right of the plates.

I was so distracted by the ambiance that I didn't notice until I returned to the table that Quinn was sitting alone. I glanced around the small restaurant and saw Jon's retreating form heading out the door. Without thinking, I followed him and called his name.

He paused. He turned slowly and stepped back into the bistro. His eyes moved beyond me to where Quinn sat, and then he met my gaze again. His expression, usually so open and unguarded, was remote and sullen.

"What's going on, Jon? Where are you going?"

He huffed, and through clenched teeth, he said, "I'm leaving."

"Why?"

Jon's green eyes looked into mine searchingly, and his expression seemed to soften. He shifted on his feet and took one of my hands in his. "Listen, Janie, no matter what he says, I want you to know that I love you. Just promise me that you'll call me tomorrow; no matter what, you'll call me tomorrow and we'll talk."

I shook my head, befuddled. "Do you two know each other?"

"No. We've never met."

"What did you two talk about?"

"It was nothing…"

"Then why are you leaving?"

He squeezed my hand. "Just promise me, please?"

I shrugged. "Fine, fine—I promise. I'll call you tomorrow. This is too bizarre."

He smiled tightly in a way that didn't reach his eyes, and released my hand. Swiftly, in one fluid motion, Jon leaned forward and kissed my cheek then turned and left. I stared at the door for several minutes.

When I turned around, I found Quinn watching me. His expression was inscrutable, as always; and, as typical, his cerulean eyes seemed to be thinly masking a mischievous flicker. I walked back to the booth that lined the wall and my pace decelerated to a slow shuffle as I approached. I stared at him, perplexed, and then I slid into the booth opposite his chair.

As though nothing were amiss, he motioned to the martini glass in front of me. "I ordered you a lemon drop."

My attention shifted to the whiskey-colored liquid in front of him and the glass in front of me. There were only two glasses.

I frowned.

I glared at Quinn, hoping to convey the intensity of my suspicion. "What did you and Jon talk about? Why did he leave?"

Quinn didn't even have enough decency to look ashamed. Instead he watched me with his up-to-no-good eyes and took a long swallow of his whiskey before responding. "You should ask him."

"I did. He insisted it was nothing." My tone was flat and laced with the disbelief I felt.

Quinn shrugged. "Then it must have been nothing…" he said, his mouth pulled to the side in a barely-there smile, "…unless Jon was lying."

I crossed my arms over my chest and leaned back to contemplate him and his dissatisfactory answer. He met my gaze steadily. At length I said, "You're not being very nice."

"What have I done that's not nice?"

"I think you're being kind of sneaky. And that's why I think you're not being nice."

His smile faded. "Sneaky isn't on your four-quadrant scatter-plot graph personality matrix."

My eyes narrowed further. "Maybe it should be. Maybe I should add honesty as an axis and make it a 3-D model."

"Do you think I'm being dishonest?" His voice was level, but his eyes seemed to flare with challenge.

"No, I think you're being technically honest, which is almost worse."

All tangible expression left his features, and his steady stare burned with intensity. I felt my cheeks redden under his scrutiny but maintained eye contact even when my heart began to race and a twisting nervousness wrestled in my chest. After a prolonged silence, he stood from his chair; his towering form moved with panther-like ease and adroit grace. Quinn slid in next to me. He placed his arm behind me on the back of the booth, and his gaze moved between my neck, lips, and eyes.

For a moment, I thought he was going to try to kiss me. Instead, he leaned close and whispered, "What do you want to know?"

It took a moment for me to form thoughts. Words followed sometime after. "I want to know what you said to Jon when I went to the bathroom."

Quinn eyed me speculatively then sighed. "We did talk. And what I said is likely the reason he left. I'm not trying to be evasive, but it's not my secret to tell."

"What do you mean it's not your secret to tell?"

"It means that Jon has something he should tell you. If you want to know what it is, then you should ask him."

"And you're not going to tell me what it is?"

He shook his head; his gaze was steady and his voice was matter-of-fact. "No. It's not my place."

I chewed on my top lip, scrutinizing him, and finally decided I believed him. "Fine," I said with decisiveness. "Thank you for being honest."

He nodded once. "You're welcome. Now I get to ask a question."

I couldn't stop myself from rolling my eyes. "Are we playing this game again?"

His smile was immediate and dazzling. "I like this game, and I definitely like playing it with you."

Before he could follow through with his question, we were interrupted by the waiter asking if we were ready to order. Quinn seemed to pull his attention from me with reluctance, but he kept his arm along the booth at my back. I picked up the menu to make a hurried selection, but for the second time in our short acquaintance, Quinn did that thing you see in movies but don't ever experience in real life: Without asking for my opinion, he ordered for me.

"We will start with the tarte aux champignons and two salade au chevrotin. The lady will have Gigot D´Agneau au jus et Romarin, and I'll have Steak Grillé au Poivre, medium. We'll also take a bottle of Chateauneuf du Pape, the 2005 Cuvee."

The waiter bowed slightly at the waist as Quinn plucked the menu from my hand and passed it to him. The waiter gave us a tight smile and said, "Very good, sir," and left.

Quinn turned his body back to me and bestowed on me his slow, sexy smile. It did strange things to my insides, like making them become a boneless mass of warm giddiness. My brain also felt hazy. I didn't feel the annoyance at his ordering for me that I should have.

Before he could follow through with his question, I asked one of my own. "Why are you always keeping score?" Wanting to do something with my hands, I pulled my napkin out of the glass; the swan dissolved into a plain, white, linen rectangle. I placed it on my lap.

His voice was low when he spoke; his eyes caressed my lips. "In every relationship or interaction there are winners and losers. It doesn't matter if it's business or family or…"

he paused for just a fraction of a second, his eyes burning a brighter blue, "…or involvement with the opposite sex. Someone always wins; someone always loses. I don't like to lose."

His words were somewhat sobering. My insides congealed and my brain managed to catapult over the fog. "That's an interesting theory." And it was. It was an interesting theory. I saw merit in it, but I also felt it was fundamentally flawed. "And, I suppose if the relationship is between two people who are keeping score, then you are right—there will be a winner and a loser. However, if no one is keeping score, then no one loses."

His eyes narrowed at me briefly, and then he leaned forward and rested one forearm along the table. "Just because you don't keep score doesn't mean one person isn't functioning at a deficit in the relationship, taking more than giving." He reached across the table and grabbed his abandoned whiskey glass.

"There were a lot of negatives in that sentence, '*don't, doesn't, isn't*.' Maybe that's your problem."

"My problem?" His eyes narrowed further.

"Yes, your problem. Maybe you're focused too much on the negative invoices on the relationship spreadsheet." I laughed. "My problem is that I miss the obvious; your problem is that you pay too much attention to it."

He seemed to smile in spite of himself; a reluctant laugh passed his lips. His gaze was unguarded and appraising as he said, "You might be on to something." He pulled at his bottom lip with his thumb and forefinger distractedly, continuing his open assessment of me, his smile widening.

I basked in the warmth of his approving gaze before I poked him. "So, what led you to this pessimistic perspective? Do your parents call you all the time wanting you to babysit their cat or install gutters on their house? I helped my dad install gutters on our house when I was sixteen. It was truly awful."

An expression that could only be described as grim melancholy cast a shadow over Quinn's face. He swallowed with effort then said, "I don't talk to my parents. I haven't talked to them since my brother died."

My own smile faded immediately, and I stared at him for a long moment. I fiddled with my napkin then set it down and clasped my hands in my lap. "Oh. Well…" I nodded, feeling like I needed to offer something in return, just in case he was keeping score on personal factoids. "I talked to my dad a few weeks ago when I lost my job. We don't really talk much, but he's a good guy. He forwards emails to me that he receives from others, but he never writes anything just to me. I don't talk to either of my sisters."

He gave me a sideways glance. "Why not?"

"We don't really have anything in common, and their career choices make it difficult to maintain a meaningful relationship with them."

"Both my father and my brother were police officers in Boston. They were not too happy with my choice of career."

"What? A security guard or consultant or whatever you are?"

Quinn's mouth hooked to the side and he paused before responding, his eyes moving over me, his expression somewhere between bemused and amused. "No, actually, when I was younger, I was something of a reverse hacker."

"What do you mean?"

"I helped people secure their computers, systems, networks—that sort of thing."

"Why wouldn't your dad like that?"

"Because most of the people who hired me to do this were criminals."

"So you created firewalls for mob bosses? As an aside, if I started a band, Mob Boss Firewall would be an excellent name." Cringing, I mentally kicked myself for the tactless aside.

"It was nothing so poetic as that." He glanced down at his almost empty whiskey and studied the amber liquid; his shoulders seemed to slump under the weight of something I couldn't see. After a long minute, he said, "Actually, what I really did was keep their data from being used against them should their computers or hardware be confiscated."

This was not something I expected to hear. Before I could catch myself, I asked, "Where did you learn to do that?"

He shrugged, not looking at me. "Mostly self-taught; I went to college in Boston for two years. My major was computer science, but I dropped out when business started to pick up."

"Why did you stop? Why did you stop reverse-hacking for criminals?"

He lifted his eyes to mine, his expression blank. "How do you know I stopped?"

"I guess I don't. Did you stop?"

"I did."

"Why? If it was so profitable, then why…"

"Because…" he interjected, his eyes looking searchingly into mine and his brow pulled low as though he were trying very hard to decipher a mystery. His attention moved to my hair cascading over my shoulder. With an absentminded expression, he picked up a curl and rubbed it between his thumb and forefinger. His voice sounded distant and distracted when he responded. "Because I was the reason my brother died."

I didn't know what to say so I just watched him.

Quinn's eyes moved back to mine; he seemed to be attempting to gauge my reaction. He smiled, but it was tinged with bitterness. "How the first program worked was that when any attempt was made to access data in the absence of an RFID transmitter, a background script would run, which wiped the hard drive clean, rendering it inoperable. Later, as my customer base grew along with the demand for larger data systems, I built a degausser. I had to add on a battery backup just in case the system was powered down. As you can imagine, the battery backup had a nasty habit of catching on fire."

I cleared my throat and swallowed, wanting to add that the risk of fire could have been tempered by insulating and cooling the degausser. Instead, I asked, "Why do you think you were the reason your brother died?"

His mouth curved into a frown and he sighed. "Because one of the guys—one of your 'bad guys' who I worked for—shot my brother."

I blinked. "I don't...I don't understand."

"Months before Des, my brother, was killed, the police had a search warrant and took all of this guy's computers, backups, everything. The program I had built for the man worked perfectly, and the police came up empty. If I hadn't put the program on his computer, and if I hadn't helped him keep his information safe from the police, then he would have been in jail instead of..."

I closed my hand around his not wanting him to finish the sentence. It was a horrible story. I wanted to say that it wasn't his fault, but I felt like that statement would come across as pandering and patronizing.

Instead, I said, "I understand why you blame yourself."

He blinked at me then narrowed his gaze a fraction as though trying to see me better. This time both his eyes and his smile were sad. "Do you blame me?"

"I blame the bad guy who actually pulled the trigger and killed him. In this situation, you sound like a person who has recognized the error of his ways and made an attempt to change. If you recall, that is the difference between a good guy and a bad guy."

He released a breath I didn't know he was holding. His eyes were still sad, but his troubled expression seemed to clear. He gazed at me with something that felt like wonder, and with his voice lowered to a quiet rumble, he said, "I don't think I'll keep score with you."

We talked. We talked, and we laughed, and we had an amazing time. Conversation flowed like a beautiful waterfall, and my senses were saturated. Food came and went. Wine was poured and appeared out of nowhere. Time passed and I had no recollection or consciousness of anyone but Quinn being in that restaurant. And at some point, the butterflies in my stomach truly ceased for Handsome McHotpants and were utterly and completely for Quinn Sullivan.

He told me stories about his family. He was the youngest and spent his youth raising hell. His sister, Shelly, was three years older and something of a reclusive free spirit who preferred to fix up classic cars and create welded metal sculptures than interact with society. His brother Desmond, Des for short, was the oldest and very responsible.

My favorite story detailed how, at the ages of thirteen and sixteen, Quinn and Shelly welded the doors shut on twenty year-old Des's car, all but the passenger side back seat. Des was forced to enter and exit the car via the back seat for two weeks, and none of them ever told their parents. At some point, Quinn's father asked to use the car, and Des tried to convince their dad that the doors had rusted shut rather than rat out his siblings.

He spoke with such affection for his brother, sister, and his parents that it made me like Quinn even more. His eyes would glaze over with memory, and he would begin to laugh before he reached the punch line of his story, which made me laugh, which made him laugh.

However, every so often, he would pause and a cloud of sadness or regret, I couldn't decipher which, would darken his features. I found myself wanting to know the specific causes for each of those episodes. I also found myself wanting to be a source of support and comfort to him.

These were not thoughts to which I was accustomed, and they would have been disconcerting if I'd spent any time allowing myself to debate them. Instead, I let the thoughts wash over me; I owned the sentiments and held them close.

And then there was the touching.

Oh. God. The. Touching.

He appeared to find any and every reason to touch me. It was maddeningly marvelous. From time to time, he would lean close and whisper something in my ear; his cheek would brush against the smooth skin of my face and neck; my toes would curl in my shoes. During most of the meal, his leg rested against mine. He touched my arm or my knee when I said something he thought was funny or interesting or just because I hadn't tried the wine yet.

All of these simple touches seemed harmless, if not meaningless, on their own; nevertheless, the reaction they elicited from my stomach was akin to descending the steepest plunging drop of a rollercoaster.

Then, when we ate dessert, he absentmindedly licked whip cream off my finger; for several seconds afterward I forgot my name and place of birth.

My level of interest in Quinn, my wanting to be with Quinn, my wanting to touch and be touched by Quinn, my wanting to prolong our conversation and, therefore, our time together, took me by surprise. I thought about having to say goodnight at some point, and it left me feeling sad, anxious, and mournful.

I did dwell on these feelings and they were unsettling. The strength of my preference, of wanting to be with Quinn rather than maintaining solitude, was a sensation I'd never experienced. In the past, I'd generally preferred solitude to company, but I'd always recognized the importance of relationships and human contact.

When we finished dinner, I felt uninhibited. Between the cocktail before dinner and the wine during dinner, I was blanked in a buzzing warmth of cozy comfortableness. I knew it was caused by that elusive, just-right amount of alcohol, where you've had just a little too much in terms of pushing the limits of your inhibitions, but not enough to make you feel ill or groggy.

We fought over the bill when it came. By fought, I mean that I insisted loudly on paying half, and he responded with beleaguered silence.

Instead of discussing it or attempting to engage in my one-sided conversation, he wordlessly put his credit card in the holder. He kept it carefully out of my reach as I continued to list all the reasons we should split the check, not the least of which was that we'd agreed earlier that this was not a date; then he handed it stealthily to the waiter as he passed. I was still oblivious, still making my case, when Quinn signed the receipt.

"Wait—what are you doing?" I looked from him to the paper slip.

Silence. *Scribble.* Silence.

"Did you just sign that? Was that the check?" My voiced hitched up an octave, and my eyes were wide with faux outrage.

He glanced up at me with something like mock innocence lighting his features, and said, "I'm sorry. Did you want to split that?"

I scowled at him, but couldn't hold on to my feeling of annoyance when he smiled. I had memories attached to his smile now, and all of them served to increase my warm fuzzies. I was drunk on good wine, delicious food, and fantastic conversation.

He shifted his attention to his wallet; a small, secretive smile was still dancing over his lips as he put his credit card away. My glower dissolved and I indulged myself by staring at him, unabashedly. I really looked at him.

He wasn't actually physically perfect, but he came close. He had a scar cutting through the center of his right eyebrow; I made a mental note to ask him about the story behind that. One ear was slightly larger than the other, and his nose was bent, just a whisper, to the left. His hairline wasn't even, and his hair was too thick; it needed to be cut and thinned. His bottom teeth were slightly crooked, but I didn't notice or see them unless he smiled his full-on one-thousand-watt smile.

I loved that when I looked at him, I didn't see the blinding McHotpants façade of perfection any more. I saw a frustratingly bossy, hilariously funny, irritatingly teasing, captivatingly intelligent, seriously sexy good guy.

"What's that smile for?"

I blinked at him and shook my head just slightly to clear it. His voice seemed to come at me from a distance as it pulled me from my musings. I realized that I'd been staring, but in my cozy, comfortable, uninhibited state, I didn't feel particularly embarrassed. I responded, "I was just thinking about my first impressions of you and how you're actually a real person."

"As opposed to…?" He lifted his eyebrows.

"As opposed to a handsome robot."

He dipped his chin and narrowed his eyes at me. "You think I'm handsome?"

"Come on. You know you're handsome." I rolled my eyes and poked him in his rib, behaving uncharacteristically touchy-feely.

"I'm just surprised that you do. When we went to Giavanni's, I thought you were going to make me put a paper bag over my head."

"What? Why? What are you talking about?" I sputtered, poking him again.

"When Viki asked if we were there together, you—"

"That's because she looked at me like I was the love child of Cerberus and a cyclops when you said I was there with you." I went to poke him a third time but he grabbed my wrist and laced his fingers through mine. Our hands settled on his knee.

He shrugged and glanced at our hands, frowning a little. "I suppose she was surprised."

I asked my next question uncertain if I wanted an answer. "Because I'm not your type?"

His eyes abruptly lifted to mine; his features lost some of their earlier unguarded ease. "You could say that."

I couldn't help my own frown or stop the sinking feeling in my chest. In that moment, I felt like a real girl; like a girl who wants to hear that she is beautiful from the boy she likes. It felt adolescent and bizarrely painful and exasperating because I knew it was adolescent. "So, what is your type? Beautiful? Blonde hair? Model thin?"

His mouth hooked to the side. "That's not what I meant."

"Well… what did you mean?"

His expression hardened slightly. "Shelly and I go to Giavani's almost every Saturday. Viki isn't used to seeing me with anyone else."

"You mean she isn't used to seeing you with a girl other than your sister, a date?"

"I don't date." His expression slipped into the mask of guarded detachment I'd grown somewhat used to over the last week. He then added, "I should clarify that; I *haven't* dated."

He's a Wendell.

Elizabeth's words from that morning were parading through my head. I tried to cover the disappointed flop of my stomach falling to my feet with a brave smile, and pushed him on the subject, asking another question I wasn't sure I wanted the answer to. "So why don't you date?"

"It's not a big mystery. I haven't needed to." His tone was matter-of-fact.

"What does that mean—you haven't needed to?" It seemed as if each time he spoke he was reluctantly giving me a puzzle piece; the finished image was looking more and more like a Wendell. Reluctantly, I was starting to accept that Elizabeth's assessment of him had been correct.

"You know what it means." His voice was hesitant, as if he weren't convinced of the statement.

I shook my head and watched him with wide eyes. "No. I really don't. You're going to have to spell it out for me."

He seemed to consider me for a moment, his gaze hawkish and searching. He then asked, "What about you? Why'd you and Jon break up?"

"First I want to know what 'I haven't *needed to*' means. Are you—" I searched for an explanation that was a Wendell alternate and could only come up with one thing, glad for my wine-fueled audacity. "Are you celibate?"

"No." A rueful smile passed over his lips, but it didn't quite reach his eyes. "Fine—it means I never needed to date someone in order to have a good time. I have..." He cleared his throat, scratched the back of his neck, and glanced to the side as though to avoid my gaze. "I had a few girls who I partied with from time to time, but we weren't exclusive."

I blinked, absorbing this information. "You mean...you mean you have certain girls that you call just to have sex with them—you mean *slamps*?"

Even under the intimately dim candlelight, I could see that his neck and cheeks were red-tinged. He didn't respond, but he did sigh. He let go of my hand, stood up, and grabbed my coat; he held it up and waited for me to shrug into it. I eyeballed him, taking his silence as confirmation. Wordlessly, he placed his hand on the small of my back and steered me toward the door.

I thought the sinking feeling would stop at some point. It didn't. Quinn was a Wendell. Even worse, he was a multiple-slamp Wendell man-whore. I felt sad but resigned and, strangely, a little angry with Elizabeth for being right.

When we stepped outside, the chilly Chicago air felt good as it whipped past me; it helped me clear my head. I glanced over at Quinn and allowed myself to dwell on the ridiculousness of my situation. I was with a really great guy who, according to Elizabeth, wanted to give me mind-blowing sex, but only mind-blowing sex, which I would be turning down as, among other reasons, he was already giving the same sex to other girls. Before I could stop myself, I stepped away and I asked, "Is it all at the same time or one at a time?"

He stopped in his tracks. Quinn met my gaze, his own betraying stunned surprise.

"What?" I pushed.

He shook his head as a reluctant smile pulled at his lips. His hand found mine and started pulling me until my feet moved. "Your turn," he said, blatantly deflecting my question.

"Not yet. I want to know more about the logistics of this." I couldn't help myself. The whole concept seemed suddenly both absurd yet strangely efficient. "How many are we talking about? What percentage of the women in Chicago are ready to have sex with you right now? What happens if one of them needs to travel? Do they have a phone tree? Is there a coverage plan or a backup plan for emergencies?"

Quinn covered the bottom half of his mouth with his free hand as his shoulders started shaking with silent laughter.

I continued, feeling a little better knowing that he was able to laugh at himself. "Is there entry criteria? An established search committee? An interview process? Skills test? What kind of radius do you require? Do you have one circling the block now? Do you always keep one nearby? Was there one at the restaurant? At the bar maybe?"

"Janie, seriously—it's your turn." His tone was authoritative, but I could see that his eyes were lit with amusement, and he was trying very hard to keep a straight face.

"My turn?" My eyebrows lifted in confusion; despite my attempts at making fun of his arrangement, I was still feeling lingering dejection from confirming Quinn's somewhat sordid sexual history; well, it was sordid compared to my history, which made it sordid by comparison. "You already know everything. I'm a one-*slamp* kind of girl."

"Why did you and Jon break up?"

I thought about the question, but I was distracted by the reality of Quinn's confession. Quinn never dated.

No—he said he never needed *to.*

Was I ok with that? What was a man-whore really? Was it such a bad thing if all the practice with slamps meant he was good in bed? If we ever slept together, would I need to cover myself in cling wrap and Lysol to protect against his plethora of contracted STDs? Did he have any STDs? Were we going to sleep together? If he had unlimited access to veteran slamps, was he even interested in sleeping with me, novice that I was? Did I want to sleep with a Wendell, especially after finding out about the multiple slamps-in-waiting? Was I going to become one of his slamps?

I was pretty sure I didn't want to become one of Quinn Sullivan's many slamps.

As an aside, I noted that "One of Many Slamps" would make a good band name or, at the very least, an album name.

"Janie?"

My eyelashes fluttered and I looked around the sidewalk unseeingly. "Yeah?"

"You and Jon; why did you split?" I noted his voice was quieter, almost coaxing. We started up the staircase for the el.

I responded without thinking. "I'm not really sure what the real reason was for our split, but I'm pretty sure the catalyst was him cheating on me."

"He…" Quinn stopped on the stairs and pulled on my hand until I met his gaze. "He cheated on *you*?"

I nodded. "Yes. But, to be fair, he said he was drunk and it only happened once."

Quinn's eyes were wide with what looked like disbelief. "I can't believe *he* cheated on *you*."

"Yes, well… I think I have some insight as to why, but I'm still processing the possibilities." I pulled my hand from his and tucked my hair behind my ears. I started up the stairs again so I wouldn't have to look directly at him when I spoke. "But there were already other issues before that. For one, he is wealthy." We reached the landing and passed our transit cards through the gate.

Quinn's eyebrows shot up at my statement. "What does that have to do with it?"

"For one thing, our priorities never seemed to align. He could, and did, spend money on whatever he wanted. I was—and am—always careful with all my purchases. Second, I always felt like I had a handicap; it felt like I was perpetually taking advantage of him or like I owed him if I accepted whatever he gave me: money, gifts, help. If I didn't accept his help, it always led to bad feelings and uncomfortable discussions where I always felt like I was the problem." My mind began to focus on our current conversation rather than the conversation of two minutes ago. I decided I would work through my slamp issues at some point later. "I'm determined to stay within one standard deviation upward of my own socioeconomic sphere."

Our train arrived, and he waited to speak until it slowed to a stop. Quinn's expression straddled the triple border of bewilderment, determination, and alarm. "So…" he said, but then he huffed out his breath and pinned his gaze on me with sudden intensity. When he spoke, I was surprised by the argumentative tone in his voice. "Would you ever date someone who earned less than you?" He ushered me onto the el and to a seat by the sliding door; when we were seated, his arm went behind me along my back and against the window.

I nodded immediately. "Oh yes, absolutely; I don't have a problem with that. My concern is being with the type of person who has enough wealth to decide on a whim to take off from real life and travel around where ever and expects that I'll be able to do the same simply because he has the means to fund it. Or who buys me extravagant gifts, like a car or expensive jewelry, for no reason, and that troubles me."

I felt a sudden shiver as if someone was watching me. I turned my head and surveyed the train. I looked from left to right and found only a smattering of what seemed to be college students. It was the same inexplicable sensation that I'd experienced in the club weeks ago.

"What is so wrong with that? If you're in a relationship with someone, why can't he buy you things and take you places?"

When I brought my attention back to Quinn, it took my mind a moment to sort through his words and their meaning; my attention still sharpened to the perception that someone was scrutinizing my movements.

I licked my lips and shook my head slightly to clear it. "I want to be financially independent. When I was with Jon, I didn't like having to constantly justify or explain that.

One time Jon bought me a car—a really nice car—and he couldn't understand that it wasn't appropriate for him to do so."

"Why wasn't it appropriate?"

I ignored the persistent impression that I was being watched, deciding it was my randomly overactive imagination, and pursed my lips in response to Quinn's question. "You know why."

"No. I really don't. You're going to have to spell it out for me." He echoed my words from earlier; his expression strangely stiff.

I huffed. "Because how can I possibly reciprocate? What do I have to offer?"

"Yourself."

I wrinkled my nose. "That makes it seem like I'm selling myself."

Quinn tilted his head to the side, studying me openly, and then he asked, "Now who is keeping score?"

I opened my mouth to respond, closed it, swallowed, and said, "It's not the same thing, and I can't believe you're taking his side in this."

"It is exactly the same thing," he countered. "If no one is keeping score in a relationship, then it doesn't matter, does it? I should be able to give you whatever I want without having to worry about you feeling guilty or like you need to reciprocate."

I frowned, studying him, really trying to absorb his logic. "Reluctantly, I admit that you have a somewhat valid point," I said hesitantly, but before a look of triumph could completely claim his features, I added, "It'll take me a while to process and potentially adjust to this perspective, though."

Quinn's gaze moved over my face, and a small smile curved over his lips. "I promise not to keep score with you if you promise not to keep score with me."

I gave him a long, sideways stare. I considered his proposal. It seemed fair. I nodded just once and stuck out my hand. "Fine. Deal."

A slow smile and a genuine look of victory brightened his expression; his eyes were as mischievous as ever when he shook my hand and said, "What should I buy you first?"

I poked him in the rib.

CHAPTER THIRTEEN

We were still engaged in easy conversation when we arrived at my building, so it didn't actually occur to me to bid Quinn goodnight at the door. We spoke about his upcoming business trip to New York planned for later that week, which naturally brought up the fact that Gotham City is based on New York City. We then talked about our favorite cities, both real and fictional.

However, once we were climbing the stairs to the small apartment I shared with Elizabeth, I felt a little flutter of nervousness at the passive invitation I'd offered.

Quinn was coming upstairs. We were going upstairs together.

I felt I should warn him that the place was small and my belongings were haphazardly strewn about and not at all organized. I wanted to explain that I was currently sleeping on the Ikea pullout couch/futon in the center of the living space, but I didn't know how to bring it up.

I also wanted to tell him that I wasn't going to be his slamp, and even though mind-blowing sex with him sounded very tempting, I was pretty certain I wanted a non-Wendell man, even if the sex would be just lukewarmly mind-blowing. Scarlet heat consumed my face with each step up the stairs, and our conversation lulled as I approached my door.

"So," he said.

I stopped abruptly in front of the door, turned to face him, and gave him a tight-lipped smile. He leaned against the doorframe leisurely, crossed his arms in front of his chest, and allowed his eyes to blaze an unhurried trail over my face.

"So," he repeated. He looked calm, confident, and confoundedly sexy.

"So…" I sighed, then pulled my gaze away from his, and glanced at the keys in my hands. "Listen, I—I had fun tonight. You—you're good to talk to, and I had a nice time, but I would like to pay you for my dinner."

His hands came up between us. "Janie, no keeping score, remember?"

"Yes, but it wasn't a date and I know it wasn't a date and I understand that you don't date and I'd like to be friends with you, but—"

"You want to be *friends* with me?" His voice sounded a little dark, perplexed.

"Yes." I lifted my eyes to his, but only briefly. His expression matched his tone. I sighed. "Listen—you should…um, you should come in so we can talk about…" I turned to the door and unlocked it with slightly shaky hands. The earlier scarlet heat turned into an inferno as I struggled with the lock. "We can talk about labels and Wendell and dinner and slamps and—oh thank God." The door opened and I launched myself inside, calling behind me, "Come in—come in. I'll make some coffee."

I flipped on the light in the hall and turned on every light on my way to the kitchen. I heard the closing of the door and hesitant footsteps behind me. I rushed through the process of boiling water and scooping the already ground beans into the French press. When everything was prepared, I walked to the couch—my bed—and noticed that Quinn's jacket draped across one corner of it. The sight did strange things to my stomach, and I'm not going to lie, to my lady bits. They may have clenched.

I hurriedly took my jacket off, almost sweating by this point, and tossed it on top of his. He was walking slowly around the small space, glancing at the bookshelves that contained my comic books and Elizabeth's record collection. He took out a Backstreet Boys LP and turned to me with a questioning frown.

I laughed lightly. "Oh, that's Elizabeth's. I live with my friend Elizabeth; you met her at that bar the night you…um, well this is her place, and I'm just crashing here—on the couch, actually—until we find a new place big enough for both of us."

His eyes drifted to the couch as he replaced the record. I tucked my hair behind my ears and cleared my throat. It was strange having him in the apartment.

Admittedly, I was just a transient visitor, and the décor and style represented nothing of me; even so, I felt like he didn't belong here, in my life. It was as if he was surrounded by an otherworldly glow that filled the diminutive space and cast everything but him in shadow, including me. He was too big, too handsome, and too graceful. He didn't fit in our small, inadequate world.

The thought made me sad, and I firmed my bottom lip with resolve. His eyes met mine just at that moment, and he frowned at my expression. Holding my gaze, he crossed to me and I crossed my arms over my chest. He seemed to hesitate at the movement but continued his approach nonetheless, and stopped just two feet from me.

Silence stretched as his gaze moved over my face; at length he spoke. "Who is Wendell?"

I blinked, startled. "Wendell?"

"You said you wanted to talk about labels, dinner, and Wendell."

"Oh, yes. Wendell." I turned, picked up our jackets, and placed them on the arm of the futon; then I sat with my legs tucked under me and my arm draped along the back of the couch. "Please—have a seat."

He sat with one of his legs under him so that our knees touched and his arm covered mine; his large hand rested on my elbow, and I focused on my breathing.

"So, who is Wendell?"

I nodded, biting my lip, not really sure how to have this conversation without putting all my oddities on display. As usual, the mouth started moving before the brain could send up a warning flare.

"You are Wendell. Or, rather, you are a Wendell and I can't be a slamp, so what I'd like to do is talk to you about dinner and labels."

One of his eyebrows rose and I felt him stiffen; his mouth opened as though he were going to interrupt me, but I, having said this much, gathered my courage and continued with loud urgency.

"The thing is—I like you. I like you a lot, and I've really only known you for a few short weeks—less than a month—but you are very likeable. I'd like to be your friend because I appreciate your honesty about being a Wendell. Therefore, I would like to have dinner with you—not a date—but I think the label applied to our dinner should be friendship and not Wendell-slash-slamp, because I don't think I'm up for that. But I understand if you aren't interested in being my friend, especially since you're already juggling a heavy load of slamps. I'd be disappointed, but I would understand."

I felt him relax slightly through my tirade; then tense; then relax. His eyes were watchful. He leaned closer and asked, "Ok, first, what is a Wendell?"

"A Wendell is a guy..." I gestured to him. "In this situation, you are the Wendell—a guy who is very...nice...looking and also very..." I couldn't look at him, so I picked a spot on my skirt and studied it. "A Wendell is very adept and/or talented in certain areas that are related to adult...bedroom activities and who also has a large selection of female companions for the aforementioned adult bedroom activities from which to choose on any given occasion."

My eyes flickered to his face and found him watching me with a confounded smile, obviously enjoying my discomfort. He cleared his throat. "Janie, just say it."

I sighed and suddenly wanted to hold his hand, likely because I was pretty sure it would be the last time I did so.

I entwined my fingers with his and squeezed. I looked at him straight in the eye and immediately felt my resolve weaken, but I plowed ahead. "Fine; a Wendell is a man who is extremely good looking and who is great in bed. Wendells do not have exclusive relationships— i.e. they do not date, but rather hook up with many women. I have no judgment for Wendells; in fact, I applaud their stamina and ability to provide excellent service to so many women. It seems like a very efficient and generous use of resources. However," I took a deep breath and swallowed, looking down at our fingers like a coward, "However, despite how equitable an arrangement that might be, I am not interested in non-dating a Wendell. Since you are, in fact, a Wendell, I think that I would be more comfortable if you and I could agree to the label of friends, not kissing friends or Wendell-slamp friends; just regular friends."

Again, silence stretched. I felt his gaze on me, heard him sigh, and then he asked, "Will you please look at me?"

I lifted my eyes to his. He didn't look relieved, annoyed, or angry like I feared. Rather, he looked contemplative and uneasy. He paused before speaking, and I thought I saw a flash of pain pass behind his eyes, but it was either imagined or hidden instantly. "I'm not used to this, so you'll have to give me a little bit of time to…to adjust," he said quietly.

"You can take as much time as you need." I offered this reassurance bravely, half-heartedly attempting to pull my fingers from his. The attempt was unsuccessful; he tightened his grip.

"I don't want…" He sighed heavily again and closed his eyes briefly, and then he met mine again with renewed composure. "I appreciate your honesty."

I chewed on my bottom lip and waited; when he didn't continue, my eyes widened in confusion. "Wait. That's it? That's all you have to say?"

He nodded. "Yes. That's it."

I drew in a breath and instinctively looked around the apartment for what I was missing. "I'm confused."

"What confuses you?"

"Are we- did you- did you just agree to the label of friendship?"

"No."

I opened my mouth to speak, closed it, opened it again, and then I licked my very dry lips. "Then what label are we going to use?"

His gaze lowered to my mouth; he lifted the hand resting on my elbow to my hair and pushed a mass of curls over my shoulder, his long fingers lingering on my neck. "We aren't going to use a label."

I took an unsteady breath; at this point, I didn't care about embarrassing myself further. What was one more debit of mortification when my balance sheet was already in the red by hundreds of thousands?

"I like labels. I like maps with labels. I like figures with labels, and I like footnotes. I don't do well not knowing someone's intentions or how to calibrate my expectations accordingly."

"That's good to know."

"Quinn!"

He fought admirably against the smile pulling at his lips and didn't meet my eyes. "You are so beautiful. I really want to kiss you right now."

His words hit me in my stomach and caused a hot tsunami of awareness that spread to my fingertips, toes, and the tips of my ears. "That's not fair. You're not being very nice."

"I've told you; I'm not nice." His gaze seemed to intensify, never leaving my lips, as he leaned infinitesimally closer.

I knew in that moment that if he wanted to kiss me, I would not stop him, but damn it, I wasn't going to sleep with him.

Undies on, undies on, high ho the dairy-o, I'm going to keep my undies on!

His hand gently cupped my cheek and his long fingers wrapped around my neck and pulled me forward. My eyelashes fluttered, and just before his mouth met mine, I said breathlessly, "You are nice. At least, you're nice to me."

He paused, lifted his eyes to mine, made a sound like a growl, and pressed his lips to my forehead. I smiled sadly, both relieved and disappointed.

After a long moment, he released me and rubbed his hands over his face, shaking his head as though to clear it. "Damn it," he muttered.

The water on the stove chose that moment to start boiling, its high-pitched whistle cutting through the thick tension in the room. I felt a little wobbly in my legs when I stood, and I hitched my thumb over my shoulder as I asked, "Do you want any coffee?"

"Do you have anything stronger?"

"I, um, let me check."

I turned abruptly and escaped to the kitchen as the teakettle screeched its alarm, and I was relieved when I took it off the stove. I knew for a fact that the only hard liquor we had in the apartment was tequila, and I had no intention of drinking tequila with Quinn.

Quinn plus tequila equaled *Quinquelia*, and that sounded like something that happens in Mexican jails.

I allowed myself a few moments to linger and compose my thoughts before I returned to the living room. Quinn was hovering in the entranceway, glancing at pictures, and I noticed, with a little twinge of disappointment, that his jacket was on. He moved to the door as I approached; he unlocked and opened it, walked a step into the hall. He turned to face me.

His gaze finally met mine as he straightened the collar of his coat. "I…" He hesitated; his features grew soft as his hands fell to his sides and his eyes gently moved over my face. After a moment, he said quietly, "I reserve the right to change my mind."

"Oh yeah? About what?" I leaned against the doorframe, looking up at him.

"About kissing you."

I self-consciously licked my lips and hugged myself, turning beet red. It seemed I was doomed to turn various and sundry shades of scarlet whenever he chose to make even moderately suggestive remarks. When I finally spoke, my voice was strained and off-pitch. "Well, ok, thanks for the heads-up. I feel duly warned."

His signature slow, sexy grin spread deliciously over his features causing my heart to flip-flop. I secretly hated him for it. That smile drove me crazy, but I suspected he knew that.

He shifted on his feet and rested a hand against the doorframe above my head, still smiling down at me. "So, are we still on for tomorrow?"

I shrugged. "Sure, *friend.* Where do you want to go to dinner?"

His eyes narrowed at my veiled sarcasm, but he spoke as though unfazed. "I thought instead of just dinner, we could have lunch and dinner."

"Um, sure. What time?"

He pushed away from the wall and withdrew his phone. "I'll pick you up at eleven thirty. Dress for a picnic."

My eyes widened with surprise. "Oh, ok. What can I bring?"

"Nothing; just bring yourself." He backed away, pressing the touchscreen of his phone, no longer looking at me.

I took a step into the hall. "Let me bring something. Or at least let me buy dinner. It's not fair for you to—"

He held up his free hand as he turned toward the stairs and gave me a devastating smile. "No keeping score."

I grumbled, but could only hear his laugh and the sound of his feet on the steps as he departed. Sighing, I turned back to the apartment, shut and locked the door, then let my head fall heavily against the thick wooden partition.

A chiming noise I now recognized as the blasted cell phone interrupted my thoughts. I turned to the living room and found the contraption on the coffee table. I glanced at the message. It was a text message. It was from Quinn.

Quote of the day: "Friendship is like peeing your pants; everyone can see it but only you can feel it."

♥♥♥

TRUE TO HIS WORD, Quinn called me precisely at 11:29 a.m. to let me know he was downstairs. I suppressed a surge of nerves and fiddled with my glasses, reminding myself that I frequently spent half-days hanging out with other friends. I could spend a half-day hanging out with my newest friend. There was nothing worrisome about that—nothing at all—nothing in the least.

I chewed on my thumbnail as I hazarded one last look in the mirror, catching Elizabeth's worried look over my shoulder. She didn't say anything, but I could feel her concern on my behalf.

I admitted that I looked nice; pretty, even. Elizabeth had helped me wrangle my hair into a braided bun. I was wearing a white silk slip and a gauzy, white summery dress with three-quarter-length sleeves. A touch of simple cotton lace gathered just under my ribcage, forearms, and around the square neckline. It ended just below the knee, and white flip-flops completed the look.

I'd never worn the dress before because it was quite see-through on its own. Elizabeth suggested the addition of the slip. The simple summer dress highlighted my best features—boobs, waist, and legs—but was subdued, even a little conservative, and was friend-picnic appropriate.

I pushed my glasses farther up my nose, purposefully wearing them instead of contacts, and turned to gather my sweater and my bag; the bag contained two fresh apples and the last of the summer peaches I could find at the market. Elizabeth fretted and twisted her hands, stopping me on my way to the door. "Oh, you should wear something else. You're so beautiful; *I* want to have sex with you. He's going to jump you in the car!"

"Oh, please!" I laughed as she pulled me in for a hug.

"Seriously, Janie," she said, and she held me by the shoulders. "If this whole Wendell McHotpants situation has taught you anything, it should be to embrace the fact that you are a total hottie, and lots of people want to get in your underpants."

I smacked her hands away and started for the door. "What are you doing this afternoon?"

"Me? Oh, I'm going to the gym, then I have to go into work to do some charting." She stretched and yawned. I knew she was running on less than six hours of sleep; even so, she'd insisted on waking up an hour before it was necessary so she could listen to the story about the Jon and Quinn dinner and the "let's be friends" discussion.

She said she was impressed with how I'd handled the situation, and she congratulated me for being courageous and honest even though I think she secretly wanted me to give in to the temptation to become a short-term slamp to Quinn's Wendell. She further pointed out that Quinn hadn't agreed to the friend label.

She pointed it out several times.

I had to cling to the label because without it, I felt adrift on a boundless sea of unknowns, so I bounced down the stairs feeling excited about seeing my new friend Quinn. Yeah, that was it: my friend—just my friend.

I exited the building and found him standing on the sidewalk at the base of my steps. He was leaning against the bottom of the cement stair rail, presumably scanning messages on his cell phone. He was crazy handsome, and I sighed quietly. Those were some lucky slamps. I put on my sunglasses.

The sun was brilliant and blinding. It was a perfect September day, and possibly one of the last mild days before the beginning of October. He must have heard the door close behind me because he looked up abruptly from his phone to where I stood at the top of the stairs. He straightened and stood perfectly still.

I dug through my bag as I descended. “I know you said not to bring anything, but I picked up some apples and peaches from the Sunday market.” I held out an apple to him as proof then tucked it back into my bag.

He groaned, and it sounded somewhat pained. “You’re not being very nice.” His voice was low and gravelly.

I scrunched up my face in response. “Oh, come on. I can bring fruit. I’m allowed to bring fruit.” I poked him and he grabbed my hand.

“I’m not talking about the peaches.”

“You don’t like apples? You should. In 2010, they decoded the apple genome, which led to new understandings of disease control and selective breeding in apple production. It really has wider ramifications…”

He stopped my mouth with a soft kiss, his hand wrapping around my waist and pulling me to him. I had the distinct impression I was being tasted in much the same way one would savor a peach. My traitorous body immediately responded by arching and pressing into his, and I kissed him back, tasting him in return. It was not a friend kiss; at least I’d never kissed a friend like that.

At length, after we’d thoroughly tasted each other, Quinn broke the kiss, rested his forehead against mine, and whispered, “Hi.”

I blinked up at him; my heart and my mind were competing in an uphill footrace, but I managed a small “hi” in return.

“I changed my mind about kissing you.”

“Well,” I said, “You did warn me.” A warm humming sensation was reverberating in my chest.

I DIDN’T HAVE much to say in the car but found myself frequently tugging at my bottom lip. Quinn was driving; it was another black Mercedes, and I wondered if it were a company car. The thought that he would be using company property for our date troubled me.

Or maybe it’s ok because it’s our non-date…our Wendell-slampcapade. Whatever.

I allowed myself to worry about the use of the car as it gave me something on which to focus. He didn’t force any attempt at conversation and seemed content to drive in silence. As confusing as it was, the silence wasn’t awkward or uncomfortable. It just was.

When we made it to the vicinity of the park, he surprised me by parking in one of the sky-rise private lots. We pulled into a numbered space in the basement. I shifted in my seat and glanced at him from the corner of my eye as he cut off the engine.

"Are we at your…do you live here?"

He quickly exited the car and rounded it to my side. Before I could pull the latch, Quinn opened my door in an unexpected, but not surprising, display of good manners. He reached out his hand to help me from the vehicle then didn't return it. Rather, he laced his fingers through mine and tugged me toward the elevator. At this point I realized that I'd become rather accustomed to the feel of his hand holding mine.

"Before we have our picnic, I want to show you something."

With no further explanation, we waited for the elevator. Once inside, we stood next to each other holding hands as the elevator ascended. Everything about the moment struck me as odd, surreal even, and I wondered how I'd arrived at this moment.

I rewound my thoughts and reviewed how I got here: It all really started that night, weeks ago, at the bar and the Saturday morning after. Fast-forward to last Wednesday when he bumped into me at Smith's. Then Thursday followed and the cell phone incident. Friday was good, normal, but then it wasn't normal, but it was still good, and he kissed me, three times. Saturday was both clarifying and confusing, which brought me to Sunday and another kiss, and this moment: holding hands in the elevator.

Despite my best efforts, I was now adrift in an unlabeled ocean of unknowns and trying to find my sea legs with no map, diagram, or figure with footnotes. I felt distinctly terrified and excited…but mostly terrified.

Despite all my brain rewinding, the elevator trip was actually very short. The doors slid open to a long, plain white hallway with four doors. Plastic sheeting covered the marbled floor, and it smelled heavily of paint. Quinn placed his hand on the base of my spine and ushered me to the end of the hall. He withdrew a set of keys and unlocked the door, and giving me a small but expectant smile, he motioned me in.

I crossed the threshold with hesitation and stepped onto an ash-colored hardwood floor. I glanced around at what I now recognized as a very, very nice apartment. It was unfurnished, so the wood panels fanned out uninterrupted and crisscrossed with the horizontal spears of light emanating from three large floor-to-ceiling windows off the living room, which overlooked Millennium Park. I walked slowly into the large living space, toward the windows, and noted the height of the cathedral ceiling as I turned to take it all in. My footfalls were loud and reverberating. The walls were painted a plain white, as were the crown molding and baseboards.

"The kitchen is over here." Quinn's voice echoed from my side; I followed where he led to a spacious, blue-gray marbled kitchen. All the appliances were stainless steel—double oven, gas range, dishwasher, giant fridge—except the sink, which was white porcelain and huge. This kitchen was meant for cooking.

The kitchen looked a little sad without small appliances, cookbooks, and food littering the countertops, like a kid waiting to be chosen for a dodge ball team.

After giving me a minute to survey the space, he placed his palm on my back and gently led me to a hallway with two bedrooms beyond. They were very similar in size, and both had en suite bathrooms. The main difference was that the slightly larger of the two also had a view of the park, and the bathroom contained a cistern-sized Jacuzzi bathtub.

My eyes widened when I saw the tub. It was an impressive tub. I don't think I'll ever quite get over the sight of that tub and the images it conjured of taking a bath with seventeen of my closest friends. I literally could have held knit-night in the tub.

Quinn seemed to sense I needed some time to absorb the enormity of the tub, so he waited for me in the master bedroom. When I emerged, I gave the tub one last longing look then turned my attention to Quinn.

Tub plus Quinn equaled Quinntub or Tubinn. I decided Tubinn sounded more alluring; I let that thought wash over me: Tubinn with Quinn.

I didn't even try to fight the blush that followed.

"Hey." He was sitting on an inset window seat; I noted it could be used for storage.

"Hey," I responded, letting out a slow breath, trying to find a subject other than Tubinn to discuss.

"What do you think?" he prompted, motioning with a tilt of his head for me to join him on the wooden seat.

"It's really nice…" I walked to him slowly, still surveying the room. "Are you thinking of renting it?"

"No, not me; I was thinking it might be nice for you and Elizabeth."

I came to a full stop about four feet from where he sat. "What?"

"You mentioned the two of you were looking for a larger place—you and Elizabeth."

"Yeah, something larger, not…" I lifted my arms around me in a movement I suspected looked like slow motion flapping. "…not Richie Rich McMansion huge."

His grin was immediate. "It's not that big."

I tilted my head at him in the way I often saw him employ, hands moving to my hips. "I am fairly certain it is well outside of our price range."

He also tilted his head. "See, that's the thing, this floor and the four beneath it belong to Cypher Systems. They were specifically purchased for employees."

"You mean… you mean the company owns these apartments?"

He nodded.

"But why would the boss want to buy apartments for his staff?"

He shrugged. "It was actually Betty's idea. She and her husband are downsizing; they want to move out of their house now that all their kids are gone, and she talked to me about helping her find a place near work so she wouldn't have to commute."

"Oh." I thought about that. "And the boss just decided to purchase five floors in a skyscraper overlooking Millennium Park?"

"If you think about it, it makes sense." He stood up, took a step, grabbed my hands in his, and brought us both back to the window seat. "It's a nice perk for employees. This is a nice place to live, near the Loop and the rest of downtown, and the park. Cypher's main business is security. Having employees spread out all over Chicago makes it difficult to ensure everyone's safety. If everyone were to live here, then it's close to work, and it's easier to keep tabs on people."

"You think the boss wants to keep tabs on people?"

"Yes and no; not in the way you mean."

"In what way, then?" I was frowning.

He sighed, ran a hand through his hair, and studied the floor for a tense moment before speaking. "You don't work much with the private accounts."

I blinked at this assertion, wondering where he was going with this seemingly random statement. "Yeah…so?"

"I can't explain what I mean in much detail."

I searched this statement and came to a speedy conclusion. "Does this have something to do with the non-disclosure agreements?"

"Something like that."

"Are they…the private clients…are they bad guys?"

He gave me an assessing sideways glance as a whisper of a smile brightened his features. "No, not exactly bad guys; just powerful."

"Hm." I began tugging at my bottom lip again as my eyes wandered over the apartment without seeing. Without meaning to speak the words aloud, I said, "Are you moving into one of the new apartments?"

He hesitated then said, "No, not one of the new apartments."

"Oh." I looked at the door leading to the bathroom. "Do you know how much the rent would be?"

"Yeah, I have an idea. It would be more than what you two are paying now; probably a little less than double."

"Oh. Well, that makes sense. It isn't a lot actually." I crossed my legs, and my foot started tapping the floor. "It would be strange to live and work around the same people. What if I quit my job? Would we have to leave?"

"Are you planning to quit your job?" His voice was monotone, but held just a slight edge.

"Well, no. Not right now. Not anytime soon, actually."

"Do you like it there? Do you still like the work?"

I nodded. "Yeah, I do. It's strange, but I never much enjoyed account management at my old job. All I could think about was applying for one of the architect positions. Now, I actually really enjoy it. It's different."

"What's different about it?"

I glanced at him; he appeared as interested as he sounded, so I drew my leg up to the wooden seat and faced him, the view of the park distracting me for a moment. "It's—well—it's just better. I'm learning about a new business, which is interesting. And Carlos and Steven are really open to my ideas for improvements to billing structure and operations, whereas, at my old place, they weren't interested in any new ideas. I also like the people."

Quinn's eyebrows lifted and he gave me a broad grin. "Oh, you do? Which people?"

"Well, let's see, there is of course Keira; she's very nice, and Steven. Dan is also very friendly. And Carlos…"

Quinn frowned. "What about Carlos? He hasn't been making the moves on you, has he?"

I chuckled, actually chuckled, and gave him a big grin. "No, no, not at all. Don't be ludicrous."

"Why would it be ludicrous?"

"Because Carlos is my boss. I'd never be interested in my boss."

Quinn's face froze; he blinked at me as if I'd said something truly disturbing. "Why not?"

It was my turn to frown. "Are you trying to get me to go out with Carlos?"

"No, no, definitely not. But, just because someone is your boss shouldn't put him into the automatic off-limits category."

"Uh, yeah it should. Dating your boss puts you at a distinct disadvantage."

"Like dating someone who is wealthy?"

I huffed. "Yeah, I guess. It's similar but worse."

"Why worse?"

"Quinn."

"Janie." His tone and his expression were granite.

"Why are we having this conversation?"

"Humor me."

"Even I, with my lack of ability to grasp the obvious, understand this concept." I poked him, not liking how serious he looked, trying to figure out what I might have said to cause the abrupt shift in mood.

His eyes narrowed as they focused on me with intensity, and his features remained impassive. "I think you're being closed-minded."

I crossed my arms and straightened my spine. "Really? How so?"

"Why do you like to assign everything a label?"

"It makes things simple."

"People aren't simple."

"But labels help make them simple. Why don't you like labels?"

His jaw ticked as his eyes moved between mine. "When you use labels as the only factor in defining another person, and therefore how you treat them, that's called stereotyping."

I opened my mouth but then closed it abruptly and swallowed. My chest felt hot with a stinging mixture of discomfort and annoyance. We were glaring at each other, and my breathing had become somewhat agitated.

"I do not stereotype people. Stereotyping implies that I make judgments with no valid data but rather based on ignorant societal shortcuts."

"Bosses can't be dated," he said. I noticed his deliberately deadpan tone.

"That's just common sense." I stood up and he grabbed my arm, not forcefully but firmly, and spun me toward him as he stood.

"Rich guys make bad boyfriends—isn't that a label?"

"That's not a label; it's a preference," I countered.

"Slamps and Wendells?" he challenged.

"Well if it walks like a duck, quacks like a duck, and has sex with multiple partners indiscriminately, then…!" I widened my eyes with meaning as my voice rose. I was moving beyond annoyance into something else that I now recognized as being very close to anger.

He growled and shifted restlessly as though caged. "I don't like being categorized."

"Don't tell me I stereotype people just because you don't like your label; if you don't like being a Wendell, then don't be one. It's your actions that dictate how you are perceived and how you are treated."

"Or you could decide to stop being such a close-minded, judgmental…"

"And what?" I pulled my arm out of his grip. "And become so open-minded that my brain falls out? Make so many excuses for people's bad behavior that I become spineless? No thanks. I have no desire to cherish each person's bullshit and call it a beautiful snowflake. I will not make excuses for all the ways they treat the people around them like garbage. If I wanted that I'd still be with Jon making excuses for his cheating or loaning my sisters money for their criminal exploits; meanwhile, I'd still be living in a state of perpetual disappointment."

His teeth were clenched. "I'm not proposing that you allow people to treat you like garbage. I'm suggesting that you make an effort to understand their behavior and the motivations behind it, rather than merely dismissing them because they meet the criteria for one of your shortcuts."

I couldn't help the sarcasm that spewed forth even though the words made me cringe as I said them. "Then correct me if I am in error: I imagine the motivation behind being a Wendell is wanting to have sex without being limited by number, variety, and frequency of partners."

He continued as though I hadn't spoken. "And also be open to the possibility that just because someone behaved one way in the past doesn't mean that's what they want now and in the future."

"People don't change." I said the words thoughtlessly even though I didn't really mean them or believe them, and I immediately regretted the statement. After what I knew, after what Quinn confided in me last night about his past and his brother, I wanted to apologize, but instead I started chewing on my bottom lip.

His eyes flashed dangerously. He swallowed as he fixed his gaze to a point over my left shoulder. I saw him shift his weight as though he was preparing to walk past me.

"I'm sorry," I blurted, and reached for him; my hands gripped his wrists in order to hold him in place. His eyes met mine and I took a small step toward him. "You're right, people can change, and motivations do matter. I don't know why I said that. It's just..." I released his wrists, rubbed my forehead with my fingers, and sighed. "It's just, growing up, my mother...she..." I rolled my eyes, hating that I was going to admit to someone that my mother's decisions had any impact on who I was as a person and the decisions I made.

Quinn crossed his arms over his chest and tilted his head to the side. "You've never mentioned your mother." He said it as though he just realized it.

I gritted my teeth. "I don't especially enjoy discussing her."

"Why not?"

I sighed again. "Because she was inconsistent and unreliable and was the female version of a Wendell."

He openly considered me, his beautiful lips twisting to the side. "A Wendellette?"

My mouth curved into a reluctant smile and I nodded. "She was..." I looked around the room, beyond him, to the window. "She was really beautiful, and my dad was just a complete doormat. She would leave for weeks, months with some guy, and then return, and my dad would forgive her and we would be expected to pretend like everything was ok."

His hands moved to his hips. "She cheated on your dad?"

I nodded. "Yes—a lot. In fact, it was ridiculous. Toward the end she was gone more than she was at home."

"Toward the end?"

My eyes moved back to his. "The end being just before she died." I shifted, suddenly feeling restless. "So, you see, being someone's slamp holds no appeal for me, nor do I wish to be a doormat. I like things defined, I dislike surprises, and I dislike the lack of clear expectations." My hands moved to my hips and I straightened my spine. "And if that makes me a little closed-minded, then I think I'm ok with that."

We watched each other for a long moment then he moved abruptly.

I felt a foreboding sense of vulnerability as he closed the distance between us, literally closed it, as in there was no space between our bodies, and I silently contemplated the way my own melted against his without my consent.

He slid his hands up my arms then around my waist, resting them on my hips just above my bottom. Much to my surprise and somewhat embarrassed appreciation, I felt every hard plane of his body including a hard length pressing into my abdomen.

Again, I blushed.

Quinn's head dipped and his mouth captured mine for a devastatingly soft kiss. My anxiety didn't dissipate; rather, a new emotion wrapped around the burning ball of trepidation in my chest and constricted it. I didn't recognize the feeling; all I knew was that it made me want to rip his clothes off.

He lifted his head just slightly, his eyes hooded. "Are you ready for our date?"

I cleared my throat, suppressing the desire to rub myself against him, suddenly desperate for friction. I cleared my throat again. "I thought you didn't date."

Quinn's cheek moved against mine so that his whispered words were hot against my ear. "I'd like to date you."

I shivered and my eyes drifted shut. My voice was tight as I asked, "Does that mean you're taking the slamps out of rotation?"

I felt him smile against my neck as he placed a lingering kiss on my shoulder. "They're already out of rotation."

He placed another kiss on my shoulder right next to where the lace met my skin. My body, my disloyal body, pressed against him more firmly, and my words came out on a sigh. "When did this happen?"

I felt him shrug. The simple movement caused his chest to rub against mine, and I had to bite my lip to keep from moaning.

"A while ago." He pulled away, one set of fingers lifting from my hip and slowly tracing the edge of my dress from my shoulder, where he kissed me, to my collarbone, to my chest, then up again. It sent goose bumps racing over my skin. My scalp felt tight.

A while ago.

My lashes fluttered open and I met his gaze; I was confused and fuzzy headed, and I wanted to know more about the disappearing slamps. Instead, I lost my locomotive of thought as he gave me a slow smile. The aforementioned fingers playing with the edge of my dress slipped over my shoulder and down my arm, entwining with mine.

He tugged on my hand. "Come on. Let's go have our picnic."

CHAPTER FOURTEEN

WE SPENT ALL day at the park. Several games of Frisbee may have occurred during which I may have gotten grass stains on my white dress.

To my surprise, there was a free blues concert at the Jay Pritzker Pavilion, and we decided to stay for the music after our day of fun together. We positioned ourselves at the edge of the lawn to allow plenty of space between us and the other park inhabitants.

Quinn reclined on the blanket with his head resting on my lap as though it was the most natural thing in the world, and I stroked my fingers through his hair. I would have stopped to pinch myself to ensure that I wasn't dreaming or that I hadn't been sucked into a *Matrix* type of alternate reality, but I didn't want to know. There would be no red pill for me.

Quinn fell asleep, and I didn't want to wake him so we stayed until the end of the last set. I watched him, mesmerized by the lines and angles of his face and the shape of his lips. They were parted slightly, and I successfully fought the urge to kiss them.

The applause woke him from his slumber. He frowned, visibly muddled by his surroundings, and blinked into my face. The color and immediate intensity of his eyes recognizing my own made my chest hurt in a really nice way. I smiled at him.

On impulse I leaned down and brushed my lips against his, intending to give my sleepy beauty a small peck. However, before I could withdraw, Quinn's hands held me in place; his giant palms on my cheeks, his long fingers stroking my neck.

He deepened the kiss even as he sat upright and leaned over me so that I was slightly reclined, the back of my head against his knee; my fingers curled around his forearms to steady myself. His tongue was warm and soft and worshipful as it gently, maddeningly gently, caressed my own. I was being tasted and savored like one licks ice cream or a gourmet dessert. The effect was inebriating.

Some passerby whistled, presumably at us, and I dipped my chin to my chest as I straightened, breaking the kiss, finding it difficult to breathe. His hands fell away. I peeked at him from beneath my lashes and the protection that my black-rimmed glasses afforded. He was in profile, glaring in the direction of the whistler; his stern expression made him look resolute, which made him look powerful, which made him look sexy.

I licked my lips, tasting him there, and sought to draw his attention back to me. "Did you sleep well?" My voice was slightly breathless.

He met my gaze, and I had the sudden sensation of being paralyzed. My limbs felt heavy and useless. He ignored my question and asked one of his own. "Why do you wear glasses instead of your contacts?"

I must have been kiss-tipsy because I answered with sincerity. "Because they make me feel safe."

His mouth hooked to the side and he blinked once. "Is that why you wear your hair like that?" He indicated to where my hair rested on the crown of my head in a severe bun. "Do you feel safer if your hair is pulled back?"

"No. I wear my hair in a bun, because if I don't, it looks like Medusa's snakes."

Quinn's trademark slow, easy smile eclipsed his features. "It doesn't look like Medusa's snakes."

"It does. Did you know Medusa also had two sisters? She was a middle child, like me. But Medusa was the only mortal of the three. Most myths have her killed by Perseus. He used a mirrored shield so he wouldn't have to look at her directly. When she died, Pegasus, the winged horse, sprang from her body, as did a sword-wielding giant."

Quinn twisted his mouth to the side, and then he gently took off my glasses and set them on the blanket beside us. "That seems unlikely."

I shrugged, feeling lethargic and somewhat giddy to be sitting on a blanket with him in the park at twilight. I also felt a bit exposed now that my glasses had been removed. "Some think she was pregnant by Poseidon at the time. Maybe his sperm was of the magical horse and giant variety instead of carrying the usual X or Y chromosome."

I reached for my water, took a long swallow, and considered Quinn over the rim of the plastic bottle. The early evening light was giving way to the darkness of night, but I could tell that he was still smiling. I was still Quinn-kiss-tipsy enough to feel no mortification when I asked, "If you could have magic sperm, what kind of creatures would you want to create?"

His smile widened; he shook his head as he looked around at the people packing up. "I don't know how much good magic sperm would do me without a snake-haired girl to put it in."

Quinn reached for his own water and took a gulp, but he choked when I said, "You could use me!"

He abruptly set his drink down, sat back on his heels, and picked up a napkin; his eyes were wide as he coughed. I reached over and patted his back soothingly.

"You should have more water."

"Thanks," he croaked, and he watched me warily as he drank from the bottle.

I sat unabashedly and waited for Quinn to compose himself. At length I asked, "Are you ok? Did it go down the wrong pipe?"

He nodded, his eyes following my movements as he gripped the napkin a little too tightly, and then he said, "You were saying something about how I could use you?"

"Oh yes. In this hypothetical situation, you have magic sperm that can make creatures." I screwed the lid back on my bottle of water, deposited it to the blanket, and began taking my hair down. "And it has already been established that I have Medusa-esque hair." I shook out the crazy curls and let them fall over my shoulders, back, and breasts. "So, now you have your snake-haired magic sperm repository. What creatures do we create?"

His expression could only be described as incredulous, even as his eyes moved over the mass of my hair with dark intensity. "What did you put in this water?"

"It's just water. What? Why?"

Quinn sighed. It sounded ragged. He pulled his gaze away from me as though it were painful or strenuous to do so. He stood and offered his hand to me stiffly, pulling me up with ease. "We should go get dinner."

I tilted my head to the side, considering him. "You're not going to answer my question?"

He shook his head, not looking at me as he gathered up the basket, the bottles, and the blanket; he tucked my glasses into the pocket of his shirt. I chewed on my lip and twisted my fingers as I watched him. I couldn't help but feel as though I'd said something wrong. I tucked my hair behind my ears and helped clean up.

We pulled everything together, and he still hadn't looked at me. I felt anxious and, therefore, my mind began to wander. I picked up the trash and walked to the waste basket, wondering whether the trash was picked up daily or whether it was every other day; wondering how much trash was generated by the park; wondering if anyone had thought about starting a recycling program in the city parks; wondering how much that would cost the city; wondering…

"Oh!"

I ran smack dab into someone and immediately tried to take a step back, but he grabbed my shoulders, not gently, and kept me from moving away. I looked into a rather unpleasant face. It wasn't an ugly face; in fact, it was a rather handsome face, but it was making an unpleasant expression, and his eyes were hard and cold.

The stranger was maybe one or two inches taller than me and extremely muscular. His head was shaved, his eyes were olive green, his rather angular jaw was flexed, black tattoos wound up from the collar of his shirt around his neck, and his full mouth was curved into a rigid frown.

I managed a small and what I hoped was a polite smile, but he merely stared at me with all the flexibility of steel. I got the distinct impression that he didn't like me. Furthermore, I had the distinct impression that he wanted to do me harm.

I swallowed and again tried to move away. "Sorry, sorry—I wasn't looking where I was going."

Instead of releasing me, he tightened his grip painfully and inclined his head forward. He whispered, "If you think you're going to talk yourself out of this, you're not."

"Hey!" Quinn's voice sounded from my left, and I turned to watch him sprint toward me. His expression was thunderous; in fact, he also looked unpleasant. He looked like he was intent on doing someone a great deal of harm.

Before Quinn reached us, the man released my arms, shoved me away, and held his hands up, palms out, as though he surrendered. He shuffled his feet backward. "Hey man, there's nothing going on here."

Quinn immediately stepped in front of me but continued to advance on the stranger. "What the hell do you think you're doing?"

The tone of his voice moved me to intercede. "Quinn, listen; it was nothing. I wasn't looking where I was going and he…"

"Listen to your girlfriend."

Quinn crowded the stockier man and leaned over him menacingly; his tone was eerily quiet. "You don't touch her, you don't look at her. If I ever see you again, it will be the last time anyone sees you."

I flinched. I didn't get the impression that Quinn's words were meant to be metaphorical or to convey an ounce of dramatic license. Instinctively, I felt the truth in them, and I would be lying if I said that in that moment, he didn't scare me.

The staring contest lasted another few seconds, until the bald man shifted uncomfortably and lowered his gaze to the sidewalk. Seemingly satisfied, Quinn walked backward a few steps then turned and, without looking at me, grabbed my hand and pulled me back to our abandoned picnic basket. My heart was galloping in my chest and I was shaking just a little. Without wanting to or meaning to, I glanced over my shoulder.

The bald man was still watching me.

Not us.

He was watching me.

He looked at me like he knew me, like he still wanted to do me harm, like the only thing keeping him from ripping me apart was the very large, angry man at my side. I pulled my eyes away and moved closer to Quinn.

For the third time in as many weeks I had the distinct feeling I was being watched. Only, this time, I knew I was right.

♥♥♥

WE DIDN'T TALK as we walked. Quinn held my hand firmly in his, gripping it almost to the point of painful. I carried the basket and the blanket and he held his phone, touching the screen every few minutes then glancing watchfully around the park. Instead of walking back to the garage, Quinn took us to South Michigan Avenue next to the Face Fountain. We stood there for less than thirty seconds before a black SUV slowed, then stopped in front of us.

Quinn opened the rear passenger door and said, "Get in."

Too flustered to question him, I climbed into the back seat and placed the basket and blanket on the bench beside me, settling myself in the middle. Quinn came in after me, slammed the door, and I immediately heard the door lock. It took a moment for my eyes to adjust to the darkness of the cab. I glanced at Quinn; his leg was pressed against mine as he twisted in his seat and peered out the window as though he were looking for someone.

The car moved and I sought the identity of our driver. All I could see was the back of his head and the impressive size of his neck. It wasn't Vincent unless Vincent had grown a foot and a half, regressed in age thirty years, and become an African American overnight. My attention was pulled back to Quinn as he settled his hand on my thigh and squeezed.

He was studying me with guarded suspicion. I could only look at him with wide-eyed confusion. I didn't understand what had just happened. I didn't understand why the man in the park looked at me with such a sinister expression. I didn't understand why Quinn felt the need to warn him with medieval threats. I didn't understand why we ran out of the park as if we were being pursued. I was at a complete loss.

My chin may have wobbled.

Quinn must have caught the movement because he moved his arm around my shoulders and pulled me to his chest. I wasn't in any danger of crying, but I didn't push his comfort away. It felt good to be wrapped in his arms, so I allowed myself to rest there, absorbed by the strength of him. He set his chin on my head and I felt him sigh.

"Do you know that guy?" I asked, my voice sounding remarkably small in the big car.

He stiffened. "No." His hand slid from my shoulder to my hip, pulling me closer. Then he said, "I don't know. He looked familiar."

I lifted my head from his chest so I could look into his eyes. "Is he one of the private clients?"

Quinn shook his head, his eyes flickering briefly to the driver then back to me. "No, definitely not. No, he looks like someone I used to know."

"Oh."

His thumb stroked my hip and his eyes traveled searchingly over my face. "Are you ok? Did he hurt you?" Quinn's voice was rough.

"No, he just startled me. He was probably just some stranger and, remember, I bumped into him, so, no big deal."

He nodded, but I could tell he wasn't convinced. I placed my hand on his chest and he covered it with his own, moving it to his heart. It was beating rapidly. He cleared his throat. "Do you—uh—want to go home?"

I gave him a small smile. "Home?"

He shook his head and said, "You should probably get home."

A dark cloud of disappointment settled over my forehead. I wasn't ready for the night to be over. I didn't understand why my clumsy encounter meant our evening had to end.

"What are my options?" I looked at our entwined hands covering his heart, then I licked my lips as my eyes moved to his mouth.

"Home." He said the word firmly.

My gaze met his and found him regarding me with a paradoxical heated stoicism; dually pushing me away and crushing me close. Something possessed me, call it wanton woman instinct, and I pressed myself to him; I felt him stiffen. I slid my body upwards, crushing my chest against his; I felt his breath hitch. My leg moved between his and I lifted my mouth to his neck then his ear and whispered, hoping the words didn't come out clumsily and awkward. "I'm hungry."

Another ragged sigh escaped him, similar in tenor to the one in the park, and his hand moved to my thigh where my dress had hitched up baring my leg. He rested it there, the palm of his hand warming my skin, for a hesitating second before he pulled the hem of my skirt down to cover my knee and shifted away from me on the seat. I felt the loss of his warmth acutely as he disentangled our limbs.

Quinn leaned forward slightly toward the driver. "We need to take Ms. Morris home."

I watched him; at first surprised then, eventually, with the understanding of stinging rejection ringing in my ears. A scarlet blush of embarrassment so deep that I felt in danger of being consumed by its incineration wound its way up my neck, into my cheeks, and to the tips of my ears. I crossed my arms over my chest and angled my knees away from him as he settled back next to me.

We sat in silence for a brief moment, and I could hear the whooshing of the blood through my heart and between my ears. My brain was overtaken by a drama-coaster of adolescent self-doubt, which I embraced as fact: *I am never going to be that girl. It just isn't in me to be sexy and seductive. Maybe with several tens of thousands of dollars in plastic surgery I can become alluring enough that, in dim light or after several shots, I might spark the interest of a biostatistician—or an actuary.*

As we approached my building, I pulled my bag from the picnic basket. Quinn surprised me by brushing unruly curls from my shoulder. I turned to look at him; he was holding my glasses out between us.

I took them and glanced away as I muttered "thank you," and then I placed them safely on my nose.

His voice was soft when he responded. "You're welcome."

Quinn didn't open the door immediately when the car stopped, and I could feel his eyes on me. In an effort to avoid his gaze, I started searching through my bag for my keys. At length he exited and I bolted past him as soon as he was clear of the door. When I launched myself up the steps, I felt him close on my heels.

"Are you going to be ok?"

"Yep. Just fine." I slipped my key into the lock on the first try and felt thankful for the little miracle.

My internal temper tantrum tirade continued: *Attracting and holding the interest of someone like Quinn Sullivan will have to go into my box of make believe with the eventual remake of Final Fantasy 7 with PlayStation 3 graphics or finding an original, pristine version of Detective Comics No. 27, Batman's debut. All attempts are futile. It is just something I will have to accept as fantasy.*

I started through the door and up the steps not waiting for the door to close and not looking back over my shoulder. To my chagrin, I heard his steps echoing mine up the stairs. I climbed faster. When I reached my door, I fumbled for my keys; once again, I was met with success in turning the locks. He stood to the side, a little distance away, watching me.

I glanced over my shoulder briefly to give him a cursory wave. "Well, good night. Thanks for the…the picnic." Just as I was about to escape into the safety of my diminutive shared one bedroom, I felt his hand settle briefly on my arm above the elbow.

"I want you and Elizabeth to think about moving into that other apartment."

I shrugged and pushed the door open just wide enough for me to set my bag down and slip halfway in. "Yeah, sure. I'll talk to her about it." I stepped farther into my place.

Quinn reached out his hand and gripped the door as though he were keeping me from closing it. "I'm serious."

"Ok." I nodded again, my eyes meeting his briefly. My brain was already several feet away, in my apartment, safe from the lingering feelings of rejection, and reading the new biography I'd borrowed from the library on Madame Curie; it was not set in the present, in the hall, where I was the pathetic queen of wishful thinking.

We stood at the door for several silent seconds; I could feel his gaze moving over me. I fought the blush of embarrassment threatening to paint the roses of my cheeks red.

Then he said, "I have to go out of town."

I nodded. "Yes, I know. You have that trip to New York on Thursday."

"No. I'm going to leave tonight. I won't be able to make our scheduled trainings this week, and I might be hard to reach over the next few days, but you should text me if you need something."

I shrugged my shoulders, and again, I heard the whooshing sound of blood filling my ears. I backed into the darkness of my apartment as the blush won and crept steadily up my neck, marching over my features and burning me with mortification like Sherman burned Atlanta.

"I'll be in Boston first, then on to New York, and I'll be back on Sunday."

Wait, what did he say? Is he still speaking?

"So maybe I can get a rain check on that dinner until next week?"

I sighed distractedly, still unable to meet his eyes. "Yeah, sure. Why don't you call me when you get back?"

I didn't expect him to call.

He nodded and started leaning into my apartment; then stopped, paused, and released the door. He shuffled backward into the hall. Quinn stabbed his fingers through his hair in a frustrated movement. "I'm really sorry about tonight."

I glanced at him. He looked upset. I frowned. Before I could say anything, he turned and left me, pulling his phone from his pocket as he went. I waited to close the door until I couldn't hear the sound of his steps descending the stairs.

I didn't turn on any lights as I walked to the couch. In the darkness of my apartment, I allowed my mind to wander.

I didn't understand anything about this guy.

One minute he was pretending he wanted to date me, the next minute he was turning down my very obvious advances, and now he was fabricating a trip in hopes that I wouldn't bother him. I was so befuddled. If he wanted to give me the brush-off, he didn't have to make up some fake business trip.

I heard my heinous cell phone chime somewhere in the apartment. The sound made me growl in frustration, but then, suddenly, I was curious. It chimed again before I made it to the kitchen counter where that devil's device was charging. I glanced at the screen. It was a text from Quinn; actually, there were several:

The first: *I am going to put some guards on you, won't even notice them, sorry about all this.*

The second: *I will call you when I get to NY on Thursday.*

The third: *A neutron walks into a bar; he asks the bartender, "How much for a beer?" The bartender looks at him, and says, "For you, no charge."*

I frowned at the phone and the messages. He might as well have sent me hieroglyphics. After a long while, I set the phone on the counter and crossed to the couch. I sat and stared then lay down in sudden exhaustion. My head was spinning. I didn't understand men. They made no sense and behaved erratically.

I knew I was still in my clothes, and I realized I hadn't brushed my teeth, but I couldn't bring myself to move. I felt paralyzed by confusion. I decided, as I succumbed to sleep, that men should come with manuals, subtitles, and reset buttons.

♥♥♥

I'VE COME TO rely on my knitting group to be my compass in all things confusing and difficult to comprehend; this usually means relationships and interactions with other humans…er, people. My ladies have helped me navigate everything from precarious office politics to dealings with my ex's mother. And this is why they were supportive and engaged when I explained to them my current situation with Quinn.

It was Tuesday night, and we were gathered in Sandra's roomy two-bedroom apartment. Fiona was the only one missing, having to stay home at the last minute because her daughter was sick with the flu. Most of us had a drink in our hand, and I'd just finished passing the evil cell phone around so they could all read the texts. I had also just finished giving them a Cliff Notes version of the last week.

They were all silent. Ashley was staring off into space, Marie was frowning at a half-knitted sweater, Sandra was standing at the entrance to her kitchen leaning against the wall as though in heavy contemplation, Kat was watching me with a cloudy mixture of introspection and trepidation, and Elizabeth was still scrolling through Quinn's texts.

Ashley was the first to pipe up; her thick Tennessee accent made even this sound charming: "I think he was upset about that guy in the park, and that's why he turned down your hot bod."

Some of them nodded in agreement; some of them continued to stare unseeingly.

I sighed. "But, how interested could he really be? By the mighty power of Thor—I threw myself at him!"

Elizabeth frowned at me. "Did you really just say 'by the mighty power of Thor'?"

"I'm trying to cuss less."

Some of them nodded in agreement; some of them continued to stare unseeingly.

I sighed. "I think I completely messed up. I think he thinks I'm pathetic, and he's just trying to avoid me by making up some trip so he doesn't have to talk to me."

Marie shook her head, her blonde shampoo commercial hair bouncing around her face. "No. That's not it." She sounded so certain. "That's definitely not it."

Elizabeth nodded in agreement. "I agree with Marie. The boy is hot for you."

Some of them nodded in agreement, some of them continued to stare unseeingly.

I sighed. "Then why did he turn down my advances?" I couldn't help the frustration in my voice. I knew part of my frustration was due to his absence. I'd been spoiled by seeing him almost every day in the past week, and now I missed him. Last Saturday, when he surveyed my apartment, I thought he didn't belong here, in my life. But now, the absence of him made me feel like I was forever trying to catch my breath.

And it had only been two days.

"Well, hell, girl! He just watched you get manhandled by a creepy neck-tattooed skinhead," Sandra said as she pushed away from the wall and joined us in the living room. "If he wasn't interested, then he wouldn't be stuffing your cell phone inbox with messages. I think he's worried about you."

"Also, hon, you may not have been as transparent with your advances as you believe. I've seen you; you're not a skilled flirter. It's usually hard to watch." Ashley grimaced.

Kat said quietly, "I don't understand his reaction to the guy in the park. It sounds like he completely overreacted. Janie, is there anything else? Did the guy threaten you?"

I shook my head. "No. I just bumped into him. He was scary, but other than grab my arms, he didn't do anything."

"But didn't McHotpants say he knew the guy?" Sandra poked me with a carrot before dipping it into a vat of blue cheese dressing and biting into it with a solid crunch.

"It was vague; something like he thought he looked familiar. I don't know." I pressed the heels of my hands into my eye sockets then allowed the back of my head to fall against the tall chair behind me. "I mean, if you think about it, the first time I spoke to Quinn was only four weeks ago. I don't really know him at all. Maybe the guy in the park actually freaked him out and I'm wrong. Maybe he's just not into me and I'm right. Maybe Quinn is an alien and is finished with his study of humankind and no longer has use for me as a specimen."

Marie shook her head. "Four weeks is long enough. People have fallen head over heels in less time than that."

"Did he actually put guards on you?" Ashley pointed the question to me, but her eyes were on Elizabeth.

"Yes. He did." I frowned at that. The first time I saw them was Monday morning as I was leaving for work. They'd approached me outside my building, both dressed casually in jeans and T-shirts and looking like regular guys, and told me that they worked for Infinite Systems. Mr. Sullivan, it seemed, put in an order for two twenty-four-hour protection teams. They promised I wouldn't notice them. They were right; over the last two days, I'd forgotten about them.

"The guards are likely outside now. We should bring them some coffee or something." Elizabeth looked up from the cell phone and handed it back to me. "The friendship one about peeing is funny. I think I'm going to use that."

I accepted the hateful phone from Elizabeth and stared at the last two messages. Quinn, true to his word, continued to send me jokes every day, which only served to confuse me further.

Marie started knitting again. "Time will tell. I say just wait and see; if he calls you on Thursday, see what he says."

I stood and stretched. "You're right! I'm done thinking about this. Done, done, done!" I swished my hand in a circle and snapped three times then walked to the bathroom, wanting to excuse myself in hopes that my absence would change the subject.

I wasn't in the bathroom long, just enough time to wash my hands, when I heard a knock on the door.

"Just a minute; I'm almost done," I called absentmindedly.

"Janie, it's Kat. Can I come in?"

"Yeah, I'm almost done."

"No..." Kat's voice dropped to a whisper. I could tell she had her lips close to the crack in the door. "I mean, can I come in and join you? I need to tell you something."

I opened the door then turned to search for a towel. "What's up? Are you ok?"

Kat's voice was heavy with hesitation. "I found...something...out." The soft click of the door closing surprised me so I turned to face her, mopping up the dampness of my hands with an amazingly fluffy and absorbent towel. I made a mental note to ask Sandra where she purchased her towels.

When Kat didn't continue, I lifted my eyebrows. "About what?"

She looked entirely too serious, like my dad did the day he told me Santa Claus wasn't real. I was fifteen.

"It's about your job." She hesitated again, tucking her brown wavy hair behind her ears while she collected her thoughts. "I found out why they let you go."

"Oh." I gripped the towel; it was so squishy. I'd forgotten that Kat had agreed to try to find out why I was let go. At present, I didn't particularly care.

"Janie..."

She said my name in a way that is usually followed with something along the lines of *Where were you the night of the murder*? or *You're going to want to sit down for this*. I increased my grip on the towel.

"It was Mr. Holsome."

I blinked. Silence stretched. Kat's eyes continued to watch me with wide-rimmed caution.

"Mr. Holsome?" I repeated, confused. "You mean, Jon's dad? My Jon's dad? That Mr. Holsome?"

Kat nodded and leaned against the closed door. She sighed.

"I don't..." I blinked at her again and sat down on the toilet seat lid. "I don't understand. Why would Jon's dad want me to lose my job?"

She looked miserable. "I don't know the why, but I can tell you I'm one hundred percent certain he was responsible. He threatened to pull out of the South Side project if they didn't let you go, and he was insistent that it had to be *that* day."

That day.

That day I found out Jon had cheated on me. *That* day I broke up with him before I left for work *that* morning.

Kat must've seen the wheels turning in my rickety brain because she said, "Do you think Jon asked him to do it?"

I shook my head. I could only huff a response. "I don't know; I can't…" My words trailed off. I thought about the accusation Kat voiced, and that I'd been thinking.

It didn't seem likely, but I was disturbed to realize it seemed plausible. Jon had said on more than one occasion, when we were together and since we'd broken up, that he wanted me to rely on him, that he wanted to take care of me, that I needed him. I didn't feel that way; I wondered why he did. Maybe it was because he felt it was true.

Maybe it was because his father had been able to end my employment with a phone call.

"What are you going to do?" Kat was twisting her hands in front of her, nervous and anxious on my behalf.

"I don't know." I shook my head then said it again. "I don't know."

It didn't seem fair that Jon should be able to, on a petulant whim, decide to make a call that made me lose my job; a job, mind you, that I was quite skilled at but that I didn't miss. I honestly didn't know what I was going to do. Part of me wondered if it even mattered. Jon couldn't do anything to me now; I wasn't dating him anymore. He and his father had no influence with my current employer. I breathed a sigh of relief at the realization. I felt secure at my new job. I felt confident and safe.

Maybe Jon had done me a favor.

CHAPTER FIFTEEN

On the Thursday of my third week, I experienced the first tremor of uncertainty about my new job, and by tremor of uncertainty, I mean lightning strike of horror.

Quinn had been gone since Sunday night, but he was still sending me text message jokes. I read them, enjoyed them, but didn't respond as I was also starting to feel silly about my behavior. When he dropped me off that night, I gave in to my seesaw of self-doubt, and it made me nauseous.

Why would he continue to text if he were trying to avoid me?

Additionally, on Wednesday night, he texted me a reminder about our phone call for Thursday. I promised myself that I would talk to Quinn on the horrid cell phone, and I wouldn't participate in any playground equipment emotional drama-coasters.

However, the incident on Sunday and subsequent time apart on Monday, Tuesday, and Wednesday allowed me some time to reflect: I didn't really know much about Quinn. I didn't even know what his job was, and I worked with him. I didn't understand Quinn's role or title in the company, as no one really spoke about him, and when they did, they always called him Mr. Sullivan.

Therefore, I gathered the nerve to ask Steven about Quinn.

Steven and I were having lunch in the break room, which was more of a long hallway along the perimeter of the building with a window view of the city, and discussing my upcoming first official business trip and client meeting.

Steven and I would be flying to Las Vegas next Monday. He explained that the client owned Club Outrageous (which made me think of Quinn) and wanted to use Guard Security for another club in Las Vegas. The client also wanted to discuss arranging personal security through Infinite Systems.

"Does Cypher Systems have an office in Las Vegas?" I dipped the chicken in my taco salad in a small cup of sour cream before taking a bite.

Steven shook his head mid-chew-swallow.

"What about New York? Do we have any office locations other than Chicago?"

Steven just finished dipping his spicy tuna roll in soy sauce and answered before he ate. "Sweet Pea—can I call you Sweet Pea? No. It's just us lunatics."

"Don't call me Sweet Pea. What about Quinn Sullivan? Where is his office?" I tried to sound ambivalent; I watched Steven over a forkful of taco salad as I tried to suppress the blush threatening to overwhelm my cheeks. I hoped he didn't notice.

He shook his head. "Mr. Sullivan has an office here in the building, but as you've likely noticed, he doesn't use it much during normal business hours. I think he prefers to be out in the field."

"Why does everyone call him Mr. Sullivan?"

Steven placed a generous portion of shaved ginger on his sushi and lifted his eyebrows at me. "What do you want me to call him? Sully? Quinning the winning?"

"No, what I mean is, we call Mr. Davies 'Carlos,' and everyone else here goes by their first name. Why don't we call Mr. Sullivan 'Quinn'?"

Steven shrugged. "I don't know. I've worked here for three years; we've just always called him Mr. Sullivan." Steven seemed to think about the issue as he chewed his sushi; then, with a half full mouth, he added, "The only time I see him is for client meetings, and it just makes sense to call him Mr. Sullivan—in front of the client, I mean. Maybe it makes him seem more important in their eyes." Steven shrugged again and swallowed. "Well, I guess he is important—strange, but important."

"What do you mean 'strange'?"

"Well, you spent time with him last Friday, right? When you had to work late? So typical. He insisted on taking you out personally to train you." Steven used air quotes to emphasize the last two words. "I told Carlos I thought he just wanted someone to glare at. I can't believe you've been so nice about it."

I wrinkled my nose at Steven. "What do you mean? He doesn't glare at me."

Steven gave me a sympathetic look. "Only you would be so gracious, Janie."

I put my fork down and stared at Steven, my tone incredulous. "What are you talking about? I've learned a lot from him. I've found the time to be beneficial." I felt the need to defend Quinn; I didn't want Steven thinking Quinn had been rude or done a poor job training me and, therefore, get Quinn in trouble.

"Oh really?" Steven lifted his eyebrows.

"Yes, really."

Steven pursed his lips and gave me a pointedly disbelieving stare. "I once spent twenty minutes alone with him during a car ride from the airport to the site. During that time he said a total of three words and his face didn't change expression once—no, wait, that's wrong." He held his hands up as though to stop me from interrupting. "He had two expressions: at first he was stoic, but then, toward the end of the twenty minutes, his expression changed to apathetic. This is all despite the fact that my conversation was obviously thrilling."

"Stoic and apathetic are synonymous." I tried not to laugh as I imagined Steven and Quinn alone in a car together for twenty minutes: Quinn glaring at Steven while Steven regaled the silent car with tales of his weekend clubbing exploits and latest furniture purchase.

"Sure, he's very pretty, I'll give you that, but you can't tell me that you don't think there is something off about him." Steven looked over both his shoulders in an exaggerated manner then offered in a faux whisper. "Did you know he sometimes joins the security guards downstairs and acts like he is one of them?"

I twisted my lips to the side, debating whether to tell Steven that I originally met Quinn when he escorted me out after being laid off from my last position. Instead, I said, "Well, isn't he? Isn't he one of them?"

Steven studied me for a moment before replying in a very dry tone. "In a small way, yes, he is. In a much larger and more correct way, no, he is most definitely not."

"Hmm." I picked up my fork again and poked at my salad, feeling pensive. "Why do you only see him during the client meetings?"

"He doesn't go to all the client meetings, really; only if there is a problem or if he is vetting a new client. Usually he sends Carlos."

My fork stopped mid-air between my plastic container and my mouth. "Wait." I could almost hear the clicking and squeaking of the gears in my head. "What do you mean 'sends Carlos'? Wouldn't the boss decide who goes to what meeting?"

Steven blinked at me three times, his eyebrows pulling up so they looked like little umbrellas over his gray eyes. "What nonsense are you speaking? Mr. Sullivan *is* the boss."

Time stopped.

Everything seemed suspended as my brain struggled to accept reality. It was one of those moments you reflect on, later in life, and wonder how your brain could have thought so many thoughts; how your heart could have felt so many feelings in the small span of a single second. The only explanation was that time must have stopped.

Quinn is my boss.

I attempted to think back over the times I'd been with him and looked for clues. I found several. Actually, I found more than several. I wanted to hide my face in my hands and cry, but I resisted the urge by biting fiercely on my bottom lip.

How could I miss something so obvious?

Quinn's words from the previous week came back to me: "*You are completely blind to the obvious.*"

Really, he was more than just my boss; he was *The Boss*. He owned the company. He owned a really impressive, profitable company. Any previous balloons of hope I had been floating in my alternate reality version of my carnival of dreams were immediately deflated if not brutally burst. This guy who I'd been fantasizing about for going on two months and with whom I thought I was kinda sorta maybe dating was not just out of my physical attractiveness league; he was out of all my leagues.

I was in awkwardly shaped head Neanderthal league, and he was in the hot ninja millionaire league.

As a coworker, Quinn and I were on somewhat equal footing. Even if nothing romantic materialized in the long term, at a minimum I thought we were building a friendship. I hoped we were building a friendship, because blast it all, I really liked him. I thought about him with alarming frequency. He was interesting and good to talk to, and I *wanted* to have a lasting connection with him.

At least, until this moment, that's what I thought. Now that I thought about all that had transpired recently—the events of the past weekend, the so-called training session, the text message jokes, our long conversations—I was becoming more and more comfortable. I thought our time together was leading toward something abiding—something shared between two people whose relationship was more than that of being coworkers.

I was blind. I was so beyond blind. I was stupid. I was wrong. We weren't becoming friends. Normal people don't have enduring relationships with hot millionaires.

What did he say to me that night after the concert? He told me that he didn't date.

Once he lost interest in me, and he was bound to sooner rather than later, I would see him periodically at best during client meetings where he was Mr. Sullivan and I was Janie Morris, his employee. These labels of *boss* and *employee* defined our relationship like the minefields around Guantanamo Bay, Cuba, define it as a U.S. Naval Base.

You don't go for a walk in a minefield.

You aren't friends with your boss.

And you certainly never set yourself up to have bedroom fantasies about him or unrequited longitudinal crushes. Lusting after your boss was like having a thing for your English teacher in high school; it made you more than a little pathetic.

My surprise must have been visible, because Steven's face changed suddenly from confusion to reluctant understanding. "Oh…oh my. You didn't know. You didn't know that Mr. Sullivan is the boss?"

I endeavored to swallow against a suddenly dry throat. "No," I said flatly.

"How could you not know that?" It was Steven's turn to sound incredulous. "He recruited you. You spent all day Friday with him. I'm sure we've discussed him before now; who did you think I was talking about when I said 'the boss'?"

I didn't hear the rest of Steven's musings. I was in the *Matrix*, and I'd just unwittingly taken the red pill; my thoughts became as agitated and circular as a washing machine on the spin cycle. We ate in silence for several minutes, and I mostly succeeded in avoiding eye contact with Steven.

After a few minutes, Steven interrupted my internal avalanche of misery. "I thought you knew when he hired you."

I met his eyes with a frown. "He said…he said that he could get me the interview, but I'd need to get the job on my own." I was having difficulty keeping my voice steady.

Quinn was wealthy. Actually, he wasn't just wealthy; he was a stinkin' rich son of a b… biscuit. And, once again, I had allowed someone else to be the captain in my sea of destiny. Once again, I was an accidental bystander to my illusion of success.

Steven seemed to understand my thoughts. "You really did get the job on your own." My features must have betrayed my doubt and unhappiness because he put his chopsticks down and reached across the table, his gray eyes softening. "No, really, listen to me, Janie. I'll admit, Mr. Sullivan has never recommended someone for an interview before. Usually he just recruits them and they start. I'll tell you what, he is always right. For instance, look at me." He gave me a wry smile.

I tried to manage one in return, but couldn't help feeling a mixture of anguished devastation and annoyance with myself. I had just discovered that either Jon or his father had arranged for my interview with the last firm and likely the job itself, and look what had happened. I didn't like thinking that the only reason I was hired at Cypher Systems was that Quinn Sullivan had decided on a whim that he wanted to kiss me, and I was good with numbers.

"Honey Cakes—can I call you Honey Cakes?" He didn't wait for me to answer. "Really listen to me. I knew you were going to be great if Mr. Sullivan recruited you. But, if it makes you feel better, I showed you that iPad spreadsheet with the wrong formulas on your first day as a test, one which you passed with flying colors."

I sighed, suddenly finished with my salad; I didn't want to eat ever again. "Thanks."

He eyed me with what I perceived to be a speculative glare. "This is his company; his baby. Do you really think he'd hire someone who wasn't amazing? Again, look no farther than your partner at this table as proof."

I tried for a half smile and rolled my eyes. "No, you cannot call me Honey Cakes."

What I couldn't tell Steven was the real reason why I felt so upset. The clarity of the moment stung. My chest hurt and I didn't really comprehend until right then that my aforementioned balloons of hope in the alternate reality carnival of dreams had been quite inflated despite all my best efforts to keep my footing on the ground.

Suddenly the idea of seeing Quinn again filled me with dread. My heart skipped two beats when I remembered my upcoming trip to Las Vegas.

"Will he…uh…" I cleared my throat and wiped my hands on my napkin. "Will Mr. Sullivan be at the client meeting in Las Vegas?"

Steven, back to eating his sushi, shook his head. "Yes, as I told you before, the boss vets all new clients for the private accounts. He'll fly over with us, God help us all."

"Oh." I thought about that for a moment. In preparation for the Vegas meeting, I'd been drafting proposals for the mysterious boss without comprehending that Quinn *was* the boss. In fact, I'd even told Quinn about one of my ideas when he interrupted my lunch at Smith's last week. I felt like I was going to be sick. I croaked my next question. "We're all taking the same flight?"

"We're all taking the company plane." Steven's voice was so nonchalant he might have said, "Wednesday is the day I cut my toenails."

I blurted out, "There is a company plane?"

"Yes."

My heart rate increased at the thought of spending four hours in an enclosed space with Quinn. "And we'll all fly together—with him?"

"Yes."

I searched the table as though it might provide me with answers, and I tried to squelch the panic from my voice. "But what if I want to fly on a commercial flight?"

Steven raised a single eyebrow at me. "And why would you want to do that?"

I huffed, not wanting to tell the truth but recognizing the strangeness of my statement. I could only think of one excuse. "I have frequent flyer miles."

Steven's thin lips curved into a broad grin then he abruptly laughed so hard that tears gathered in the corners of his eyes. I could feel myself turning red then eggplant purple with embarrassment. His laughter was, however, contagious, and I managed a self-deprecating half-hearted chuckle.

"Oh, Janie, you are a peach." I think he meant it as a compliment, but I only heard *you are a fuzzy fruit*. "You won't mind forfeiting some frequent flyer miles, I promise. It's a pretty stress-free way to travel. And we'll be briefing the boss and talking over strategy en route, so there is actually a good work-related reason to travel together. He's not so bad if you stick to business topics."

I didn't know how stress-free it would be; I already felt pretty stressed out just thinking about it. "Who else will be on the plane?"

Steven wiped at his tears of hilarity and gave me an open smile. "Well, you and me, Carlos, Olivia, and the boss—you know, Quinn Sullivan."

I glared at Steven. "Thank you. I get it now."

He gave me a sweet smile. "Just making sure."

Suddenly, I had a headache.

THAT NIGHT, I cancelled my tutoring session on the South Side and I called Jon.

I didn't call Jon last Sunday as I had promised I'd do. At first, it was an oversight, but after talking to Kat during our bathroom pow-wow on Tuesday, I'd been purposefully avoiding him. I didn't know what to say. I wasn't certain he'd been the reason I'd lost my job, and I didn't want it to be true.

However, for some reason, now I really wanted to see him. Elizabeth didn't say anything about my abrupt decision, but she gave me plenty of disapproving stares before I left the apartment and, as I pulled on my boots, said, "Isn't Quinn calling you tonight from New York?"

A sharp pang reverberated in my chest; her words had found an unintended target: I missed Quinn and I wanted to talk to him. I missed talking to him, seeing him, touching him. Despite my confusion after he left on Sunday, I'd been looking forward to his call all week. I swallowed the knot in my throat and set my jaw.

I currently had no plans to tell Elizabeth that Quinn was my boss's boss. I needed to process it first, decide what it meant. Right now, in my current mindset, it meant that Quinn and I were already over.

In response to her passive-aggressive query, I shrugged my shoulders and stood to leave.

She lifted her chin toward my cell. "You're not taking that?"

I shook my head. "Nope." And I pulled on my coat.

She crossed her arms over her chest, her glare heavy on my retreating back. "Well, if he calls, I'll just let him know you're out with your *friend*."

I paused at the door, took a deep breath, and called over my shoulder as I shut it behind me. "Don't wait up."

I thought I heard her growl as I walked down the hall, but I couldn't be certain.

As I left the building and walked toward the el platform, I was acutely aware of the two guards behind me. I wondered if they were in frequent communication with Quinn. I wondered whether they would tell him what I was up to and who I was meeting. The thought made my stomach turn a little sour. I didn't like the sensation of being leashed. The cell phone felt like an albatross around my neck, and I'd only had it a week. The guards also were starting to grate on my nerves.

With a literal shrug of my shoulders, I tried to shrug off the mounting irritation and redoubled my efforts to focus on the task in front of me. I walked faster.

Jon and I met at one of our previously regular haunts. It was an Italian restaurant on the North Side with tall burgundy leather booths, dim lighting, and really good fried cheese. I didn't return his embrace when I entered, but rather, my arms hung limp at my sides, and I felt no nostalgia when the heady tomato, wine, and sausage aroma wafted over me. But I did allow him to lead me to our usual table. We placed our drink orders. I wanted only water, but Jon ordered a bottle of expensive Sangiovese and two glasses.

No sooner had our waiter left when I asked, "Why did you cheat on me?"

It wasn't the question I meant to ask. In fact, I didn't really care about the answer. I was just stalling before confronting him with Kat's evidence about his father's role in my job loss. Also, for some reason, I was craving drama. I wanted to yell at someone.

"Janie…" Jon sighed, his head dropped, his shoulders slumped. "It was a mistake. It was the biggest mistake of my life."

"Jon, I'd like to know."

"This is going to sound crazy. You have to…" he reached out like he was going to grab my hands but then seemed to think better of it. "I'll tell you, but you have to promise me that you'll stay—you'll stay and talk to me after. Don't get up and walk out."

"I asked, didn't I? I want to know; I want to talk about it." I winced at my own lie. I really just wanted to yell at him for being a liar and a manipulator.

"But you might not stay after I tell you why I did what I did. You just have to promise me you're not going to shut me out after. I don't think I could live with that."

I pursed my lips and scowled. "Fine, I promise. I promise I will continue to talk to you after you tell me. Would you feel better if I attached a timeframe to the promise? Ok, I promise I'll stay and speak to you for no less than one hour after you tell me."

"Honestly, yes; it would make me feel better." He looked relieved and a little desperate.

I blinked at him, incredulous, but I promised anyway. "Ok, I promise to stay and talk to you for the period of one hour after you tell me."

He sighed again, nodding, and looked like he was going to be sick. He swallowed. He affixed his gaze to a spot on the table and began. His voice was so quiet that I had to lean forward to hear him. "You have to understand," he said. "I've loved you from the very first moment I saw you. I just knew you were the one for me. Do you remember?" He smiled sadly, still looking at the table. "You were arguing with our professor on the first day about using linear equations as an approximation of non-linear equations. You were so angry."

"I wasn't angry."

He glanced at me, his green eyes, still somewhat sad, glittering with amusement. "Not every equation is solvable. If we didn't use linear equations as estimates, we would be left with chaos."

I smiled in return and shook my head. "Nah. We're not talking about this now. Besides, I don't get angry. I was annoyed."

The shadow of amusement faded from his expression. "But, it's relevant. What you just said, you just said that you don't get angry. This is true, you don't. All these years we've been together, I've never seen you more than one standard deviation from baseline. You're never excited. I've never even seen you embarrassed. Even when you drank too much that one time when we were in the Hamptons, you were so calm. If you hadn't thrown up, I wouldn't have been able to tell whether you were drunk."

"I still don't see the relevance."

He cleared his throat and stared at the table again. "I did it to be closer to you."

I waited for him to continue. When he didn't, I leaned farther forward and folded my hands on the table, prompting him. "What? What do you mean you did it to be closer to me?"

He took a deep breath then met my gaze; his olive green eyes were ripe with sadness and regret, and a touch of accusation. "I did it to be closer to you. Sometimes you are so…" His hand on the table balled into a fist. "You are so distant, almost apathetic about me, about us. It's like you don't care whether or not I'm there. Do you know how that makes me feel? I love you so much. I burn for you. I ache for you." He reached across the table and gripped my hand; the force of the action startled me. "I just want you to feel something for me—just one-tenth of what I feel. I can't stop thinking about you, and damn it, Janie…"

For the first time in maybe ever, Jon made my heart beat faster. His voice was filled with such raw emotion I imagined I could almost reach out and touch his words. At one point in my life, I was convinced this was the person I was going to marry, and with whom I would have a dog, a house, and two babies. I thought he was consistent, safe, and reliable.

Now, suddenly, I was faced with *passion.*

There were, for lack of a better word, stirrings; something akin to when my leg falls asleep. The stirrings weren't pleasant or unpleasant. They just were. But I had to ignore them; I needed to sort through and comprehend the explanation for the cheating and the employment sabotage before I could focus on defining the depth of feeling which may or may not exist.

"I don't understand, Jon. How could you cheating on me possibly bring us closer together?"

His grip on my hand increased, and he clenched his jaw. He released a slow breath that whistled between his teeth before he confessed. "I slept with Jem."

My jaw dropped, my lashes fluttered. I assumed I misheard him. My voice was a whisper. "What did you just say?"

I watched him swallow; his eyes seared me; his expression was plain agony. "I slept with Jem. I slept with your sister."

The beating of my heart reached a crescendo between my ears. "That doesn't make any sense. Jem isn't…Jem lives in…" I sighed. Jon's mouth moved but I couldn't hear what he was saying. I thought I heard my name. I searched the table as though it held answers, and I said again, "This doesn't make sense."

His hand tugged on mine and roused me out of my indefinable state; he was mid-sentence when my mind engaged. "She called me and said she was in town. She said she wanted to surprise you, so I met her." His words were an avalanche, increasing in pace, the next more urgent than the last. "I hadn't seen her since she visited us that one time in college, and when I saw her, I couldn't believe it; she looked just like you. I mean, just like you. She is taller than she was before; she's your height, and her hair and her eyes are even the same color as yours. I thought it was you at first, from far away, but when I got closer, I saw the differences. Her voice doesn't sound anything like yours. She's not anything like you. I know that now, but then…but then she was so interested in me, and she seemed so like you but yet so different—animated, uninhibited—and I thought…I thought…"

We stared at each other for a long time, my mind playing catch-up with his words. He said she looked like me, but then he only mentioned her hair and the color of her eyes. It didn't make any sense. Jem and I had always looked more alike than June and I did, but Jem had always done everything in her power to change that. She cut her hair short, dyed it purple, or bleached it. She wore contacts to change the color of her eyes. She had nose piercings and lip piercings and other piercings. It was true that the last time I had seen her was going on six years ago when she'd been seventeen and I'd been nineteen. I looked basically the same.

The rest of his words fell over me: *She's not anything like me; instead, she's interesting and animated—she's uninhibited.* When I thought of Jem, I never thought of her as being interested in anyone other than as a means to an end, and she was never animated. If possible, she was even more withdrawn than I was; I always thought of her as coldly focused. However, she certainly was uninhibited.

I sighed again. My forehead fell into my free hand. Jon took it as a sign to continue, and I closed my eyes when he spoke.

"I drank too much, but that's not an excuse. I was drawn to her. She reminded me so much of you, but it was different because…" He let out an unsteady breath. "I just wanted you. But you never seemed to want me like I wanted you; you were always so detached. She acted like she wanted *me*, and I liked that." He swallowed the last word.

I lifted my head and watched him. He looked truly undone. I cleared my throat and drew his attention to me. "Jon, why didn't you ever say something about this when we were together? I never knew. You never told me there was anything wrong. You never said anything about me being distant."

"I tried. Really, I tried. When we were first together, I just thought you would come around. I mean, I was your first boyfriend; I was your first…but then I thought that maybe you just weren't that interested in the physical stuff. I thought I was ok with that. I thought I could handle it if it meant being with you." He had to take another breath, and when he next spoke, he sounded choked. "But now, I can't stop thinking about you. When I said I ache for you, I meant it. Every day it's like I'm counting the minutes until I see you, and I think *maybe today. Maybe today she'll change her mind and forgive me.*" His eyes were watery and red-rimmed. "Janie, can't we try again? Can you forgive me?"

A sudden thought occurred to me. "Is this what made you leave that night when I introduced you to Quinn? Does he know about this?"

Jon silently considered me before responding. "Are you dating him?"

I thought about his question and answered honestly. "No."

His eyes bored into mine. "Did you call it off or did he?"

I huffed impatiently. "Does he know? Does Quinn know about you and Jem?"

Jon shook his head slowly. "No, not that I know of anyway."

"Then why did you leave that night at dinner? What did he say to you?"

If possible, Jon looked even more uncomfortable. "I can't talk about it yet. I just told you…" He pulled his hand through his hair. "Can't we get through this one thing? You haven't answered me yet; can you forgive me?"

I pressed my lips together in a firm line before asking him again. "What did you and Quinn discuss last Saturday? Why did you leave?"

Jon shook his head, seemingly unwilling to meet my gaze.

But I knew. I was suddenly certain.

"It was about my job, wasn't it? The one you had your dad fire me from."

Jon closed his eyes and leaned back in the booth. His head hit the back of the leather cushion. I thought I heard an expletive whisper from his mouth. He looked wretched.

I tried to swallow, but confusion layered with viscous emotion made my throat feel thick. "How…" My throat worked to swallow, and then I started again. "How did he know? How did Quinn know that your dad had me fired?"

Jon shook his head, his eyes still closed, and his voice was very soft when he said, "I don't know. He just knew."

CHAPTER SIXTEEN

"QUINN RECRUITED YOU, didn't he?"

I blinked at Olivia a few times. I was confused by her abrupt question, but then I recovered quickly. "Yeah, you could say that."

It was Friday afternoon, the Friday before the big business trip to Las Vegas—the big business trip to Las Vegas that I was now dreading—the Friday of what was turning out to be the strangest week ever, and I was trying to function on two hours of restless sleep.

I wasn't tired when I arrived back to the apartment earlier that morning even though it was past 2:00 a.m. Elizabeth was asleep; I could hear her soft snoring, so I stealthily removed my boots and closed her door so as not to disturb her slumber or incur additional wrath.

My mind was active; I felt unsettled but strangely numb. I checked my email, suddenly curious about Jem. I wanted to see if she'd replied to the message I sent last Saturday. Had she been in town this whole time? Why did she sleep with Jon?

I navigated to Gmail; there were no new messages.

I thought about emailing her again, but everything I wanted to ask, despite my mostly ambivalence toward Jon and the end of our relationship, would likely come across as crazy, jealous ex-girlfriend. My life was coming dangerously close to resembling a Jerry Springer episode; all that was missing was a question of someone's paternity.

I started typing: *Hi Jem, I was just emailing to ask you if you are in town. Jon mentioned something about seeing you a few weeks back. In your last email, you said you wanted to see me. Do you still want to meet up? Janie*

I hit send then stared unseeingly at the screen until it blurred.

Jon was right about so many things. I avoided emotional intimacy. I hated relying on others. I wasn't good at it, and I turtled any time I encountered a difficulty. Because of this, I bent on things that mattered to me or, using Jon as a case study, I abruptly broke off relationships. I also entered our relationship with extremely low expectations, and as long as I kept my expectations at a minimum, I was able to justify my somewhat marginal personal investment in him. It hadn't been fair to Jon.

Regardless, he *cheated* on me with my sister, and when I broke up with him, he asked his father to pull some strings so that I would be *fired.* Neither his motivation nor his desperation justified his actions. I could not and would not forgive Jon.

And then there was Quinn...

"How did you meet him? It seems like you two know each other pretty well." She raised her eyebrows at me expectantly.

Olivia and I were meeting to tie up loose ends before our departure on Monday for Las Vegas. She had thus far been somewhat unhelpful, but not unhelpful in a specific enough way for me to have a valid complaint. We were finished with our meeting but she hadn't left yet; I wanted to scowl at her and tell her to get back to work; instead, I said, "Why do you say that?"

Olivia shrugged, her pale blue eyes watching me a little too closely. "Keira said he's called for you, like, three times today, and you haven't taken any of his calls. Anyone else would be fired."

When I'd gotten home earlier this morning, I had turned off my cell phone without looking at it. I tried not to obsess about how oblivious I'd been or about how obvious my obliviousness must have been to him. I didn't want to think about it, so I didn't.

Likewise, when I arrived at work this morning, I set my phone to automatic voicemail. When Keira appeared at my door, indicating that Mr. Sullivan was on the phone, calling from New York, and needed to speak with me, I told her I was just about to go into a meeting and promised to call him back. I'd done this three times.

It was true; I didn't want to talk to him. I didn't know how to talk to him. In my sleepless examining last night, I realized that he'd never exactly lied to me about being my boss. But now I knew that he was *the* boss, and everything was different.

I ignored the implication that I'd been dodging Quinn's calls, and I thought about how to answer Olivia's question truthfully without including real details. "I met Mr. Sullivan at my old job."

"Did he recruit you away from there?"

"No."

"Hmm." Olivia seemed to contemplate me for a moment with a sideways glance before she said, "Carlos hired me. I'm the only person at the company who wasn't recruited by Quinn."

"Oh? I didn't know that." I was distracted by all the revelations of the past week, and thus was tempted to succumb to the pleasant void of apathetic numbness, but I just couldn't seem to muster enough energy to feign interest in what she was saying.

"I think..." She leaned closer to me and lowered her voice to a conspiratorial whisper. "I think I make him uncomfortable."

My brow lifted of its own accord, and I regarded her with open confusion. "Who? Carlos?"

Olivia laughed lightly and flipped rolling sheets of chocolate brown hair over her shoulder. "Quinn, of course!"

I tried not to grimace when she used Quinn instead of Mr. Sullivan. "Why do you think that?"

"Well, other than Carlos, haven't you noticed that everyone Quinn hires is so...so..." She looked upward as though trying to search for the right word. "Everyone is...you know, so plain; or they're odd." She paused, her eyes settled on the top of my head. "You're very big for a girl."

I didn't miss her meaning; in fact, her words hit the bull's-eye in my stomach. I was discovering that I was not as immune to the scorn of pretty people as I thought. I blinked at her and said nothing, but in my thoughts I retorted, *You are a twatwaffle.*

Twatwaffle being a new word I'd found on Urban Dictionary. I hadn't yet said it out loud but I found myself liking the way it sounded in my head.

She continued. "Carlos has insinuated that Quinn is really a terrible flirt." Her pretty mouth curved into a knowing smile. "I think Quinn purposefully hires women who are plain or odd looking, so he's not distracted at work. At this point, he must be desperate. I bet he's even flirted with you."

I gave her my best imitation of a smile, but I was pretty sure it looked like a dog baring its teeth. "That's an interesting theory."

"Hmm," she said again, leaning back. "Has he flirted with you?"

I shook my head and looked at the portfolio on my lap. "Not unless you call kissing flirting."

Olivia's eyes opened very wide for a split second; then she laughed. "You're funny!" She tapped my leg with manicured nails, then flipped her long, shiny, straight hair over a slim shoulder. "Well," Olivia said on an audible sigh, "it's a good thing he's not attracted to you; otherwise, he likely wouldn't have hired you in the first place."

I kind of wanted to stab her in the neck.

"Janie, are you two finished yet?" Steven's form appeared at my door, and I immediately jumped up from my seat, thankful for the murder-attempt-distraction and the chance to escape. I crossed to my expansive desk in order to improve the distance between Olivia and the pen in my hand.

"Yep, all done. I think Olivia has what she needs."

"If I have any questions, I'll just stop by later and ask." She stood and gave Steven a wide, friendly smile.

Steven shook his head; his lips were pursed. "Olivia, Janie doesn't have any more time to work on this with you. She needs to get ready for next week, and that report needs to be done by tonight. You better have all you need from her."

Olivia's eyes met mine, and her smile widened. "Yeah, I think I got everything I need."

I WORKED IN the office over the weekend, enjoying the solitude. It allowed me the space I needed to avoid thinking about anything confusing and/or unpleasant.

I didn't really need to go into the office over the weekend. I could have accomplished just as much on my laptop in the comfort of my slippers at home. However, in all honesty, avoiding Elizabeth was the intentional byproduct of my industrious two days away from the apartment. I hadn't yet told her about Kat's knit-night revelations, or finding out that Quinn was *the* boss, or that Jem and Jon had engaged in *coitus extremeous*. I didn't know how to tell her, and it just felt like too much to deal with right now. I wasn't ready to talk about it, and I knew she would make me talk about it.

I justified my absence by insisting to myself that I needed to finish the billing presentation that I hoped the boss would adopt as the new business practice for Guard Security. However, now that I knew I would be making my pitch to Quinn instead of some unknown entity, I was beginning to have second thoughts about the initiative. I'd discussed it with Quinn previously, on the day he'd met me at Smith's Take-away and Grocery, not knowing he would be making the decision regarding whether it moved forward.

Now I felt like I needed to prove myself. My job didn't seem like it was really mine, or like I deserved it. The combined pressure of performing at the client meeting and proving I deserved to work at Cypher Systems, along with the thought of seeing Quinn for the first time in a week, now knowing him as *the* boss, caused my stomach to become like hair trapped in bubblegum—a massive tangle of heinous, untenable knots. I spent my time working tirelessly on the billing presentation. I finally went home and lost myself in comic books until 1:00 a.m., and then I woke up early and buried myself in work once more.

I didn't know how I was going to face him. What would I say? What would he say? I had no roadmap for this situation. We'd held hands, we'd kissed, and I liked it—a lot.

On the Monday morning of the trip, I was so exhausted that Elizabeth had to shake me awake; she informed me that my alarm had been going off for seven minutes without me so much as reaching for the snooze button. I showered, braided my hair then twisted it into a bun on the crown of my head, and dressed in my black pantsuit in a haze.

At the last minute, I decided to wear my glasses instead of contacts; I told myself this was because my hands were shaking too much to put them in. I went through my head-box-closet coping exercises several times in the taxi on the way to the airport, thankful to find myself almost detached by the time I arrived.

Steven met me at a prearranged spot with coffee, a blueberry scone, and a reassuring smile. He guided me to the private airstrip, all while telling me about a disastrous date from the weekend with a lawyer named Deloogle—at least, that's how the name sounded. It seemed all his dates' names rhymed with Google or Bing. It was not unusual for him to regale me with stories on Mondays regarding his weekend exploits. Typically, the evenings ended with some hysterical calamity.

I was so wrapped up in his story that I didn't really notice where we were going. When we boarded the plane, he handed my bag to an attendant and we took seats next to each other.

He reached the end of his story. "It was so disgusting that I had to arrange for the carpet cleaners to come fix the spot on Sunday." He shook his head. "That's the last time I go out with someone who wears a live ferret as an accessory."

I smiled and laughed then abruptly realized where I was. The calm numb from before was pierced by a pang of awareness. We were seated near the front of the corporate jet, and I fought the urge to crane my head around to see the rest of the aircraft. Instead of attempting to discern the occupants, I concentrated on the interior of the jet.

I had no comparison, as I'd never traveled via private plane, but my surroundings were impressive; everything looked new and shiny. The seats were beige leather, the trim and carpet were navy blue, and the bulkhead was lined with elaborate wood paneling. Seats were clustered in groups of four facing each other: two facing forward, two facing backward. I assumed this was to facilitate conversation during the flight.

An attendant walked over to us; she was very pretty and, I guessed, in her mid-forties.

"Can I get you two something to drink before we depart?"

I cleared my throat. "No thanks, I'm good. But…uh…do I have time to use the restroom before we leave?"

She nodded. "Sure do, hun. The head is at the back of the plane." I smiled my thanks and stood to walk toward the back when I came face to face, or rather, chest to chest, with a solid man wall.

"Oh, sorry." I backed up a step and grabbed the seat to maintain my balance, my eyes automatically lifting to the face of the barrier.

I immediately regretted the movement when my gaze met that of Quinn McHotpants Sullivan.

By the power of Thor!

CHAPTER SEVENTEEN

His hands reached out to my upper arms, presumably to steady me, and we stood looking at each other for a long minute, me gaping, him steadily watching me with an impassive mask and fiery blue eyes. He was even more devastatingly and unfairly handsome than I remembered. It didn't help that he was wearing a nicely cut black suit, obviously custom, and a white shirt with a stunning blue silk tie.

I was the first to break the gaze.

I stepped back and out of his grip, letting my attention drop to the navy carpet as I fiddled unnecessarily with my glasses. I mostly succeeded gathering my wits, finding it helped to focus on how annoyed I was that, once again, the man's mere presence turned me into a complete flustering kerfuffle of hormones.

I thrust my hand forward in an offer to shake his hand. "Mr. Sullivan. It's very nice to see you again." I glanced up at him as he fit his hand into mine, ignoring how nice his skin felt against mine and that stupid—yes, *stupid*, because it was inconvenient, and my vocabulary was suffering due to his mere presence—stupid shock of something like delightful pain when we touched. I tried to give him a professional, firm handshake.

"Ms. Morris." Even though I felt a small twist of sadness at the formality of his greeting, his voice sent little shivers down my back, and I was further set off-kilter. His eyes moved over me in the same open, plain assessment that he always seemed to employ: lips, neck, shoulders, lower.

Our hands hung suspended between us, no longer moving, and I battled to keep myself from turning completely scarlet under his attention. I didn't move to withdraw, nor did I have any desire to break the contact. I felt certain this man had no idea what he did to me just by looking at me and holding my hand. For a split second, I imagined that hand elsewhere on my body, and I lost the battle against my blush.

I tried to cover my heated embarrassment and, as usual, started speaking without thinking. "This is a nice plane you have here." His eyes lifted to mine abruptly. "I don't know much about corporate or private jets. It seems like fuel efficiency is a real problem, though, as planes are just about the least fuel efficient means of transportation."

Quinn tipped his head to the side, arresting my attention with his intense stare. "Are you saying you'd prefer to drive to Las Vegas?"

"Well, trains can be very nice. Maybe you should invest in a corporate train. There was a study conducted by AEA Technology comparing a Eurostar train and an airline journey between London and Paris. It demonstrated the trains emitted ten times less CO_2 on average per traveler than planes. Don't forget, trains also have sleeping cars for…sleeping."

Quinn's mouth curved in an almost nonexistent smile, and the shade of his eyes seemed to darken. "Planes can have beds, too. Maybe I could have one installed on this plane for the next time we travel."

"How would you decide who gets the bed and who has to sit in a seat?" I blinked at him.

He opened his mouth as though to respond but then suddenly shut it and withdrew his hand from mine, frowning at me. "Good point."

The sound of someone clearing their throat pulled my attention away from Quinn. Olivia Merchant and Carlos Davies were standing to the side of us, watching our exchange. Carlos gave me a small smile as his eyes narrowed and moved between Quinn and me. But Olivia, who had been the one to clear her throat, was frowning. I hadn't noticed as they'd approached. In fact, I hadn't noticed anything but Quinn from the moment I collided into his chest.

"Excuse us, Janie. We're trying to get through to our seats." Olivia motioned with her hand toward the empty seats across from Steven and me.

"Oh, sorry." I stepped to the other side to let them pass then ducked around Quinn, careful to avoid further eye or physical contact, as I sprinted toward the bathroom at the back of the plane.

Once in the safety of the onboard toilet, I let my head thump against the wall behind me and caught my reflection in the mirror. I admit it; I am not above talking to myself in the mirror. In fact, I do it quite often. The image I found looking back at me was covered with splotchy red remains of an impressive blush, and a grim expression.

I wanted—no, I *needed* to find some way to turn off my intense involuntary reaction to Quinn. He'd only been gone one week, and all the progress I'd made toward comfort and ease in his presence had dissipated. I was acting like a ridiculous teenager.

Ok, Janie, remember: Quinn is your boss—the boss.

The Boss.

I groaned.

I took a couple of deep breaths and attempted to calm the momentous beating of my heart. Why was it that I felt so painfully self-aware? Was it that I now fully understood how off-limits he was, and how wretchedly doomed I was to live in a state of perpetual unrequitedness? To my utter despair, his presence seemed to make the invisible box in my head explode instantly on eye contact, scattering my once neatly folded thoughts and feelings all over my pretend closet of calm.

It wasn't just his physical superiority that flustered me, not anymore. Undeniably, as demonstrated during our initial elevator encounter, the magnificence of his features seemed to render me painfully inept at normal conversation. Now I knew him. Now I had memories attached to him. I could recall with vivid detail the way he tilted his head when he listened; the sound of his voice; the sound of his laugh; his ready responses to my hypothetical questions; the way he teased me; the touch of his fingers brushing my hair over my shoulders; the heat of his gaze as it moved over my body; *what his chest looked like after a shower.*

The last thought made me groan again as a new tidal wave of tingling embarrassment rushed from my stomach to the tips of my fingers.

I glanced around the small bathroom and wondered how much longer I could remain without raising suspicions as to the state of my physical or mental health. It was the second time in two months I'd considered taking up residence in a bathroom stall. I glanced at my watch; we were scheduled to depart in less than ten minutes. I needed to pull myself together.

I closed my eyes and I went through the normal coping exercises of folding up my reckless feelings, but they all seemed to take the shape of black and red lacy lingerie. Frustrated, I bit my bottom lip, hard, and resolved to wash my hands. If I could focus on something as simple as washing and drying my hands, I might make it through the next four hours on Quinn Sullivan's private jet.

I took one last significant breath, then exited the safe confines of the toilet stall, smoothing my hands over my thighs to ease my nerves. I walked with measured steps to the front of the plane and tried to look unconcerned like a normal, capable, confident human being instead of the awkward, bigheaded Neanderthal I was.

I nearly ran back to the bathroom when I saw that Carlos had taken the seat I had previously occupied next to Steven, and Quinn was seated opposite Carlos. This left one vacancy in the four-seat cluster: the one next to Quinn. I swallowed with effort and hesitated. The men hadn't yet noticed me. My eyes moved over the cabin and fell on the back of Olivia's head; she was by herself in the adjacent cluster. The seat across from her might as well have been labeled *Janie's best option.*

Making up my mind, I closed the distance and moved to take my best option, but Steven—*damn Steven!*—foiled my plan.

"Janie, sit here." He motioned to the seat next to Quinn. "Olivia will take notes. Mr. Sullivan needs you to review the latest invoices. I was also just telling him about your thoughts on managing Guard Security's expenditures using the billable tracking software."

"Oh. Ok." I looked from Steven's smile to Olivia's frown, which, if possible, seemed to deepen as I slipped into the seat next to Quinn. I didn't look at Quinn, however. I didn't look at him as I explained the purpose of the software, how I'd come across the open source project when I was in graduate school, and how I'd used it as an effective way to track time spent on tasks and to assign effort to each task.

The plane taxied and took off. Steven's encouraging grin, Carlos's warm brown eyes, and even Olivia's somewhat hostile stare settled my nerves. When I finished explaining how the system could be tailored to improve the efficiency and profitability of billings and collections over the current time-based system they were using, I was almost calm.

"Based on historical data, I ran an analysis which, even though hypothetical, demonstrates that we could increase revenues even in the short term. Carlos, will you please hand me my iPad? I think it's under your seat." I shifted and pointed to my bag.

"Sure thing." Carlos leaned forward to extract my case.

"It's an interesting idea." Quinn's voice sounded thoughtful, and I sensed him shift next to me, leaning closer as I opened the iPad to the bulleted list I had prepared on the impact of implementing the software.

"We won't be able to use the open source product, but we could have our team develop something similar in house," Carlos commented.

"It's actually a really great product." I scrolled down to a description of the system. "I checked last week, and they just pushed a new release."

Quinn's voice was very close to my ear as he spoke, and I could feel the air around me change as he leaned over my shoulder. "That's not the point. I'm sure it's a great product, but we can't use open source software."

"We also couldn't apply it to the Infinite Systems group." Steven sounded matter-of-fact as he chimed in and shrugged his shoulders. "But, for our corporate partners, it would answer a lot of their questions on the billing structure."

I frowned, looking from Carlos to Steven. "What am I missing here? Why can't we use open source?"

Quinn placed his hand over mine and pulled the iPad between us, forcing me to turn toward him. He wasn't looking at me but rather at the screen as he mumbled, "Data security issues."

My voice was slightly unsteady as I tried to focus on something other than the feeling of his hand covering mine and holding me in place. "Well, why can't we use it for the Infinite Systems group?"

Quinn lifted his gaze to me abruptly, his eyes narrowed, and silence stretched. I thought he wasn't going to answer. His jaw seemed to be set, and his mouth was drawn in a particularly thin line as though he were considering something unpleasant. I took the opportunity to look at him, really look at him. A twisting pain originating just under the left side of my rib cage made my breath catch; I missed looking at Quinn, and I missed talking to Quinn.

But he wasn't Quinn. He was Mr. Sullivan, *The Boss.*

I licked my lips and broke the silence. "I guess it doesn't really matter, I just thought…I just thought it would be good to keep things consistent."

A momentary flash of something that looked almost like alarm crossed Quinn's features, and he turned to Steven; his voice sounded accusatory. "I thought Janie only worked on the public accounts."

Steven lifted his hands slightly as though he were defending himself. "She does. We split the two. I handle all the private clients on the back end, but…" Steven's eyes met mine for a brief moment before he continued. "But Carlos and I were thinking that some of the Infinite Systems clients might respond well to her."

"I thought I was very clear." Quinn's voice, although quiet, had the cadence of a growl, and he pulled the iPad completely out of my grip, arranged it on his lap, and turned his attention to the figures on the screen.

Carlos cleared his throat, and I could only watch the strange exchange with wide, confused eyes. "Mr. Sullivan, Janie is very talented. Please consider—"

Quinn huffed. "I won't. Don't bring it up again."

He was angry. Quinn looked even more amazing when he was angry. The silliness of my priority in thought process dawned on me sluggishly as I watched him review the information I had prepared. I knew that instead of focusing on his good looks I should be focusing on why I was being purposefully excluded from participation in Infinite Systems. Maybe it had something to do with my suspicion that I didn't deserve my job—that I'd been hired based on a whim, not on ability.

I pulled my attention from him and swallowed; my throat felt thick and tight. I surveyed the group. Steven briefly met my gaze and gave me a strained, apologetic smile. Carlos's expression was one of stormy frustration directed at his hands on his lap. Olivia seemed to regard me with something resembling displeasure and suspicion.

Before my mind could wander, Quinn abruptly dropped the iPad in my lap and his voice was aloof when he spoke. "Send the web link to the development group and have them use the open source product to start drawing up requirements. Now, before we touch down I want to review the invoices for Club Outrageous and the scope of work for the Las Vegas properties."

With the subject of my involvement with Infinite Systems now closed, we turned to the subject of the upcoming meeting.

Throughout the two-hour gauntlet that followed, I did my best to stay focused on Quinn's questions, and where he pointed, and not on his mouth and hands. I swear, whatever pheromones Quinn Sullivan secreted were the equivalent of Janie catnip.

The most difficult and dangerous moments were when he would shift close to me and lean over my shoulder. I found myself resisting the urge to lean into his coat lapel and smell him. At one point, I became slightly fixated on the pulse point at the base of Quinn's neck and nearly missed one of Carlos's questions.

Carlos seemed to take my distracted response as a sign of fatigue; he suggested we take a break. Everyone agreed immediately. Thankfully, Quinn excused himself, and he pulled his cell phone out of his pocket and walked to the back of the plane to make a call.

I didn't allow my gaze to linger on his backside as he walked away, even though I wanted to. Instead, I lifted my eyes to Steven's, and he winked at me. His small gesture served to calm my nerves, and I forced my hands to relax on the case of the iPad.

"You did really great." Carlos was the first to speak; his tone was quiet. I wasn't sure if he was trying to be respectful of Quinn's telephone call or if he just didn't want to be overheard.

"Thanks." I gave him a tight-lipped smile. "Is he always like this on trips?"

Steven nodded. "It can be pretty brutal. But, you know, he's the boss. He gets the job done, and so must we."

Olivia leaned over the aisle. "I don't mind. I think he's brilliant."

Steven muttered something under his breath, but I couldn't hear it. I frowned at him and he mouthed, *"I'll tell you later."*

"Looks like we're almost there," Carlos remarked absentmindedly as he glanced out the window.

As if on cue, the attendant appeared and told us all to buckle up. We were about to land. As I buckled my seat belt, I noted that Quinn was taking a seat in one of the four-seat clusters at the back of the plane and hadn't yet ended his call. His eyes briefly met mine, and I thought I saw him smile—one of his whisper-light, barely-there smiles. Then he looked away and frowned one of his serious, fiercely irritated frowns.

The plane began its descent, and I was still firmly seated on my drama-coaster of uncertainty.

Just... *great.*

♥♥♥

I OPTED TO hide in the bathroom until I was certain everyone had deplaned.

As soon as I stepped off the plane and into the dry heat of the Las Vegas private airport, I was immediately struck by how colorful and colorless the landscape was. The desert was rich hues of browns, reds, and oranges, but nothing else. It was an unholy blend of heat and sand and fire and gasoline and cigarettes. I was abruptly thirsty.

When I finally descended the steps, I saw two black limos parked a short distance from the airplane. Steven, Carlos, and Olivia handed off their bags to one driver, and Quinn was standing next to the second limo engaged in a conversation on his cell phone. I pulled my roller bag after me and headed toward Steven and the first limo; however, before I could hand off my bag, I heard Quinn's voice behind me.

"Ms. Morris, you'll be riding with me."

I turned just my head toward him and hesitated. I was having some difficulty comprehending that I wasn't going to be taking limo #2 with Steven, Carlos, and Olivia. I would be taking limo #1 with Mr. Sullivan Boss McHotpants.

Steven reached forward, squeezed my hand, and kept me in place for a brief moment. His voice was low enough to ensure the comment was not heard by the others. "He's going to subject you to the silent twenty-minute car ride from hell. After the meeting this afternoon, we'll order room service and have a sleepover. We can commiserate, and you cry on my shoulder."

I lifted my eyebrows in alarm, remembering Steven's story about riding alone with Quinn, and wondering if, now that it was established he was my boss, Quinn would stop speaking to me. He seemed so different on the plane; so distant and aloof. I imagined we would sit silently in the limo while his expression vacillated between stoic and apathetic.

My stomach suddenly hurt.

Driver #1 reached to take my bag, and I followed him dutifully. Quinn was still on his phone and pacing back and forth behind the limo when I reached the open passenger door. I slipped into the dark car; it took my eyes several seconds to adjust.

This was the second time I'd been in a limo; the first time was on my worst day ever. I wondered what Vincent, my driver, was up to at this moment.

This limo was significantly larger than the first one. Black leather benches stretched in long lines on either side of the car's interior. What looked like a fully stocked bar sat just under the privacy window toward the front. The inside had that new car smell plus the thick, earthy scent of fine leather.

In lieu of sitting in a bench facing forward, I opted for one of the side seats. I didn't particularly want to sit next to Quinn. I felt distance in proximity might make the imminent car ride from hell a bit more bearable.

Quinn entered the car on the same side I had. The door closed behind him and he glanced to his right, paused, and surveyed the interior. His eyes rested on me almost immediately. I did not return his gaze, but rather felt his stare as I concentrated on the crystal decanters at the front of the cabin.

"Do you want something to drink?"

I shook my head no; even though I was thirsty, I was having difficulty swallowing. Instead, I folded and refolded my hands on my lap then clasped them over my knees. The car engine started and the limo moved forward. I glanced out the window directly in front of me, but the glass was so dark that it significantly dulled the landscape beyond.

Several long moments passed in silence, and for once, I welcomed my mind's wanderlust. I counted the lights along the wood panel of the ceiling and tried to imagine the robot on the manufacturing assembly line responsible for such detailed work. I liked the idea of robots and hoped I would live to see robots become assimilated into households as pets or companions. Rover would become Robo-rover and the elderly might own a Robo-panion.

Quinn's voice was quiet when he interrupted my musings. "What are you thinking about?"

I cleared my throat and shrugged, and found myself answering with honesty before I could think to stop myself, "Robots."

"Robots." I heard him shift on the bench then move to the seat directly across from me. Our knees and ankles touched, his long legs invaded my space. "Why are you thinking about robots?"

My heart skipped then galloped at his closeness. I shrugged and focused my attention on the blue silk of his tie. It looked dark purple in the dim cabin. Despite my best intentions and attempts at self-control, the physical contact of our legs made my stomach erupt in an angry wasps' nest of nerves. I remained silent because I found my mouth no longer functioned.

He leaned forward, resting his elbows on his knees; his hands were clasped and hovering above my thighs. "Janie, why haven't you returned my calls?" His voice sounded tightly controlled, as though he were struggling to keep his temper in check.

I lifted my gaze to his, surprised by the use of my first name. I swallowed. "I—Mr. Sullivan—"

"Don't do that." He half groaned, half growled and covered my hands with his.

I studied him for a moment; a thick knot was in my throat, and the wasps' nest was swirling furiously in my stomach, incited by his touch. I finally managed to choke out a reply. "I'm not sure what you want me to say."

He narrowed his eyes in a slight outward indication of frustration, but then they flickered to my lips. "Why did you turn off your cell phone?"

I ground my teeth; the buzzing wasps were turning into an angry Africanized bee colony. Their feelings of hostility spread through me and set my body humming with aggravated resentment. I was surprised by how angry I was when I responded. "Why didn't you tell me that you were the boss?"

His gaze met mine and pinned me in place. "I did."

I stiffened then pulled my hands from his and gripped the seat on either side of my legs. "Oh, was I asleep during that conversation?"

He frowned. "Are you angry with me?"

I blinked at him, maybe three times, possibly four, in stunned confusion. "I…I'm not—" I stuttered then finally managed to get out a complete sentence. "I'm not angry with you."

"Well, then you do a good impression of angry."

"Mr. Sullivan…"

"Don't call me that." He interrupted me again but his voice was softer now. "Don't call me that unless you want to."

"I do want to."

My statement was met with silence; his expression was hard, frustrated, determined. He watched me for what seemed like several minutes. I tried, but couldn't quite meet his gaze. My anxiety increased with each passing second, and, therefore, my mind began darting in every direction. The car rolled along, and I thought to myself that it must have extremely good shocks because it felt like we were gliding. I imagined the car on ice skates gliding across a frozen lake, being pushed by robots.

Finally, very quietly, he said, "Why?"

"Because." I swallowed; my chest felt impossibly tight. "Because I have a habit of saying some wildly inappropriate things, as you know. And you are not just my boss; you are the second B in B and B, which is Betty and the *Boss*. I can recall at least seventeen things I've said to you that I should never say to the boss. And, if I keep calling you—" I took a deep breath, my fingers dug into the leather seat. "And, if I keep calling you Quinn, I'll say at least seventeen more, if not thirty-four more or two hundred-eighty-nine more."

"Then you should most definitely keep calling me Quinn."

I sighed and eyed him warily.

Suddenly he leaned forward and gently lifted one of my hands from the bench. His thumb moved in slow motion over the back of my knuckles as he held it between both of his palms. "Look. I've really enjoyed all of the seventeen wildly inappropriate remarks you've made, and if you recall, I've said at least seventeen of them myself."

The sensation of his thumb moving over the back of my hand was doing something unexpected to the middle of my body. In an effort to mask the effect, I swallowed rigidly, firmed my lips into a stiff line, and said nothing. What I wanted to do was to unbutton my shirt and ask him to mimic that motion elsewhere.

"I would be very disappointed if you started behaving differently around me." His features and his tone were serious and imploring; his eyes were a dark, fiery shade of cobalt blue in the dimly lit limo, but his circling thumb was my undoing.

I felt flustered and confused, which made my tone sound more accusatory than I intended when I asked the first question that came to mind. "Why did you hire me?"

His thumb paused, just briefly, before he responded. "Because, despite your insistence to the contrary, you do have a photographic memory, you have an extremely analytical approach to business practice, you are a fantastic accountant, and your legs looked amazing in those shoes."

I pulled my hand out of his grip, and, for lack of knowing what to do with the trembling appendages known as my arms, I crossed them over my chest. "You can't say things like that. You are my boss."

His jaw flexed, and he balled his empty hands into fists. "But I'm not just your boss, am I?"

"You're right; technically you're my boss's boss."

He ignored my comment. "We're dating."

"Well, I don't date my boss, so…" I closed my eyes and sighed. I wanted the car ride to be over. If I just closed my eyes, maybe all the drama would go away.

I heard him sigh; it was an angry sound. His legs were still pressed against mine, and I could feel the warmth of him through our layers of clothing.

My eyes were still closed when I asked, "Why didn't you tell me who you were?"

"I did—more than once."

I released a slow breath before countering. "You know what I mean." I lifted my lids and met his seething gaze. "You knew that I misunderstood. Why didn't you correct me?"

His eyes flashed with blinding intensity. When he spoke, his tone was severe. "Would you have stayed with me at the concert if I'd told you? Would you have let me kiss you? Would you have gone out to dinner with me? Stayed at the park?" His eyes were narrowed, and my stomach dropped to my feet when I saw his expression slide, with each word, deeper into a mask of indifference.

I shook my head slowly and answered honestly. "No. No, I would not. But you knew I was going to find out eventually."

He looked away from me and straightened his tie, smoothing his hand down the blue silk, his tone sodden with superior sarcasm. "By then I'd hoped it wouldn't make a difference."

The car slowed and stopped. I swallowed a giant lump in my throat. I didn't want to ask the next question, but I needed to know; it was better to know. "What are you going to do now?"

His voice and his face were devoid of emotion, and he almost sounded bored when he responded. "What do you mean?"

"I mean, do I still have a job?"

He flinched as though I'd slapped him; his lips parted and his dark brows lowered over eyes that seemed to be shooting fire in my direction. "What?" For a moment, he looked truly stunned.

I lifted my chin and grabbed the leather bench to steady my hands. "Do I still have a job?"

The car door opened and my eyes moved automatically to the light—my escape.

When he didn't move or respond, I reluctantly focused my attention on him again, he didn't look quite so severe. Rather, his gaze had softened considerably. If possible, the quiet understanding of his expression troubled me more than the cold stoicism he'd employed earlier. I sighed and shifted along the seat toward the door, lying to myself that I wanted to forget this car ride and forget that Quinn was ever anything but my boss.

I exited first and walked toward the trunk, hoping to grab my bag and disappear into the large casino lobby. I felt as though I might even cry. Limo #2 was maneuvering into the casino but was still some distance away.

I felt Quinn hovering behind me, and then his hand closed over my arm just above my elbow; the heat of his words on my ear and neck made me shiver despite the warmth of the Las Vegas sun.

"I'll find you later."

I turned toward him, but he'd already released my arm; he was walking toward the hotel lobby and away from me.

CHAPTER EIGHTEEN

I WAS BASICALLY Rudolph the Red-Nosed Reindeer; except, instead of a blinking red nose, I had a crimson blush. Quinn Sullivan made my light blink on and off. You could guide a sleigh by it, or a private jet. It was a beacon of embarrassment, mortification, pleasure, turpitude, awareness, frustration, and, yes, anger.

At present, however, I was a normal shade of whitish-beige. I was listening with all outward attentiveness to Quinn as he finished the presentation our team put together for the meeting. It was an overview of the security in place for Club Outrageous, a schematic of the new club in Vegas overlaid with identified weaknesses in current operations, a comparison of approaches to security management of the entire property, casino included, and so forth. It was a strong presentation. I knew it by heart.

I didn't hear any of it, partly because I knew it by heart and partly because it was Quinn delivering the presentation. I spent the entire half hour trying to appear attentive to the content rather than the fine, agile movements of the speaker, the cadence of his voice, the depth of his cobalt eyes, *the shape of his...*

I blinked, with purpose, and shook my head just a little in order to redirect my thoughts. The room was dimmed for the presentation, and for that, I was thankful.

The afternoon up to this point had been somewhat of a blur. After Quinn had left me standing outside by limo #1, Steven, Carlos, and Olivia's limo pulled in behind ours. Carlos didn't seem surprised to find me there by myself and warmly folded me into their group, helping me navigate hotel check-in. Really, all I had to do was follow him into the casino; he did everything else. He even handed me my key, told me what room number was mine, and how to find the elevators.

We were then dispatched with instructions to meet in the hotel lobby in one hour. I went to my room and didn't do much of anything but frown, use the facilities, brush my teeth, look at the list of in-room TV channels, and then head back downstairs armed with my portfolio and iPad. Carlos and Olivia were sitting across from each other on large, golden, jewel-encrusted settees. They weren't talking; rather, they were independently together, engrossed in the contents of their own cell phones.

I glanced around with not a little trepidation. Neither Quinn nor Steven was present in the lobby. Carlos noticed me first, and he and Olivia both stood in lagged unison as I approached. That was when I saw a third person, also standing in lagged unison, and he was engrossed with his phone also. He was of normal height, a little taller than I was, and had normal blondish-reddish hair and normal bluish eyes and a normal smattering of freckles—though light—over his cheeks but, strangely, not his nose.

Introductions were made swiftly; the unknown person was the nephew of the casino owner and the manager of the new club; his name was Alex or Adrien or Aiden or Allen something like that. I was introduced rather formally as Ms. Morris, Senior Fiscal Project Coordinator and manager of the account. We shook hands. He may have smiled and held my hand a little too long; he might also have winked. I wasn't in the mood to notice anything about him.

Allen or Aiden (or whoever) was going to escort us and give us a tour of the new club, the club for which we were to provide security, the club for which we had prepared the presentation. I tried to push myself to feel at least some professional interest in the tour if not some normal inquisitiveness.

On the elevator ride up, I was informed by Olivia that Quinn and Steven had a separate meeting with the client to go over the private account—a meeting I wasn't invited to attend. I spared her a waxy, unconcerned smile.

The tour was fine. The club was fine, although it looked peculiar as it was empty of partygoers and was rather brightly lit by several west-facing windows. It didn't look anything like Club Outrageous; it just appeared to be a typical nightclub; although, in its defense, they hadn't yet finished decorating. There were several men, I assumed construction workers, coming in and out of the main area, but I expended no mental energy noticing them.

We ate lunch at a black table near one of the windows. I didn't notice the view of the Las Vegas Strip or the landscape of rust-capped ridges and canyons beyond.

I drifted through these happenings, not tasting my food, speaking when spoken to, answering questions but not really asking any of my own. I was wholly uncurious, which should have concerned me, but it didn't.

There were a few more tours of the casino floor, the lock room, and a few sections of the basement. Finally, after an indeterminable amount of time and banal chitchat, we were taken to a conference room and prodded with coffee, tea, and cucumber water. The club manager left briefly while Carlos and Olivia set up for the presentation, he pulled out a thumb drive, and she placed hardcopy packets in front of each of the conference table's large leather seats.

Then, in walked Steven and Quinn and, suddenly, my brain engaged. I started noticing.

In fact, I couldn't stop noticing.

I noticed that he didn't look at me or speak to me, and he seemed to sit in the seat farthest from mine.

I noticed that Carlos made all the introductions as the client entered: Mr. Northumberland, a tall, tanned, trim man in his fifties with black eyes and pepper hair. He owned the casino. His nephew, the one who was either called Aiden or Allen or Alex or something starting with 'A', entered the room behind him, and an entourage of four men and three women followed. I suspected their names didn't matter. They weren't making decisions; they may as well have been curtains.

There were some initial niceties, such as comments about college football; someone pointed out that it was hot outside; I was asked if I'd had a chance to spend any time gambling since we'd arrived. I wanted to respond that life was a gamble, and we were all losers. Instead, suppressing my emo-moroseness, I replied in the negative and settled into my seat.

Then the presentation began. Though my color was normal throughout, I knew it was only a matter of time before he would say something or do something to set my Rudolph light blinking. The man had my button in his possession, and he pressed it repeatedly.

I couldn't help but notice that Mr. Northumberland seemed very impatient—impatient to get the presentation started, and then during the presentation, impatient to ensure that our security implementation would be completed by next month. He interrupted Quinn frequently, asking questions such as, "How much time will that take?" and "Don't you already have everything you need?" and "Is that going to delay the project?"

When the presentation ended, Olivia stood and adjusted the lights in the room, and Quinn requested that the casino staff open their information packets. He took the group through the implementation plan, the timeline, the resources we would provide, the cost; suddenly he surprised me, and I guessed the rest of our team, by adding, "These budget numbers are initial estimates. We're planning an overhaul to our billing structure in order to provide corporate clients with a greater level of granularity. The next time you see the cost estimates and, for that matter, the invoices, they'll have line item detail."

Mr. Northumberland nodded with what I guessed was appreciation because he said, "That's good, that's good; just as long as it doesn't hold anything up."

Quinn assured him the changes would not preclude moving the project forward, and then Quinn was discussing networking and wiring requirements of the space. I could only watch him with mystified incredulity.

I felt Steven's foot tap against mine under the table and swung my gaze to meet his. He had the ability to enlarge his gray eyes and narrow them at the same time; it often impressed me. He gave me this look now; it was meant to convey surprise and suspicion. I shook my head almost imperceptibly, hoping he understood my silent communication. I had no idea why Quinn chose that moment to mention my idea about billing changes, or why or when he'd decided that Cypher Systems was going to commit to the new software one hundred percent.

I did know that Olivia was also watching me; the daggers she was throwing with her glare were difficult to overlook, even in my peripheral vision. Instead of focusing my attention on her knife-wielding propensities or Quinn's continuing recitation of the deal's details or Steven's sideways glances, I stared unseeingly at the two-dimensional, top-view diagram of the club space within my packet.

It was such a small thing, the new billing technique. It really was such a small thing. I doubted Mr. Northumberland or any of his lackeys cared about line item detail on billing invoices.

But why had he done it? Why had Quinn even brought it up?

It was nothing. It meant nothing. Stop obsessing about it.

My eyes followed the lines of the blueprint. I distracted myself by studying the digitally rendered topical design and comparing it to the tour we'd taken of the space earlier. This, as it turned out, was a very effective distraction.

I frowned, blinked, and rechecked my examination. My frown deepened.

The schematic in the packet did not match the actual size, layout, or features of the club we'd toured that morning.

I must have sighed loudly or made some other overt sign of displeasure, because the room became quiet; somewhere to the right a throat was cleared. I glanced up. Everyone was looking at me, including Quinn.

"Ms. Morris..." Quinn was very Mr. Sullivan in his expression and tone. "Is there something you wish to add?"

I looked from Quinn to Carlos to Steven to Allen (or Alex or Andrew or whatever his parents had named him that was so forgettable) to the client, Mr. Northumberland. I was on a precipice. It was my first client meeting, I was the most junior member of the team; I didn't even know if I deserved the job or if my zebra print stilettos had been the deciding factor. I should smile politely and apologize, or cough wildly to cover up the unintended sound. I could also feign Tourette syndrome.

Or I could publically announce that all the team's cost estimates had been based on a grossly inaccurate rendering of the space due to an oversight or, more alarming, the purposeful deception of the client.

Well, what do I have to lose?

I licked my lips then placed my hands, folded, on the table. "Yes. I do. Before we move beyond the AutoCAD rendering, I would like clarification as to why the space we toured this morning doesn't match the plans sent by the casino last month, included here in our packet. We based all our cost estimates on the AutoCAD rendering."

There was a slight pause as the group apparently absorbed this information before all eyes swung to the nephew—AllenAlexAndrewAiden. I followed their stares.

He looked decidedly uncomfortable. The man's eyes bounced around the conference room then settled on Mr. Northumberland's before he issued a small, nervous laugh. "The differences are minor, really. It's basically the same."

I frowned severely as several sets of eyeballs ricocheted back to me, but I focused my attention on the nephew. "I must respectfully disagree. There are two partitions—non-weight-bearing walls—that are not present on the digital design rendering; the current space has west-facing windows and an outside patio, but the design depicts no windows and no patio; additionally, the square footage of the actual space is at least eleven hundred feet larger, not including the patio." I shifted my gaze to Quinn's.

I couldn't read Quinn's expression, which may have been due to my current unrest regarding all topics McHotpants rather than any surreptitious attempts on his part. I did comprehend that his stare was neither hostile nor warm; in fairness, I could only describe it as attentive.

The nephew moved from side to side in his seat as though he couldn't get comfortable. "That's absurd. Clearly you can't read architectural schematics."

"Actually…" Quinn paused, pulling his eyes from mine and addressing Mr. Northumberland, who, for the first time since the meeting began, hadn't felt the need to interrupt. "Actually, Ms. Morris is very familiar with such schematics as she graduated summa cum laude from Iowa State University with a dual major in architecture and mathematics. You see, Iowa State is one of the top schools in the nation for architecture."

I flinched, just a little, barely perceptible to anyone who may have been watching me, when Quinn recited my qualifications. I was not aware that he was so acquainted with my academic credentials. It made me wonder what else he knew about me and how he came to be such an expert.

Mr. Northumberland's expression of surprise boiled into sudden impatience; to my relief this thunderous glare was directed at his nephew. "Allen, this is entirely unacceptable! If this causes another delay in—"

Quinn smoothly interrupted. "Mr. Northumberland, we can modify our implementation strategy and meet the deadline if time is the issue here. However, the cost…" Quinn sighed, closed the packet of papers in front of him, and leaned back in his chair. "I cannot guarantee that the cost of the project will not be impacted."

Without any overtures or pretense, the client leaned forward and pointed a finger at Quinn. "If you can meet the deadline, you can have triple your original budget." Then his black glare moved to his nephew. "I can't have any further delays."

Quinn nodded once then abruptly stood; I watched his long fingers button the top button of his suit jacket. "In that case, we're finished for today. I see no further need for pretense and discussion; what's important now is getting started."

Northumberland stood as well, almost eagerly. His entourage also stood; they reminded me of synchronized swimmers, only in business suits. Their boss said, "Good man. I couldn't agree more." He reached across the table and shook Quinn's hand. "You have an impressive team."

I caught Steven giving me a meaningful look, and I returned it with a raised eyebrow and a shrug of nonchalance even though inwardly I was breathing a ragged, yet guarded, sigh of relief.

I'd taken a chance. I only hoped it would be enough to prove that I was worthy of keeping my job.

♥♥♥

CARLOS AND QUINN disappeared together directly after the meeting adjourned, and I begged off dinner with Steven, claiming a headache. Of course, Steven still threatened to keep his promise of a sleepover. I was noncommittal and laughed at his good-natured teasing, but I didn't feel like company. I felt like stewing in my room alone with a bottle of wine and a hamburger and HBO.

Before I ran off, Steven reminded me that our meetings for the following day had been canceled and that the plane would now be departing at 3:00 p.m. He suggested we meet up during the day and try to see a little of Vegas before leaving. I was, again, noncommittal. I felt kind of like a jerk.

I did have a headache. I had a cornucopia of confusion to sort through. I needed to figure out what I needed, what I wanted, what was right, and where they all intersected.

What I needed was to keep my distance from male humans—Jon and Quinn—and keep my job—and reorganize my life so that calm and order were restored.

What I wanted was to throw myself at Quinn and continue behaving like an infatuated teenager.

And I didn't know what was right.

When room service arrived, I took the bottle of wine into the bathroom and had a bubble bath. The hotel tub was nowhere near the awe-inspiring, spectacular feature in the apartment Quinn had showed me last Sunday, but it was perfectly adequate for my current needs.

Nevertheless, after an hour in the tub drinking alone, I felt no closer to solving my dilemma. Instead, I was left with an empty bottle of wine, pruney fingers, and more questions.

I was getting dressed when I heard a confident knock on my door. It was just past

9:30 p.m. Naturally, I assumed it was Steven making good on his sleepover threat. Due to this perilous assumption, I didn't check the peephole; I just opened the door.

It was a crucial, if not monumental, mistake.

If I'd seen Quinn first through the fish-eye opening, I might've had time to compose myself. I might have decided to pretend I was asleep. I might have trapped myself under a heavy immovable object or jumped out the thirty-story window.

As it was, I could only return his smolder with stunned, albeit tipsy, surprise. My internal organs and major muscle groups were helpless against the chemical reaction reducing them into frozen yet gelatinous goo. My heart, likewise, spring boarded to my throat. I was abruptly aware that I was attired only in a white tank top, bra, and bikini bottoms; so, basically, my underwear.

I'd like to say that, when faced with the smoldering indigo eyes of Quinn Sullivan after a bottle of wine, his impressively massive and muscled form hovering outside my hotel room door and big hands gripping the frame, I felt very little in the way of intense physical or emotional response.

If I said that then I'd be a dirty liar—a dirty, dirty liar.

Quinn, suspended like a metaphor on the abyss of in-my-room/out-of-my-room, was still in his custom cut black suit, white shirt, and blue silk tie.

However, he was emphatically mussed.

His tie was loosened haphazardly and hung a little off balance around his neck; his shirt was wrinkled from hours of wear; his hair was askew and spiking about at odd angles; his chin and jaw were shadowed with a full day of stubble. Of course, he still looked like a *GQ* model, but instead of the well-groomed variety, he looked like the well-tousled variety.

The fact that he said nothing at all didn't help. He just…looked.

At first, he held my gaze for a long moment; then he looked up, he looked down, he looked all around. This was done with such a deliberate languorous insolence that I feel like I was being perused for purchase. I blamed my slightly inebriated state when I was tempted to ask if he were looking for something in particular or just window-shopping.

Regardless, his eyes were the bull, all my previous attempts at detachment were the china shop, and he was smashing it to pieces—*smash, smash, smash.*

I managed a deep breath but couldn't seem to release it. I maybe resembled a red-nosed reindeer caught in headlights.

Then, he moved.

"Can I come in?" Quinn asked the question like it was a statement and, without even pretending my response mattered, he walked into my room leaving me to stare after him as I held the door.

"I don't. I—well—if—you—I guess—how… ok."

As he walked by, I smelled whiskey, and the aftershave or soap he had used still clung to his skin and his suit.

He smelled delicious. *Smash, smash, smash.*

I released the breath I'd been holding after a further three or four seconds then, on fragmented autopilot, hesitantly closed the door. I kept changing my mind as I moved in slow motion, reconsidering the correctness or appropriateness of closing the door while my boss's boss sauntered around my hotel room.

My internal dialogue went something like this: *Leave it open! But that would be strange if someone walks by. Who cares? I care! Why do I care? Just close it! You can't close it; you're in your underwear! And if the door is closed, you might... do... something. Here is the situation: I'm in my underwear in my room with Quinn, and my alcohol-laden inhibitions are low, low, low. It's like closing yourself up in a Godiva chocolate shop; of course you're going to sample something. Don't sample anything! Don't even smell anything! If you smell it, you'll want to try it. Don't smell him anymore— No. More. Smelling. I hope he doesn't see the empty bottle of wine... Put some clothes on. Is it weird if I dress in front of him? I want some chocolate. Ah! Clothes!!*

Finally, the door closed even though I hadn't made a conscious decision to do so. I took a steadying breath then turned and followed him, trailing some distance behind and crossing to the opposite side of the room from where he was currently standing. I spotted my workout shirt on the bed and attempted to put it on surreptitiously.

Quinn's back was to me, and he seemed to be meandering around the space; he didn't appear to be in any hurry. He paused for a short moment next to my laptop and stared at the screen.

He looked lost and a little vulnerable. *Smash, smash, smash*

I took this opportunity to pull on some sweatpants and a sweatshirt from my suitcase. The sweatshirt was on backward, with the little V in the back and the tag in the front, but I ignored it, grabbed my jacket from the closet behind me, and slipped it on too.

He walked to the window and surveyed the view as I hurriedly pushed my feet into socks and hand-knit slippers, given to me by Elizabeth last Christmas.

I was a tornado of frenzied activity, indiscriminately and quietly pulling on clothes. I may have been overcompensating for my earlier state of undress. However, it wasn't until he turned toward me with leisurely languid movements that I finally stopped dressing; my hands froze on my head as I pulled on a white cabled hat, another hand-knit gift from Elizabeth.

Quinn sighed. "I need to talk to you about your sist…" But then he stopped speaking when he lifted his gaze to me.

His features, shaping into something resembling dumbfounded astonishment, were cast in a warm glow from a nearby lamp.

He looked earnestly surprised and a little boyish. *Smash, smash, smash.*

His mesmerizing eyes narrowed as they looked over my now completely covered form; the only skin showing was that of my face and hands. If I'd been thinking clearly and soberly, I might have felt ridiculous. Instead, as I was most definitely not thinking clearly and was most definitely not sober, I was cursing myself for leaving my gloves in Chicago, and I was looking for my glasses.

He shifted on his feet, stuffed his hands in his pockets, and studied me with open and growing amusement. "Are you going somewhere?"

I swallowed and tried to shrug, but the movement was lost under the layers of clothing. "Yes." I lifted my chin, feeling suddenly hot, which reminded me of how hot it was outside, even at 9:30p.m. I then quickly amended. "No." I lowered my hands from the hat on my head and tugged at the sleeves of the jacket. "I haven't decided."

He tilted his head just so, his mouth tugging upward on one side, and then he slowly, slowly started crossing to me like he was stalking prey; like he was afraid sudden movements might send me into another tornado of clothing myself. "Where were you thinking of going?"

"To gamble," I blurted. It was the only thing I could think of in my slightly imbibed state; after all, we were staying at a world-famous casino in Las Vegas.

"Really?" he asked conversationally, like I was telling him about a good bargain down at the Save-A-Lot. "What were you thinking of playing?"

"Poker." I wanted to cross my arms over my chest, but due to clothing, boobs, and a lack of coordination, I encountered too much bulk; my movements were restricted.

"Poker." He nodded once, holding me in place with a clearly skeptical if not entertained expression. "Is it very cold—this place where you're going to play poker?"

Without me really noticing, he'd crossed to me. One moment Quinn was at the far side of the room by the window, and the next moment he was standing directly in front of me with no more than three feet of air and clothes separating us.

"N-no—not necessarily. I just wanted to be prepared."

"Prepared for arctic temperatures?"

"Prepared for any eventuality."

"Like what? Poker in a freezer?"

"Like strip poker." I said the words before my brain thought them and, due to his proximity, I saw something the opposite of calm flash behind his eyes. I chewed on my top lip to ensure I didn't say anything else. I knew that my own eyes were overtly large, and watchful, and very repentant for the most recent sounds of my mouth.

Quinn swallowed, and his expression had changed: less teasing but no less intense. "We could..." His gaze flickered to my lips then settled on my forehead. "We could play strip poker here."

CHAPTER NINETEEN

My already large eyes widened further, and I blinked several times in rapid succession. "I-I-I." I reached for something to hold on to and ended up leaning against the wall behind me. "I can't—we can't do that."

"But you'll play strip poker with strangers?" He seemed to be studying me very closely.

"Well, yeah—" This was a strange conversation to be having, as I was speaking in the theoretical sense and in the literal. Theoretically, I'd play strip poker with strangers, depending on the circumstances and the strangers, but I had no literal intention of doing so.

Quinn quickly countered. "And if I happened to be playing poker—strip poker—at the only table in the casino, would you still play?"

I hesitated; I felt like I was being led into a trap that involved Quinn getting naked, which actually sounded really nice. I reluctantly said, "No."

"Why not?"

"Because… I—you're you." I congratulated myself for not slurring the words even as sweat was beading on my chest and upper back.

"Do you trust me?"

"Sometimes."

"Sometimes?" He lifted his eyebrows just slightly in challenge. "Haven't I always been honest?"

"You've been technically honest."

"Do you think I'd ever hurt you?"

His questions were rapid-fire, and the way he looked at me paired with my self-imposed heat suit and questionable policy of drinking alone made me a lot dizzy.

I hesitated again, then said, "I don't know."

He frowned at my response but didn't relent. "Don't you think everyone deserves a chance?"

"A chance?"

"Yes, a chance."

"What…what kind of chance?" My words were a little shaky, and his expression remained inscrutable, but his eyes—his eyes were dark, purposeful, and almost menacing in their glittering intensity.

Damn smoldering eyes. *Smash, smash, smash.*

"A chance to prove themselves, to defy shortcuts and preconceived expectations, preferences… labels."

I pressed my lips together. This was one of those questions that are impossible to answer correctly, such as, *When did you stop beating your wife*? Did I believe everyone deserved a chance? Yes. But he knew that. I breathed in through my nose but stopped when I smelled him: whiskey, aftershave, and Quinn.

He smelled great. *Smash, smash, smash.*

In a moment of weakness, likely caused by my smelling him, my voice was quiet and laced with a note of resignation when I responded. "Yes. Everyone deserves a chance."

He gave me one of his barely-there smiles, just a hint of a smile, and licked his lips. "Then I want my chance."

"And how do you propose I give aforementioned shhh—ance—" I swallowed in order to correct my slur. "…this *chance*…to… you? What vehicle will you use for the chance?"

We'd said the word 'chance' so much it was starting to sound distorted and funny: *chance, chance, chance, chance, shance, shance, shanz, shanz… shnaz*

Without preamble he said, "I want to date you, be exclusive. I want us to spend time together like we did before I had to go to Boston last week. And, if I have to travel, I want you to answer the cell phone when I call, because I want to hear your voice."

With every syllable that left his mouth, I felt my button being pushed again and again, and the resulting crimson blush was truly massive. I cleared my throat and said, "Oh, is that all…?"

"No." He shook his head, interrupting me. "That's not all. I want to touch you and kiss you, frequently, and I want you…" He shifted on his feet as though steadying himself then his hand reached out; he stepped closer and cupped my cheek in his palm. "I want you to touch me."

Gah! His words!! *Smash, Smash, SMAAAAAASH!!*

"And…" he said, but then he paused, his fingers threading through the hair above my temple and beneath the hat covering my head. He pushed it off and we both let it fall to the floor. "I want to play strip poker, with you, right now."

I was careful to take my next breath through my mouth. I didn't want Quinn-sniff to influence my already wino-impaired brain function. A little voice in the back of my head said, *Don't trust him! You're not special! You're weird and awkward and a bigheaded Neanderthal freak with Medusa hair! He's confused you with someone else!*

Almost immediately, I told that voice to eat shit and die.

I wanted to believe him.

My palms lay flat against the wall behind me and I slanted my chin upward so I could really look at him. His expression straddled between guarded and hopeful. I recognized it so acutely because it was how I'd been feeling since we met.

I cleared my throat and took another steadying breath, through my mouth, releasing it slowly before asking, "What if I said no?"

Quinn became very still. "Are you saying no?" His tone felt just a wee bit dangerous.

I shook my head. "No…I mean, I'm not saying no. I just want to know what happens if I say no."

He paused again, staring at me as though the answer to my question was written on my face. He no longer looked hopeful; he just looked guarded. Silence stretched for almost a full minute, and we stood there watching each other. Then he blinked suddenly, and an expression resembling dawning comprehension made his eyes flash.

"Janie," Quinn shifted away; his hand fell from my hair; his countenance darkened. "You're not going to lose your job."

I twisted my mouth to the side and made sloppy work of crossing my arms over my chest. "You won't be upset?"

"Yes, I'll be upset—" He cleared his throat, looked away briefly then met my gaze again. "I'll be disappointed." He said the word disappointed very carefully, measured, like it was meant to be four words in one. "But, I'm not going to disadvantage my company because you don't…" He lifted his hands between us then rested them on his hips. "Because you're not interested."

I surveyed him for a moment then asked, "Would it be the same job that I have now? Or would it be something else?"

His jaw ticked. "The same job."

I nodded absentmindedly. Even though he was looking increasingly reserved and upset, I found my nerves had calmed significantly.

I took a step forward and shrugged out of the jacket. "Would we be friends or just Mr. Sullivan and Ms. Morris? Could we still hang out?"

He let out a deep sigh, and I didn't like the hard expression setting his mouth in a firm, unhappy line, or the way his usually fiery eyes were growing cold and distant. "Listen." He said it slowly, like a rumbly growl. "I'm not an overbearing asshole, but I'm also not a masochist. So, no…I'm not interested in being friends."

"Hmm," I said, studying him. If I were honest with myself, I would have to admit that his answer made me happy for some strange reason. I didn't understand why, so I tucked the data point away for future analysis. Regardless, it made me happy, and I allowed myself a small smile. The alternating lava and ice emoto-craziness I'd been living with since last Sunday settled down to a heated simmer of unease.

"What if—"

"Janie—" He lifted his hands, hesitated, and then placed them on my upper arms. I found it interesting that sometimes he seemed to need to touch me or make contact between us before he could speak. "What can I say to convince you that a relationship between us isn't going to affect your job?"

"But what if we were to break up?"

"I still wouldn't fire you."

"How can you be certain of what you would do? What if I kidnap your dog?"

"What? Why would you—" He huffed impatiently then shook his head. "I don't have a dog."

"That's not the point. What if I turned bat-shit crazy on you but still was a great employee?"

"I'm professional enough to keep my work life and personal life separate."

I sighed unhappily. "But you don't know—"

He slid his hands down to mine and held them. "You can't prepare for every scenario or eventuality in life."

"But what if getting involved turns out to be a horrible mistake?"

"What if it turns out to be the best decision we ever made?"

"I'm risk averse." Even as I said the words I squeezed his hands with mine, afraid he would let go.

He studied me with frustrated contemplation, his brow furrowed deeply. Quinn shifted closer and leveled me with a deliberate gaze. "Ok, what if we didn't decide? What if we left it to chance?"

I swallowed. "How so? How do we do that?"

"We'll play poker."

"One hand?"

"No, we'll play until midnight. Whoever has the most clothes on at midnight wins."

"Wins what?"

His eyes flickered to my lips and he licked his own. "If I win, we date for a month, during which time I get to buy you whatever I want." I started to protest, but his voice rose over mine, and his hands held me in place. "And you stop looking for reasons or labels or whatever for why we shouldn't. If you win, then…" he shrugged lightly, "… then you decide what happens next."

I swallowed again, eyed him warily, and then I pulled my hands from his grip and stepped to the side.

Still hot, I pulled the sweatshirt over my head; the workout shirt also came off at the same time and I tossed them across the discarded jacket. This left me in my tank top, bra, sweat pants, underwear, socks, and slippers—six pieces of clothing; nine if you counted the socks and slippers as separate articles.

The room tilted a little and I wobbled. My state of intoxication hung around me like a fur coat, and would likely continue for several hours. Any decisions I made would probably be impaired.

Impaired judgment- check.

His gaze drifted to my neck, chest, stomach, and then back up again. The usual fire reignited in his eyes, but it was mixed with something else; something I couldn't place or, more likely, didn't comprehend. It was like I'd just slapped him but not quite.

I stopped trying to read his thoughts and instead tallied his clothes with a sideways glance. He was wearing a tie, shirt, jacket, undershirt, pants, socks, shoes, and either boxers or briefs. That was seven pieces of clothing or ten if I counted the socks and shoes as separate pieces.

"We're not evenly matched." I pointed to his tie then put my hands on my hips and mimicked his stance. I hoped bravado and wine-haze would prop up my resolve. So far, so good.

He glared at me, looking resentful, and his voice was steely as he asked, "What, specifically, makes you think so?"

I lifted my chin and indicated his tie again. "Your tie, Quinn. I have on nine pieces of clothing, and assuming you're wearing underwear of some sort, you have on ten. I can either put on my hat, or you can take off your tie."

His glare morphed into a perplexed frown as I spoke, but when I reached the end of the last sentence, his features transitioned into something like petulant yet amused understanding, and most of the rigidity left his shoulders and neck.

We stared at each other, again for almost half a minute, before I broke the silence.

"Or, you could take off your jacket…?"

Quinn's mouth hooked to the side; he smoothly removed his jacket and tossed it to the pile of my discarded clothes. He began unfastening his cufflinks, and the breath he released while pinning me with an irritated stare sounded relieved. It made me smile.

"You're going to pay for that."

I widened my eyes. "For what?"

"Hmm…" He fought a smile. "Do you have cards, or do we need to get some?"

I stepped around him unsteadily and crawled across the bed to my luggage. "I have cards. I like to play solitaire when I travel."

"Why don't you use your laptop or the iPad?" He turned to watch me dig through my bag.

"I like the feel of the cards." I fished them out then crossed to the couch. There was a desk against the wall but no table near the couch. There was, however, an ottoman. I placed a magazine on the ottoman and decided it would make a flat enough surface, and I shuffled the cards.

Shuffling helped. It kept my hands from shaking when the faint voice of my sober self asked *What am I doing? Am I really doing this?*

He was… blindingly beautiful, and wealthy, and my boss. All were really good reasons why *we* were not suitable.

But I really, really liked him. He was damn sexy and interesting and crazy smart and annoyingly insightful. I had to trust that there was something about me that he saw and liked enough to abandon his slamps and his Wendell lifestyle. I didn't like trusting, and I didn't like setting greater than mild expectations, but I wanted to have faith in him. Call it wine, call it Quinn-sniff-induced obscurity, but I felt too warm and fuzzy to dwell on the scary side of strip poker.

Impaired judgment… still check.

"So…" I heard Quinn's voice from behind me; it sounded like he was still standing in the same spot. "I did actually come here to talk to you about something."

I glanced over my shoulder. "What's that?"

He pulled one hand roughly through his hair and put the cufflink in his pants pocket with the other. "I need to talk to you about last Sunday; about that—uh—guy, in the park."

I was kneeling on the floor next to the ottoman, but something about the tone of his voice made me sit back on my heels and turn my entire torso toward him. "Ok." I placed the cards on the magazine. He had as much of my full attention as was possible, given my current lack of sobriety.

Quinn hesitated, sauntered as he spoke, not looking at me. "So, when I left Boston years ago, I wasn't very popular with… anyone." He fiddled with the contents of the room: a lampshade, the mini-bar, the instructions for Internet connectivity. "I made some data copies in order to make sure that I wouldn't be…bothered in Chicago."

He paused over the mini-bar, touching a doll-sized bottle of Johnnie Walker.

"Data copies?"

"The people I worked for—I made copies of their data when I installed the wipe script and degausser."

"You mean, the bad men?"

He gave me a small smile and nodded. "Yes, the bad men." Quinn walked to the couch, hesitated for a moment, and sat down. He placed his large hands on his knees as if he might stand up at any moment. "Janie…" He leveled me with a vacillating, undecided gaze.

"Yes…?" He was quiet for so long I felt the need to prompt him. I was beginning to feel a renewed sense of anxiety. This was a long buildup for him; he was usually a straight-to-the-point kind of guy.

He sighed then asked, "Have you had contact with your sister Jem recently?"

I'm sure I looked comical, gaping at him in response to his question. He could have asked me, "*Do you want tampons or pads for your Bat Mitzvah?*" and received a less dumbfounded reaction.

I breathed out heavily and responded with the first words that occurred to me. "How do you know Jem?"

He shook his head, his eyes focused and attentive to the expressions that must have been kaleidoscoping over my face. "I don't really know her. But in an effort to be more than technically honest, I can tell you that I know who she is."

"What do you mean, you *know who she is*?"

"I mean, just before I left Boston six years ago, I met her when I was at a…a business associate's house. She was—she was involved with him, and was… introduced to me briefly."

"Six years ago?" I frowned at this. Jem would have been seventeen or eighteen at the time. "Are you sure? And you remember her?"

"It's hard to forget someone who tries to set your car on fire."

My mouth gaped open, and I slowly released a breath in that sloppy, overly exaggerated way you only achieve when you're nearly drunk. "That sounds like Jem."

Quinn pulled his gaze from mine, leaned forward, and picked up the cards. He started to deal them for our game of poker. "Right before I left Boston, before Des died, I was securing systems for a group that, well, the particulars aren't important. It wasn't a typical operation, though. The main guy—his name was Seamus—was basically a skinhead, a thug, but he happened to be a very smart thug." Quinn replaced the deck, picked up his cards, and began rearranging them, frowning as he did so. "The trusted members all had these neck tattoos." Quinn offhandedly gestured to his throat, drawing curving lines from his collar to his ear and around the back of his neck.

I drew in a deep breath. "The guy in the park, last Sunday—he had a tattoo on his neck."

"Also, Dan, the security group leader at the Fairbanks building, used to be one of them."

"What did Jem do that has this guy's panties so twisted?" I wrinkled my nose in what I surmised was an exaggerated way, because Quinn's gaze softened as he looked at me, and he smiled.

"Does it matter?"

"No…yes." I rolled my upper lip between my teeth and chewed on it. "No, I guess it doesn't, but I'd like to know."

"She helped one of his rivals raid a cash house of his."

"Why would she do that?" I continued to bite my lip.

"Because she wanted to make him angry. Because she is crazy." His tone was flat, as though the explanation was rudimentary, obvious.

"I can't believe you used to work with these people." I switched lips and started nibbling on the bottom one.

Quinn's eyes met mine. "When I saw the guy in the park last week, I thought that he was there because of me. But when I went to Boston and met with Seamus—"

I flinched. "You met with him? The skinhead leader in Boston?"

He nodded, his jaw flexed. "When I met with Seamus—"

"Isn't he dangerous? Why would you do that?" I interrupted him again.

He ignored my interruptions and continued. "Seamus said he was looking for Jem. That guy in the park thought you were her."

A new kaleidoscope of expressions, mirroring my thoughts, must've mounted my features because Quinn quickly added, "I've had guards on you since last week, and I told Seamus that you are not Jem. He also knows that you work for me and are not a viable option for…" He paused as though choosing his words carefully. "I think he believes me that you're not a viable option for initiating contact with Jem. But, to be on the safe side, I want to put guards on you when we get back to Chicago."

I nodded until it felt like I was bobbing up and down on a boat, and I cleared my throat. My hands were rigid in my lap, and I noted that they were balled into tight fists. With effort, I relaxed my fingers, picked up my cards, and forced myself to look at them: *ace of hearts, two of clubs, three of diamonds, ten of clubs, nine of clubs*. It was a shitty hand.

"Why—how—" I fanned out my cards and laid them on my lap. "Why did Jem try to set your car on fire?"

Quinn shrugged, not meeting my gaze. "I don't remember; I don't think there was a reason. I just remember that she was crazy."

I felt sorry for myself; for being dealt a shitty hand, and for having a sister whose most recognizable trait was criminality. Some people have annoying relatives who drink too much during the holidays and corner everyone with one-sided conspiracy theories about the government being both heinously incompetent and capable of staging elaborate hoaxes like the moon landing, or Pearl Harbor, or the theory of relativity.

I had a sister who didn't limit her antics to holidays, and she liked to sleep with my boyfriend and/or attempt murder when faced with boredom.

I didn't allow myself to dwell in the land of defeatism for very long. I couldn't do anything about the hand I'd been dealt. I could only make the most of it, hope for the best, and accept my fate.

Or I could cheat.

"Did you—do you—" I picked my cards up again but didn't look at them; I kept my attention fixed on Quinn, blinked twice so he would come into focus. "Do you think I look like her? Like Jem? Did you think I was her?"

Quinn frowned at his cards then met my gaze. "Yes."

I waited. When he didn't elaborate, I craned my neck forward and widened my eyes in disbelief. "Yes? Just yes?"

He nodded.

"Which part? Yes to which part?"

"You look like her. I thought you were Jem when I first saw you." He looked like he would have preferred to discuss anything else, including, perhaps, the menstrual cycle of koalas or the regulations surrounding peanut butter manufacturing.

I slid my teeth to the side. "Is that why you wanted to kiss me? Because you thought I was her?" I quoted Quinn's admission from the night of our first kiss. Something hard settled in my stomach and made my mouth taste sour, like stale wine and postage stamps.

He shook his head. "No—God no. I think I noticed you at first because of the resemblance. I can honestly say I've never wanted to kiss your sister."

"When did you figure out that we weren't the same person?"

He folded his hand of cards and held them on his lap, and he leaned forward with his elbows on his knees. "The day after I first saw you, weeks before we spoke. I did a very thorough background check on you to make sure you weren't Jem." I was impressed by the starkness of his tone even though the admission looked like it cost him something. His eyes were weary.

I was also impressed by his continuing more than technical honesty, even if it felt like I was prying the answers out of him.

I considered this information as I considered him. "Is that why you escorted me out when I lost my job? You thought I might blow something up?"

"No. Like I said, I knew you weren't her."

"Then why did you pose as a security guard?"

"I didn't pose. I like to spend time on the floor with my team, especially when we take on a new project. We'd just taken over security for the building and moved into the top floor. I wanted to…" He looked away, sighed, and met my eyes again. "I wanted to get a sense of the other people who worked in the building."

"And you escorted me out because you wanted to get a sense of who no longer worked in the building?"

"No," he said.

"No?" I prompted.

"No," he said, this time a little more firmly, pronounced.

"Hmm…" I surveyed him for a long moment, and we entered into an old-fashioned staring contest. He had an unfair advantage because I was, basically, intoxicated.

Finally I spoke. "Why did you escort me out?"

He flexed his jaw even though his eyes were lit with mischief. A Mona Lisa smile pulled at the corners of his mouth. "How many cards do you need?"

"Don't avoid the question."

"I'm not avoiding—I escorted you out because—" he swallowed then huffed, "When the request came through I recognized your name and I wanted to… see… what you were like." Quinn glared at his cards.

I smiled, a big goofy smile, "You wanted to see what I was like?"

He didn't respond. He placed three of his cards in the discard pile and took three from the top of the deck.

"Were you watching me?" The bigness and the goofiness of my smile increased.

He glanced at me, the corners of his mouth tugging upward. "For the record, I know you were watching me too."

I blinked at him. "Watching you?"

He nodded, his eyes narrowed wickedly. "In the lobby, hiding behind the plants. You would come down with your lunch and watch me while I worked."

Button pushed, I blushed to my ears and quietly turned my attention to my cards. After a long moment, I gave him all four but the ace. I felt like I'd been caught with my hand down my pants, feeling embarrassed, but pleased that he'd noticed (and seemed to like it.)

"I wasn't watching you," I mumbled.

"Yes, you were."

I glanced at him for a brief moment and found him *watching* me with a look that bordered on menacing; I smashed my lips together to keep from smiling.

"You better have an ace." He handed me four new cards.

"I have an ace." I plucked them from his outstretched hand, careful not to touch him. "Do you want to see it?"

"Oh, I'll see it soon enough."

I glanced up from my new cards and met Quinn's steady gaze with an unsteady one of my own.

Smolder, *schmolder*. His eyes held such an intensity of promise that I wondered if it would be best just to forfeit and strip naked now. I knew the only way I was going to win this game was to cheat.

My main problem was that I wasn't sure I wanted to win.

CHAPTER TWENTY

I GLARED AT him.

Through my bottle-of-wine-induced haze, I'd been counting cards; so I knew he'd been cheating for the last few hands. But I couldn't admit to counting cards; otherwise, I would have to admit that I had been cheating the whole time. Also, I was down to my underwear, tank top, bra, and one sock. Meanwhile, he was down to his tie, boxer briefs, and one sock.

This last hand meant that we were tied.

He laughed, shuffling the cards, his blue eyes actually dancing with merriment. "So, sock or shirt?"

I was sitting on the floor with my back to the bed, he was sitting on the couch, and the ottoman was between us serving as a table.

I thought about which article of clothing to remove even as I let my eyes move over his chest approvingly. I'd been dreaming about that torso for weeks, ever since he made his shirtless, just-showered entrance the morning of my hangover. I'd thought about what I wanted to do when or if I actually had it within my possession.

I blinked hard and tried to focus on the footstool we were using as a table. I pressed my thighs together for no reason whatsoever, and ignored the building warmth in my lower belly.

Quinn's soft voice pulled me from my mounting aimless frenzy. "Janie: sock or shirt?"

I met his gaze abruptly and wondered if he knew what I'd been thinking; but looking at his face was almost worse. We were two minutes away from midnight. He wore a very serious expression, and his eyes were freaking smoldering again, moving between mine with what felt like violent concentration.

I huffed impatiently. "Fine. Neither."

He raised a single eyebrow. "Neither?"

I tilted my head to the side, removed my gaze from his, allowed my hair to curtain my face, and leaned forward, pulling my bra straps from my shoulders and through my arms in one swift movement. Then I unclasped the bra and, like magic, pulled the white lacy brassiere from my body without removing my shirt.

Never mind that my shirt was a thin, white, tank top that was practically see-through. I didn't want him thinking he'd won just yet, or that he could guess my *moves*. I was quickly learning that a bottle of wine convinced me of all sorts of fantastical things, not the least of which was that I had *moves*.

I tossed the bra over my shoulder and leaned back against the side of the bed.

"Ok, deal the cards," I said without looking at him. He was too distractingly beautiful. Instead, I pulled my fingers through my hair as I stretched and arched my back.

I heard his breath catch.

I looked up.

His eyes were no longer smoldering; they were now suddenly and forcefully ablaze, and he was gritting his teeth, watching me as I stretched. His look told me I was steak and he was a tiger, and that made me dinner and dessert.

"You shouldn't do that." The dark heat in his gaze, the set of his jaw, and the white knuckles of his fists betrayed the force of his concentration. He was concentrating… really, really hard.

I stilled my movements and froze mid-stretch. "Do what?"

"That." His words were ragged. "Don't do that unless you're finished playing with me."

I licked my lips, finding them suddenly dry, and my eyes moved hungrily over his form.

In truth, in that moment, I didn't remember what we were playing for, which may have explained why I suddenly no longer had any desire to continue to the game.

Then again, it could have been the impaired judgment.

I let my hands fall gradually to the carpet on either side of my thighs; my hair crashed over my shoulders and down my back. I licked my lips again as I watched him and his tightly reined reaction with wide eyes. Slowly, slowly, I righted myself to my knees and, without plan or forethought, pushed the ottoman to one side. Despite what I thought were measured movements, the cards spilled off the makeshift table and onto the floor.

His eyes followed me with intensely guarded attentiveness as he sat perfectly still on the couch. I crawled over to him and knelt between his legs. I lifted then rested my hands lightly on his bare thighs for balance. He flinched when my skin made contact with his.

"Quinn." I whispered his name. I don't know why I was whispering, but I suspected that my vocal chords were incapable of cooperating. "Quinn."

Abruptly, he wrapped the long fingers of one hand around the back of my neck, cupping it, and before I could think or react, he dragged his mouth over mine and ransacked me. He was fervent and wet and hot, and the warmth in my stomach fluttered and twisted until the pressure between my thighs was unbearable. I pressed my knees together again and clenched.

His mouth pulled away from mine, and began alternately biting and sucking and kissing my neck. The scruff of his unshaved face was pleasurably painful, and each skillful stroke of his tongue soothed the scratches left by the stubble.

I closed my eyes against the sensations of his hands and his mouth everywhere at once, and I think I lost consciousness.

Let me clarify that last statement. I think my alcohol-saturated forebrain lost the ability of conscious thought. My lower brain—the Id, the part that is associated with automatic responses and instinct and pleasure-seeking behaviors and wanting ice cream for dinner every night—that part may have slipped my forebrain some benzodiazepines so that it could assume control and have its way with my body. For purposes of simplicity, I will call that part of my brain Ida.

And Ida did have her way with my body. Let me make that perfectly clear.

On the long, long journey to the bed, Ida had her way on the couch and the floor and the dresser; at one point Ida had her way against the wall.

For maybe the first time ever in my life, my mind spent a significant amount of time not wandering because it couldn't engage or gain any traction. All forebrain surfaces were slippery; everything and nothing was distracting at once. I was utterly focused on the moment, on the feeling and sensation of being with and over and next to and under and against Quinn.

I was crushed and grabbed and stroked and admired and savored and, by God, aroused. I was aroused like it was going out of style and on sale. At one point, I thought it was going to sever me in two, and I panicked in much the same way a feral animal panics when approached with unfamiliar kindness.

To my wonderment, Quinn seemed to innately comprehend what I needed. He knew when I required tenderness and when I craved—well, not tenderness. He calibrated his movements, caresses, and kisses as the counterpoint to desires I had no idea existed within me but which, now, I was certain I could never live without. With one arresting look, one devastatingly raw gaze that stole my breath and held me captive, one moment of connection, he made me fearless.

The jarring part, because there is one, is that Quinn seemed to be just as lost as I was, and my body, my hands, my mouth, and my eyes seemed to know how to be his counterpoint, how to reassure and ignite and move and respond. If my forebrain were engaged,

I'm sure I wouldn't have recognized this suddenly fearless creature who found boldness and bravery, and who shed cowardice within the dreamy chaotic perfection of physical intimacy.

When Ida—sated, satisfied, smug Ida—allowed the curtain to be pulled back, albeit briefly, Quinn and I were collapsed against each other in a Chinese knot of limbs and sheets. I was slightly less drunk on alcohol, but a great deal drunker on the euphoria that apparently accompanies mind-blowing sex.

Ida whispered in my ear that Quinn felt warm and good and very, very right. I nodded at this assertion even as a small pain originating in my heart made it suddenly hard to breathe. I suppressed the sensation, swallowed it, and put it on a shelf to think about later.

Abruptly, I had three rapid thoughts:

Quinn still has his tie on.

I wonder if he'll let me keep it.

I wonder if he'll let me use it to—

And then, just like that, Ida was in control again.

CHAPTER TWENTY-ONE

LIFE IS FUNNY.

And I don't mean just ha-ha funny; I also mean cunning, curious, capricious, and, "The joke's on you, Batman!" funny.

Sleep gradually receded and I blinked against unforgiving brightness. The first thing I saw was the staunchly, almost glowingly white pillow and empty sheets next to me. To my still drowsy eyes, the sheets did not look familiar and the room was too bright. I frowned, closed my eyes, and opened them again, and then I remembered.

Naked.

On a bed.

In a hotel.

In Las Vegas.

Having just spent the better part of the early morning engaging in insouciantly indulgent lovemaking with Quinn Sullivan.

I sat up abruptly and unthinkingly. My eyes were no longer drowsy. I was shocked awake as though an electric current had just been passed through my spine. My gaze tried to absorb everything at once: the room, the window, the door, the clock, the bed, my nakedness, the discarded piles of clothes peppering the floor like anthills, and the equally discarded pile of cards next to the ottoman.

Rigidly, I listened intently for sounds—footsteps, breathing, shower, faucet—and spent several seconds holding my breath until I was convinced that I was alone. I released the breath I'd been holding slowly, and allowed my muscles to relax just a little. I allowed my brain to turn its attention to thoughts and feelings other than alarm and battle readiness as my eyes slowly took in my surroundings. I looked at the details rather than ascertain whether or not I was in immediate danger of encountering Quinn.

Because, impulsively, on first recognizing and realizing where I was and what I'd done, that's what it felt like: danger.

Since I spent much of my childhood being left behind and ignored, one might think that, as an adult, moments of perceived abandonment would feel old hat. The truth is, as an adult, I am always waiting to be left behind. I'm always ready to be discarded and, therefore, I spend a significant amount of time preparing for this eventuality.

I lower my expectations, I don't seek out meaningful relationships, and I don't engage in any sort of real intimacy, physical or otherwise.

Engage is the key word here.

Except, when I do engage, when it happens, when I'm left behind it doesn't feel old hat. It feels like it did the first time, and it takes me by surprise.

So I don't let it happen.

I swallowed, then licked my lips, absentmindedly pulled the bottom one through my teeth with worry. I glanced around the room and noted with cool detachment that the clock read 9:31 a.m. The only clothes strewn about belonged to me. I was alone.

There was, however, a note.

A white piece of paper lay on the bed next to me. I recognized the hotel logo at the top and Quinn's efficient script beneath. The note was illegible from where I sat, so I stared at it.

I stared at it.

And, I stared at it.

Then, I stared at it.

After that, I stared at it.

Dragging my attention elsewhere, I pushed my heavy, long hair away from my eyes and behind my shoulder then rested my forehead in my hand; my thumb and index fingers rubbed my temples. Tangible memories, not just initial scattered fragments, of what occurred before I fell asleep, of what I'd done and said, of what we did together, flooded into focus, and a faintly familiar small pain originating in my heart made it suddenly difficult to breathe.

Impaired judgment.

It wasn't anxiety or fear. It was something like wishing, or longing—or hope. The sensation reminded me of when my mother would actually be present for one of my birthdays when I was a child, or when my parents would sit us down, the three girls, and tell us that my mom would be staying this time.

I was uncomfortable with the sensation, and it made me feel despondent and weary. So I pushed it away as I'd done last night after we made love the first time, and I walked to the bathroom to take my shower. I encouraged my mind to wander, to think about something other than what Quinn's note said and what, if anything, had changed because of last night, whether, in the light of day, my decisions had been good ones; where Quinn was; or when I would see Quinn again.

However, to my disappointment, despite my desire to daydream about anything and everything else, all I could think about was the what, whether, where, and when of Quinn. This might have had something to do with the fact that signs of him were everywhere; and, by everywhere, I mean all over my body.

I was sore from… exertion, as evidenced by nail marks, bite marks, and scruff marks. I stared at my reflection in the mirror for an indeterminate amount of time and, gritting my teeth, I turned on the shower.

It wasn't just that I'd never experienced anything like the connection, the intimacy, or the sensations of the previous night. Rather, it was that I'd never realized the desire existed.

I felt wholly disconcerted by the fact that what had been a previously unidentified want now felt more like a need, like water and breathing and comic books and shoes. I didn't like it that something had been awakened in me. I preferred to be in control of my cravings. Furthermore, I preferred only to have cravings I could satisfy without the requirement or assistance of another person. This was, after all, the definition of self-reliance.

I tried to remind myself that I had been drunk, so nothing that happened last night *really* counted or mattered.

Impaired judgment.

Surely, he would realize that I'd been exhibiting impaired judgment.

After the shower, I towel-dried and applied hair product to my curls. My cheeks were flushed, and it had more to do with the memory of the previous night than with the steam of the shower.

I walked into the main room and, still avoiding the note, scaled the perimeter of the bed, picked up my discarded clothes and folded them into a neat pile next to my suitcase. I picked out another business suit from the closet and started to dress, on autopilot.

It was now 9:47 a.m., and the plane was due to leave at 3:00 p.m.

I was facing five hours alone with the note. I eyed it despairingly.

The other disconcerting realization originating from last night was the moment of what I thought was shared trust. I gave him something in that moment, when our eyes met and I became fearless; it was a part of myself. And now, in the very bright light of day, I wasn't so sure that I'd made an especially wise decision.

He hadn't earned that trust. I gave it to him based on weakness called faith, and the faith had been based on wine-pickled-brain-impaired-judgment.

I didn't want to read the note. I felt certain I knew what it said. He was, after all, a

Wendell at heart, and *I'd just become one of his slamps*. I swallowed thickly at the thought.

But I wasn't. I wasn't a slamp.

Instead of being controlled by the girly-drama-hysterical Janie, the more logical Janie endeavored to make her presence known: *Having the hot sex over the course of several hours does not a slamp make.*

These thoughts didn't help either.

With a huff, I crossed to the bed and picked up the note; girly-drama-hysterical Janie was certain it was a blow-off. Logical Janie decided to reserve judgment until the note was read.

JANIE,

I'll be right back with breakfast and coffee. Call me as soon as you wake up.

-Quinn

I STARED AT THE NOTE.

I stared at it.

And, I stared at it.

Then, I stared at it.

After that, I stared at it.

The longing was back, along with the hope. It spread like a wildfire through my heart and brain and body so fast I nearly lost my breath. Therefore, I did the only thing that made sense.

I panicked.

CHAPTER TWENTY-TWO

I WONDERED IF Quinn had ruined me for everything that was not-Quinn in much the same way that his private plane had ruined me for commercial airline travel.

I left Las Vegas at 11:35 a.m. on an Alliantsouth direct flight to Chicago. The security line made me feel like a refugee, and it all went downhill from there. While waiting at the airside, an escaped pet turtle stole my glasses and snapped them in half at the nose. I was severely jostled when I boarded the plane, and I was pretty sure the man behind me copped a feel. When I took my seat by the window, the woman next to me took off her shoes.

The smell of swamp feet was all I lived and breathed for two hours. I wondered if the thieving turtle would have enjoyed the aroma.

Mercifully, more than a thousand miles and one taxi ride later, I was sitting at my desk, checking my email, sipping on coffee, and modifying the original project plan for the Vegas club. It was just after 6:00 p.m. and the office was quiet. I allowed myself to get lost in spreadsheets, calculations, formulas, and pivot tables.

My office phone rang, and after inspecting a calculated value on my screen for veracity, I lifted the receiver to my ear.

"Janie Morris."

"What the hell, Janie."

Electric shock, that's what it was.

He was irate, and the sound of his voice caused the sensation to travel down my spine and through my limbs until it stung my fingertips, toes, and ears.

"Hi—Hi Quinn." My chest was tight, and I was having trouble breathing; even so, I struggled to sound unflustered and calm.

Silence.

"How was your trip?"

Silence.

"It's nice to hear your voice…" The statement came out sounding like a question, as though I were playing *Jeopardy* and I'd chosen my category.

I heard him sigh, and I could almost see his beautiful face and the frustration marring his features.

Finally, he said, "*What's going on?*"

I picked at the plastic of my desk calendar with my thumbnail and felt nothing but contrition.

I closed my eyes. "I'm sorry."

His voice was less irritated. "*Why are you sorry?*"

"I just…" I hesitated, letting my forehead fall into the palm of my hand.

I couldn't tell him the truth. I couldn't tell him that I was sorry for exhibiting poor, wine-induced judgment and sleeping with him, because I wasn't. I wasn't sorry. I was glad I'd been inebriated, because it allowed me to do something that was so very, very unwise. I was glad my judgment had been impaired.

I couldn't tell him that I left because I was an idiot who was confusing fantastic sex with depth of feeling.

I couldn't say I was hoping for a future with him. I couldn't admit I was desperate for it.

So I lied.

"I kept thinking about the plane ride with everyone, and you, and I don't think there is a handbook for this, but if there is then please send it to me, because I didn't want to say something wrong in front of everyone. I mean, we haven't talked about how this is going to work—us working together and you being you and me being me—and I…I don't want to jeopardize my working relationships with the team here…"

He interrupted me when I paused to take a breath. "*Janie, Janie- it's ok. Ok? I understand.*"

I stopped, hesitated, bit my bottom lip, and wondered what he understood, because I wasn't even sure that I understood. "You do?"

"*Yes. I do. I know you like labels and defined expectations. I can do that when it comes to work. We can put in place some sort of agreement that defines expectations and such at work.*"

"So you think we need one too?"

"*Yes, if it will make you feel more comfortable, and definitely yes if it keeps you from disappearing again.*"

I blurted before my brain could stop the words. "Why are you even interested in me?"

I closed my eyes and scrunched my face as mortification (from me) and stillness (from him) greeted my question. My self-recrimination was swift: *Don't ask that question; he might not have an answer.*

I heard a soft *click-click* then silence.

I opened my eyes and looked at the report on my desk without really seeing it. "Quinn?" There was no answer. I swallowed thickly. "Quinn? Are you still there?"

"That's not a conversation I want to have over the phone." Quinn's voice came from my left.

My head shot upward. I looked for, and found, the source of the words. Quinn was there, leaning against the frame of my office door, his phone still in his hand. I slowly lowered my phone to the desk as I stood. My face decided to give him a stupid shy smile; it was an uncontrollable response to his presence.

"Hi..." I breathed the word.

"Hi." His smile was unhurried, and the warmth in his eyes was doing strange things to me, like making me want to bite him.

He stepped in the door, closed it, and locked it. He set down a bag and slipped his phone into his pocket as he entered. He was wearing a white dress shirt and a patterned tie but no jacket. We gazed at each other. I was afraid that he might dissolve, thus proving to be a figment of my imagination, if I moved or spoke. I didn't want him to disappear.

Then, as though it were the most natural, expected thing in the world, he crossed the room to where I stood and kissed me. It immediately told me he had missed me, and that he'd been thinking about kissing me all day.

The kiss also made me want to bite him.

After he was satisfied, he straightened and tipped his head to the side; his eyes were half-lidded as he studied my face. I gazed up at him with another shy smile claiming my features through no conscious decision of my brain, and I allowed myself to appreciate the sight.

"You're not wearing your glasses." His tone was conversational, but his voice was deep, rumbly, quiet, and very intimate. I loved it.

"No, they were taken."

"Taken?"

"Long story involving a turtle."

He smiled at me, his eyes full of man-mirth. "A turtle? Really?"

"Yes." I breathed him in. He smelled good. I loved it.

"What are you doing tonight?"

"I'm meeting my knitting group at seven o'clock."

"I didn't know you knit." He lifted his eyebrows.

"I don't."

His eyebrows lifted slightly higher. "Oh, ok. Well, how about later?"

I answered truthfully. "I was planning to sort my comic books based on level of second-wave feminist influence."

"As opposed to first-wave feminist influence?"

"Yes, well, Susan B. Anthony laid the foundation for those who would come after her. It's all really interrelated, but she didn't have direct influence over late twentieth-century comics."

He closed his eyes and shook his head, a very reluctant looking smile claiming his mouth.

"Why? What are you doing tonight?" I asked dreamily. In that moment, I felt like such a weak girl.

He met my gaze again with a heavy-lidded one of his own. "I was hoping to show you one of the reasons why I'm interested in you, because there are many. But, if you need to sort your comic books, then I guess I could just show you now." His hands slid down my arms to my waist, my hips, and then my bottom. He didn't so much as rest them there as firmly plant them on my body and press me to him while caressing my backside.

The movement made my insides explode. I felt a nuclear blast of awareness so keenly that I almost lost my breath.

I said, "Oh," because it was all I could manage.

He grinned and dipped his head; he kissed me just behind my ear then down my neck. I, of course, angled my head to the side to give him better access.

And then I lost consciousness—and by lost consciousness, I mean Ida woke up and asserted her dominance.

IT'S TRUE.

I had really hot sex in my office, with my boss, on my desk.

That happened.

I've experienced these singularities before: these surreal moments where some combination of the lighting in the room, the situation, the smell, the people I'm with, and the clothes I'm wearing make me feel like I'm in a movie.

Standing in my office, simultaneously trying to adjust my undergarments and hair while buttoning my shirt with Quinn in my peripheral vision, I felt very much like I was in a movie.

Nothing about the moment felt very plausible.

"I need to come into the office more often." I could hear the playfulness behind his words, but I didn't smile. My palms itched to touch his bare skin, and my heart fluttered in my chest.

We'd just finished mauling each other in my office, literally on my desk, and already I couldn't stop thinking about when I'd get a chance to climb all over him again. It was not a feeling with which I had any experience, and the intensity was somewhat troubling.

"I know where we should go to dinner tonight," he said. His voice came from somewhere behind me. I guessed he was standing by the window. "But we'll need to change first."

My fingers began to tremble and, therefore, I stopped buttoning my shirt. Placing my hands on my hips, I leaned against my desk and ducked my head. I allowed the coppery spirals to curtain my features as I tried to absorb the fact that last night and several minutes ago were real events in my life. They were allowed to be my memories.

I brain repeated: *That happened, that happened, that happened, and this is happening.*

And this time, I couldn't blame the wine for my impaired judgment.

I heard him cross the room. Through the filter of my curls, I spied his black leather shoes stop directly in front of me. He paused then tucked my hair away and behind my ears. The infinitely gentle gesture made me feel cherished.

"Hey," he said.

I glanced at him through my eyelashes, and we stared at each other. His tenderness filled me with the acute need to invade the silence.

I cleared my throat, met his gaze fully, and wanted to say something that would ease the growing discord in my Bermuda triangle of brain-heart-vagina; finally, I decided on praise and honesty.

"For the record, that was really enjoyable."

His lips quirked to the side as his gaze moved over my features. "Is there a record? Have you been keeping a log?"

I nodded. "Yes. I keep a log of everything. Data is immeasurably valuable, which is why there are such stringent data access policies for medical research."

I noted that his eyes abruptly affixed to mine in the middle of my statement. "You…do you…" He licked his lips. "Do you actually keep a written log of every time you've had sex?"

I frowned at him. "Don't be ridiculous. I don't write it down. I keep a running log in my head; you know, of things I liked and didn't like; things you liked or seemed to like—that kind of stuff."

He blinked once slowly. "Oh." His eyes were filled with plain bemusement, an unusual expression for him.

Growing uncomfortable under his stalwart scrutiny, I dipped my chin, once again not wanting to meet his gaze directly. It was perhaps too soon to share my freakish tendencies with him.

However, it abruptly occurred to me that perhaps it was *exactly* the right time to share my freakish tendencies with him. Perhaps now was precisely the right time to send him running, which he would inevitably do, before I *really* changed and some Quinn-related biochemical process, likely methylation, flipped on all the girl-gone-wild genetic markers of my DNA and I started zealously pursuing him to get my next Quinn fix.

"It's like shoe sizes," I said, studying him closely.

"Shoe sizes." He blinked slowly again. "What are you talking about?"

"Well, they only make so many shoe sizes. If your feet are larger than the largest shoe size, then you are considered to have freakishly big feet." I touched my thumb and forefinger to the buttons of my shirt, ensuring they were all completely fastened and rigidly buttoning the last two. "You should know that I have similarly inescapable freakish attributes."

Quinn immediately smiled but then suppressed it; he cleared his throat. "Well, what about clowns? They wear freakishly big shoes."

"So?"

"So—big shoes have their place."

"Yeah. In the circus…" I crossed my arms. "You know, with the freaks."

He mimicked my stance. "You are not a freak."

"You should know this about me before this, whatever this is, gets out of hand. I am, indeed, a freak."

"Define out of hand."

My cheeks flamed at how he made the colloquialism sound sordid.

Regardless, I straightened my spine and attempted to come across as reasonable and logical. "You know, before this turns into something else, and you think I'm one way when actually I'm another way."

"Janie, you're not the only one in this room who is freakish."

"No you're not. You're a falcon, and I'm an ostrich."

Looking very predatory, he narrowed his eyes. "First, you are using too many analogies today, and second…"

I interrupted. "See?" I pointed to myself with both hands for emphasis. "Freak!"

He ignored me. "Well, I have to admit that I can totally see the similarities between you and an ostrich."

This surprised me; I thought he would try to defend me against my own insults.

"I…uh…you can?" It was my turn to slow-blink.

"Yes." The slow sexy grin gradually claimed his features.

"Is it because I'm a strange bird who buries my head in the sand?"

He laughed as he rubbed his chin lightly. "No, it's because you have long legs, large eyes, and—" his eyes moved over my hair, "a lot of plumage."

Unthinkingly, I reached for the dreaded crazy-town curls and twisted the bulk of them, hoping to calm their chaos, but to no avail.

He smiled at me.

The full force of his smile felt almost painful.

"So, about dinner…"

"I…uh…I can't go out with you tonight." I was somewhat surprised by how normal my voice sounded. "You know, I'm meeting my knitting group. I told you before, before we…before you…" I huffed.

Quinn tilted his head to the side and he lifted his large hands to cover my shoulders. It was so strange to think that he could touch me at will and wanted to do so; that it was now suddenly ok and expected because the seal had been broken; the line had been crossed.

I held certain truths to be self-evident—truths about myself, about people, about the world, and about how everything fit together—and those were changing.

Everything was changing so fast—everything. The only thing that was constant was change.

His hands moved down my arms and he tugged me toward him, away from the desk. I allowed him to pull me to his chest as he swept the drape of hair from my face. He tilted my chin upward and kissed me softly on the mouth.

He didn't release me right away; his long fingers were now under my chin, but he did shift his head far enough away so that his forehead and nose were in focus. Quinn's eyes gazed into mine; I was once again struck by how blue they were, and I lost some of my breath when I endeavored to exhale.

He frowned. "You still want to go to your knitting group tonight?"

I nodded.

His gaze moved over my features as though looking for the veracity of my head-bob answer.

"You could always skip this week and spend some time with that guy you're dating." His hands moved to my waist, ostensibly to keep me in place.

I swallowed and pressed my lips into a smile. "That is very tempting."

His mouth hooked to the side; he looked hopeful, an expression that seemed all kinds of strange on his typically reserved features. "We could go out to a movie."

I wanted—no, I needed to keep my knitting group commitment. It suddenly felt very important that I be there.

"It's my night to bring the wine. If I don't go, they'll start prank-calling senior citizens and then blame me for the ensuing arrests."

The truth was that I needed time to figure this out. I was very attached to Quinn, but I worried that it was a bit premature. Forming an attachment to someone typically took me years. I'd known him less than six weeks, and already I felt more for him and thought more about him than I'd ever felt for Jon.

For the love of Thor, I was missing him even when we were in the same room together. The force of the feelings, and the virtually all-consuming nature of them, made me want to hide under my desk until my brain and my heart and my vagina came to a consensus.

Therefore, I pushed him away, albeit gently, and insisted on meeting my friends.

His expression morphed into one that was familiar: taciturn. I noticed that Quinn's jaw ticked and his mouth curved downward.

He sighed. It sounded pained.

"Janie I thought that—after—" Quinn licked his lips, released my waist, and stepped away. He crossed his arms over his chest and stood with his feet braced apart as though posturing himself. "What is it?" His tone was chipped.

I swallowed before answering. "What is what?"

The predatory look returned; what felt like hostility reticulated through his glare. "We just…" His voice started to rise, and I watched as he swallowed with difficulty, glanced away, looked back into my eyes, and sighed again. "You want to go spend time with your knitting group, tonight, after what just happened? After what happened last night?"

I started to worry my lip with my teeth, my eyes wide with feelings I found it difficult to explain. "Yes?"

"Yes?" His eyebrows rose expectantly. "Is that a question?"

"No?"

Quinn's eyebrows pulled into a sharp V. "Are we on the same page here at all?"

"I don't know what to say." I hugged myself, gritting my teeth.

We stared at each other; the moment was protracted and stiff like a heavily starched shirt. His gaze—weary, accusatory, but searching—made me feel like I was an imbecile. Maybe I was.

In fact, I knew I was.

I had the opportunity to spend the evening with Quinn, who I really, really liked in every way, and I was passing it up because I was scared—yes, scared.

Fe, fi, fo, fum, scared.

Unable to hold his penetrating glare, I let out a slow breath, closed my eyes, and turned my face away from him, but just my face, and I shook my head.

"I don't know what to say." My voice sounded strangely lost to my own ears.

I felt rather than saw him shift closer. "If you're not interested in me as something permanent, then you need to tell me now."

My short laugh was involuntary and immediate, as were my words. "God, Quinn, you have no idea how permanent I'd like this to be. I'd like us to be Twinkies and cockroaches, death and taxes. But I…"

His hands were on me again, on my waist, slipping around to my back, pressing me to his chest, pulling me into an embrace. I automatically grabbed fistfuls of his shirt and clung to him.

"Then stay with me tonight." His words were warm against my ear, and the earlier saturation of irritation was now absent. He sounded almost relieved.

"I just need..." My breath was ragged. I'd journeyed into uncharted waters, and my unintentional confession didn't calm my unease, but it didn't exacerbate it either.

I was in emotional limbo.

I rested my head against his shoulder and breathed him in; he was so warm, like a furnace. I closed my eyes.

Finally, I said the only thing that made sense, which was made easier by the anonymity of darkness behind my closed eyelids. "I don't know what I'm doing. I'm afraid. I'm not used to it."

I felt him smile against my neck where he'd dipped his head, and his lips brushed against my shoulder. He pulled away, slowly, with obvious reluctance.

One of his big palms caressed my cheek; his fingers pulled through my hair and forced my head back.

"Look at me."

I took a deep breath, then opened my eyes.

Most of his earlier frustration was absent, and the way he looked at me made me feel uncomfortably but deliciously aware that we were pressed together from the waist down.

"We'll go out tomorrow night, ok?" He kept his thumb on my face, rubbing it slowly over my cheekbone in trance-inducing circles.

I nodded.

"And you'll spend the entire evening with me?" Quinn's chin dipped to his chest so that he was peering at me through his eyebrows. "No feminist comic book organizing? No wine club knitting?"

"It's a knitting group with wine drinking involved, but yes: I will spend the entire evening with you." My chin wobbled just a little, making my voice shaky and raw.

He may have detected the flimsiness of my emotional limbo because he smiled at me in a way that relieved the pressure of his earlier frustration and began calming the muddled upheaval.

"Ok." His fingers dropped from my hair, and he leisurely gained a step backward, his hands stuffing into his pants pockets like they needed to be restrained. The smile grew somewhat wistful as his eyes moved over my face. "I can wait."

CHAPTER TWENTY-THREE

It was Marie's turn to host knit night. Quinn insisted that he would drive me to my knitting group leaving no room for discussion. He walked me to the door of Marie's apartment building and kissed me goodbye. It was a devastating kiss, and when he left, I felt part of me leave with him.

Needless to say, it was a disconcerting sensation.

He also insisted, before he left, that I promise to call him while I sorted through my comic books later that night. He claimed to be interested in learning all about how second-wave feminism influenced comic books of the late twentieth century.

Somehow, I found the assertion dubious.

Elizabeth met me at the door, and I floated through Marie's well-decorated apartment without really seeing anything or noticing anyone. Had I been more self-aware, I might have detected the stares following my entrance and the quizzical glances exchanged.

My mind was engaged in wanderlust, and not the predilection for wandering; rather, my mind was wandering lustfully. I pressed my fingers to my lips and recalled how Quinn had lifted me to the desk like I weighed nothing, his hot fingers under my skirt, above the lace of my stockings, and…

"Janie?"

I blinked several times, pulled out of my trance, and focused on the person standing directly in front of me, staring at me with what appeared to be mild concern.

It was Ashley.

"Yes?"

"Honestly, girl, where did your mind just go, and do you need a traveling companion?" Ashley's Tennessee twang was hushed. "Are you ok?"

"I...uh..." I continued to blink at her and looked around the room and its inhabitants as if seeing them for the first time. They were all watching me with open concern and curiosity; the only sound breaking the silence was Sandra munching on potato chips.

"I'm sorry," I finally managed. "Were you talking to me?"

Elizabeth was sitting on the couch, her eyes wide and watchful, and she patted the seat next to her. "I asked if you wanted to sit down, but you just stood there."

"Oh! Yes. Yes, sure, I'd love to sit." I ducked my head and moved to claim the seat beside her, letting my purse drop from my shoulder to my feet.

"Where is your travel bag? Did you drop it off at the apartment already?" Elizabeth eyed me with suspicion, but her tone was light and conversational.

"No, not yet. I went to the office after I landed."

Marie handed me a plate with potato chips and onion dip and shared a look with Fiona over my head. "How was your trip?"

"It was..." I blushed uncontrollably as a giant grin mounted a hostile takeover of my face. I tucked my chin to my chest and allowed my hair to fall forward and shield my expression.

There was a sharp intake of breath. "You didn't!" Elizabeth exclaimed. "Oh, my God!"

"Wait...what? What happened?" Ashley said, overhearing Elizabeth's outburst.

I squeezed my eyes shut as the room erupted in voices. Elizabeth was bouncing up and down on the couch next to me, spilling my potato chips all over the place. She was chanting, "You did it! You did it!"

"What? What did she do?" Kat's quiet but curious words cut through the noise.

"She had hot monkey sex with McHotpants!" Reverberations from Elizabeth's bouncing almost made me topple off the sofa onto the floor. I abandoned the paper plate to my lap and gripped the cushion on either side of me, which proved to be a very good thing when I was, a moment later, tackled by a bear hug.

"Praise the Lord!" Sandra had me in a death squeeze with one of her legs crossed over my lap. A split second later, greasy potato chip fingers were on my cheeks, and she lifted my face to hers. Her Texas drawl was even more pronounced than usual. "When Elizabeth told us you were giving him the cold shoulder, I was terribly afraid I'd never be able to live vicariously through your sexcapades." She gave me a sudden, fast, closed-mouth kiss then held my head to her breast as one would do with a child. "If you didn't climb that man like a tree, I was going to have to get all lumberjack on his ass."

At this point, I was laughing and, admittedly, snorted.

"What does that even mean?" Marie, also laughing, was trying to detangle Sandra from my limbs. "And give the poor girl some space so she can tell us everything, and I do mean everything." Marie succeeded in pulling Sandra off me and began gathering the scattered chips. I tried to help.

Elizabeth *squeeeeeed* again and shifted on the couch so that she was facing me; she hugged a pillow to her chest, her eyes lit with excited merriment. "Start from the beginning! Leave nothing out, and tell us exactly what happened."

"And make sure to describe everything in inches. I can't do the metric conversion in my head," Ashley added, leaning back and sipping her red wine.

I covered my face with my hands and shook my head. "Gah! I don't even know where to start!"

"Start with the taking off of the clothes!" Kat's suggestion made me burn a brighter shade of red.

"You don't understand; a lot has happened." I sighed; my hands dropped to my skirt and I picked at the hem. "I found out that Quinn is not…well, he is my boss, and then there is Jon and my sister, and then Kat, and the reason I was laid off…"

"Give her a minute!" Fiona said, scolding the group, and then she added, "Let her gather her thoughts; otherwise, she might leave out the best parts."

I TRIED TO tell them what happened, and I managed to relay the facts, but I was a woefully inadequate storyteller when it came to reciting intricate details.

At one point, Ashley said, "Oh, my God, Janie. How can you make everything sound like a boring police report?"

"Oh, geez…" Marie bit her lip, her blue eyes pinning me with concern. "Are you ok, hon? I can't believe all that happened in one week."

"Obviously she's ok," Sandra interrupted, setting her knitting on the table and taking a gulp of her beer. "What I want to know is who won the game of strip poker?"

Elizabeth grabbed my hand. "I can't believe he owns the company. I did not see that coming."

"I can't believe Jon slept with your psycho sister," Ashley chimed in. "That bitch is *cr-aaaaa-zy*."

"Who won the poker game, Janie?" Fiona's soft voice drew my attention, and her perceptive eyes were narrowed in a way that made me nervous.

I swallowed. "It was a tie."

"Hmm…" Fiona pressed her lips together in a contemplative line. "So the two of you are dating?"

I shook my head as though to clear it. "I guess so."

"And is that what you want?" Fiona pressed.

I nodded before I realized my head was moving. "Yes." My chin trembled a little. "Yes, but it's scary, you know?"

"Oh, Janie." Fiona smiled at me, her elfish eyes twinkling. "That's how you know it's real."

♥♥♥

I texted Quinn that night when I left knitting:

Won't be organizing my comic books; instead am planning to pass out from exhaustion as soon as I make it home.

He responded:

Ok. I'll take a rain check on the call. See you tomorrow after work. FYI guards will make sure you get home ok.

Then, a minute later:

I miss you. You should spend the night here tomorrow.

Then, thirty seconds later:

Or you could come over now. I promise I'll let you sleep.

I thought about it.

I thought about it; my head said no and my vagina said yes and my heart said *I don't know! I'm emotionally inhibited! Leave me alone!*

I was peripherally aware of and recognized the guards shadowing me on my short walk home. Marie lived in our neighborhood just three blocks away. Elizabeth had a night shift at the hospital and left the group a little early. It was a cold night, and my cheeks stung as the Chicago wind whipped against my face, threading through my loose hair and tossing it fretfully around my shoulders.

The cold air felt sobering. I responded to Quinn's last text:

If I come over, I won't want to sleep. Go to bed.

I slipped my cell into my coat and ascended the steps to my building. Almost immediately, I felt the phone buzz in my pocket. I glanced at the screen as I undid the lock and headed for the stairs:

You should definitely come over now.

I smiled, my skin warming, my cheeks turning pink. He could make me blush via text message.

I climbed the flights distractedly, touching the screen of my phone and typing a reply while grinning like a doofus.

No. We both need sleep. Go to bed.

As a second thought, and before I could stop myself, I added one last bit because it was true, and I suddenly wanted him to know:

I miss you too.

I opened the door to my apartment as I hit send on the phone, shut the door, and slid the lock. I took a deep breath and leaned against the partition. I allowed my head to fall against it as I closed my eyes and wondered how it could be possible that I'd only been away from home less than forty-eight hours. So much had changed since the last time I'd been here.

"What the hell is wrong with you?"

I stiffened, my eyes opening as wide as saucers as I searched for the owner of the voice. Even before I saw her, I knew who it was.

Jem.

CHAPTER TWENTY-FOUR

SHE STOOD IN the hallway with her shoulder against the wall. Her arms were crossed over her chest, and her chin was tilted up in the proud, stubborn way she usually employed when faced with—well, anyone.

She was dressed in dark wash jeans, brown boots, and a white long-sleeve shirt—clothes that were considerably tamer than what she usually wore; however, it was cold outside, I reasoned, and I didn't actually *see* her anymore. Her hair looked like mine: long and curly, and generally unruly. It was even the same color. Even though she was at least two sizes thinner than I was, I immediately understood how I could be mistaken for her doppelganger, especially at a distance.

I blinked at her, wondering at first whether she were real or imagined, and hoping for the latter. Before I could think to speak, Jem's raspy Peppermint Patty voice interrupted my internal debate.

"Well?"

I considered her for a long moment before asking, "How did you get into the apartment?"

Jem shrugged. "I pretended to be you. I told your super that I lost my keys. He let me in."

"Well, that's just great." I sighed heavily and stepped into the apartment. I pulled off my brown wool jacket, hung it on the coat rack, and eyeballed her.

"Aren't you happy to see your baby sister?" She shifted, her lips pressing into an irritated line.

I walked past her into the living room then moved to the kitchen. I suddenly needed a drink. Jem followed me and hovered at the counter, leaning across it. She watched me as I poured myself orange juice and tequila.

"You sure that's a good idea?"

I ignored the question and mixed the liquids together with a spoon.

"You any better at holding your liquor? Last time I saw you drink you passed out from five shots of vodka."

"I didn't pass out. I puked on my SAT proctor." I wasn't upset about it—not anymore. I just knew that when Jem was around, it was important to be as accurate and precise as possible.

"Whatever."

"Why are you here?" I took a long swallow of my drink.

"I told you I was coming to visit."

We stared at each other for several long moments, and then I asked her again. "Why are you here?"

She straightened slowly and crossed her arms over her chest. "I'm visiting Chicago, and I need a place to stay for a few days."

I shook my head. "You've been in Chicago for weeks. Why now?"

Her eyes narrowed almost imperceptibly as her chin lifted. "What do you know about that?"

I took another swallow of my juice then set it down on the counter. "I know a lot."

As she studied me, I noted that her glare was hard and guarded, just as I remembered it. She spoke slowly as though choosing her words carefully. "Who told you I've been in Chicago for weeks?"

"Jon." I rolled my glass between my palms to keep my hands busy, wanting to move, wanting to escape, wanting to punch her in the face, wanting to eat a granola bar.

Her expression didn't change; her gaze didn't even waver. "He's an asshole, you know."

"So are you." That granola bar was sounding better and better. I set my drink on the counter and started pilfering the pantry.

"Yeah, but I don't pretend about it. He justifies all his douche-baggy behaviors by calling it love. Get me a glass."

I glanced over my shoulder, watched her unscrew the tequila. "Now you're going to drink my tequila?"

"Yes."

I shrugged then moved to the cabinet that held the cups; passed one to her then turned my attention back to the Hunt for the Red Granola.

"What was the plan, Jem? Why did you do it?" I didn't precisely care why she slept with Jon. Rather, I didn't like the silence, and it seemed like a reasonable topic of conversation given the circumstances.

"Blackmail, of course."

"Of course." I found the granola bars and pulled out two, passed her one and ripped the other open with my teeth. I always struggled with opening single-serving items such as bags of M&M's or condoms.

"He, of course, fucks it all up by telling you the truth." Jem poured a hefty amount of tequila into the glass but didn't drink.

"Why the blackmail?"

"I needed the money."

"Why?"

Jem held my gaze for a long moment, sniffed, and then moved her eyes over the contents of the small kitchen as though taking inventory. She took a swallow of the tequila but didn't grimace.

I took this opportunity to study her; for the first time I could recall in a long time, Jem looked patently uneasy. Abruptly, I found that I was enjoying the silence. I enjoyed smacking my lips when I took a sip of my Tequila and orange juice, and I enjoyed the way the loud crunch of the granola bar sounded magnified by her tense disquiet.

When it became clear that she had no intention of answering my question, I decided to ask, with my mouth full of crunchy candied oats, "Can I guess?" A few of the loose pieces of my cereal bar flew from my lips and landed on the counter. It was obnoxious and gross, and I loved it.

Jem shifted her weight from one foot to the other, swirling her neat tequila, still not meeting my gaze. "Sure."

"Ok, I'll take three guesses." I set my food on the counter, gulped my orange juice, and cracked my knuckles. "Guess number one: You need the money to go to college."

Her eyes lifted to mine; a small, genuinely amused smile tugged at the corner of her lips. "Yep, that's it. I got into MIT, but I just need the two hundred and fifty grand to cover the books for my first semester."

I returned her smile. I couldn't remember the last time I smiled at her, sincere or not.

I shook my head slowly. "No, no. That's not it. Let me try again." I cleared my throat, pursed my lips, and narrowed my eyes. "You plan to start a nonprofit organization and need the startup principal."

She nodded. "Ok, you got me. I want to help orphans learn how to fish for lobsters. If they don't learn about lobster fishing from me, they'll just learn about it on the streets."

"It's not generally called lobster fishing. The main method for catching the Norway lobster is *trawling*, although the large Homarus lobsters are caught almost always with lobster traps."

"Fuck off with the Wikipedia bullshit, Janie."

My smile broadened, but I could feel the bitterness behind it; my mouth tasted like vinegar. "Ah, but I think that's not it either. Ok," I placed my index finger on my chin. I was surprised that she was playing along, joking with me, and it occurred to me that Jem might have no expectation that I would guess correctly. I inhaled deeply. "Let me think…"

"Maybe it's both of those. Maybe I want to go to college so I can start a nonprofit."

I snapped my fingers, almost startling her. "I've got it!"

"You found me out. I want to adopt all the Dalmatians in Boston and turn them into a fur coat." Her voice was, of course, deadpan as she said this. Jem lifted the tequila to her lips.

"No…" I hesitated, and then took another deep breath. "You're running from a skin-head named Seamus who has crazy neck tattoos, and he wants to kill you."

Jem held perfectly still, her eyes boring into mine, her glass mid-air. I allowed several seconds to pass. I noted that she didn't appear to be amused anymore.

My hand found and closed over the discarded granola bar wrapper. I crinkled it with my fingers and continued. "And you need the money so you can hide."

Jem took another gulp of the brown liquid then lowered the glass. Her expression was inscrutable. This was the Jem I knew. I couldn't remember a time when she didn't look at the world (and me) with a granite-like inflexibility. Her chest expanded slowly as if she was taking a calming breath.

"How do you know that?" So quiet; her voice was so quiet that I almost didn't hear the words.

I tried to mirror her impassive mask, but I knew I was failing. I could feel the heat of resentment pour out of my fingertips and eyeballs. I felt the chilling warmth of it in every breath I took.

"Lucky guess." I licked my lips; they tasted sweet from the orange juice.

We stared at each other in silence for a long time. I wanted to yell at her. I wanted to ask her if she ever thought about anyone but herself. I wanted to ask her when and why she decided to be the crazy Morris girl instead of the sweet, or gregarious, or well-mannered, or any other version of girl she could have chosen to be besides crazy.

She broke the silence. "I need the money."

I sighed and glanced at my almost empty glass. My fingertips rubbed my forehead. I was going to have a headache.

"I know."

"No, Janie, I *really* need the money."

My gaze flickered to hers, and I was surprised to find that fear had replaced some, not all, of the boulder of inflexibility. I sighed.

"I don't have any money."

"But Jon has money."

I shook my head. "I doubt he'll give you any money."

"But he'll give it to you. If you ask him, he'll give you anything."

I bit my top lip to silence my abrupt and unexpected urge to scream at her. The impulse was so sudden I had to swallow. My hands were shaking.

I was angry.

I couldn't speak, so I shook my head again.

"Fuck, Janie! It's the least he can do after cheating on you."

And then I laughed. At first it was a short burst, completely involuntary. Then, when I met her glare, another hysterical giggle spewed forth and I was lost. Soon I was laughing so hard that my side and my jaw hurt. I had to stagger to the couch to keep from falling to the floor.

Nothing about this situation was funny. I was pretty certain I had just cracked up.

"So, what? You're not going to forgive me for sleeping with your douchebag boyfriend?"

My mouth fell open. I didn't think it was possible for her behavior to surprise me at this point. I was wrong.

However, I was so practiced at numbing my feelings around my family—in their presence, when I thought about them, when I recalled my childhood—that my surprise was short-lived. It was like looking at them and my past through a microscope; they were an unfortunate science experiment.

"Jem." I lifted my hands from my lap and pressed my palms to my chest. "I can't forgive you if you're not sorry."

Her green eyes narrowed into slits. "Yeah, I guess you're right." Her head bobbed in a small movement, and her voice was quiet. "I'm not sorry. I'd do it again. And if you had another rich boyfriend who I thought I could get money from, I'd sleep with him too."

Her words made me flinch. I closed my eyes so I wouldn't have to look at her.

Her raspy voice was closer when she next spoke. "We're not so different, you know."

I didn't open my eyes at this ridiculous statement; instead, I leaned further into the couch and willed her gone.

She continued. "I don't think Jon is a guy who is as faithful as his options. He thinks you're it; you're the one. You don't seem to care that he cheated on you, and you don't give a shit about him."

I huffed at this. "One minute you say he's an asshole for cheating on me, and the next minute you're telling me I'm the bad guy for not caring enough that he cheated on me. Jem, I broke up with him."

"Yeah, but you don't seem too depressed about it."

I opened my eyes, but I was slumped so deeply into the sofa that my gaze made it no higher than the edge of the coffee table. "This isn't going to work. I'm still not going to ask Jon for the money."

Jem's face was unsurprisingly void of emotion. "You are just like me, Janie. You left Jon, an annoyingly nice guy who you dated for years, and who loves you more than anything, and now you feel nothing but relief; am I right? You're relieved that you don't have to be bothered about taking his feelings into account anymore. You have the means to save your baby sister from certain death, and you can't even muster enough pretend sentiment to try. You're incapable of feeling any depth of emotion, Janie, just like me—and just like mom."

I met her gaze calmly, even though her words met their intended target with swift precision. Jem's overly simplified assessment of the Jon situation was very close to my current view of reality, but I wasn't yet finished sorting through all the reasons why that relationship ended. It was true; I hadn't been as attached to Jon as he may have been to me. It was also true that I was feeling mostly relief about the end of the relationship. However, he cheated on me, then tried to lie about it, and then had me fired. Those were all his decisions.

I knew that I wasn't blameless, but I was not the first girl in the history of forever to stay with a guy because he was ideal on paper. For the love of Thor! He was my first boyfriend. I was allowed to make mistakes.

The other charge, about not having enough *pretend sentiment* to save Jem, was the one that made me furious. That fury reassured me that I was capable of emotional depth.

I hated her.

I shifted my gaze from hers, and when I spoke, I spoke to the room.

"You can stay here if you want. I usually sleep on the couch, but you can have it."

She was quiet for a long moment, and I knew she was debating whether to push me further. To my surprise, she didn't.

"Where will you sleep?"

I inhaled, then released, a deep breath. "Elizabeth is at the hospital for a shift, so I'll sleep in her bed."

"You're still friends with Elizabeth?"

I nodded, hesitated, and then lifted my eyes to hers. Her expression was unchanged, still inflexible, but her eyes moved between mine with a touch of approaching interest. It was a subtle yet rare demonstration of feeling.

Jem swallowed, licked her lips. "That's good. She seems to care about you."

"She does." For reasons I couldn't immediately understand, Jem's words made my eyes sting, so I blinked.

Jem twisted her lips to the side and let her arms fall from her chest. With a small sigh, she walked to the entryway and picked up a black leather jacket.

"I can't wear this anymore. You can keep it or whatever. Get rid of it. I don't care." She tossed it to me on the couch and I automatically caught it; it smelled like her: cigarettes, clean soap, and violence. Memories careened over and through me so suddenly that I had to grip the jacket to steady myself.

I loved her once.

When she was little, maybe three or four years old, I used to give her piggyback rides around our neighborhood, or pull her in a wagon behind my bike. She liked everything fast.

She started to smoke when she was eleven. There was nobody to tell her no, even though I tried. She laughed at me then. Growing up in the same house, I often felt she was laughing at me. It didn't anger me. It made me sad.

The stinging in my eyes intensified. I bit then pulled my top lip between my teeth. I couldn't speak; there was a giant knot in my throat. I watched her as she picked up my brown wool coat from the rack and pulled it over her shoulders.

"I'm taking this."

My mouth hitched to the side and I leaned back against the couch, her black leather jacket still on my lap.

"That's fine," I responded, even though I knew she wasn't asking my permission.

"I'm leaving. I don't know if…" Jem fingered the middle button of my coat, her eyes rigid but intense. She buttoned the coat.

When she didn't continue, I cleared my throat and found my voice. "Where will you go?"

Jem shrugged and shook her head; she stuffed her hands into the fur-lined pockets of my jacket. "I don't know."

Without pausing, without a wave or a smile or a goodbye, Jem turned and left.

My door made a soft, final click as she closed it.

CHAPTER TWENTY-FIVE

I SLEPT HARD and had strange dreams.

The dreams were the troubling kind where I thought the action and events were genuine, but on waking and in retrospect, I realized they were obviously completely implausible.

The one I remembered most intensely on waking was about losing my teeth. The fragments of bone fell out of my mouth every time I opened it to speak, and they ran away, though they had no legs, which, in the dream, sent me into a panic.

There is nothing quite like watching one's own legless teeth running away.

Tourists kept accidentally stepping on my teeth. I was forced to chase my molars and canines down Michigan Avenue while dodging black-socked sightseers wearing shorts, white Keds, and rainbow visors. When my alarm went off, I actually ran my tongue over the back of my teeth to make sure they were all still present, in my mouth, and securely situated.

By the time I arrived at work and greeted Keira at the front desk, the last miens of my dental-nightmare had almost completely dispersed. However, a lingering sense of disquiet and a completely irrational foreboding remained. My chest felt tight, heavy, and uncomfortable, as if I had some terrible combination of bronchitis and gastroenteritis.

During the short walk down the hall to my office, instead of dwelling on my increasingly complex feelings for Quinn or the unpleasant altercation with my sister, my mind ambled. I wondered about and made a mental note to check on the content of carpet fibers. More precisely, what made the current generation of carpets stain resistant? Were eco-friendly approaches to carpet manufacturing currently the norm? What country could claim the title as leader in office-carpet exports?

Still studying the carpet, I opened the closed door to my office and was startled out of my floor-focus by the presence of unexpected company.

Olivia was inside my office standing behind my desk. Her back was stiff and her eyes were wide as they met mine; her hand flew to her chest, and she sucked in a loud breath.

I hesitated, frowned, and glanced at the name outside the office to ensure I had the right door. When I confirmed that it was, indeed, my office, and she was, indeed, in my office, I returned my gaze to her and waited for an explanation.

A protracted period of silence stretched as we eyeballed each other. She looked very well assembled, as usual, and, even though I was the one to find her unexpectedly in my office with the door closed, she appeared to be waiting for me to explain my presence.

I waited two beats longer, then lifted my eyebrows as my chin dipped. "Well?"

"Can I help you?" Olivia crossed her arms over her chest and leaned her hip against my desk.

I blinked at her and wondered if I were still dreaming. "What are you doing in my office?"

"It's not your office; it doesn't belong to you; it's the company's office."

She huffed.

She actually huffed.

It was a breathy sound, overly exaggerated, and combined with a bit of an exhaled snort.

I crossed my arms and mimicked her stance, mostly to hide the fact that my hands were clenched in fists. "Olivia. What are you doing in the office that has been assigned to me by the company, with all my papers and confidential reports, with the door closed?"

She raised a single, impressively well-groomed eyebrow. "I'm looking for the updated schematic of the Las Vegas space."

I shook my head. "It hasn't been sent to us by the group in Las Vegas yet; they said they would email it by Friday."

"Oh. Well, then, just send it over to me when you get it. No one can move forward with the new plans until you send it to the group." Olivia's tone and manner were so flippant that I almost actually felt like it was my fault that the client hadn't yet sent the schematic.

I clenched my jaw. "As soon as I receive it from the client, I will distribute it to group."

Olivia issued me a tight-lipped non-smile and moved passed me into the hallway without any further remark.

What. The. Hell...?

Somewhat grudgingly rooted in place, uncertain whether I wanted to push the issue by hall heckling her or just simply mope somberly. I watched her retreating form as she left; her steps hurried, her pace almost road-runner frantic. Then, shaking myself, I eye-rolled all the way into my office and heaved a gigantic sigh; my earlier uneasiness had been replaced—or, more accurately, substituted—with immense irritation.

I approached my desk and glanced at its contents; all the papers and folders were neatly stacked into piles, just as I'd left them yesterday. I checked the drawers and found that they were still locked. My desktop PC was also locked. If she'd been looking for something in particular, I could see no outward sign that anything had been rummaged or disturbed.

The tightness in my chest constricted, and was now vacillating between annoyance and anxiety. I fell into my office chair. I attempted to clear my mind by staring out the window, and for a few moments, I allowed myself to drift on white, puffy clouds visible in the distance.

For the first time in recent memory, I successfully endeavored to sit and be still, and to think about nothing at all. I gazed at the sky until my eyes felt dry.

At some indeterminable time later, the sound of laughter and normal office conversation pulled me out of my trance. I blinked, rubbed my closed lids, and decided to make an honorable attempt at getting work done. I didn't think about carpet, or Quinn, or Jem, or Olivia. Instead, I clung to the impersonal numbness of my task list.

Thus, ignoring the stack of memos and printed reports on my desk, I lost myself in spreadsheets and glorious pivot tables, and to requirements, documents, and billing-software workflows. The tension around my lungs eased with every passing hour, with deeper immersion into numbers and Visio swim lane charts.

The sound of my office door closing abruptly brought my attention back to the present and to the man who'd just entered.

I blinked. I gaped. I stood.

Simmering warmth slid from my stomach to the tips of my ears, inexplicably relaxing any remaining tightness in my chest like a salve as I registered that Quinn was standing in front of the closed door. He was smiling in that odd, quiet way of his, not with any perceivable curve of his mouth but rather with a subtle glint in his eyes and a lift of his chin.

My very obvious grin at his presence couldn't be helped any more than I could catch those errant teeth in my dream. I loved that he was wearing faded blue jeans and a long-sleeved black shirt. He hadn't shaved since I'd last seen him.

"Hi."

"Hi," I auto-responded; spreadsheets and pivot tables immediately forgotten.

He crossed to me and gave me a quick, soft kiss before I could discern or properly appreciate his intention. Immediately he straightened and held a paper bag between us. It was yellow and grease-stained; black writing spelled out *Al's Beef.*

"I have Italian beef and French fries."

I pulled my attention from the bag and met his narrowed blue gaze. Again, a sincere automatic smile further opened my features to him. "You brought me Al's Beef for breakfast?"

His lips pulled to the side, his eyes moving between mine, and he turned his head just slightly. "No, I brought you lunch. It's almost three."

My mouth opened and I glanced at the watch on my wrist. It was, indeed, almost 3:00 p.m.

"Oh my gosh."

Quinn placed the bag of food on the desk and started distributing its contents: sandwich and fries for me; sandwich and fries for him. He even pulled out two green food baskets, presumably so that we could enjoy an authentic Al's Beef dine-in experience within the comfort of my office.

"Sit." He motioned to my chair as he claimed the seat on the other side of my desk.

I obeyed, but I didn't unwrap my food immediately; instead, I opted to watch him until my stomach grumbled, demanding my attention. It presumably just now realized that I hadn't eaten all day. The smell of fries and roast beef made my mouth water.

Mimicking his movements, I dumped my fries into the basket and pulled the paper away from the Italian beef, revealing a deliciously soggy sandwich. He was already eating, the sandwich disappearing by fourths with each bite. He seemed so completely at ease, as though his appearance at the office and bringing me lunch was an everyday occurrence—as though it was expected.

Closing the door for privacy, sneaking a swift kiss, bringing lunch to eat together; people who were dating did these things. I knew this. I used to date someone. But with Quinn, everything felt meaningful in a way it never had with Jon.

I picked up my sandwich and lifted it to my mouth but didn't take a bite.

I was too busy noticing things about him that I couldn't recall caring to notice about anyone else. I was acutely aware of Quinn's movements; of the placement of his hands on the sandwich; his nonchalant, carefree mood; how he was dressed and the amount of skin he'd left exposed; the length of his hair. The number of details felt overwhelming, but I was greedy for specifics, greedy to know and memorize everything about him.

I felt like a kettle set to boil; any minute I was going to steam up from all the details and start screaming.

I blurted, "I'm not really sure how to do this." I abruptly dropped the sandwich into the basket and leaned backward in my chair.

Quinn waited until he finished chewing to respond; his eyes moved from me to the sandwich. "Do what?"

"Be the girl you're dating."

His mouth curved upward in a trace of a smile. "Do you want a handbook for that too? Because I'd like to be involved in sketching the diagrams if you do."

I pressed my lips together and pummeled him with a single French fry. He laughed, obviously unable to contain himself, and my face flamed.

"You know what I mean." I didn't look at him; rather, I stared at my basket of Italian beef and seasoned fries.

He stopped laughing but not all at once; he allowed it to taper off gradually. I glanced at him through my eyelashes; a huge smile still asserted itself over his features, and he was looking at me with a sanguine, untroubled expression.

He looked happy.

My heart fluttered; yes, it fluttered uncontrollably. The flutter morphed into a flapping monsoon as I watched his smile fade from broad to slight and his gaze darken, intensify, and scorch.

"You're so beautiful." It was said on a sigh, as though he had said and thought the sentiment at the same time and hadn't quite realized the words had been spoken aloud.

I felt the compliment acutely, but in a slightly scary and thrilling way. I lifted my head and blinked at him, my mouth slightly agape. His eyes traveled over my lips, hair, neck, then lower. I noticed he was holding his napkin as though someone might be inclined to steal it.

He also seemed to be greedy for details.

I tucked my hair behind my ears and rubbed my neck. Everywhere his eyes moved itched and tingled.

I cleared my throat. "You too."

He met my gaze and studied me; his smile was still slight. "It's different with you; it's not just the way you look."

In a surprising turn of events, the comment on my inner beauty made me squirm to a much greater degree than the compliment aimed at my physical features. I wasn't so sure that inner Janie was at all a beautiful person. Jem's words from last night; the apparent callous disinterestedness with which I regarded the end of my relationship with Jon, my unwillingness to help my sister in her time of need, had me doubting whether I was anything other than a selfish and vapid replica of my mother.

"Are you admitting your beauty is only skin deep?" I tilted my head to the side, wanting to tease him rather than dwell on how high, on a scale from one to ten, I would rank on the vapid meter.

Quinn breathed in through his nose, his eyebrows lifted, and his attention shifted to his hands; he loosened his grip on the napkin and began twisting it between his thumb and forefinger.

He didn't respond. I took his silence as confirmation.

"I think you're wrong."

He continued to twist the napkin wordlessly until it resembled a short length of rope.

I considered him at length. There was still a lot I didn't know about Quinn, and therefore, I deliberated the possibility that he was right. He could be a virtually empty shell of a person with a stunning façade, impressive intellect, and a foil wit.

Then, I frowned because the prospect felt dissonant with reality.

"No, you are a good guy." I tilted my head to the side and allowed my gaze to move over his lips, hair, neck, then lower to where his heart was beating. "We see the strengths and faults in others that we do not or cannot recognize in ourselves."

"Janie." His small smile, more of a grimace, struck me as brittle when our eyes finally met.

"Are you trying to scare me off?"

He nodded his head, but on a sigh, he replied, "No."

"Do you have any current nefarious plans? Are you plying me with Italian beef as part of an evil plot?" I motioned between us and asked, "Is this an elaborate lie? Are you planning to lure me into a false sense of security, have your way with me, light me up, and then toss me aside like a match or a Christmas tree?"

His face was serious. "No."

"Then why do you believe that you lack internal beauty?"

"Because I only do things for selfish reasons."

"Like dating me?"

"Dating you is completely selfish."

The comment struck me mute, but I recovered. "If…if you were being selfish, then you'd still be a Wendell and I'd be a slamp."

He shook his head. "If you were a slamp, then we wouldn't be exclusive, and you could be with other people."

"And that makes you selfish?"

"That makes me selfish." His eyes pierced me, and his voice was low and sandpapery.

I took the opportunity to munch on a French fry, now cold, and deliberated his words.

"I will say this." Quinn held me with his eyes, his expression increasing in severity as though hovering on the precipice of a meaningful confession. "You make me want to be less of an asshole."

My lashes flapped at him. "Really? Wow." I gulped.

It was a confession of sorts, but it was the type of confession that encouraged my sarcasm rather than my appreciation. The statement struck me as the epitome of noncommittal, pseudo-subtle, self-deprecation; I was amazed by its definitive tepidness.

"That's so poetic. You should write greeting cards: *Dear Dad, thank you for helping me become not as big of a jerk as you are. I'm still a jerk, just not a big jerk like you.*"

Quinn laughed again, but this time with complete abandon; it was a deep, rumbly belly laugh, which, since I was within earshot of the blast radius, was extremely infectious, and I felt it acutely like a touch rather than a sound. He held his hand over his chest and my attention loitered on the spot. Even as I laughed I felt a twist of discomfort emanating from a mirrored location in my own chest.

I ached. I wanted to be close to him. I wanted to know everything about him.

The suddenness of the pain caught me by surprise, and I closed my eyes against it, breathing out slowly, collecting myself so I wouldn't give in to my desire to climb over the desk and tackle him where he sat, Italian beef sandwich on his lap, napkin in his hand.

"Janie."

My eyes remained closed but I gave him a slight, evasive, closed mouth smile.

"What are you thinking?"

I swallowed but didn't answer. My heart was racing. I wanted to tell him I was thinking about the fiber content in stain-resistant carpet, but that would have been a lie. Even if I wanted to, and I did want to, I couldn't seem to distract myself from the reality of being with him and all the irrepressible terror and hunger that accompanied it.

"Why are you so afraid?"

"Because I'm not thinking about the fiber content in stain-resistant carpet." My eyes remained stubbornly shut.

"What does that mean?"

"It means…" I lifted my lids and found him surveying me with simple curiosity. I swallowed a new thickness in my throat, knowing that I needed to tell him the truth. "It means my brain finds you more interesting than all the *really* interesting trivial facts I could be contemplating or researching at present."

His answering smile was leisurely and measured. "I think that's the nicest thing anyone has ever said to me."

I returned his smile even though I felt suddenly sober; my eyes were inexplicably watery. "Quinn…" I took a deep, steadying breath. "Quinn, you need to be a good guy. I *need* you to be a good guy."

He nodded, his expression reacting to and echoing my sudden seriousness. "I know. I want to be." Quinn licked his lips as his eyes moved to my mouth. "I will be for you."

CHAPTER TWENTY-SIX

WE LEFT WORK shortly after 4:00 p.m.—together.

Quinn reached for and grabbed my hand. He flashed me a smile and gently held it as we walked down the hallway past a gaping Keira and onto the elevator within plain view of the security desk and its inhabitants, then straight to the lobby. As we walked, fingers threaded together, Quinn caressed the wrinkles of my knuckles with the pad of his thumb and spoke of the dilemma with the corporate client in Las Vegas.

At first, I was fairly preoccupied by our public display of physical contact and managed only single-syllable responses. However, once we were settled in a large black limo, I tried to focus on his words rather than the predictably astonished glances from my coworkers.

But then we sat close together on the bench seat; he lifted my legs so that they were positioned across his, and he fiddled distractedly with my collar, his eyes on the buttons of my business shirt.

I was watching his lips as he spoke. I tried to find my place in the conversation, but the way he looked at me, the closeness of him, the feel of his hands—one on my thigh, one brushing against my neck—made me feel fuzzy-headed and unfocused.

"Janie?"

I blinked, saw his mouth form my name before I heard the word. My eyes widened then met his.

"I'm sorry, what?"

"Are you…did you hear what I said?"

"No," I answered truthfully, my attention moving to his mouth again, which, at the moment, was an attention-hogging lodestone.

Quinn squeezed my leg. "Am I boring you?"

"No." I sighed, allowed my head to rest against his arm behind me, still focused on the bottom half of his face. "I was just thinking about your mouth."

He licked his lips and, to my surprise, his neck and cheeks tinted slightly hot. "What were you thinking about my mouth?"

"I like it."

"What do you like about it?"

Without hesitating, I responded, "Everything: the shape of it, how big your lips are, your tubercle, the curve of your philtrum. Did you know that in traditional Chinese medicine, the shape and color of the philtrum, also called the medial cleft, is supposed to have direct correlation to the health of a person's reproductive system?"

I noticed his eyes flicker to the space between my nose and mouth, seemingly without his expressed consent, and then quickly back to my eyes. "How about that."

I nodded. "There are a lot of fascinating and unusual studies out there that link the shape of a person's mouth to other parts of the human anatomy and its abilities or proclivities."

I noticed his breathing had changed. He swallowed. "Like what?"

I traced my finger over the top of his lip, enjoying the fact that I was actually using my knowledge of random facts as some sort of brainy, academic foreplay, and that Quinn seemed to like it and respond to it.

"Like the Cupid's bow, the double curve of the upper lip. A study out of Scotland reported that women with a prominent cupid's bow are more likely to experience orgasm during sex."

Quinn's attention once again affixed to my lips and then he promptly groaned. "You shouldn't say things like that when I can't do anything about it."

I enjoyed the tortured sound he made and once again met his gaze, which had darkened considerably.

I tried to keep my face straight.

"Then there is the distinction between extrinsic and intrinsic musculature of the tongue."

"You need to stop talking." Quinn grabbed a fistful of my hair and yanked my head back, claiming my mouth with his, and ending my involuntary bubble of laughter.

When he lifted his mouth, I whispered, "Most of the tongue's blood supply comes from the lingual artery."

He kissed me again and again.

If I'd been listening to our ensuing kiss-sloppy conversation, been an observer rather than a participant, I might have rolled my eyes in judgmental exasperation. Admittedly, it was improbable that peer-reviewed medical research citations and correlative studies of human anatomy could get a person, let alone two people, hot and bothered. But there we were, pawing each other with mounting urgency as I recounted theories linking the amount of hair on earlobes and genital arousal.

By the time the limo stopped, we were half dressed, and the buttons of my shirt were scattered all over the floor. Naturally, Quinn had ripped the shirt open with a growl when I mentioned mammary glands.

I frantically pulled away and grasped the useless edges of my shirt. "Oh shit!"

Quinn was still somewhat lost in a fog of lust and moved his hand further up my inner thigh, his mouth seeking mine again. I swatted him away despite the fact that everywhere he touched me protested in delicious agony. Nonsensically, I tried to smooth my hair, *tsking* when my shirt opened again.

"What am I going to do?"

Quinn, finally drawing away from me, pulled a sweater over his bare chest with not a trace of hurry. He lifted a single eyebrow as he adjusted his pants and zipped his fly. The sound made my back stiffen, and I realized how close we'd just been to copulating in the back of a car.

"I think you look good just like that."

I stared at him for two seconds before I smacked him on his infuriatingly well-muscled shoulder.

"My shirt is ripped open, and..." I frantically twisted in my seat and may have shrieked. "Where is my underwear?"

There was no amusement in his voice when he responded, "Someplace safe."

My eyes widened further, and I knew that my mouth was hanging open dumbfounded. I was about to lose my mind.

"Give them back."

"You don't need them."

"Give them back to me right now."

"You should try new things."

"I am not leaving this limo while commando!"

The passenger door on Quinn's side opened, and I yanked the skirt I was wearing back to mid-calf. I didn't miss his dark smile when it was clear that I was not likely to push the underwear issue further until we were in private. By then, it likely wouldn't matter.

Quinn reached for his leather jacket and draped it around my shoulders, zipping the front up to my neck. I swam in the largeness of it, but at least I wasn't going to be walking around with my shirt hanging open. He exited the limo, then held his hand out to me at the threshold. I moved and stood as demurely as possible. When he cleared his throat, I met his gaze and he winked at me, surreptitiously yet suggestively licking his lips.

I followed where he led.

♥♥♥

SOMETIME LATER, NEAR midnight, Quinn gave me my underwear back on the promise that I would wear only underwear until sunrise. The only other option was my birthday suit as he'd confiscated all my other clothes and hidden them somewhere within the massive penthouse he called home.

Of course, he lived in the penthouse.

It was the same building where the boss had purchased five floors for Cypher Systems staff. At first, when we arrived, I thought we were headed to the apartment he'd shown me before. My imagination filled with images of us together in the giant bathtub.

Quinn's tub, as it turned out, was far superior, as was the view and the kitchen, and the bedrooms were more spacious.

The apartment was nearly as sparsely decorated as the unfurnished and unfinished apartment downstairs that we'd toured weeks ago. There was no couch and no chairs in the living room, no table in the dining room, and only a single dresser and bed in the bedroom. The box spring and mattress were on the floor; there was no bedframe. There were no pictures either.

I had a sheet wrapped around myself and, turning away from him, I glanced down at my underwear. They were white cotton and, as I contemplated it, not at all sexy. Most of my undergarments were chosen for comfort, cost, and practicality. I eyeballed him as I pulled on the granny panties, keeping the sheet in place to nonsensically preserve my modesty.

"Why did you hijack my underwear?"

Quinn was lying on his back, his long form stretched on the unmade bed, his hands behind his head, watching me.

He was completely naked. No sheet for him. Nope. No modesty for Quinn. He appeared to be entirely, mindlessly at ease in his own skin. I envied his unabashed ability just to be naked.

I also appreciated it.

"I hate them." His gaze swept from where the sheet covered my bottom to my bare shoulder then back to my hidden thighs; the way he perused my body made me shiver.

I snapped the elastic at my waist beneath the sheet. "Is it because they lack frill?"

He shook his head lazily. "No. I don't care what they look like. I hate all your underwear."

I frowned. "So you're an equal opportunity underwear hater?"

"Only your underwear."

"Underwear serves a critical purpose."

"I don't want to know."

He sat up, swung his legs over the edge of the bed, and reached for me by moving aside the edges of the sheet and hooking a finger in the band of the much-discussed panties. He brought me to his lap, encouraged me to straddle him, and then he peeled the sheet from under my arms. He kept his eyes on mine while he extracted the material, crumpled it, and tossed it away from us. I shivered. He wrapped his arms around my middle so that his arms crossed behind me and his hands warmed the skin of my sides and stomach and brought my front against his.

"You're staying with me tonight. No escape."

I spread my palms over his bare biceps. "You haven't given me much of a choice; you've even taken my sheet. I can't go home clothed only in granny panties. It's supposed to be cold tonight."

He nuzzled my neck and tightened his grip, pressing our chests together. Although I was thoroughly mussed and mollified from our evening of marathon lovemaking, my heart skipped at the contact.

"It's supposed to be cold tomorrow, too. Why did you leave your coat at work?" He asked the words against my skin, kissing a path across my collarbone then biting my shoulder.

I was really and truly enjoying physical contact to the point of craving it, yet I did not allow myself to wonder at this inexplicable transformation. My spoken reply was an automatic, thoughtless, breathy sigh. "I didn't. Jem took it."

Quinn immediately stiffened, and his movements stilled. Abruptly his hands moved to my forearms and he pulled away even as he held me in place. "You saw Jem?"

I met his astonished glare, and my mouth struggled to make sound. I squeaked once or twice before I managed to respond, "Yes."

His eyes seared and scorched, and pinned me with an accusatory stare. "When? Where?"

"I-I-I saw her last night. She was at my…she was waiting for me at my apartment."

"Damn." Quinn clenched his teeth, his jaw and temple ticking, and pulled me abruptly against him in a fierce hug. "Damn it, Janie. You should have called me."

"She didn't stay long." I held on to him tightly even though I didn't precisely understand the ferocity of his reaction.

We held each other for a long moment. My encounter with Jem had been weighing on me like a squatting Sumo wrestler all the previous night and through the morning; but I hadn't thought about her since Quinn showed up in my office with his greasy lunch offering.

I moved my hand in a slow circle over his bare back, a motion I hoped would sooth the unexpected shift in mood. I kissed his temple and whispered, "I don't understand why you are so upset."

"Because Jem is dangerous." I felt his chest expand; he sucked in a capacious breath as though greedy for air. "I don't want her anywhere near you."

I leaned back and forced him to meet my gaze. "She would never hurt me."

His eyes only narrowed. "You're wrong. She would." His voice was like steel. "I really think you should move into this building."

I pressed my lips together but didn't respond.

His hands moved to my face, giant palms cupping my cheeks, long fingers pushing into my hair behind my ears and at my temples. "Please. You don't have to stay here forever. Just please show Elizabeth the apartment and think about it. Think about staying until this Jem business is resolved."

"Quinn, I…" My hands moved up his biceps and settled lightly on his forearms. "You are my boss. You are also the guy I am dating, and now you want to be my landlord?"

He winced then gritted his teeth. "It's not like that."

"Just one of those things—relationships—can complicate, *does* complicate interactions between two people. You can't be everything to me. I have to stand on my own."

He studied me, his stare turning hawkish. "You could move in with me."

I smiled even though my heart felt heavy. "We've been dating less than a month, and besides, I can't afford even one-tenth of the rent on this penthouse."

"I own this place. There is no rent."

"Quinn…"

He cut me off with a kiss and turned us in one fluid movement so that I was lying under him on the bed.

"Just don't say no." He kissed me again. "Not yet." He kissed my neck, and his words and breath were hot and urgent. "I'll give you the key and the code to the building. Promise me you'll show Elizabeth the apartment." He nibbled on my ear and whispered, "And promise me that you'll think about moving in with me."

I nodded, but not mindlessly. I wanted to pacify him so we could get to the good stuff.

He pulled away and his eyes surveyed me. "Promise me."

I nodded again and lifted my hand to tousle his hair. "I promise."

AT SOME POINT in the last forty-eight hours, Quinn had brought my bag from the Vegas trip to his apartment. Therefore, and thankfully, I was able to dress in fresh clothes, ones with buttons, before heading to work.

I learned a bit more about Quinn as a consequence of spending the night at his place;

he doesn't really sleep, he exercises every morning, he eats pastries for breakfast. Quinn was up by five and back from a long run by six thirty.

After his shower, he woke me up in the most pleasant way imaginable.

Yes. That way.

I was standing at his kitchen counter drinking a really delicious latte from one of those marvels of modern mechanics one-touch espresso makers and eating a cherry and cheese Danish by 7:20 a.m. At 7:40 a.m., we were walking to work, a short six-block stroll, holding hands and talking about the day ahead.

Since I had tutoring on Thursdays, we made arrangements to go out again Friday night. He kissed me goodbye at the entrance to the building, leaving me wobbly headed and kneed, at 7:58 a.m. I was in the elevator at eight o'clock on the dot.

What a difference a day makes.

I was still smiling dazedly as I walked down the hall to my office, not really noticing anyone or anything. I sat behind my desk and mindlessly shuffled through the folders. I didn't yet want to lose myself in spreadsheets, so I opted to read through the pile of memos threatening to spill off my desk. It would allow me to continue to revel in all the warm and silky feelings from the previous night and morning.

The first ten or so were actually about my new billing software. The last memo suggested moving the conversation to email. This was typical. Most conversations were initiated via hard-copy memo. After they were determined to be benign in nature, they were moved to email. All memos were to be shredded after they were read.

As he was responsible for the private clients, most of Steven's internal correspondence was hard copy. Since I was responsible for the corporate clients, most of mine was electronic.

I sifted through the correspondence quickly, but then my attention was abruptly ensnared when I spied both my name and Quinn's listed together in a printed copy of an email. I'd never received a printed copy of an email before, and my gaze moved to the email address of the sender. I recognized it as one of the French Tweedle Dee lawyers I'd met on my second day. At first, I skimmed the email, but then after the second sentence, I forced myself to start at the beginning and really, truly read it:

Hi Betty,

Per Mr. Sullivan's request and as discussed during our phone conversation, Jean and I have consulted on the matter of Ms. Morris at length. It is our opinion that Mr. Sullivan's best course of action would be to terminate Ms. Morris's employment as soon as is feasible (without interrupting operations). In such cases as these, it is not unusual or unwarranted to offer a large severance package and release her from the non-compete agreement she signed on initiation of the position.

The reason for termination should not be stated explicitly to Ms. Morris nor inferred/alluded to in any documentation in order to mitigate risk for future recompense.

Furthermore, we advise that Mr. Sullivan not be charged with conducting the dismissal interview. I've taken the liberty of cc-ing Mr. Davies and his administrator to this email as it is our recommendation that he handle the matter as Mr. Sullivan's designee.

The other option is for Ms. Morris to resign her position. In either case, we've drafted a release form that Ms. Morris should sign, and which, regardless of future outcomes, should, as much as is feasible or possible and to the extent allowable by law, absolve Cypher Systems from any related future litigation. I recommend that she sign the release as a condition for receiving the severance.

Please let us know if Mr. Sullivan decides to proceed so that we may move to nullify the non-compete agreement. Likely, Ms. Morris will have great difficulty finding new employment until it is expunged.

Henry LeDuc, JD

CHAPTER TWENTY-SEVEN

"HAVE YOU SHOWN this to him? Have you asked him about it?"

I shook my head and chewed on my thumbnail, staring over Elizabeth's shoulder at nothing in particular.

We were in the Starbucks four blocks away from my building. As soon as I found the email, I used the dratted cell phone to call her and beg her to meet me for lunch. As it turned out, I woke her up at home, and she immediately left to meet me for coffee. Thus, she was dressed in pajamas and boots.

"I have to be honest, Janie. I don't speak lawyer gibberish, so I'm not really sure what this says. But," Elizabeth reached for and held my hand, drawing my attention to her. "I think you should ask him about it before you jump to any conclusions."

I swallowed. "I know. I will."

Elizabeth's frown deepened. "How did you get a copy of this? Did they accidentally email it to you?"

"No, it was with my memos on my desk. Someone must've…" I blinked, my eyes losing focus again, and then I shuttered my lids.

Of course.

"What? What is it?"

"Olivia." Blood drained from my face even as heat spread up my neck. "I found Olivia, Carlos's assistant, in my office yesterday morning. She must have left it there."

"The one who gives you dirty looks at work? Any chance it's fake, then?"

"I don't think so." I debated the theory for a moment but dismissed the possibility. "It's real. She wanted me to find it."

Elizabeth rolled her lips into her mouth and between her teeth, surveying me. Finally, she said, "After everything you've told me about him, about Quinn, I seriously doubt he wants to fire you."

I nodded and was surprised to find that I agreed with Elizabeth's assessment. "I don't believe it either."

She smiled a wry hopeful smile. "So, does that mean, despite this strange email and its indecipherable but damning contents, you trust Quinn?"

I nodded again without thinking and spoke my thoughts aloud. "It does. I do." I met her clear blue eyes. "I do trust him. I think there has to be a perfectly reasonable explanation."

"Yay!" Elizabeth's smile was full and immediate; she squeezed my hand. "Although I don't advocate love as a rule, I can honestly say yay for you and Quinn!"

My head tilted to the side in a very Quinn-like gesture before I could stop the movement. "What are you talking about?"

"You and Quinn." Elizabeth sipped at her black coffee. "You are in love, Janie."

"I'm not in love! I'm in lust, I'm in deep infatuation, I'm in—in—in definite *a lot of like* with Quinn, but I'm not…"

Was I in love?

Though I loathed to admit it, that was a distinct possibility.

I loved being around Quinn. I loved talking to him. I loved his laugh and, at times, his bossiness. I loved his self-doubt and I loved his determination. I loved that he seemed to be changing, wanted to change, even as I was changing. I loved that we were growing into something new, together. I loved trusting him. I loved making love to him—really loved making love to him.

If it walks like a duck and quacks like a duck and loves like a duck…

Well, Thor!

My ears were suddenly ringing.

Elizabeth wiggled in her seat and wagged her eyebrows. "You l-o-o-o-o-o-ve him."

"You don't even believe in love." I leveled her with a severe glare, hoping to quell the unexpected dawn of realization. If I could just think about it a little more without Elizabeth's wagging eyebrows, I might be able to analyze the situation with the pragmatism it deserved.

She shook her head and averted her gaze from mine. "You know that's not true. I believe in *one* love, *first* love."

I knew not to press her on this point or to dissuade her from this belief, especially in relation to herself. I knew Elizabeth's history, and I didn't want to make her hash through a topic that was so painful for her.

I tried to make my argument relevant only to the present situation. "What about Jon? I loved Jon."

"No, you didn't. You tolerated Jon in much the same way that tolerance is taught in the workplace or at school." Her mouth curved downward as though she tasted something unpleasant. "I think you loved him as a fellow human being, but you never felt more than tolerance for him."

"But Quinn wants—he's my boss, and now he's my boyfriend. And then there is that apartment in his building. I promised him I would take you to see it."

She shrugged. "We'll go tomorrow afternoon before you meet Quinn for your date." She was wagging her eyebrows again.

I held my breath for a moment then sighed. My forehead landed in my palm and I directed my question to the table. "What am I going to do?"

Elizabeth cleared her throat then brushed her fingertips against my wrist. "Well, you are going to go back to work and not let Ms. Olivia Von Evilpants think she made any impact on your relationship with Quinn. Tonight, you'll tutor down on the South Side. Tomorrow, we'll go look at the swanky apartment. Then, afterward, when you go on a date with the man you love—aka Quinn Sullivan, aka Sir McHotpants—you'll ask him about the email."

She made it sound so simple, so reasonable, and so possible.

I could only nod, agree, and hope she was right.

IT ALL WENT ACCORDING to plan, until it didn't.

I did go back to work. I did ignore Olivia even though she seemed overly eager to throw herself in my path and speak to me for the rest of the day. I did go to tutoring that night, and I successfully avoided thinking about being in love with Quinn until he messaged me his nightly text, which had turned somewhat math-mushy recently:

If I were a function, you would be my asymptote. I always tend toward you.

He followed it with *I miss you.*

I allowed myself to enjoy it and wonder that I may have fallen into the pit of love with this man. For it was, truly, a pit. It was dark and unknown. It was scary, and I was surrounded on all sides by it.

Therefore, in an effort to avoid dark and definitely frightening pits, I made up my mind to make up my mind about the in-love question when I saw him next.

The next morning I was feeling better about the lawyer-speak email. I was feeling calmer and more certain. By mid-afternoon, I was actually looking forward to taking Elizabeth to see the apartment, and by the time I met her at the building, I was trying to contain my pre-Quinn-date excitement.

It all went wrong when I inserted the key into the apartment door. Before I could turn it, the door adjacent to it opened, and Quinn bolted out of it, his expression thunderous, and his chest bare.

That's right. He wasn't wearing a shirt.

Elizabeth and I took a startled step backward as he, also startled, rocked backward on his feet, his expression instantly mirroring ours.

"Janie." He said my name in a breathless whoosh as his hand reached behind him and he grabbed for the door he'd just exited.

My eyes moved to his naked chest, then lower to his jeans. I lifted my gaze to his again, and I could sense Elizabeth shifting sideways behind me as she tried to peer into the apartment behind him.

"What are you doing here?" Quinn asked the question without malice or accusation; he sounded genuinely astonished.

"I'm…you made me promise to show Elizabeth the apartment."

His attention shifted from me and flickered to where Elizabeth was standing. He blinked at her.

"So, Quinn…" Elizabeth's voice sounded at my shoulder, and didn't lack malice or accusation. "Who is in there with you, why the hell don't you have a shirt on, and what the hell is that on your neck?"

Quinn visibly flinched, either surprised by Elizabeth's words or the harsh tenor of her tone.

Before he could respond, Elizabeth stepped forward and pointed to a mark on his neck. "Is that a bite mark?"

His hand automatically lifted to his neck.

Elizabeth turned to me, her voice rising. "Did you give that to him?"

I shook my head. Everything was happening so fast; there were too many data points, and I couldn't absorb any of them. They were scattered on the floor and running away from me like legless teeth. I could only look mutely between Quinn and Elizabeth, and the door he was trying to close.

Elizabeth turned back to him and pointed to another mark in the middle of his chest. "And that is a cigarette burn; what the hell?" She was shrieking. "I *know* Janie didn't give you that."

His eyes found mine and I saw fear. "Listen—listen for a minute; you both need to leave. You shouldn't even be here; where the hell are your guards?" Quinn seemed to be trying to collect his wits, and his voice was laced with firm yet panicked urgency.

The door behind him swung all the way open and, in that moment, my brain and heart stopped.

Jem was behind him dressed in her bra and jeans, smoking a cigarette, a hard smile curving her lips.

"Hey, big sister."

Quinn glanced over his shoulder distractedly then almost jumped into the hall. "What the hell?"

My mouth opened and I heard something break, a small snapping noise, in the back of my mind followed by an intense rush of physical pain starting behind my eyes and in my chest. I couldn't breathe. Quinn, Elizabeth, and Jem were all talking at once, but I heard nothing.

I heard nothing.

♥♥♥

IN RETROSPECT, when I dwelled on the next several minutes in hindsight, all I remembered was blurriness. Somehow, Elizabeth pulled me out of the hallway and out of the building. She shoved me into a taxi. At some point, I recognized that my face was wet, and I thought that I must be crying. We made it to the apartment and I followed behind her; she held my hand. Once inside she steered me to the couch and left me there for a moment, coming back almost immediately with the last of our tequila.

After setting it on the table, Elizabeth shook my shoulders. "Janie! Janie, listen to me." Her voice sounded very far away.

I turned to her, meeting her eyes. They were large, and I registered concern. She pulled me into a full body hug and held me tightly. I heard her mutter, "That son of a bitch; I will kill him… everyone is going to want to… we'll all take turns giving him cigarette burns… they're coming over…"

I blinked, pulling away. "Who is coming over?"

She pushed my hair away from my face in a way that, heartbreakingly, reminded me of Quinn. "While you were sitting catatonic in the cab, I texted all the ladies. We're having an emergency meeting tonight."

I shook my head and was surprised when a sob vacated my chest. "No. I don't want to see anyone."

"Yes, they are coming over. Yes, you will see people tonight, people who love you and want to support you. You can wallow over the weekend. Tonight you're going to get drunk and eat too much ice cream."

I only partly heard her and barely comprehended the words. I was crying again, and everything went blurry. She pushed the bottle of tequila into my hand and encouraged me to drink.

It burned in my mouth and down my esophagus, and I held the discomfort close to me. It was a relief to feel pain from some source other than my heart. Elizabeth pulled the bottle from my hand and took a long, answering swig before slamming it on the table with a loud *thunk.*

"I am so sorry, Janie." She put an arm around my shoulders and brought my head to her chest. "I am so sorry."

The door buzzed and Elizabeth stood to check the receiver. I heard Marie's voice over the speaker. I mechanically reached for the tequila bottle, feeling a little disappointed when it burned with less intensity on my second swallow.

Nevertheless, as I took my third pull from the bottle, I welcomed the numbness.

Moments later Marie's arms surrounded me and buried my head on her shoulder. I noted vaguely that her shampoo-commercial-ready hair smelled like lemon and lavender. Next, Kat's arms encircled me from behind. I heard Sandra's voice some time later, and she took Marie's place on the couch.

"Come to Mama, baby girl." Sandra kissed my forehead and held me in a tight embrace; lest I forget her profession as a psychiatrist, she soothed me with a coaxing voice. "Now, you don't need to talk about it until you're ready. We are here to support you and love you." She took a deep breath and then, lest I forget she was Sandra the Texan, she continued. "And when you're ready to cut his balls off, I will provide the knife."

Dimly, I was aware that someone was laughing. I lifted my head and, with a little surprise, realized that I was in fact laughing. I met Sandra's green eyes, sparkling but rimmed with concern, and I managed a soggy smile.

I glanced around the room. Elizabeth was hovering by the door with her hands clasped together against her cheek; Marie was sitting in a chair by the couch giving me a sympathetic smile; Kat was behind me rubbing small circles on my back; Sandra was holding my shoulders. Their wide stares all mirrored my vulnerability to me and to each other as though they wanted to and even expected to shoulder and share in my burden.

I really loved them.

Kat smoothed my hair to the side and laid her head on my shoulder. "Oh, Janie, we are all going to get so drunk."

My eyes blurred over with new tears even as a small, involuntary laugh passed between my lips. The buzzer for the building door sounded again, and Elizabeth pressed the release button without checking who was calling up.

"It must be Fiona; she said she was getting a sitter until Greg could get home. Ashley has to finish her shift, but she said she'll be here by seven o'clock." Elizabeth moved to the apartment door and left it ajar for our friend.

Sandra took the bottle of tequila from my hand and held it to Marie. "We need to get some cups. I love you girls, but I have no desire to drink y'all's backwash all night."

"Let's order takeout." Kat hugged me from behind, lifting her head from my shoulder. I placed one of my hands on her arm and returned the squeeze.

"Chinese food or pizza?" Marie stood and crossed to the kitchen, pulling takeout menus from their place on the fridge, still holding the bottle of tequila in her hand.

I wiped at my eyes, sniffing, feeling the warm numbness one associates with good friends and three rapid-fire shots of tequila. Love really was a pit, and I was at rock bottom. I didn't know how but I knew these women were going to help pull me out of the dark place I had plummeted into headlong. But first, I needed to order my thoughts and organize the data. I needed to process the last half hour and figure out what precisely I saw, felt, and believed.

However, before I could even begin to pick up the pieces of reality let alone study them with the careful attention they required, the sound of Quinn's voice saying my name was a proverbial chainsaw to the fragile remnants of my heart.

"Janie!"

I glanced up confused and wide-eyed, and I saw Quinn hurrying toward me. He pushed the table out of the way and knelt in front of me, reaching for and sliding his arms around my waist. It took me a moment to register that he was searching me, my body, for something, as though he expected part of me to be missing or damaged.

It took me several more seconds to understand that he was there, that he was touching me, and that he was speaking.

"Are you ok? Has anyone approached you? And why the hell was your door open?"

As soon as I overcame my shock, I pulled away from him and held my hands up between us. My mouth opened and closed as my brain struggled to understand his abrupt presence, the anger behind his words, and the relief in his eyes. I was clearly lagging behind real-time event comprehension.

I broke the stunned silence. "Quinn, what…what are you doing here?"

As though everyone else was equally dumbfounded by his presence and my words were the cure to their stunned silence, the room erupted in noisy feminine outrage.

"The hell!" I registered Elizabeth's angry growl somewhere over his shoulder.

"Listen, Mister." Sandra tried to insert herself between us.

"I think you should leave." Marie walked into the living room from the kitchen holding the bottle of tequila as though it was a viable weapon.

Kat squeezed my hand.

Quinn tried to talk to me over the insistent gaggle of my friends and Sandra's angry-body barricade. "Janie, please listen: You are not safe; your guards should have been with you today; we need to get out of here. They never would have let you come to the building."

The buzzer sounded again and, amidst all the chaos, I discerned Fiona's voice over the speaker. Elizabeth pressed the button while continuing to shoot daggers at Quinn. "Because you were there 'hiding the salami' with her sister?" Elizabeth accused, pulling out her cell phone. "I'm calling the police, Quinn. You need to leave. Now!"

Quinn didn't move from his position in front of me and met her censure with all the flexibility of granite. "I wasn't with Jem."

"We saw you!"

"No, you don't understand." He turned to me, but Sandra anticipated his movements and blocked me from view. "Janie, I wasn't *with* her, we weren't 'hiding salami'; I was trying to help."

"Then why was your shirt off, Quinn, if that *is* your real name?" Elizabeth asked, sounding like a suspicious Sherlock as she punched in three numbers on her cell.

"Because Jem is bat-shit crazy and burned me with a cigarette then bit my…" He huffed. "We don't have time for this!"

"Seriously, big guy, you just need to make like a shepherd and get the flock out of here." Sandra crossed her arms over her chest, her voice low with warning.

Quinn stuttered for a moment, his eyebrow lifting at Sandra's crude dismissal. "I can't leave until I know she is safe."

Marie crossed her arms over her chest. "Safe from who?"

Elizabeth spoke into the phone at her ear, giving the 911 operator our address before adding, "I need the police."

Elizabeth didn't finish the sentence because the phone was roughly pulled from her grip and she was knocked to the floor. A collective shocked breath fanned through the room; all eyes rested fitfully on three very large, very sinister-looking skinheads with neck tattoos who invaded the small apartment, made significantly smaller by their looming thickness.

One of the men was holding Fiona around the waist. He had a gun in his hand that was pointed at Quinn, but their collective attention was rigidly affixed on me.

"Well, hell, Jem. It's been a long time."

The taller one of the three addressed his comment to me, and I recognized him as the scary stranger from the park.

"What the hell are you doing, Sam? Does Seamus know you are here?" Quinn stepped in front of Sandra, Kat, and me, hiding us from two of the goons and Sam.

I heard rather than saw Sam's harsh reply. "You shut the fuck up, Quinn. You said you didn't know where she was."

"You are making a serious mistake." Quinn's voice made me shiver. Even though they held a gun on him, his tone made it perfectly clear that he was not to be bothered with trivial things like bullets. "Like I told Seamus, this is not Jem."

I noticed Marie shifting on her feet; her hand was still around the bottle of tequila, and her eyes were wide as they moved between Quinn and the skinhead called Sam.

I heard the click of something, which I guessed was the safety of a gun, because Quinn became suddenly rigid, and the threatening tenor of his carefully spoken words was almost tangible. "What do you think you're doing?"

"I'm taking that bitch. I'm taking her back to Seamus, and he can decide if she is Jem or not, but I'm sick of dicking around Chicago."

Unexpectedly, it was Marie who spoke next. "Like hell you are."

A few things happened at once.

I didn't really see everything as I was behind Sandra who was behind Quinn, and Kat was to my right, also partially blocking my view. But what I did see was the aftermath, and I was therefore able to put the pieces together.

Marie must have thrown the bottle of tequila at one of the skinheads, the one who had been holding Fiona, because his gun went off and the bullet hit the wall somewhere above the window. He staggered backward holding his head. Fiona must have been preparing for this moment, because she withdrew two long Susan Bates knitting needles from her project bag, the long thick ones that beginners typically learn on with the white nobs at the end, and she stabbed him in the shoulder. Immediately the gun dropped from his hand.

Elizabeth, who had been on the floor the whole time, reached for the gun as goon#2 tripped over her legs and fell heavily against the bookshelf.

Kat yelped when the gun went off, and she grabbed my hand. To my surprise, she threw both of us behind the couch. I landed on the floor quite ungracefully, taking the brunt of my fall on the left side of my body.

Quinn flipped the coffee table up on its side, presumably to offer a modicum of cover against the potential impending rain of bullets, and he reached for a previously hidden Glock in the back of his pants, training it on the skinheads just as Sam pulled out his handgun. However, before Quinn or Skinhead Sam could fire a round, diminutive and petite Fiona screamed and pushed Sam forward.

She was small and he was big; therefore, other than a momentary inability to balance, Sam quickly recovered and turned his rage and weapon on Fiona. At this point, Elizabeth was able to fire one round. It hit Sam in the stomach, and he promptly doubled over with a gurgled curse before goon#2 reached Elizabeth and wrestled the weapon from her grip, elbowing her roughly in the face as he did so.

"Oh, shit! Ow! That hurt!" Elizabeth cried.

Before goon#2 could raise the weapon, however, Marie and Sandra launched themselves across the room, Sandra yodeling like Tarzan. I heard Quinn exclaim, "Damn it!" before he jumped over the coffee table a second later.

Surprisingly, Marie and Sandra made very efficient work of tackling the big man to the ground. Admittedly, he was still on his knees, trying to scramble up, when they reached him, and yes, Marie kicked him in the groin area with pointed boots immediately on entering his sphere of personal space. Sandra grabbed the 9mm from him while he was distracted, and to my very great surprise, after promptly switching on the safety, she clobbered him with the butt of the gun.

"I

Clobber.

"—am going—"

Clobber.

"—to fuck—"

Clobber.

"—you up—"

Clobber.

"—bitch!"

It took me a moment to realize that Sandra was holding a ball of yarn in her other hand, the one not holding the gun. She stuffed it in the mouth of goon#2 even as she brought the gun down for another bone-crunching blow.

Fiona scrambled over to Elizabeth and cupped her face, trying to shield her from further violence, and Quinn pistol-whipped Sam, knocking the tattooed menace out with a single blow.

Marie picked up the tequila bottle and swung it wildly at goon#1 who, seemingly, had just recovered from the shock of being stabbed with a Susan Bates knitting needle. Goon#1 lifted the hand of his good arm over his face but was a little too late; Marie brought the bottle down with a resounding *crash*, and the tower of a man fell backward, unconscious.

Kat and I were peeking under the couch. The only sound in the small apartment was labored breathing until someone, I guessed Marie, said, "Oh, shit! Sandra! Is that the Madelintosh Aran limited dye lot yarn you just stuffed into that asshole's mouth? You know I can't replace that!"

CHAPTER TWENTY-EIGHT

THE POLICE ARRIVED not ten seconds later. It was a good thing, too. Marie was holding a broken bottle of tequila, shards of glass in every direction, and Sandra was holding a gun; they were arguing about the apparently very expensive and hard to find skein of yarn that Sandra had stuffed in the mouth of one of the skinheads.

Quinn turned toward me as soon as the police entered. His eyes met mine, and what I saw there was a potent mixture of tension and relief. Nevertheless, he didn't come to me. Instead, he placed his weapon on the ground then moved his hands to the back of his head, waiting for the Chicago police. The room felt unbearably large, and the distance between us felt impossible.

It wasn't until hours later, after statements and questioning and a pseudo-physical administered by an EMT, that we were all released; actually, all of us but Quinn. Soon after the police arrived, they handcuffed him and took him to the police station despite protests from Kat, Elizabeth, Sandra, Marie, Fiona, and of course, me.

Ashley arrived exactly when she said she would, and she was quickly filled in on the details by Sandra. As she listened to the story, I watched a spectrum of emotions flicker across her features.

Finally, she settled on exasperation. "Why does everything good happen when I'm not there? I swear, the next time Janie's hot boyfriend saves y'all from neck-tattooed skinheads, y'all better wait 'til I'm done with my shift or else I'm gonna be pissed."

"He didn't save us; haven't you been listening?" Elizabeth held an icepack to her chin where she'd been hit by a meaty elbow. "Fiona stabbed one of them with a Susan Bates needle, Marie was wielding a tequila bottle, Sandra pistol-whipped the other, and I shot the third."

"Where were Janie and Kat?" Ashley looked from me to Kat.

"Hiding behind the couch like sane people!" Kat said before anyone else could speak.

Ashley gave us a sudden watery smile. "Damn it, if something had happened to any of you, I would have been very upset. What were you thinking?"

She initiated a group hug, which lasted well past what would have been considered typical, as none of us wanted to let each other go.

♥♥♥

AFTER ALL THE LADIES LEFT, Elizabeth leaving with Marie, but before the last police car drove away, I approached a short, stocky guard who I instantly recognized and who'd been watching me since the police escorted us all out to the ambulance for our EMT checkups. It was Dan, the security man from the Fairbanks Building.

We walked toward each other, meeting halfway. His large brown eyes were big and kind, and he gave me a small smile; it almost looked apologetic.

"Ms. Morris." He nodded to me.

"Dan, the security man." I nodded to him.

He sighed. "Are you ok?"

I continued to nod. I didn't want to say yes because I wasn't sure how I was doing. However, I didn't want to appear to be a basket case when I needed his help.

"Listen, Dan, I was hoping you could take me to Quinn—um—Mr. Sullivan's place."

"It's ok; I call him Quinn, too." Dan pointed with his thumb to a car behind him, a black Mercedes coupe. "That's actually why I'm here."

I smiled and released a short breath. "Of course."

"Come on." He motioned with his head for me to follow.

When we were settled in the car, and he'd pulled into traffic I noticed he was giving me long, sideways glances, as though he wanted to say something, ask something, but he wasn't sure how to start.

Taking pity on him, I prompted, "Is there something you want to say?"

"Yes." The word tumbled out of his mouth. "Yes, I wanted to tell you how sorry I am."

I blinked at him, wondering how I'd missed his very distinctive Bostonian accent during all the times I'd talked to him before now. "Sorry? Why are you sorry?"

"Because Seamus is my brother, and he is a complete fu—er, he is a very bad guy."

I shifted slightly and pressed my back to the passenger door so that I could study him more fully. "Yes, well in that case, I suppose I should apologize for my sister. She is also a very bad…guy."

He chuckled. "Yes. Yes she is."

I squinted at him. "Did you know Jem?"

He nodded. "She is still just as crazy as she was when I knew her."

"Oh—you saw her recently?"

He nodded. "This afternoon when you came to the new building with your friend, I was in the apartment with Quinn and Jem." He glanced at me as he turned the steering wheel to the right and merged onto Michigan Avenue.

I stiffened. "So, you were there?"

"Yep, that bitch—er, your sister—is crazy, but you know this. Quinn was trying to help her. He offered her money to disappear, but she started ranting and shit, and taking off her clothes. I swear, if I didn't know her already—how nuts she is—I would have thought she was on something. Then she bit him and burned him with her cigarette, right through his shirt. It was crazy; blood was coming from his neck."

I winced, thinking about Jem biting Quinn with such force that she drew blood. "Why was she taking off her clothes?"

He shrugged his shoulders. "I dunno. 'Cause she's *crazy*? When you got there, he was cleaning the bite mark and all the blood. He was leaving to get some new clothes. I would have taken a bath in alcohol and hydrogen peroxide if she'd bit me."

I chewed on my lip as I took all this in; I felt relieved, stupid, and anxious. Dan parked the car in the basement of the building and escorted me up to Quinn's penthouse. He opened the door for me but didn't go inside.

I'd been quiet since the car, wanting to sort through my tangled mess of emotions and the evening's events. But I was restless to see Quinn and not really capable of dwelling on anything until I wrapped my arms around him and felt, rather than saw, that he was safe.

"So…" Dan handed me the keys to the penthouse. "Quinn should be home sometime tonight. When he called me they hadn't charged him with anything, and they shouldn't 'cause he has a license to carry that gun."

I stopped him as he turned away. "Dan, can I ask you something?"

His eyebrows lifted as he nodded his assent. "Sure."

I shifted the keys from one hand to the other and tucked my hair behind my ears. "How long have you known Quinn?"

He shrugged. "Since we was kids."

"Do you know why Quinn left Boston?"

He hesitated; his eyes narrowed as his lips twisted to the side. "Yes."

I couldn't help but smile at his one word answer, the very picture of cautious loyalty.

"So do I…I think."

He stood very still, watching me, his eyes moving over my features with concentrated intensity; at length he said, "You know, he is really crazy about you; not *crazy* like your sister Jem crazy, but trying-to-become-a-better-person crazy."

I pressed my lips together, and my heart, now whole again, skipped wildly in my chest before I replied, "The feeling is mutual."

♥♥♥

AT FIRST, I DIDN'T even contemplate sleep. I did laps around Quinn's bare apartment, wishing I'd brought a comic book with me, realizing I didn't even have my stupid cell phone. In a fit of petulant annoyance, I threw myself onto the bed and promptly fell asleep.

When I awoke, I was confused. The panorama of the park and the lake and the city told me that it was still the middle of the night, but I had no idea how long I'd been asleep. I stretched, planning to get up and check the time on my watch via the light of the bathroom, but I acutely realized that I was not alone.

There was a body next to me.

In fact, I was curled around that body.

And the body was not asleep.

My breath hitched. "Quinn?"

The arm around my shoulders squeezed gently before he removed it then shifted on the bed and propped himself up on an elbow so that he was facing me.

"Hey." His other hand immediately entangled itself in my hair, and he was tugging my head back so that he could cover my mouth with his. I leaned into his kiss, pressing my body to his, and feeling an overwhelming mix of indescribable joy, relief, and gratefulness.

We kissed, just kissed, for a long time; sometimes I was over him, sometimes he was over me, sometimes we were sitting up, sometimes we were lying down. It went on and on, and if it weren't for the necessity of air, we might have kissed for the rest of our lives. I would not have complained.

I was straddling his lap and we were on the middle of the bed when he pushed my hair from my face and rested his forehead against mine.

"Oh, Quinn, I am so sorry." I hugged him to me, my arms around his neck.

"Janie, there is nothing to be sorry about."

"But I assumed the worst. I saw you with Jem, and I assumed that you…that you and she…"

His arms tightened around me. "You assumed we were playing 'hide the salami,' as Elizabeth called it." Despite the evening's events, this made us both laugh.

When the short burst of laughter ended, I nuzzled my head into the crook of his neck, careful to avoid his injury. "Dan brought me here and told me what happened with Jem. I am sorry she bit you."

His hand rubbed circles over my back, and with each pass his hand moved lower until he was stroking the base of my spine just above the curve of my bottom. "It's ok. I don't care about Jem."

I pulled just far enough away from him to see his face. He looked tired and weary.

"I don't either," I said, and then I sighed at the memory of all the trouble my sister had caused. "You should know that I do trust you."

He offered me a small smile that didn't quite reach his eyes. "We can talk about it in the morning."

"No…no, listen." I shifted backward, and at first, he didn't let me go, but then he finally allowed me to move to the edge of the bed and stand. I reached into my pants pocket and pulled out the folded email, my voice was still thick with sleep, "Olivia—at least I think it was Olivia—left this on my desk yesterday. I was going to show it to you today." I shoved the paper at him.

He looked from me to the paper, and then with clear hesitation, he took it from my hand. I crossed to the bathroom and flipped on the light, which gave him just enough illumination to read the contents. He pushed to the edge of the bed and stood, his long form unfolding, straightening, then stiffening as he read. A rush of breath escaped his lungs and his eyes flickered to me.

"I haven't seen this, but Janie, I can tell you…"

I covered his hand holding the paper with mine. "No; it doesn't matter. What I wanted to say was…what I want to say is that I saw this yesterday, and yes, admittedly, I had a momentary freak-out, but then I thought about it, and I realized that I trust you. I knew there had to be a reasonable explanation, and I was going to show it to you today, tonight, before everything went from Judd Apatow harmless to Quentin Tarantino horrifying."

Quinn took a step toward me, shaking his head. "I asked them to."

"You don't have to explain. I trust you now, and I trusted you when I read it. I just wanted you to know that I wasn't worried. I-I-I have faith in you."

This time his small smile did reach his eyes, and he looked almost proud of himself, and a little mischievous. His gaze moved over my face in a slow sweep as he licked his lips. "Let me tell you what this is about, ok?"

I nodded. "You don't have to."

"I want to." Quinn dipped his chin and leveled me with a measured stare. He glanced briefly at the email and handed it back to me. "After you and I talked on Tuesday, when you told me you didn't want to take the plane back with everyone else, I knew that you felt uncomfortable leaving things undefined at work. I called Betty and tasked her with asking the lawyers to put a proposal together to define our work expectations in such a way that would allow us to continue our relationship outside of work."

My attention moved back to the email as he explained, and I read it again with this information in mind.

"Obviously they misinterpreted the request. I wanted them to set up something tangible, something legal that you could feel good about, something that would protect you in case our relationship ever…ended." One of his hands moved to the back of his neck.

"It reads as though they interpreted your request, your main objective, as protecting the company. They want me to resign so that you and I can date without putting the company at risk."

"I'll get it straightened out." He shifted closer, running the back of his knuckles against the skin where my scoop-neck shirt met my chest.

I surveyed the email once more before stepping away from him to place it on the dresser. "I know you will." I couldn't meet his eyes. Part of me wondered if it would just be better for everyone if I did quit. Then I could date Quinn without making others uncomfortable about putting his company at risk.

"Hey." He tilted my chin back until I met his gaze. "What are you thinking about? And don't tell me it's robots."

Despite myself, I gave him a brittle grin. "Maybe I should quit."

He shook his head. "No. That's not acceptable."

"Quinn."

"That would be bad for my company."

"But at least…"

"What are you so afraid of?"

"I'm afraid that if you get to know me, you'll think I'm weird." The words, words I didn't even know I was going to say, blurted forth like a disobedient hiccup.

His gaze refocused and met mine directly. "I do know you, and you're right; you are weird."

"I'm afraid you're laughing at me instead of with me."

He shrugged. "There is nothing I can do about that. You're funny."

"I'm afraid that your money and my lack of money will come between us."

He placed his hands on his hips. "It won't. I won't let it."

"I'm afraid that I feel more for you than you feel for me."

He shook his head slowly. "That's not possible."

"I'm afraid that we're moving too fast and that this is just infatuation."

"I don't know what this is." He breathed in as though he was going to continue, but then he paused.

Quinn studied me, held my gaze. He seemed to be considering his next words carefully.

I knew what I wanted him to say: I wanted him to tell me that this wasn't infatuation, that he was certain we were meant to be together into eternity, that I looked pretty and ask me if I did something different with my hair, that I was the most beautiful woman in the world to him. It was what I wanted to hear because I was falling in love with him.

I'm not falling in love; I am in love with him.

Finally, his words deliberate and cautiously crafted, Quinn said, "I think about you all the time." His gaze narrowed and his jaw ticked as though the confession had cost him. "And I can't guarantee that this isn't infatuation because sometimes I think it has to be. But…" His gaze moved upward then to the left and over my shoulder. "I don't think of you as perfect."

I frowned at him.

I don't think of you as perfect.

"Oh…ok." My eyelashes blinked in rapid succession, and my brain started compiling the list of all my imperfections. "Is it because of my height? My seepage of trivial facts? My granny panties?"

"No, listen." His attention swiftly moved back to me. "That's not…" He shook his head and swallowed. "If this was just infatuation, then I would, we would become disillusioned at some point, yes?"

I nodded, and I was sure it was unconvincing.

He continued. "I don't have misconceptions that you're flawless. And you don't have any illusions about me. You're too practical, and if you did, you wouldn't have reminded me on Wednesday that I need to be a good guy."

I nodded again, this time more convincingly albeit more warily.

"I don't think this," he motioned between us, "I don't think this is infatuation." He shifted closer, and I thought he was going to touch me, but instead, he crossed his arms and his voice became softer and gentler. "I know that life, in general, terrifies you; I know that you are frequently oblivious to the obvious, and I know that you are completely irrational at times."

I opened my mouth automatically because my brain was telling me to object, but surprisingly, I didn't actually feel any outrage at being called terrified, oblivious, and irrational. His assessment was, more or less, on target. The fact that he knew these things about me, and he seemed to accept them regardless, made me feel better and worse.

"And all that drives me crazy. *You* drive me crazy." His voice deepened, and he leveled me with a narrow glare as he continued. "But, in spite of how totally nuts you are, I wouldn't change anything about you."

I pressed my lips together and started biting the inside of my cheek. I bravely met his pointed stare. "You think I'm totally nuts?"

He nodded and sighed. "Yes. And I…" his eyes moved over my forehead, eyebrows, nose, cheeks, lips, and chin. "I can't stop thinking about you."

I inhaled deeply, trying to breathe him in, trying to understand this desire to take him within myself and carry him with me always. He lowered his head and my eyes drifted shut.

"Janie…"

I sighed. "Yes?"

"What are you thinking?" His voice was a whisper, his breath against my cheek.

My eyes fluttered open and I licked my lips, wanting his mouth on mine, driven to mad honesty. "I love you."

I sensed rather than saw his self-satisfied smile. "Good."

He softly brushed his lips against mine. My immediate confession-induced panic dissolved as his nearness blanketed me in a frightening sanctuary I never knew I wanted, but now recognized was necessary to my continued existence.

I lost myself to him and to myself; to trust and to faith; and in that moment, I was fearless.

EPILOGUE

QUINN, FOUR MONTHS LATER

WHEN I WALKED into the luxury plumbing fixture store on West Lake Street, I was immediately struck by the fact that they had rows of toilets hanging on the walls. The floor was plain cement. The walls were ordinary red brick. Covering the floor and walls was an array of sinks, tubs, faucets, and toilets. The space was large, but it felt small due to the large selection of bathroom fixtures.

Automatically I did a sweep of the store, located exits, sized up the other customers, and so forth. Habits come naturally. Once comfortable, I walked to Elizabeth; she was about forty feet away, studying a row of faucets on the wall.

She didn't look up when I approached but merely tipped her head in my direction as a greeting. "McHotpants."

"Elizabeth." I rubbed the back of my neck. I didn't mind the nickname when Janie used it. But it just didn't seem right with her friends, particularly Elizabeth. I hoped that today's meeting would improve our strained interactions. "Thank you for meeting me."

Elizabeth shrugged. "No problem. Anything for Janie. She said she'd meet us here at six." She reached out and twisted the knobs on a faucet.

If Janie was going to arrive at six, then that meant I only had a half hour to work through whatever issues Elizabeth obviously had with me dating Janie. I waited for Elizabeth to look up, but instead she frowned at the metal spigot and walked farther into the store.

I scowled at her, trying not to grind my teeth. "Why did you want to meet here?"

"I want a new faucet."

"What's wrong with the faucet in the apartment?"

"I don't like it."

With a great deal of effort, I managed to keep from rolling my eyes. "Ok."

She fiddled with another series of levers. "Ok? So you're ok with me changing the sink?"

I glanced around the store again, counting three more people I'd missed in my first sweep of the space. "Elizabeth, you can remodel the bathroom if you want. I don't care."

"And you'll pay for it?"

"Sure, whatever; whatever you want."

She looked at me then. Her pale blue eyes narrowed, and she inspected me as if I was a disease.

Since we'd first met some four months ago, I had felt at cross-purposes with Elizabeth. She was irritable every time I was alone in a room with her. Just last week, which was the last time Janie and I had spent the night at their place, Elizabeth made passive-aggressive remarks about my inability to make a good cup of coffee.

I know how to make coffee. I make really good coffee. She just doesn't like me.

Usually I wouldn't care, but her best friend happens to be the woman I want to spend the rest of my life with. It is necessary to make an effort.

I met her glare with one of my own; finally, she spoke. "So, Mr. Granite Face, what is this about?" She motioned between the two of us. "Why did you want to meet before Janie arrives?"

I crossed my arms over my chest, preparing to negotiate. "We need to figure out some way to get along."

"You're right." She didn't look surprised by my statement.

"What is it about me that you dislike?"

She lifted her blonde eyebrows. "I don't dislike you."

I didn't want to call her a liar, so I didn't respond.

After a protracted moment, she continued. "It's not that I dislike you. I just don't trust you."

"Why not?"

"Because I don't understand your motivations, and I still think you're hiding something." She mimicked my stance, crossing her arms over her chest. She was small and looked silly when she tried to appear tough.

"I'm not hiding anything."

"Oh, really?" Elizabeth started rubbing her chin with her thumb and forefinger. "What did you do with Jem? What happened to all of those thugs from Boston? Why didn't they press charges?"

"Janie and I discussed all of this. She knows that I took care of it."

Elizabeth didn't hide her anger very well. "Well, Janie won't tell me."

"That's probably for your own good."

"I want to know what happened. I don't want to be patted on the head and sent on my way! What if they come back? What about Janie?"

"Janie is stronger than you think, and I'll protect her."

"I need to know so I can take care of her; you can't protect her forever!" Elizabeth waved her arms around wildly. She was starting to draw attention to herself. I didn't particularly care, but it was annoying.

And because I was annoyed, I responded without thinking. "Yes, I can. When we get married, she'll be—"

"You're getting *married*?" Elizabeth's shouted exclamation echoed against the porcelain tubs and drew all remaining eyes to our position.

I glanced around the store, offered nothing but an unfriendly glare in apology for her outburst, then took Elizabeth by the arm and escorted her to the back of the store. When I was satisfied that no one was listening or watching, I responded in a low voice. "I haven't asked her yet."

Elizabeth blinked at me; her mouth opened and closed. I gave up and rolled my eyes.

When she finally spoke, her voice was a tight whisper. "I can't believe you're going to ask her to marry you!" To my surprise, she sounded excited and happy.

I blinked at her; my mouth opened and closed.

"Oh, my God, you have to let me help! I want to help! This is so exciting!" She hopped back and forth on her feet, clapping her hands.

I responded through gritted teeth. "No. I don't need your help. I can do it on my own."

She stopped hopping and abruptly frowned. Her voice was still a whisper although somewhat louder. "See, this is why I don't like you!"

"I thought you did like me."

"No, I do like you, I like you for Janie, but I don't like that you hide things! Why do you do that?"

I studied her. Elizabeth's hands were planted on her hips, and at least she didn't appear angry. She looked hurt. What I knew about Elizabeth I'd learned from Janie; it was obvious that Elizabeth had been taking care of Janie in one way or another since college. It occurred to me that I might need to modify my approach.

I licked my lips and glanced toward the door; what I was about to admit would be easier if I didn't have to look at her. "I'm not used to *sharing*—not information, not resources, and definitely not people."

I heard her sigh before she spoke. "Well, me either. But I love Janie, and what is important is *her* happiness. I want *her* to be happy."

"You know I love her." I growled; the preachy tenor of her words and tone irritated me, and my response and resulting glare were perfunctory.

"I know...I know you love her." She held her hands up, her eyes wide and pacifying, and her tone softened. "But we have to find a way to get along; you said it yourself," she added on a sigh. "We have to learn to share."

I released a slow breath and reluctantly admitted to myself that Elizabeth was right; we had to share Janie. This was the issue. I didn't know how to share her. I wasn't even sure that I wanted to. Part of me wanted to stay in bed with her every second of every day and explore her perfect body. There was a ferocity behind the sentiment that still surprised me, caught me off guard. But I loved Janie, and that meant I needed to do things just because they were good for her and made her happy.

"Also, you might find that I'm pretty handy to have around." Elizabeth's mouth curved into a beseeching smile. "I'm a valuable ally. For example, I am exceptionally good with wound care."

I allowed a small smile, but I knew it didn't quite reach my eyes. I comprehended that befriending Elizabeth was a much better strategy than merely tolerating her.

I rubbed my hand over my face; before I changed my mind, I quickly consented to her interference. "Ok, fine."

"Ok? Fine?"

I refocused my attention on the short blonde and found her watching me, her hands clasped together hopefully.

"Ok, fine; you can help me."

A high-pitched squealing sound met my ears and I winced; then, she hugged me. I patted her on the back, hoping to pacify this bit of overzealous effervescence.

"You won't regret it! Oh, my God, I'm so excited! Have you picked out a ring?"

I was already regretting it but decided to keep that to myself.

"No. I haven't done anything yet." Crossing my arms over my chest, I glanced at my watch then at the front door. Janie would be arriving at any minute, and I didn't want to be talking about engagement rings with Elizabeth when she showed up.

"That's ok, I know what she likes. I can help with that, but don't get her a diamond unless it's synthetic because…"

"I know, I know, the atrocities of the African diamond trade. I was, uh, actually thinking about getting her something antique."

Elizabeth glanced up thoughtfully then nodded. "Yeah, that's a good idea; did you know she really loves rubies?"

The question promptly caught my attention. This was actual valuable information. "No, I didn't know that."

Maybe Elizabeth could be helpful after all.

"It's something about the fact that any other color makes the gem a sapphire, but if it's red, it's considered a ruby."

I felt my lips curve into a smile. A ruby would be perfect for Janie.

Our attention was drawn to the front of the shop by the jingling of a bell announcing the entry of a new customer. I knew it was Janie before I saw her. It was the most ridiculous thing, but my heart constricted then expanded whenever she entered a room. I'd come to expect the uncontrolled response, but I hadn't yet grown accustomed to it.

My feet were carrying me to her before my mind grasped their intention; I was too busy noticing that she was wearing a skirt, which likely meant she was wearing thigh highs with lace at the tops. She knew that drove me crazy. I was already plotting to get her alone so that I could confirm my suspicion. Also, she was wearing her hair in a bun, and I immediately started formulating plans to hide all her hair ties as soon as possible.

I caught her eye as I approached, and again, my heart lurched when she smiled. Warmth radiated from my chest outward, and I automatically returned her smile because I had to. I simply did not have a choice.

"Hey." We reached for each other, and her soft palm rested on my cheek briefly as she gave me a small kiss.

It wasn't enough. It never seemed to be enough.

I fought the urge to deepen the shallow contact and stuffed my hands in my pockets. I'd never been one for public displays of affection. Now, however, I had difficulty keeping my hands off Janie's body regardless of where we were. I also had difficulty concentrating on anything or anyone but her.

"Hi," she responded, her focus split between our surroundings and me. Our surroundings finally won the battle for her attention. "I love this place." She breathed the words as if she was in awe.

I watched her spin a slow circle. Her eyes brightened as they took in the dually sparse and cluttered atmosphere.

"Why do you love it?" I had a sense that I would enjoy her answer. I knew it would be unexpected and unique. Everything about her was unexpected and unique. She was my bright light of eccentricity in a very predictable and ordinary world. She made everything new and interesting or funny.

Janie issued me a skeptical glare. I'm sure she meant it to look distrustful, but instead she just looked adorable and gorgeous. "You're going to make fun of me."

I smiled despite myself, something that was becoming very common when we were together. "I'm not going to make fun of you. I really want to know." I reached for her hand, losing the war against restraint, wanting to feel the warmth of her skin against mine. "Why do you like it here?"

She tilted her head, her big hazel eyes moving over my face, then meeting mine. I guessed they were looking for the sincerity of my statement. I wanted to kiss her again but knew that she would never answer the question if I did.

"It's actually embarrassing, and it's about my worst day ever, which actually turned into one of the best days ever because it was the first time I talked to you and looked at you in the eye. Did you know that I had a really hard time doing that? Looking at you in the eye was hard for me, and in my defense, there are actually a number of cultures where it is a sign of respect not to look someone in the eye. For example, in Japan, school-aged children—"

"Janie." I moved our hands behind her back, drawing her against me. "Why do you love it here?"

She blinked, her soft mouth parted. She blushed. It was devastating and made my pulse quicken.

I used to try to make her blush on purpose. I enjoyed flustering her and watching the way her eyes heated, and I especially loved the way she would glance at me through her lashes. Janie was brilliant and beautiful. I loved that I seemed to be one of the few who could surprise her enough to elicit an involuntary reaction.

It's not that Janie was cold; it's that she was naturally aloof. Whenever I watched her at work or in a group, she seemed to be holding herself apart from the action, but it never struck me as purposeful. She appeared to be more comfortable watching. Maybe that's why her impulsive reactions were so gratifying.

"It's the bathroom fixtures." She cleared her throat and lifted her chin, meeting my gaze directly, bravely. "I am a fan of bathrooms. I have found them to be exceptionally good for meditation."

I couldn't help but laugh. "Meditation? You meditate in the bathroom?"

She nodded, fighting a smile. "Well, it's meditation of a sort. I used to wrap all my thoughts up and put them in a box on a shelf in a closet in my head, but lately, I just sit in the bathroom and work through things in there. Something about all the porcelain and tile, I think." She pulled away from me, glancing over my shoulder. "Hey, Elizabeth! I didn't know you were already here."

Honestly, I'd forgotten Elizabeth was there. I released my hold on Janie and stepped back as she greeted her friend.

"Yep. Got here a little while ago." Elizabeth smiled warmly at Janie and hitched a thumb over her shoulder. "I've been looking at faucets."

"Are you done looking? What time is our reservation? Because I wouldn't mind looking around if we have time..." Janie's hopeful eyes moved between Elizabeth and me.

"We have plenty of time; the reservation isn't until six thirty, and we're only ten minutes away," I reassured her and won an immediate smile.

Elizabeth took Janie by the hand. "Come look at these; the lever release is really smooth."

I watched as Janie and Elizabeth approached the row of sink fixtures and fiddled with the knobs, *oohing* and *ahhing* at intervals. I hung back and just studied the pair of them: Janie, tall and perfectly round in all the right places contrasted with Elizabeth's shorter, slimmer form. They were opposites in many ways, but they interacted with the practiced ease that only time and trusted friendship brings.

When they'd exhausted their time and returned to where I stood, I was pretending to check my email on my phone. I didn't want to admit in front of her friend that I'd been merely watching her for the last quarter of an hour, enjoying her animated expressions and the way she moved. Also, studying their interaction allowed me to recognize how relaxed Janie was around Elizabeth. This friendship meant a great deal to Janie. It meant a great deal to both of them.

I glanced up and met Janie's smile with one of my own. "Are we ready?"

Janie nodded, biting her lip. "I am very ready. I am so hungry I could eat a horse, but not in the demonstration of great wealth way or the sacrifice to the gods way, but in the colloquialism way in which I am stating that I am very hungry."

Elizabeth chuckled at Janie's earnest explanation and caught my gaze. She gave me a small smile then abruptly narrowed her eyes at me.

"Uh…" Elizabeth suddenly pulled out the hospital pager from her purse. "Well, look at that; shoot." She looked up at Janie and her expression was apologetic. "It looks like I won't be able to come to dinner tonight." Elizabeth glanced at me briefly then added, "I guess it's just you two kids tonight."

One of my eyebrows lifted, as is my habit when I am suspicious of a person or a situation. The timing of her page seemed very remarkable, and I knew immediately what Elizabeth was doing. She'd just had fifteen minutes of uninterrupted Janie time in a bathroom fixture store. Elizabeth was showing me that she, too, could share Janie by gracefully bowing out of dinner.

Janie frowned. "That's too bad." Her gaze flickered to me then back to Elizabeth, and the volume of her voice was slightly lower when she spoke again. "I was really hoping that you and Quinn might have a chance to…you know, talk and get to know each other a little better."

I watched as her blonde friend gave her a soft smile. "I'll have to take a rain check; I'm sorry. I really have to go." Elizabeth squeezed Janie's hand then moved toward the door. "Have a good time!"

My lips twisted to the side as Elizabeth moved past me and I gave her a grateful smile, which I was sure reached my eyes. She issued me a meaningful glare that told me unequivocally: *You owe me one.*

I nodded to let her know that I understood and that I intended to pay her back. In fact, I fully intended to exploit Elizabeth's knowledge of Janie's tastes when choosing an engagement ring and planning the proposal. My future interactions with Elizabeth would be mutually beneficial, and surprisingly, I was actually looking forward to becoming friends with her. I was looking forward to how happy it would make Janie.

Janie's sigh pulled my attention back to her, and I enveloped her in my arms as the bell jingled on the front door announcing Elizabeth's departure.

"That's too bad." She snuggled against my chest.

"There will be a next time."

Janie grunted noncommittally then leaned back, catching my eye. "Did you two talk before I arrived?"

I nodded.

"What did you talk about?"

I tilted my head to the side and allowed myself to study her features. She had a beautiful face, perfect lips, light freckles, big eyes. The color of her eyes was mossy gold, and it made me want to write crap poetry and hire a skywriter.

"Quinn?"

I blinked at her upturned face. "Uh…what?"

She blushed and glanced at me through her eyelashes. "What did you two talk about before I arrived?"

I cleared my throat to stall. I didn't want to lie, I wasn't going to lie, but I couldn't give her the whole truth, either. Instead, I settled for what she called *selective truth.* In this case, I felt completely justified.

"We were discussing a project of mine. She thought she could help me as she has familiarity with the subject matter." I shrugged and surreptitiously started to unwind her hair.

"Oh." Her eyes moved between mine, searching, and I held her gaze boldly. "Are you going to let her help?"

I nodded. "Yes. She's going to help me. I think it'll be good." I succeeded in releasing her hair and felt my body tighten at the openness of her expression framed by the mass of wild plumage.

Her smile was slow, delighted, and it made my breath catch. "I am so glad."

I considered her for a moment, and seriously thought about falling to my knees and proposing right there in the luxury-plumbing fixture store on West Lake Street. I looked at this beautiful woman, and all I could think was *Want. Mine. Need.*

Before I could make good on the Neanderthal impulse, Janie gave me a quick kiss and stepped out of my arms. She slid her fingers between mine and tugged me toward the door.

"Come on; the sooner we go eat that horse, the sooner we can go back to your place." Janie's eyebrows wagged very clumsily, and I allowed her to lead me from the store. I was busy admiring her backside and the shape of her legs in the ridiculous stilettos she was wearing as she pushed open the door.

We walked down the street toward the restaurant and she held my hand. I was silent because my mind was still racing; the thought of her as my wife overwhelmed me. I was undeserving of her brilliance and sweetness, but I would marry her if she'd have me, and I would never let her go.

"Hey." She poked me in the ribs. "Why is your face like that?"

I swallowed the thickness in my throat; my voice sounded raspy to my own ears. "Like what?"

"Like all serious and determined. It's the look you get when you're about to rain down a world of hurt."

"*Rain down a world of hurt*? Where did you pick that up?" I tilted my head to the side, narrowing my eyes.

"From Steven. We were talking about how you *rained down a world of hurt* on Olivia last week."

In fact, I'd fired her. I hadn't been gentle either. I had no tolerance for incompetence.

I grimaced. "She was bad at her job. She needed to go."

"I agree, but don't change the subject; why is your face the world of hurt face?"

"It's not—it's not." I shook my head then pulled her to a stop. My arms encircled her. I pressed her body against mine and kissed her, softly, catching her off guard. Despite her initial surprise, she responded beautifully and allowed me to take what I needed: her warmth and her blind acceptance.

Except she wasn't blind—she was smart. She knew me and loved me anyway.

I pulled away, just far enough so that her eyes were in focus. Her lashes fluttered open and she gazed at me, trusting and happy.

My voice was a growl. "I love you."

She smiled. "I know."

I released a slow breath and lost myself in her mossy gold eyes. "I don't deserve you."

She licked her lips, her gaze lowering to my mouth, and her smile widened. "Oh, you deserve me." She nodded, her eyes moving back to mine. "You've made me fearless."

It was a confession, and I felt it like a heavy weight in my chest. I wanted to give her a confession too. I swallowed with effort then brushed my lips over hers. My words were a whisper that only she could hear.

"And you make me a good guy."

THE END

Subscribe to Penny's awesome newsletter for exclusive stories, sneak peeks, and pictures of cats knitting hats. Subscribe here: http://pennyreid.ninja/newsletter/

Pre-Order Penny Reid's next release Marriage and Murder, Book #2 in the Solving for Pie: Cletus and Jenn Mysteries Series.

Coming March 2nd, 2021!

ABOUT THE AUTHOR

Penny Reid is the *New York Times*, *Wall Street Journal*, and *USA Today* Bestselling Author of the Winston Brothers, Knitting in the City, Rugby, Dear Professor, and Hypothesis series. She used to spend her days writing federal grant proposals as a biomedical researcher, but now she just writes books. She's also a full time mom to three diminutive adults, wife, daughter, knitter, crocheter, sewer, general crafter, and thought ninja.

Come find me -
Mailing List: http://pennyreid.ninja/newsletter/
Goodreads:http://www.goodreads.com/ReidRomance
Facebook: www.facebook.com/pennyreidwriter
Instagram: www.instagram.com/reidromance
Twitter: www.twitter.com/reidromance
Patreon: https://www.patreon.com/smartypantsromance
Email: pennreid@gmail.com …hey, you! Email me ;-)

OTHER BOOKS BY PENNY REID

Knitting in the City Series

(Interconnected Standalones, Adult Contemporary Romantic Comedy)

Neanderthal Seeks Human: A Smart Romance (#1)

Neanderthal Marries Human: A Smarter Romance (#1.5)

Friends without Benefits: An Unrequited Romance (#2)

Love Hacked: A Reluctant Romance (#3)

Beauty and the Mustache: A Philosophical Romance (#4)

Ninja at First Sight (#4.75)

Happily Ever Ninja: A Married Romance (#5)

Dating-ish: A Humanoid Romance (#6)

Marriage of Inconvenience: (#7)

Neanderthal Seeks Extra Yarns (#8)

Knitting in the City Coloring Book (#9)

Winston Brothers Series

(Interconnected Standalones, Adult Contemporary Romantic Comedy, spinoff of Beauty and the Mustache)

Beauty and the Mustache (#0.5)

Truth or Beard (#1)

Grin and Beard It (#2)

Beard Science (#3)

Beard in Mind (#4)

Dr. Strange Beard (#5)

Beard with Me (#6)

Beard Necessities (#7)

Winston Brothers Paper Doll Book (#8)

Hypothesis Series

(New Adult Romantic Comedy Trilogies)

Elements of Chemistry: ATTRACTION, HEAT, and CAPTURE (#1)

Laws of Physics: MOTION, SPACE, and TIME (#2)

Irish Players (Rugby) Series – by L.H. Cosway and Penny Reid

(Interconnected Standalones, Adult Contemporary Sports Romance)

The Hooker and the Hermit (#1)

The Pixie and the Player (#2)

The Cad and the Co-ed (#3)

The Varlet and the Voyeur (#4)

Dear Professor Series

(New Adult Romantic Comedy)

Kissing Tolstoy (#1)

Kissing Galileo (#2)

Ideal Man Series

(Interconnected Standalones, Adult Contemporary Romance Series of Jane Austen Reimaginings)

Pride and Dad Jokes (#1, coming 2021)

Man Buns and Sensibility (#2, TBD)

Sense and Manscaping (#3, TBD)

Persuasion and Man Hands (#4, TBD)

Mantuary Abbey (#5, TBD)

Mancave Park (#6, TBD)

Emmanuel (#7, TBD)

Handcrafted Mysteries Series

(A Romantic Cozy Mystery Series, spinoff of *The Winston Brothers Series*)

Engagement and Espionage (#1, coming 2020)

Marriage and Murder (#2, coming 2021)

Home and Heist (#3, coming 2022)

Baby and Ballistics (#4, coming 2023)

Pie Crimes and Misdemeanors (TBD)

Good Folks Series